PRAISE FOR
THE CONNECTIONS SERIES

Mended

"Kim Karr is one of my few autobuys. Romantic, sexy, and downright gripping! I read it in one sitting because I just couldn't put it down!"
                    —*New York Times* bestselling author Vi Keeland

Torn

"I was riveted from the first line and couldn't put it down until the last word was read."   —*New York Times* bestselling author A. L. Jackson

Connected

"I was pulled in from the first word and felt every emotion . . . an incredibly emotional, romantic, sexy, and addictive read."
    —Samantha Young, *New York Times* bestselling author of *Fall from India Place*

"Emotional, unpredictable, and downright hot."
                    —K. A. Tucker, author of *Ten Tiny Breaths*

"This book had all my favorite things. Sweet, all-consuming romance, smart and real characters, and just enough of every emotion to keep me unable to put the book down. This was one of those holy-smokes kind of books!"   —Shelly Crane, *New York Times* bestselling author of *Significance*

continued . . .

"It's been two weeks since I finished *Connected* and Dahlia and River are still in my head." —The 2 Bookaholics!! (5 stars)

"I am now in awe of Kim Karr." —Shh Mom's Reading

"I can't say enough about this book! I LOVED IT! You will be sighing, swooning, and smiling often but you will also be crying, yelling and you will have your jaw drop to the floor once or twice." —The Book Enthusiast

"I can't wait for more of [Karr's] books!" —Aestas Book Blog

"Grabbed my attention and held on to it from beginning to end. . . . The romance, the heat, the angst, the storytelling, and the characters are all captivating and very well-balanced." —Bookish Temptations

"A sexy, emotional, and wonderfully romantic debut. . . . Kim Karr has a fantastic 'voice,' which will only continue to grow and refine."
—Swept Away by Romance

ALSO BY KIM KARR

The Connections Series

Connected

Torn

Dazed (digital novella)

MEN DED

The Connections Series

KIM KARR

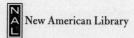
New American Library

NEW AMERICAN LIBRARY
Published by the Penguin Group
Penguin Group (USA) LLC, 375 Hudson Street,
New York, New York 10014

USA | Canada | UK | Ireland | Australia | New Zealand | India | South Africa | China
penguin.com
A Penguin Random House Company

Published by New American Library, a division of Penguin Group (USA) LLC. Previously
published in an InterMix edition.

First New American Library Printing, June 2014

LIBRARY OF CONGRESS CATALOGING-IN-PUBLICATION DATA:
  Karr, Kim.
  Mended: the connections series/Kim Karr.
    p. cm.— (The Connections series; 3)
  ISBN 978-0-451-47067-6 (pbk.)
  I. Title.
  PS3611.A78464M46 2014
  813'.6—dc23   2014000346

Printed in the United States of America
10 9 8 7 6 5 4 3 2 1

Set in Bulmer
Designed by Spring Hoteling

For Kimberly . . .

♥ *For making this book as much a part of your soul as mine* ♥

Mended Playlist

MENDED

PROLOGUE
Let Her Go

Xander, 18 Years Old

A black Jetta with heavily tinted windows swerves around the corner and comes to a stop in front of me, blocking my path as I walk through her school parking lot. The window rolls down and the thumping of the stereo's bass assaults me. I grin, recognizing the song immediately.

Logan Taylor pokes his head out to meet my stare. "Hey, dude, where you been?"

"Hey, man. Good to see you. I've been here and there. You?"

He hangs his arm out the open window. "Same. It's been weird not jamming with you every day."

"I know. Talk to your aunt."

"Do I look suicidal?" he says, then blows the hair out of his eyes.

I just shake my head because there's nothing else I can say. Not wanting to discuss Mrs. Taylor, I check out the curves he's sitting in. "New car?" I ask as my eyes sweep the sleek, shiny body in front of me.

He shakes his head. "I wish. It's my dad's, and anyway you know

I'd never pick a yuppie-mobile if I had my choice. I'd much rather have a car like yours any day, but no chance of that."

I laugh. I do love my car. It used to belong to my father—it was his sixteenth birthday present from my grandparents and he kept it all these years. When I was little I always admired it even if it only sat in my grandparents' garage. My dad never drove it anymore. He said it wasn't a family car. So when my dad gave me his shiny red Corvette for my own sixteenth birthday, I couldn't have been more excited.

"You here to see my cousin?"

"You know it," I say with a grin.

"She'll be glad to see you, man. She's been in a funk. Her mother has her going out on auditions almost every day."

I roll my eyes and sigh at the same time. I can't wait to get her out of this town. I take a deep breath before responding. "She told me you've been getting her where she needs to go. Thanks for looking out for my girl."

"Hey, she's family and I love her. I'd do anything for my cousin. . . . You know that. Listen, I have to jet, but call me and let's get together," he says, then speeds off.

I shuffle onward with a slight smile on my face from knowing I finally get to see her. I take the short walk over to our meeting spot and the bell rings just as I arrive. The doors open and she walks my way. Her earrings glitter where they dangle from her ears—the sun reflecting off the star-shaped sapphire stones that are the exact same color as her eyes. Watching the way she moves, I can't help but think she's the total package . . . looks, personality, brains, and a rocking body. There's a mysterious allure about her that I can never explain—she has an innocence that I'd do anything to protect. She's confident yet shy, strong but not, a rebel and a conformist all in one. And I fucking love her.

A huge smile breaks across her angelic face when she sees me standing near the basketball court and my heart goes crazy. Her small frame whisks in my direction and her long, platinum blond hair blows in the wind. She lifts her hand to her mouth and forms a perfect O as she blows me a kiss. She looks beautiful, and all I can do is grin. My gaze quickly drifts to her chest and then down to her narrow hips. She's wearing a white button-down that's a tad too tight and a navy skirt that's a little too short. Don't get me wrong—my body reacts to hers with just a single glance. That's how much I love the way she looks. But I hate the thought of all the other guys seeing what's mine, especially when I'm not around to put them in their place.

Pulling off my red Brent Academy polo and tossing it on the bench behind me, I slide my shades on and stand in my khakis and white T-shirt waiting for my girl, Ivy Taylor, to get closer. I keep my eyes fixed on her, ignoring all the other students around me. Sure, some of the guys walking by give me crooked looks, but that's as far as they take it anymore. They're used to seeing me by now—I've been waiting for her most days after school since I started driving. At first they didn't like me on their school grounds, but after a few fights they learned to leave me alone or get the shit kicked out of them. Just because I dress like a preppy ass doesn't mean I am one.

Today I skipped out of school early—leaving my brother at the pristine private school we attend so I could see my girlfriend. Ivy attends a magnet school in the heart of LA. She lives nearby in a rent-controlled apartment building with her mother and three much younger sisters. Their father took off on them long ago and Kelly Taylor, Ivy's mother, is nothing if not resentful about it. In fact, her spiteful attitude is sometimes directed at me, and lately she's restricted our time together. She says she got a new job with later hours, so now Ivy has to go home right after school and I'm no longer allowed over when she's not there. Coincidental? I doubt it. I can see through her—she views me as a threat to her golden ticket.

There's no one to blame except myself for not keeping my big mouth shut, but I couldn't help it. Her vendetta against me started when she overheard Ivy and me planning our rehearsal schedule. She made the idiotic statement that her daughter was a born actress and she should be spending her time rehearsing for parts and preparing for auditions, not playing in a band. She even went so far as to ask me, "Don't you agree, Xander, that with Ivy's looks she should be an actress, not a singer?"

"Do you even know Ivy?" I asked with a dry laugh.

"Yes, I know my daughter. And I know that with her beauty, she'll be an instant superstar. She just needs a push in the right direction. She needs to put herself out there more is all. Did she tell you an agent contacted me?"

I looked at her, dumbfounded, shaking my head. Because no, Ivy hadn't told me.

She grinned. "Well, one did—last week. He spotted Ivy when the band was playing at that school in Anaheim and thought she'd be perfect for a TV show airing in the fall. She auditions for it next week."

Ivy's head dropped as she spoke. "Mom, I told you, there's no way I'm wearing a bathing suit on camera."

Mrs. Taylor snapped, "Ivy, maybe the lifeguard part isn't right for you, but that doesn't mean there isn't another role you'd like in the series. You need to go for the exposure, if not for the practice."

"Mom, I don't want to act," Ivy reluctantly told her mother.

"We've talked about this. Singing in a band will take you nowhere. The money is in acting."

"She doesn't care about where the money is," I retorted, glaring at her mother. I mean, come on, Ivy's a modest, shy girl. It took forever for her to feel comfortable around me. Traipsing around a movie set half-dressed isn't exactly her thing, and honestly, I don't think I could handle it anyway. I didn't even bother to address where the money is. That was just a ridiculous statement. "I'm sorry, Mrs. Taylor, but everything isn't about money. Ivy's never even expressed the slightest bit of interest in acting—it's always been you making her go on auditions that she doesn't want to go on. I think Ivy needs to decide what she wants to do herself."

"That's easy for you to say. Money has never been an issue for you or your family," Mrs. Taylor said.

I didn't respond. She was wrong. Yes, my grandfather had money, but my mother had been living paycheck to paycheck over the last couple of years. My father's erratic work schedule never guaranteed enough to even pay the mortgage, and if it weren't for my grandparents we'd have lost our house. But that wasn't something I was going to get into with her. I may have had a smug look on my face, I don't know, because she stared at me for the longest time and so did Ivy. The difference? Ivy's stare said, "Thank you." Mrs. Taylor's stare said, "Fuck you."

The truth is, I know Ivy very well. We've been together for four years. We met through Logan. He and I were playing on the same basketball team when he told me he was looking to put a band together. I asked who he had lined up. He told me he played the drums and he had a cousin who sang, played guitar, and wrote songs. When I asked what his cousin was like, he said, "She's a talented girl whose voice draws you in the minute you hear it, and the beautiful tone of her guitar playing only sucks you in further."

His description of her intrigued me enough to make me consider joining. When I met Ivy, I could tell right away that she was a soulful artist who sang about what she knew, what she experienced. Once I heard her sing, I definitely wanted to hear more, and before I knew it, I was playing guitar with Logan and his cousin, Ivy Taylor. We called ourselves Poison Ivy and modeled our band after No Doubt. Which is fitting, because Ivy looks like a young Gwen Stefani. For the record, I agreed to play in the band because I was hot for Ivy, but I stayed because she really could write a song, sing a note, and rock a rhythm guitar like no other girl I knew. It didn't hurt that I fell in love with her the minute her fingers hit the chords. That smile she gave me when she played and sang was one I knew I couldn't live without.

Now it's been almost a week since we last saw each other, and my train of thought is instantly derailed the minute she jumps into my arms. "You made it! I've missed you so much."

I fall back onto the bench with her on my lap, my hands gliding up her warm thighs, and I tug her skirt down. "Hi, gorgeous. I told you I'd be here. I just couldn't skip out of school early this week until today. I'm sorry."

"It's okay. I get it, but it doesn't make it any easier. I hate not seeing you. It sucks."

Circling my hands around to her fine ass, I push her closer to me and grin. "I think what you mean to say is you love me so much you can't bear to be without me that long."

Her fingers travel to my hair and she yanks on it and says softly, "Stop putting words in my mouth, even if they are true."

Reaching up, I take her hands in mine and stare into the depths of her blue eyes. Today they are the darkest of blues—stormy. "Fuck, I've missed you." I breathe out. Then after another moment I whisper, "God, I love you."

A quiet sigh escapes her lips and the look in her eyes tells me everything I already know but still love to hear. She nuzzles her nose close to my ear and the warmth of her breath on my skin instantly excites me. "I love you, too, Xander. And I can't wait until the fall so we can see each other every day without our family issues getting in our way."

I attach my lips to hers and kiss her with the passion that always ignites between us whenever we touch. I think about the freedom we'll have to be together, and I get lost in just the idea of it. Pulling away, I brush my tongue across her lower lip. "I can't wait either," I murmur. The thought of us on our own together has my body going into overdrive. The muscles in her thighs tighten and the sound of her breathing becomes louder. I hold her face in my hands and just look at her—she takes my breath away. She always does . . . she always has and she always will.

She leans in and kisses me slowly. It's not the same as the way I kissed her. Her kiss is one of need, not want, and I can feel it. I respond with slow, steady flicks of my tongue, but before I'm done letting her know I'll always be here for her, someone is tapping me on the shoulder. I twist around to see a short, gray-haired woman in a yellow suit pointing her finger at me. "Excuse me, young man, but that kind of behavior is not allowed on school grounds. I'm going to have to ask you to leave."

Ivy scurries off my lap, smoothing her skirt. "Sorry, Vice Principal Myers. It won't happen again." She forces a smile at the woman, who has scolded us a few too many times over the years.

"Oh, Ivy, I know it won't, my dear," the iron-faced lady says while shooting daggers at me with her eyes.

It happens every damn time, and I wonder if she remembers me or thinks Ivy's kissing a different guy each time she catches us. I try to apologize, but like usual she turns around in a huff and marches toward the other end of the basketball court to break up another couple heading in the same direction we were. Standing up, I wrap my arm around Ivy's waist and lead her to my car. Leaning over, I whisper in her ear, "Your skirt is a little short, don't you think?"

She looks down as if she forgot what she's wearing. She shrugs her shoulders. "Honestly, I don't."

"All you have to do is bend over and every guy will think your ass is just begging to be spanked."

She laughs. Before I can comment further she snakes her arm around my waist. She looks up at me trying to stifle her laughter. "Xander, I'm pretty sure you're the only guy that thinks that way when he looks at me."

"Trust me, baby, I'm not. But keep it up and I'll be doing more than just thinking it."

She giggles again. She thinks I'm kidding—but I'm not.

The hot sun beats down on us and reflects off the paint of the cars in the parking lot, nearly blinding Ivy. I turn to face her. I walk backward and remove my sunglasses to place them on her pretty face. Twisting back, I slap her ass and clutch her by the hand, then sprint for my car, about fifty yards away. We are both panting when we reach it. After I open the door for her, she pushes the seat forward and throws her red sack on the floor, but fails in her attempt to swat me with it first. I shake my head and grin. When her eyes adjust to the shade, she removes my sunglasses. Her face is a vision as she props herself back on her elbows and pulls her red combat boots into the car. With love written all over her face, I decide to drop the clothing issue. "You all set?" I ask.

She nods and I quickly close the door and dart around to the driver's side. By the time I slide in, she's buckled up and grinning at me. As I start the engine, the throaty roar of the 5.4-liter V-8 comes to life. I turn to her, barely able to speak with thoughts of what I hope to have time for shifting through my mind, and ask, "What time do you have to be home?"

She leans over and slides her tongue around the shell of my ear. "I have at least two hours. I was hoping you'd make it today, so I told my mom I had a study session and to ask Mrs. Cooper to babysit if she couldn't get home before the girls' bus."

Turning my Corvette around the corner a little too fast, I drag my mind back to the road, but my dick twitches as I try to decide where we should go. My grandparents are in the process of moving from their house in Brentwood to a condominium in Beverly Hills and I'm pretty sure yesterday was moving day, so the house should be empty today. I know they have until the end of the summer to fully vacate, but I think we're safe going there now. I glance at her as she settles back in her seat and fumbles through her bag with a look of concern on her face.

"Everything okay?" I ask.

Her eyes flutter as we turn the corner and the sun makes them sparkle. "Of course," she says with a smile.

"Where do you want to go? Pool house or pier?" I ask. Of course, getting her naked is what I really want to do, but I'd be cool with just hanging out and talking if that's what she's up for. I know she has a lot going on with her mother.

Pulling a CD out of her bag, she ejects my Nirvana disc and tucks it into the sleeve above her visor, alongside the many others. Then she inserts hers into the player and kicks her feet up. Staring at her legs has me wishing I hadn't given her a choice of where to go. She doesn't answer right away. Instead she reaches for the sunglasses she threw on the dash and puts them on. Then she looks my way, raises her head, and quietly says, "The pool house is fine with me."

My mouth goes dry and my breathing becomes forced. I'm a little more than excited with her choice. I try to deflect my anticipation by pointing to the player. "What CD is this?"

Dropping her feet, she turns toward me and just a glance has me looking at her tits overflowing from her pushup bra. Fuck, a week has been a long time. How am I going to make the two months this summer? I hope my mom will let me make calls from France.

"Stop staring at my chest," she chastises me, not even attempting to pull the puckered fabric of her shirt together.

"How can I be staring when I'm driving?"

"I don't know, but you are," she says, turning bright red.

"Don't be embarrassed," I tell her.

"I'm not," she says shyly and searches in her bag again. She offers me a piece of gum and I decline as she sticks one in her mouth. She blows a bubble and pops it before hitting PLAY. "I made you a mix tape so that when you're thinking of me you can listen to it and know I'm thinking of you. I also made you a photo album," she says, pulling a black canvas album out of her backpack. Glancing at it, I can see it has a picture of us inserted in the front. It's a photo from last summer when we went with my family to Niagara Falls to see Third Eye Blind perform. Ivy and I are standing on the *Maid of the Mist* in yellow ponchos—

both of us have a look of awe on our faces as the water rushes all around us and the sound of the falls roars above us.

"The pictures aren't to share. And don't look at them until you're in France. This is to keep you away from all those hot French babes."

"Baby, I'm only interested in you."

"Two months is a long time, though."

"It is. But all it means is a lot of hand action," I joke.

Her face blazes with color. "That's why I'm giving you a few pictures."

I glance back at the album with what I know must be a shit-eating grin.

"Caution" plays through the speakers, and the song pulls me back in time. It was the first song she wrote that we played together and the only song I ever had a vocal spot in. Both of us seem to lose ourselves in our memories. We've been dreading the time we'll be apart this summer. I thought I was taking it harder than she was, but I'm no longer so sure. Sometimes I forget that underneath her seemingly hard exterior is that fragile, sensitive girl who captured my heart. She always seems undaunted, unmoved—but I know she's not.

Taking her hand, I pull it to my lips. "You're crazy with those thoughts. You know that, right?"

She shrugs her shoulders. "We've never been apart for two months."

I hesitate, trying to find the right words, but I'm not sure what they are, so I settle on, "It'll be okay. It's not that long. But thank you." I pause, then chuckle. "How did I get so lucky to snag a girl like you?"

She leans over the console and kisses the corner of my mouth, then whispers in my ear, "It's because you're so good in bed."

She quickly sits back in her seat, but I capture her hand first and look over at her. "You know it, baby," I joke. Her cheeks blaze and I laugh. We were both virgins when we met and have only been with each other, so really there are no comparisons, and I like it that way.

"Caution" ends and so does the playful mood in the car when Keane's "She Has No Time" starts playing. The lyrics of the song cast a wave of sadness over me and I swallow the huge lump in my throat as it plays on. Ivy isn't one for openly expressing her feelings, but sometimes she tells me things that make me want to snatch her and just run away. And this song triggers that protective instinct I have for her. It reminds me of her life so much that I have to press STOP. I think it's better for me to listen to this CD when I'm alone.

This is one of our last days together for a while, so I want to keep things light and fun. I always tell her our relationship is so entangled with our messed-up family lives, but really it's hers that is the sadder. My father might have turned into a drunk, but my family is close—something she doesn't have. She loves her sisters, but they are so much younger than she is—she's more like their mother than their sister. And her mother—I don't even want to think about her.

As the CD ejects, I turn to her and mouth, "Thank you." Then I tell her, "I'll listen to it later," and place the CD in the console.

"Technically, do people really make mix tapes anymore? Or are they called mix CDs?"

Laughing at her attempt to lighten the mood, I say, "I have no fucking idea, but great question."

She twists sideways to pick up the photo album again and freezes. "Whose pink bag is that?"

I quickly glance back. "Tessa's I think."

"Why are Tessa Bloom's things here?" she asks. Her voice is harsh.

I shrug. "She must have left it in here when I gave her a ride home."

"Why are you giving her rides home? Doesn't she have her own car?"

I place my hand on the bare skin of her leg. "Baby, not rides. *A* ride. And her car was in the shop, so she needed a lift."

She leans back in her seat and fidgets with the seat belt. She turns away but replies, "I don't really like her or her friend Amy hanging out with you when I'm not around."

I squeeze her thigh and inch my fingers under her skirt. "Don't be jealous. We're just friends. You know that."

She pouts. "I can't help it. I know she likes you, Xander."

"She doesn't. But even if she did—I love you."

She looks at me uncertainly. I reach my hand over and catch the back of her neck, pulling her in my direction. "Do you hear me?"

She nods and I let the silence sweep the car. Again, I want to keep today light, not argue about a girl who doesn't matter. I finally pull into my grandparents' driveway, and as I park my car, I see that she's looking straight ahead, ignoring me. I lean over and kiss her cheek, then nip her ear. "Come on—we don't have much time. Don't be mad at me over a stupid ride." She turns her head and I tug on her lip.

She finally smiles and playfully tries to tug mine back. Then, knuckling me in the side and wrinkling her nose, she says, "No more rides."

"Okay," I reply. "No more rides. Now stay put." I push open my door and head over to her side of the car.

We walk quickly, straight to the pool house. It's where we've spent most of our alone time over the past four years. Lately, I've had to share it with my brother, but when I found out my grandparents sold their house, I told him in no uncertain terms that the pool house was mine for the time we had left.

I swing open the unlocked opaque glass door. Ivy walks in first and I follow. The built-in window seat, ceiling fan, light blue walls, and bamboo wooden floor are all that remain. The furniture and pool table are gone, but I don't think either of us cares. Once I close the door we become two silhouettes in a darkened room. She turns around and stands on her tiptoes. With the blinds closed, there is barely enough light to illuminate anything, but I can see the gleam in her eyes. I bury my face in her neck. "Fuck, I missed you," I say again.

My hands roam her body, and her fingers skim mine right down to the front of my pants. Her fingertips trace up the length of my zipper and when she finds the tab, she slowly pulls it down.

"Fuck," I say, and let my head fall back—her gentle touch only excites me further. When I can't take it another minute, I circle my arms around her waist and suck on her earlobe. "Ummm . . . that feels so good."

She drops her hands and leans into me—and the strain in my pants actually becomes painful. I quickly pull her shirt over her head and feel my way to the inside of her bra. "Unsnap it," I tell her and when she does I feel the full weight of her breasts in my hands and then with my mouth. Heat blazes through me and I can't help but think about the looming summer separation that's just a few days away—it's really going to suck. I'm going to spend the next two months in Paris with my aunt, and Ivy will be taking her sisters to their grandparents' place in Indiana. I hope those pictures she gave me help me get through it. I'm sure I'll be doing a lot of fantasizing, so I try to capture every second of right now to use then as well.

When my lips return to hers, she's trembling. "Are you cold?" I ask her.

"No," she responds, her eyelids fluttering.

In the next moment, with our breathing loud and heartbeats louder, she pulls my shirt over my head. Running one hand along my abdomen, she teases, "Wow, have you been working out more?"

I catch her hand in mine and her smile lights up the room. I yank her to me and cover her mouth with mine in a hungry kiss. She responds immediately. My mouth caresses her soft lips and I want to taste every inch of her sweetness with my tongue.

Once I feel like I have thoroughly kissed her, I pull away, "Yeah, I've been working out every day, trying to exhaust myself to keep from climbing in your bedroom window and fucking you. And if I didn't think your mom would have me arrested, I would have."

She laughs halfheartedly. "It won't be long and we won't have to worry about my mom." I can hear a sadness in her voice and I hope it's only that she'll miss her sisters when she's away at college She kisses the very corner of my lips and runs her hands back down my stomach.

I hold her tightly and claim her mouth. With her eager return, my breathing quickens and my pulse races. It doesn't take long for me to lean back and crook my finger, leading her over to the window seat. Feeling a sense of uncertainty in her that isn't usually there, I take my time. I want her to feel how much I love her . . . to know she doesn't have to worry about us being apart. I unbutton her skirt at the waist and then tug the zipper down, and the skirt falls to the floor.

"Open your legs," I command.

When she does as I ask, I cover her pussy with my hand and slip my fingers inside her panties. She is so wet. I suck in a breath, wanting to savor the feeling. It's hard to believe two people could ever want each other as much as we do.

The room transforms around me. I see nothing but her as I quickly remove my pants. She watches me, and then I clutch her hips so I can lower us to the cushion, where I plan to spend all of the hour we have left making love to her. This time the sex won't be frenzied, the fucking won't be hurried—no, it will be a reflection of how we feel about each other. I wish we had more time . . . I wish we had all the time in the world. However, right now we don't. I know I have to get her home and then head back to school to pick up River. But I push those thoughts aside and sink into her. As I thrust in and out, the world as I know it fades away and pleasure is all that remains.

CHAPTER 1
The Wire

Xander, 30 Years Old

The magic of rock and roll—it casts a spell on you. And I'm no exception. I'm a band manager and I'm living the dream, touring with the Wilde Ones, helping them secure their well-deserved place in the music industry. I love being a part of it all, especially watching the band perform live—the crowds, the cheers, the music. It's a high and a low all at once, and I wouldn't trade it for anything. Every step of the way with this band has been fun, exciting, stressful—every possible emotion. Obviously we've had some breaks, but mostly we all put in a lot of hard work—myself, Garrett Flynn the drummer, Phoenix Harper the bassist, River Wilde the former lead singer, and now Zane Perry the new lead.

"Can you hear me now?" Zane bellows.

I nod my head as my heart pounds in my chest. My hands feel cold and clammy and a nervousness that makes me weak and shaky takes over. Doubts race through my head and I'm questioning if he's going to make it through this. A vague awareness that something bad could happen has been kicking around in my mind, and I can't shake it. The Wilde Ones are doing a sound check onstage and Zane's not on his game.

It's July and the weather has been brutally hot. But today it seems cooler. Maybe it's the California weather. Maybe it's the excitement of being home. The Beautiful Lies tour bus finally rolled back into our home state of California after six months away. While we're in town, I have a laundry list of shit to do—meet with the accountant for the band, catch my assistant, Ena, up on changes to upcoming stops, and stoke some fires in the publicity department at the label to ease the questions about the lead singer transition. I'm actually thinking some of the more mundane tasks of my job are suddenly looking better and better. On the road my day is always the same, but never the same— posting dailies and arranging rehearsals are automatic, but the rest evolves with the location, the people, and the needs of the band.

When the bus eased into the amphitheater, we could see tanned kids in board shorts and bikini tops already lined up at the will-call window. Security guards in polo shirts directed us to the artist parking lot, and we were officially home. Tonight we'll be headlining our biggest show to date. We're on tour without my brother, and still more than half of the shows are sold out, including tonight's. River quit the band—touring just wasn't for him—but even so, the album is on its way up the charts. Who knows—it may even hit gold status. The songs on the album were written and sung by River, but are performed in concert by Zane. Having him as my brother's replacement has been the key to our successful transition in a world where replacing leads is normally unsuccessful—simply put, we're lucky as hell to have him. However, River did promise to make a surprise appearance at our next stop. It's going to be epic.

But tonight is all about the arena—Mountain View and the Shoreline. "That's enough," I yell to the band and call rehearsal. This place is the biggest outdoor venue we've played, and I couldn't be more stoked—or more nervous. A sold-out show and a rocking opening band—what a combination. But a lead singer with another cold and a weakened voice that can't be heard throughout an amphitheater scares the shit out of me.

I head straight for the bus and spend the next few hours hashing out a song with Nix that he calls a jumbled mess of muscular sense and big-riff sunshine—whatever the hell that means. All I know is that it needs help and that's why he's turning to me. I hadn't played guitar since I was eighteen, but for some reason, I've picked it back up over the course of this tour. At first I played on whichever guitar was lying around, but last month I had my mother mail my old one to me, and it feels like home. It's a light blue and brown Gibson—it's the same guitar that Slash uses. Playing again seems to help pass the time and brings a sense of calm to me that I haven't felt in a while.

Hours pass, and before I know it, it's almost showtime. We make our way over to the amphitheater, do the typical festival schmooze fest, and then settle back until it's our turn. Waiting for the band to take the stage is always the most nerve-racking time. I'm sitting in the practically vacant makeshift meet-and-greet area backstage and sipping a beer in a worthless effort to calm my nerves when a voice travels through the sound system. It's a powerful and emotive mezzo-soprano range that is nothing short of explosive. She sounds unlike any singer I've ever heard before—with only one exception: Ivy Taylor. I push back the memories and emotions that her name evokes; they are just too painful. I can't see her onstage, but I know that the voice belongs to Jane Mommsen. Her band, Breathless, is playing right before the Wilde Ones.

A hand on my shoulder startles me. I twist and glance up as Amy sits down beside me, crossing her legs. "Hi, Xander. I thought I saw you earlier at the hotel."

She's a beautiful woman—long, wavy dark hair, petite figure, very natural-looking. She's wearing jeans, a blue shirt with some kind of foil design, and silver sandals. Grinning at her, I say, "Finally we catch up. Can I get you a drink?"

"I'd love that. How's life on the road been?"

"You know, it has its ups and downs, but actually not bad. You?"

"Jane's been going full force for a while now. But the tour ends with the summer and I'll be glad to be back in LA."

Standing up, I laugh. "I know the feeling. Let me get us that drink—I'll be right back." Tossing my empty bottle, I make my way to the coolers lined up under the tent and grab two beers. I know she'd rather have a glass of Chardonnay, but beer it is. Amy is Jane's assistant, and I've taken her out more than a few times. We went to high school together, and we know most of the same people, so whenever I need a date, I ask her. Last time I saw her was almost nine months ago when I took her to River and Dahlia's wedding.

Heading back to the table, I hear Jane yell out to the crowd, "Are you ready for three of the hottest guys in music?" The audience starts screaming and the overhead lights dim, cuing the guys that it's the fifteen-minute countdown until they take the stage. I can see the band members huddle together in their typical pre-performance stance. I'll have a quick drink with Amy and then join them. As I hand her the bottle, my fingers touch hers and we both grin, knowing that we'll end up alone by the end of the night.

"You sticking around for the whole show?"

"I think I might." She smiles.

"How about we ride back to the hotel together and have a real drink at the bar?"

"Sounds like a plan."

"Great. Time for me to get back to work."

She rises from the table, and I do the same. She stands up on her toes and kisses me quickly on the lips. "See you tonight," she whispers.

I give her an expectant look and cross the room to join the band.

"You're late," Nix says with a snicker. "What's with you two anyway?"

I shrug my shoulders. "Nothing. We see each other casually once in a while."

Garrett raises an eyebrow. "Chicks are never cool with casual."

Shaking my head at him, I don't bother to disagree. Amy and I have been doing this for years. It works for her and for me. We like each other's company but see each other only sporadically. I'll call her every now and then and we'll go out, but we are in no way exclusive. I don't ask her about other men and she doesn't ask me about other women.

I grab the bottle and pour the amber liquid into the shot glasses stacked beside it. It's our preshow routine. A shot and a prayer, so to say. It's Garrett's turn tonight to "pray"—this should be good.

He raises his glass. "Here's hoping Xander gets laid so he'll get off our backs."

Tipping my glass back, I quickly down the liquid. It burns as it makes its way down my throat. Once we've all drunk our two-shot maximum before a show, Garrett follows his toast up with, "Seriously, man, you need to get laid."

The guys laugh and I actually join in. Jerking off in the small bathroom on the bus is definitely one of the downsides of touring. I've slept with a few girls at some of our stops, but screwing groupies isn't really my thing. I'm not one to have time for a girlfriend, but I'm also not about to pull my dick out backstage. So it's been a long six months.

Zane coughs after he slings back the shot and I look at him with concern. "You're going to a doctor tomorrow."

He shakes his head. "Yes, Mom, if you say so."

"I'm not kidding. Your voice sounds like shit."

"It's a fucking cold. I took some medicine. I'll be fine."

"Doctor. Tomorrow. I mean it. I'll have Ena set it up."

"I can always sing," Garrett chimes in, and I smack the back of his head.

"Hey. I can," he responds, offended.

The lights start to flicker and I look at Zane with that feeling of uneasiness again. Second time this tour he's coughing and hacking. We're screwed if he really gets sick. He nods at me as I pat him on the back. Slinging his guitar over his shoulder, he heads out first, raising his arm in the air. The crowd goes crazy. The six-foot-tall guy is a chick magnet and no one is missing my brother tonight. Garrett heads out next, yelling, "Great to be here, Mountain View!" and Nix follows with his trademark nod. Zane skips his normal charming banter, and I know he must be saving his voice. Again I think about how fucked we are if he gets really sick.

I stand at the edge of the stage all night, until they finally come to their last song. "It Wasn't Days Ago" is a simple but crowd-affecting ballad, and Zane belts it out. Shouts from nearly thirty thousand fans call for an encore. Turning away from the microphone, Zane coughs again. He bites his thumbnail, looks over at me, and I slice my finger across my neck.

"One more song for tonight," he tells the screaming fans, and my blood pressure rises. "This one is a cover, an 'ode to' I'll call it. It's for Xander Wilde, the band's manager, and it's his favorite song. Everyone ready?" As he starts to sing Linkin Park's "Iridescent," I close my eyes and listen. When he hits the chorus, his voice gets so low my eyes snap open. Zane turns to grab a bottle of water while the guys continue to play, but I can tell something isn't right.

CHAPTER 2
Something Beautiful

Last night definitely didn't go as planned—a visit to the ER, then sleeping in a chair next to Zane all night on the bus because the steroids he was given freaked him out wasn't what I had expected. It's noon and Amy and I are just arriving at Pelican Hill Resort. She invited me to join her at some party being thrown tonight by her band's label. I would rather have skipped, but since we are here anyway, Ellie, the tour manager, insisted we all go for the good PR.

I'm exhausted and really need some sleep before dealing with the press and tomorrow night's show. The paparazzi have been everywhere—by the bus as we exited to the waiting car in LA, outside the doctor's office, at the gates of Zeak Perry, Zane's father's house, and now they're here in Irvine at the hotel.

To avoid the chaos awaiting us in the lobby, I called Ellie and asked her to check me in and meet me at the pool bar with the room key. I drape my arm around Amy, and we head that way. I've been here a few times, so I know my way around. Cutting through the grotto and over to the pool and cabanas, I steer Amy to the right and stop in my tracks as all the air rushes from my lungs.

My body floods with adrenaline and my gut twists. I don't even have to do a double take, since I'd know her anywhere. There's no mistaking her. She's just so beautiful—the elegant planes of her face, those high cheekbones, the red lipstick, and her platinum hair, which may be shorter than it used to be but is still tucked behind her ear like it always was. She looks the same. No, she looks better. Her skin glistens in the sun and my gaze automatically follows the shape of her long legs. They look smooth and tan against her white bathing suit. An ache forms in my chest as I think about running my fingers up them. She still looks like that eighteen-year-old girl I once knew, but now she has the body of a woman—lean and toned and full of curves. The sight of her is so familiar it doesn't seem like a day has passed since I last saw her—and everything I ever felt for her, it's all still inside me.

My pulse races at the mere memory of us. She's reclining in the cushioned lounge chair, reading a magazine just outside a cabana. My heart slams harder in my chest when she sticks her earphones in her ears and it transports me back to the last time I saw her do the very same thing. We'd skipped school and were at my grandparents' house—their pool. She was lying on the lounge chair listening to music and singing along—her voice so full of soul. I'd moved to sit with her under the guise of putting lotion on her back. She sat up and smiled that shy smile she didn't need to have when she was with me. I squeezed the tube into my hands. And after rubbing them together, I slowly applied it to her back, kneading my way up and down, touching every inch of her that I could.

Suddenly she sits up and looks over at me. Her eyes pin me in place, bringing me back to the here and now. She looks at me as if she remembers me for who I was, what we were. Not what I did to her. With my chest pounding, memories of us keep flashing through my mind. Fighting a smile, I wonder if she's thinking the same thing—remembering what we were, what we shared, how we loved.

She quickly breaks our connection when she averts her eyes and turns toward the man handing her a drink. I suck in a deep breath, trying not to feel sick at the sight. He's nearing fifty, wearing a terry-cloth robe. He's about my height, dark brown hair, meticulously groomed facial hair, and not exactly ripped, but fit. I've never actually met him, but I hate him all the same. Damon Wolf. I've seen his picture on TV and in magazines. He's her agent, her fiancé, and I'm sure he's the reason she's not singing anymore.

She looks up at him with that same forced smile she used to give people she just wanted to appease and mouths "thank you." I have a sudden urge to go over and deck him, but then her gaze shifts back to mine. After a few moments, he pulls her chin back to make her look at him, and I can sense some discomfort between them. We could always sense each other's feelings even when we weren't near each other.

Amy's hand slides down my arm and I have to blink a few times before I can hear what she's saying. Glancing one last time at Ivy, I see that she's staring at me again. Then suddenly her mouth forms a scowl and she flicks her attention away from me. Hooking her arm around Damon's neck, she pulls him down for a kiss and I think I might throw up.

"Are you okay?"

I nod, not able to say a word.

"Isn't that Ivy Taylor over there? The girl you used to date in high school?" Amy asks. There's an irritated tone to her voice I'm not used to hearing, and it makes me agitated.

"Yeah, it is." I try to sound casual. She's not just a girl I used to date . . . she's the only girl I ever really loved. She's also the girl whose heart I broke. Seeing her now brings back all those feelings I blocked, ignored, cast away. So many times over the years I wanted to go after her and tell her the truth—but I never did. Why, I don't know. Then one day it was too late—she had gotten engaged.

Amy chatters on. "I think that's Damon Wolf with her. We should go say hi."

My body goes cold at the thought. I straighten and just as I'm about to say, "No fucking way," my phone vibrates in my pocket. Squinting at the screen, I see that it's my brother. I look over to Amy and motion toward the bar. "Hey, this is River. I need to take it. I'll meet you over there in a minute."

"That's fine. We can catch up with them later. I'll go order us a drink." She smiles and starts toward the bar.

Turning around to avoid staring at Ivy, I answer the phone. "It took you long enough to call me back."

"I was in a meeting and stepped out as soon as I could, so don't start. What did the doctor say about Zane?"

"He's out for the rest of the tour and we're fucked." I hated the sound of the harsh truth in my own words.

"You sure? You're back in LA for almost two weeks after tomorrow night, right? Isn't that enough time for him to heal?"

"Technically, yes. But his old man wants him out. The doctor said that he couldn't be sure as to how long the blood that had accumulated under Zane's vocal cords had been there, but obviously last night, the degree of ruptured vessels was severe enough to cause his voice to freeze. The doctor advised at least two weeks of rest before another evaluation to see if surgery is necessary. Zeak wants his son to take a longer period of time off. He's afraid that if Zane keeps singing and it keeps happening, scar tissue will build up and cause his voice to change forever."

"Do you blame him?"

"No, I don't." I feel like shit that I have to put River in a position to do what he didn't want to do in the first place. But I also know that if I don't, the band won't survive. If I have to cancel this tour, the Wilde Ones are done. So I ask, "Did you talk to Dahlia?"

He sighs. "Yeah, I did. She's cool with it, Xander. I'm just trying to figure it all out."

"You know I'll do whatever you need me to do, right?"

"Shit, why can't you just be an ass and make it easy for me to say no?"

"Because you have no idea what this means to me."

"Actually I do, and that's why I'm going to make it happen. But, Xander, remember I can't play a twelve-string."

Laughter and relief take hold of me. I feel a huge weight lifted off my shoulders. "Right now I wouldn't care if you only played the mandolin," I joke.

He laughs and I add, "You'll be here tonight?"

Now he sounds slightly annoyed. "I said I would. We might be a little late, so don't get your panties in a wad."

"That's cool. Thanks for everything. Hey, one more thing."

"What?"

"Ivy Taylor's here."

"No way. Have you spoken to her?"

"Fuck, no. You know she won't talk to me. And besides, she's with that asshole."

"You should talk to her. Tell her the truth."

"What's that going to do now? She'll just think I'm lying."

"You want me to talk to her? I can explain everything."

"No. I don't need my little brother to fight my battles. I'll talk to her if I feel the time is right. Do you hear me?"

"Whatever you say. Look, I have to run, but I want to discuss this later. And, Xander . . . you don't know he's an asshole. Just because Dad said his name once doesn't mean shit."

"Right. Okay, see you tonight," I say and end the call. My head is spinning from knowing that after all these years I'm actually in the same place she is. I want to talk to her, tell her everything, but I can't see how that would change anything anyway. Glancing behind me, I catch another glimpse of the two of them that turns my stomach. He's such a slimeball. Since his father was hospitalized and he took over the business, he's been scooping up labels, tearing them apart, and rebuilding them with bands he thinks are better fits. My guess is he picked up Jane's label—that's why he's here. I heard they were having some financial difficulty, and he's just the kind of bottom-feeder that would want to capitalize on being not only Jane's agent but now also her producer. The sight of him touching Ivy makes my skin crawl.

Damon Wolf, now turned music mogul, is the agent to a select few stars. Damon Wolf—two of the last words my father spoke to me before killing himself, and I never knew why. Of all the guys in the world Ivy had to end up with—why him? I look up and they're gone. I'm anything but relieved, though. Rubbing my chin, I'm antsy, agitated, pissed as hell, but I feel more alive than I have in years.

Our breakup is permanently etched in my mind—it's something that, although done, was left unfinished. What matters the most is that she didn't stay in LA for college. She got away from her mother's influence and didn't go into acting. She ended up right where she belongs—in the music industry. I felt at peace with what I did when her career started to take off. I was even okay with the fact that somewhere along the way she traded the alt-rock edge for the pop culture route—following in the path of Britney Spears instead of Alanis Morissette. However, whenever I watched her perform I did notice she seemed uncomfortable, unsure, and uneasy with the show she was putting on. Perhaps if she had taken the other route her comfort level would have been there, but who knows? I have to admit, though, that Damon Wolf did help create Ivy Taylor the vocalist, as the world knows her today. She may not have been at the top of the charts but she certainly wasn't at the bottom. She was made for the spotlight—and I really want to know why she stopped performing.

The resort club is filled with staffers, managers, agents, musicians, and reporters sipping their drinks and talking—all waiting to hear the news from the label about the fate of Next Records. I'm on my second Jack and Coke when I notice Ivy enter the room. Damon surprisingly isn't by her side. Gorgeous and alone—she looks incredible. At five seven, she is perfectly proportioned from head to toe. She joins a group of people on the dance floor. Her pin-straight hair moves across her bare shoulders as she sways among the guests. Her short black dress shimmers under the lights and accentuates her curves in the best possible way. It's tight—longer in the back than the front, showing an edge only she could pull off. And my rebel girl has turned in her combat boots for thigh highs—flashing a bit of leg that is sexy as hell, but maybe just a little too much skin. No matter what she wears, I've never been able to take my eyes off her. And now, my mind can't turn off how I once felt about her. But the large diamond on the fourth finger of her left hand signals a reminder that she's not mine anymore.

I make my way around the room, networking, talking about the band, but somehow I never lose track of where she is. She catches my gaze at one point, but I'm unsure what she's thinking. I wonder if what I did killed what she once felt for me. Just seeing her has made me want her all the more, and I know I have to talk to her. When I'm standing next to Amy and the guys, I notice Jane pat her on the shoulder. They move off the dance floor and close enough to where I'm standing that I can just barely hear their conversation. I can't help but eavesdrop.

"It's so good to see you. I've heard nothing but great things about that successful whirlwind tour of yours!" Ivy tells Jane. Hearing her voice puts a smile on my face. Her tone is still soft, but she seems more confident. It makes me feel somewhat proud.

"Well, you could be the next major tour to hit the road, but I heard you and Damon are actually thinking of starting a family," Jane responds.

Hearing those words cripples me.

I turn to Amy. "I'll be right back."

"Everything okay?" she asks.

My feet are already moving. I have to get away. I don't want to hear Ivy's response. I dart outside, needing some air. I wonder if she's already expecting a baby. Fuck. His baby. My head spins. I haven't seen her in so long and now everything I've pushed away, locked away, is back. So many emotions I never wanted to feel again. When I thought we'd be together, there was a life I envisioned I'd have with her. I've never thought about that life with anyone else since then. I haven't let myself—I let her go and my dreams went with her.

Wrenching my mind from the past, I reenter the room and look around at everyone shooting the shit, dancing, and flirting. I look for Ivy, but Amy finds me first.

"How about a drink?" she asks, unfazed as to where I've been.

"Sure," I answer and lead her to the bar—I need another drink.

Soon I'm leaning against the bar facing the crowd and Amy is sitting on the stool next to me. Ellie is on the other side of her, talking to Garrett.

We're talking about Lou Reed and Metallica cutting a new studio album and the buzz that the artists' collaboration is perfection, but when I glance up and see my brother and his wife walking in, I smile for the first time all day. I can't believe I've missed that pain in my ass and the muse, too. I haven't seen Dahlia in a few months and I have to say River was right—she looks amazing. Seeing his happiness means everything to me. Years ago I promised my grandfather I'd look out for him and not let the same things that happened to our dad happen to him. I did the best I could and then I had to let him make his own decisions, and I'm glad to say I think he's much happier because of it. I know my grandpa would understand, and I think he'd be proud.

Amy must see me staring because she turns around on her stool. Twisting back, she's smiling too. "You didn't tell me Dahlia was pregnant."

"Sorry. With everything that happened last night, I never even thought about it."

"How far along is she?"

"Three or four months, I think."

"She's got the cutest baby bump. She really makes pregnancy look good."

I have no clue about pregnant women, so I just nod my head in agreement. River sees me and heads toward the bar with what I swear is a protective shield around Dahlia. Honestly, I feel sorry for Dahlia, because his overprotectiveness will probably reach a level of insanity. Ivy crosses his path before he reaches me and I can tell she recognizes him right away. He seems to play it cool. Giving her that same look he always gave her—the half smirk that seems to put girls in a frenzy, the one I used to think meant he was hot for my girl and the millions of other girls who were on the receiving end of the look. It actually wasn't until River brought Dahlia around that I figured out the look didn't mean anything. The look my brother gives his wife, the one with a full smile that brings out his dimples, is the one that matters. I realize now it's the same look I used to give Ivy. He introduces her to Dahlia, who appears to be gushing. I watch as the two ladies seem to hit it off. Ivy points to Dahlia's stomach and then Ivy is the one gushing.

"So are they both going?" Amy asks, and suddenly I feel like I must have missed half of the conversation. My phone vibrates in my pocket. Pulling it out, I glance at the screen and put a finger up before I answer it. "Hey, Zeak, everything okay with Zane?" The music is so loud I can't hear him, so I step outside. After a ten-minute phone conversation with Zeak trying to persuade me that I should postpone the tour, I finally head back inside.

The lights dim and the music gets louder as the DJ invites people to the dance floor. Making my way through the crowd, I come face-to-face with pale arched eyebrows delicately framing the most perfect feline eyes. However, their stormy blue color offers up a hint of her unease at seeing me. Only inches from me, she takes my breath away with just one look. Her normally colorless cheeks are flushed and her breathing is shallow, telling me she's affected by my presence as well.

"Ivy," I breathe softly, almost not believing that she's right here in front of me.

She quickly diverts her gaze, looking anywhere but at me, and it doesn't take long for her pouty red lips to form a frown. "Excuse me," she says a little too politely as she tries to step around me. The tone of her voice is so soft, so feminine, that my body hums just from the sound alone.

I clutch her elbow, my fingers tingling from the touch of her warm skin against mine. I pull her closer to me. The feel of her body is so familiar. I whisper in her ear, "Don't act like you don't know me. Talk to me."

She stiffens the moment physical contact is made. Her breath quickens and when her eyes shoot to mine they seem to sparkle. For a moment I think their hardness is fading. But just as she opens her mouth to speak, the room brightens, the music quiets, and a voice comes over the microphone.

"Hello, everyone. Thank you so much for coming tonight. For those of you who don't know me, I'm Damon Wolf, head of Sheep Industries," he says from the front of the room, flashing a fake smile. He's wearing an expensive suit with a tie and has swapped his sunglasses for matching glasses with clear lenses. The crowd claps as he pauses, and Ivy holds her arms up high, clapping with a pride that guts me. I scan the room and see River and Dahlia talking to Garrett. Ivy's eyes flick between the stage and the parquet floor beneath us. Her eyes go dull—there's not an ounce of admiration in them as she looks at him. But when she also doesn't look back toward me, I walk away.

The announcement was just as I thought—his father's company had bought Jane's label. At least, by the looks of it, her label is one company he doesn't plan to dismantle. Most of the bands it holds are solid and their dynamics seem to work the charts well together. River, Dahlia, Amy, and I leave shortly after the announcement and head to my brother's suite to discuss the tour, but there's more than just the tour on my mind. I can't wrap my head around Ivy being with Damon. Watching them function as a couple killed me. I knew they were engaged, but seeing them together is like one of my worst nightmares and just makes it all the more real. Every time I saw him touch her today it set my insides on fire—it was unbearable, intolerable, and I knew that if I stayed, I was going to have to drop him.

It's five eleven a.m. and before I brush my teeth or take a leak, I roll over and snag my laptop from the nightstand to read what everyone on Facebook and Twitter has to say about the band and its lead singer. Surprisingly, not much, and I'm thankful. I want to wait to announce anything until after tonight. Before I close out, I search Ivy's name. Why, I don't know. She has a Twitter account but hasn't tweeted since her engagement announcement. Hmmm . . . I wonder why.

Amy wakes up and sleepily looks over at me. The computer screen's glow is the only light in the room. "What are you doing?"

"Hey, go back to sleep. I just need to send a few e-mails to Ena so she can get River and Dahlia set up for the tour." I lie because I don't want to tell her I'm stalking my ex-girlfriend and because I shouldn't be thinking of Ivy when Amy is lying in bed next to me.

She rolls over and I set my laptop down and get out of bed. Once I've done a quick workout in the hotel gym, I head back to my room and hit the shower. I turn on only the hot water and let the steam fill the bathroom. Rubbing my eyes, I lean against the cool marble and think about Ivy—about how I didn't realize how much a part of my life she was and how much I have really missed her. When I'm done, I head out to the living area and turn the TV on to find something mindless to watch. I'm slurping down my coffee when Amy joins me.

"Did they win?" she asks, pointing at the replay of the Brooklyn Nets game on the screen.

I nod. "Ninety-eight to eighty-five over the Lakers. It sucks, but I have to say the Nets have the best music sound bites in their game, so I watch them over and over."

She laughs. "Only you would notice something like that."

"I might even consider trading teams just to get one of our songs boomed over the PA as Johnson races toward the basket."

"Are you serious? That music isn't just prerecorded crap on replay?"

"No. Not at a Nets game, anyway. A guy named Period sits on the platform and punctuates games with amped remixes. It's like he's deejaying every game. It's genius."

"Well, you sold me," she says, flopping down in a chair and pouring a cup of coffee.

"What's your plan for the day?" I ask her. Today is pretty much a down day. I want to avoid the calls about Zane until after tonight's show, and the guys are doing their own thing during the day. We'll meet up for a short rehearsal before the show later tonight, so I'm up for whatever until then.

"I have to shower first. I tried to join you earlier, but the door was locked."

I blow off her comment with a partial truth. "Sorry, a bus habit. I didn't even realize I locked it. So, thoughts for after your shower?"

"I need to cut out by noon, but I wouldn't mind lounging by the pool for a few hours first."

"Sounds like a plan. We'll eat some breakfast and head out there when you're ready."

"Pancakes?" she asks with a grin.

I shake my head no. That's the one food I never eat—Ivy always made me pancakes. "Waffles sound great," I respond.

I'm relieved that she's leaving soon but feeling guilty that my mind has been consumed with Ivy. What the hell is wrong with me? I need to stop overthinking this. Amy and I have always been casual. Everything is cool between us.

After breakfast we're sitting by the pool when Ivy and Damon set up a few cabanas over. I glance at Ivy, then study her. I know I shouldn't, especially with Amy lying next to me in her skimpy green polka-dot bathing suit, but I can't help it. Ivy looks amazing in a red bikini—seeing her makes my body ache. Her hair's down and falls freely around her chin, making the angles of her heart-shaped face less pronounced—softer, not harder, even more beautiful. As she sits down, her head snaps in my direction. She squints and must see that I'm staring. I don't care.

Damon follows Ivy's glare and my eyes cut from hers to his. His expression goes dark, as he seems to recognize me. Does he know me? Or does he sense what Ivy and I have—*had*? He sneers at her, and I swear if I could bury him with just a look I would. He sits down on her chaise longue and pulls her to him, kissing her. Tension flows through my veins until she pulls away. He moves closer, speaking with animated gestures. Her facial expression signals that she's not happy. My body goes rigid as I'm forced to watch this arrogant son of a bitch's attempt to tame a girl who should never be tamed.

He practically fucks her with his eyes, and I squeeze my fists at my sides, resisting the urge to smash his face in. Ivy pulls her robe out of her bag and wraps it around herself. For some reason this helps ease my rage. Then suddenly he stands up and snatches hold of her elbow, pulling her out of the chair. I stand up as well. She snaps at him and steps back, but he grasps her shoulders. A smirk spreads across his face as he presses himself against her. The vulgarity of his actions hits me like a punch. She whispers something in his ear, and he drops his hold but doesn't surrender. He touches his fingers to her cheek and tilts her head toward him. As if to make a point, he slides his hands down and unties her robe, his gaze lazily scanning her body before shifting over to me. I know what the asshole is doing—he's demonstrating to me that she's his. He obviously feels the need to antagonize me further by running his hands down her hips and slipping his fingers inside her bathing suit bottom. My stomach twists. She flinches, then gathers her things and walks away. But he quickly catches up to her.

At the sight of his seemingly aggressive behavior, I have to fight the urge to go over there and sock him, but my chance is lost when they both exit the pool area. My frustration and aggravation are surpassed only by my concern. I try to hold back my rage—how dare he touch her like that, look at her like that? With adrenaline coursing through my veins, I slip on my T-shirt.

Amy glances at me. "Where are you going?"

"I'll be back. I'm going to run up and see why my brother isn't down here yet."

She giggles. "Have fun with that." I just shake my head. I know why he's not down here, and I'm not really going to his room. I promised myself that if he did this for me—made the decision to help us out—I'd cut him some slack.

I don't know where I'm going, but my anger toward that arrogant asshole has already taken hold. She might not be mine, but that doesn't mean anything right now. I follow their path through the grotto and try to talk myself down, because I know where this is leading. With my fists balling at my sides, I can hardly control myself. When I turn the corner at a rapid pace, her stormy blue eyes slam into mine. For the briefest of moments, I stop in my tracks. My stomach lurches at the sight of what he did. There she is—my angel—with blood dripping from her lip and tears streaming down her face.

I rush over to her. "Ivy—" I whisper, my voice catching on her name. I take her face in my hands. Pulling my T-shirt up, I wipe the blood from her lip and blot the tears from her cheeks. "Are you all right?" I ask finally, filling the silence of the last twelve years between us.

For a few moments she lets me take care of her—like she used to. Then she blinks as if remembering that this is not then. She presses her lips together, but her scrutiny doesn't waver from me as she pushes me back. I reach to help her, but she shrugs my hand away. "I don't need your help," she says forcefully. Her voice getting higher with every word, she unleashes what I can only assume to be years of pent-up anger at me. "I can take care of myself."

I don't blink. "Did he hit you? Does he hit you?"

She shakes her head, sadness mingling with determination on her face. "That's none of your business. Leave it alone, Xander. I mean it."

I reach for her face, my fingers brushing her cheek. "Tell me the truth. Does he hit you?"

"No, he doesn't. Do you think I'd be with someone who does? Men with loose fists and men who cheat—they're grown from the same mold and they can both go fuck themselves."

She stares at me for the longest time and without another word she storms away—cold, guarded, and angry. The girl I knew with the hard exterior, but so fragile and sensitive, appears to be gone. Now she's all hard edges, and she's pissed as hell—at that asshole, and at me.

CHAPTER 3
Under the Water

Listening to the beat, I can feel the strum of each chord in my chest, and my ears ring and my heart pounds as the green, yellow, and red fluorescent lights illuminate the stage and the darkness cascades above us. A feeling of relief takes hold of me. They're almost done—they did it. My throat might be dry, and I'm out of breath from yelling, but I don't care. Tonight they did it old-school and they killed it. No opening act, no fire, no smoke, no extras—just the Wilde Ones onstage at the Verizon Wireless Amphitheater.

River's certainly not planning on jumping back into doing another nine months in the studio, but my brother is in top form right now as he sings the last song of the night. In an "I'm in love croon," with his six-string standing in for the synths and bludgeoning rhythms of the produced track, River gives "Once in a Lifetime" all he has. His raspy, soulful tone stands out as he sings the ballad acoustic style to his wife. The unplugged version is making the fans go crazy. Cheers and yells come from behind me and I feel like I'm part of the audience tonight.

I'm not backstage like I usually am. Instead I'm standing with Dahlia in the VIP section. She and River are staring straight at each other. Their connection seems to be pulling out all he has. And I have to say, her good mood has definitely rubbed off on me. Despite the events of the last two days, I'm having the best time I've had since the tour began. It's just her and me and a select dozen or so other people in the roped-off orchestra section, and it's been a blast. My cousin Jagger and his girl, Aerie, are here somewhere. Jagger arrived in town after I hit the road, so I never got to catch up with him. But I've talked to him on the phone a number of times and finally got to meet him before the show. So strange having a cousin you've never met, but when you live so many miles apart for most of your lives, I guess it happens. Jagger and Aerie together, though—that still makes me laugh. She's so uptight and he, well, I don't know him that well, but I'd say he's anything but. He seems to be a lot like River. I invited them to join us up here, but Aerie was in full-on work mode and wanted to be out in the crowd, interviewing people. She said she'd catch up with us after the show. Unfortunately, my mother and stepfather, Jack, are in Paris, so they couldn't be here. And my sister, Bell, had to work. She just recently started her own event-planning business in addition to keeping her day job, so catching up with her lately has been hard. But she seems to have found her place in this world. She's happier and more put together.

Dahlia nudges me. "Hey, you watching? You seem someplace else."

The show ends with crazed fans screaming at the top of their lungs for an encore. "More! We want more! Give us more!"

I give her a look as if to say, "Where else would I be?" but her attention is riveted on the stage again at the sound of my brother's voice. River smiles at the crowd and catches us in his vision as he slips the microphone out of the stand. "More? You want more?"

Their response comes in unison. *"Yes!"*

He hits the edge of the stage and drags his fingertips along Dahlia's outstretched hands. "I think we can do that." He finds the microphone stand again and clips it in place.

Dahlia leans over to me. "I really have to use the restroom. I don't think I can wait."

I laugh and nod my head. "Come on. I'll take you backstage now." It's my job to be her personal bodyguard tonight, and actually I don't mind it. It obviously puts my brother at ease, and my sister-in-law and I get along really well now, after a bumpy start. Turns out she is exactly four months pregnant. She and River have decided not to find out the sex of the baby, but she showed me an ultrasound picture and the baby was sucking his thumb. I have to believe it's a boy, for River's sake, because another girl in his life to watch over just might push him over the edge. The thought makes me laugh, though.

I'm standing at the perimeter of the stage, watching the end of the spectacular show, when I feel a tap on my shoulder and an unfamiliar voice asks, "Are you Xander?"

Without turning around, I give a cursory nod, not sure why she's asking until she says, "There's a woman in the bathroom who has asked me to tell you to get her husband and come right away."

I whirl around and see the woman in uniform. "What's wrong with her?"

"She didn't say. I'm sorry. I have to get back to work." The woman then turns and walks away, pushing her cleaning cart in front of her as she goes.

I look out onstage and River glances over, looking for Dahlia, I'm sure. I slice my finger across my neck, giving him the "cut it now" signal, and his smile instantly fades. His panicked voice trembles over the mic.

"Thanks, everyone!" He darts toward me. His eyes search mine on the way, but I don't wait for him to cross the stage.

Heading toward the bathroom, I knock and open the door. "Dahlia?"

River pushes past me into the long rectangular room. "Dahlia, what's wrong?"

"I'm not sure," she cries as she swings one of the stall doors open. He rushes in and disappears behind it.

"Xander, call nine-one-one," he yells.

"No, I don't think I need an ambulance. It seems to have stopped. Let's call my doctor first," Dahlia nervously tells River.

His breath coming fast and hard, he does as she asks. I can't quite make out what he's saying because the toilet is flushing over and over. My pulse pounds louder than the sound of the running water as I wait to see what the hell is the matter. When I see his feet moving, I yell, "What's going on?"

There's fumbling behind the door, and then it opens and he carries her out. In a shaky voice he says, "We need to take her to the hospital. She's bleeding. Take my keys and get the car."

I'm sitting in the family care area waiting to hear how Dahlia and the baby are doing. My thoughts are drifting to seeing Ivy after so many years and how things could have been so different. When you believe a lie for so long . . . does it become the truth?

Behind my closed lids flashes a memory from twelve years ago. Looking back on it now, I think we were more like adults and less like sex-crazed teenagers. We had crossed the line from lust to love, from adolescent to adult. When we left my grandparents' place that last day we spent there before graduation, the fractured afternoon light peeked through the clouds and I drove her home. I pulled over a good distance from where she lived. Dropping her off on the corner was something I really hated. But I understood. I had my own home issues, so who was I to talk? I'd had to bring my brother home and pick up my sister every day since my mother went back to work because my drunk of a dad couldn't get a job. I couldn't wait for the fall when Ivy and I would head to the University of Chicago together. Ivy got a free ride, my grandparents were paying for me, and we both got to get the hell out of LA.

As soon as I put the car in PARK, she bolted out. She didn't even wait for me to open her door, which was a habit she knew I really hated, but I didn't say anything. She leaned against the large black stripe of the hood as I approached her. Some kids were sitting on their stoops playing games, others were yelling and screaming, but I blocked all of that out as I caged her with my arms on either side of her and rested my forehead against hers. "I don't think I'll be able to meet you after school again at all the rest of the week. Tomorrow I have to pick up my cap and gown, Thursday is graduation rehearsal, and Friday is some kind of senior dinner."

She wrapped her arms around my neck. "I know you're busy. I can't believe our ceremonies are both on Saturday. At least my mom said I could go to dinner with you and your family after graduation."

Leaning into her, I circled my arms around her waist and kissed her lightly. "It'll be our last day together before our summer trips, so I'll pick you up as early as possible. Make sure your mom thinks you're sleeping at Jody's house."

She kissed me and I leaned back to look at her. Her blond hair fell past her shoulders and she was smiling shyly at me. "It's already arranged," she said, flushing. A nervousness that I'd seen many times presented itself in her expression.

"What's the matter, gorgeous?"

She broke away and in the quietest voice said, "I'm really going to miss you this summer."

"I'm going to miss you, too. But, hey, we talked about this. It won't be that long. The summer will be over before you know it and then we'll be together." I hugged her tightly, reassuring her.

"I know you're right," she whispered, and the sadness in her eyes broke my heart.

I had tried my best to get my mother to cancel or at least shorten my trip to my aunt's. Since she called it my graduation present, I really thought I should have gotten to choose if I wanted to go or at least for how long. She hadn't said I couldn't, but she hadn't said I could, either. I knew I would continue to work on her.

I kissed Ivy one last time and trapped her fingers in mine before she twisted away and broke the connection. She walked backward for a beat, then turned around and sashayed down the sidewalk toward her apartment building.

"I'll call you tonight, sexy thing," I yelled to her.

She turned, gave me one last heart-stopping smile, and blew me a kiss. She wouldn't even let me walk her to her apartment building because she was afraid her mother would see her with me when she was supposed to be studying. So I waited on the corner until she reached her door. As soon as she did, she came rushing back. She threw her arms around my neck and whispered in my ear, "I hope you can call me because if you can I'll practice what we've talked about."

I stepped back and looked at her with what I knew was a sly, wicked grin. She was flushed on every exposed body part. "Really . . . ?" I asked.

"Yes," she mouthed, her cheeks changing color from pink to red with that one unspoken word.

"Christ, just you saying it is so fucking hot."

She kissed me, softly at first, then harder. "You better get out of here or you're going to be late," she said, and just as quickly as she had turned and come back to me, she was gone. Once she disappeared through the doorway, I got in my car and grinned for the longest time. Finally, I drove away and headed back to school to pick up River. I had to drop him off before picking up my sister, since my car didn't have a backseat. I was late, and I already assumed I'd probably catch shit for it. As we walked into the house, I knew immediately something was wrong—Bell's backpack and shoes were in the foyer. She was already home.

"Hello?" I yelled.

"Daddy, I can't do it," a small voice cried from the landing—it was Bell.

I began ascending the stairs. "Stay here," I called over my shoulder to my brother.

I stayed silent as the wooden stairs beneath me squeaked.

"Don't say you can't. You can. You're just not playing the right chords. Do it again," my father said.

I bolted up the remaining stairs two at a time to the wide-open loft that acted as his music studio. Bell was sobbing and her fingers were bleeding. They were fucking *bleeding*. Seeing my little sister sitting there on a stool while my shaggy-haired, unshaven, drunken father barked orders at her triggered a rage I'd never felt before. I couldn't take another minute of his drunken insanity—he wasn't only ruining his own life, he was tearing ours apart.

He gave me a passing glance as he pointed to the chord he wanted my sister to strum. "You're late," he muttered.

"What the fuck are you doing?" I yelled.

"Teaching your sister how to play correctly."

My jaw clenched tightly. "The hell you are. Bell, go downstairs with River."

She looked at me, sobbing.

"No, Bell. Stay here," he ordered, glaring at me.

"Go. Now!" I yelled to her as River came racing up the stairs. "Take her now and get her out of here," I told him.

My hands were shaking as I took another step toward my father. It was strange, because he looked at me with vacant eyes, but I could have sworn I saw a flicker of fear in them. I had a feeling in the pit of my stomach that I couldn't explain. It made its way through me as an urge to kill him. I lunged at him. He went flying backward and hit his head against the wall. A few of his framed *Sound Music Magazine* covers came crashing down. He scooted away from me, but my fists moved toward him in a hard, thrusting motion. He didn't duck, he didn't move. Hit after hit, my father just took it.

"I hate you! You're a worthless excuse of a man!" I screamed.

"I know," he cried. "I tried, I did. I tried to protect you all. But now with Damon Wolf, he . . ." The rest of his response was incoherent. I had no idea what the pathetic man in front of me was trying to say.

"Xander, stop it!" my mother screamed. She wrapped her arms around my waist and pulled me back.

She leaned down to him but looked toward me. "What's going on? What happened?"

I stiffened and took a deep breath, but he blurted out what had happened himself. Through his incoherent mumblings, he finally managed to make my mother see him for the worthless piece of shit he really was.

Without tears, she stood tall and told my father, her husband, the almost famous Nick Wilde, that it was time for him to leave.

He didn't even plead for forgiveness. He didn't say anything. He just stood and weaved down the stairs with his head down—a drunken mess. My mother pulled me to the kitchen and put ice on my hand. She finally broke down and cried. She asked me questions I couldn't answer because my mind was jumbled with all kinds of thoughts—good, bad, love, but mostly hate.

Then out of nowhere an earsplitting bang rang through the air for a good thirty seconds. I knew immediately what it was. Running to the bedroom, I saw him lying unconscious on the floor in a pool of blood with his gun next to him. The sight filled me with as much rage as sorrow. He was dead—I knew he was. I could hear my mother's shoes in the hallway and I ran over to the door, slamming it closed and locking it.

"Call nine-one-one now!" I screamed to her.

She beat on the door, tormented screams coming from her mouth. I heard River's voice in the background and yelled to him to make the call and to call Grandpa too. I didn't know what to do—I couldn't let her see him like that. I scrambled to pull a sheet off the bed and that's when I saw it—his suicide note.

It read, "I love you all. Boys, take care of Mom and Bell and don't ever settle for not being at the top, because I know you can do what I couldn't."

As I covered him, both pain and contempt rushed through me. I slid down the wall and cradled my head in my hands. "What did I do?" I sat there with him for what felt like forever, blocking out my mother's cries. When the fire department arrived, I was forced to unlock the door. The police and the coroner arrived at different times, asking the same questions, making us tell the story over and over again. The medics gave my mother something to calm her hysterics. My grandfather showed up and, even grief-stricken, he took charge. He always did; that was who he was—a man in control. He made my brother go back to the neighbors' to stay with Bell until my grandmother got there to take them to their house. He talked to the police, the coroner, made a million other calls, and then finally he took my mother and me back to his house.

The next few days passed in a blur—the arrangements, the wake, the funeral. River, Bell, and I didn't finish the last few days of the school year. I skipped graduation, much to my mother's and grandparents' dismay. But the funeral was the day before, and I couldn't face anybody or even attempt to act normal. I was too broken. We were all broken—even my strong grandparents.

I remember the last night I talked to Ivy. The conversation was short. She wanted to see me, but I said no. I couldn't do anything but think about what I'd done, what I'd caused. She begged to come see me, but I said no. She'd offered to take her mother's car once her mother fell asleep, but again, I said no. She didn't need to piss that witch off. I couldn't deal with that shit. As it was, my "I" trip to Paris became a "We" trip to Paris—the family was going. So because I couldn't pull myself out of my own sorrow, Ivy and I said goodbye over the phone, and her sadness ripped me apart.

I look up at the dim lights through the window in the grim waiting room, and a shiver sweeps through me as I remember how it happened. Our summer trips were both over and it was the night we had planned to meet again. I hadn't yet told her I wasn't going to the University of Chicago with her, and I wasn't looking forward to it. I couldn't go that far—I couldn't leave my family when they needed me most. But it never mattered anyway, because instead of being the night we reunited, it was the night we ended. We never formally broke up. We were just no longer together. I loved her, and that was it—I loved her enough to do what was best for her. So even though we were a part of each other, when I got the opportunity to set her free—I did.

My eyes fly open when the overhead lights come on and pull me out of my own darkness. The only person who knows the truth is standing in the doorway of the waiting room. To everyone else I was a cheater, but I didn't care what people thought because leaving LA made her who she is today—I know it without a doubt. Standing up, I approach my brother. He looks exhausted. Clapping my hand on his shoulder, I ask, "Is she okay?" I want to ask if the baby is okay as well, but I'm afraid.

"Dahlia and the baby are fine." The relief in his expression can't be denied, but his voice is strained.

"What happened?"

He sighs. "She has something called placenta previa."

I give him a questioning look.

"It means her placenta is lying unusually low in her uterus."

"But you said Dahlia and the baby are okay?"

"They are for now. The doctor did an ultrasound and said the friction of the two organs being so close is what caused the bleeding. There is a chance as the pregnancy progresses the uterus will lift and there won't be any more bleeding, but there is also a chance it won't."

I can see his throat working to fight back his fear. "River, plain English, please."

He clasps both his hands around his neck. "The doctor advises that she take it easy. Avoid activities that might provoke any more bleeding."

His green eyes assess my reaction. He nods and I do the same. Both understanding what this means . . . he won't be going on tour. I pull him to me and hug him—something I can't remember doing since our father's funeral. "You do what you have to do. I understand."

CHAPTER 4
Just Beneath the Surface

The moon hasn't quite disappeared, but the sun hasn't yet risen—it's dawn and the streetlights are still on. I exit the cab with my bag in hand and climb the steps lit by the faint glow from the road to my condo in Beverly Hills. A car drives by, tossing the newspaper in the driveway, and I just leave it—I'll catch up later. I stayed at the hospital all night with my brother, and now I'm contemplating the phone calls I'll have to make later today. I've been taking risks, learning things, and making new relationships since I started to manage the Wilde Ones. But this—being left without a lead singer in the middle of a tour isn't an evolution, it's a regression, a detriment . . . it's the end.

Once I shower, I sit down and think about how I'm going to tell the guys. It makes me sick to think about it, but it has to be done. They aren't going to take it well, but I know I can't put it off. Announcements have to be made so shows can be canceled and money refunded. Time seems to creep by before I finally decide to pick up my phone. I call

Garrett and then Nix and tell them both to meet me at my place. I know they're not going to be happy, but at this point there are no other options. Garrett arrives around four with a six-pack in one hand and a new flick in the other.

"It's not date night," I tell him.

"Fuck off," he snorts. "I just thought you could use the company. You sounded like shit on the phone. What's going on?"

I slap his back. "We need to talk about existentialism."

He shakes his head in confusion, but I'm saved from explaining when Nix walks in right behind him.

"What's with the emergency meeting?" Nix asks.

"How about a drink?" I ask and motion for them to have a seat on the couch.

"Is it that bad that beer isn't strong enough?" Garrett questions, holding up the six-pack that he brought in.

These guys have been my brother's friends for longer than I can remember. Actually, although I've never admitted it, they're my friends too, and what I'm about to do is the hardest thing I've had to do in a really long time.

"How's Dahlia?" Nix asks.

Walking over to the bar, I say over my shoulder, "She'll be okay . . . but she can't travel."

Pouring whiskey into three tumblers, I turn around. Nix's and Garrett's jaws are on the ground, and it's clear they know what that means. I hand them each a glass of whiskey and toss mine back. "Remember when Brian Chase accidentally hit himself in the nose and blood squirted out everywhere?"

Nix's eyes narrow and Garrett just knocks his drink back, moving around me and stepping up to the bar.

I go on. "The more he bled, the harder he drummed, and the harder he drummed, the more he bled."

They both nod, confused about my reason for telling them this,

I'm sure. I continue. "That's how I feel about our band. We keep go-ing and going, but I really feel there's a time for the bleeding to stop and I think it's now. No more Band-Aids to stop the wounds from oozing."

Nix clears his throat. "I disagree. I think we could take a different approach."

I peg him with my stare and wonder where he's going with this. Garrett sits down and I do the same as Nix keeps talking. "Do you re-member the first time you heard Neil Young sing and you were like, 'Really? This guy is popular?'"

I raise an eyebrow. "Yes. What's that got to do with anything?"

"Everything. It means anything can happen when you don't ex-pect it," Garrett interprets for me.

"What's going on?" I ask them.

Garrett looks at me a little warily. "Well, someone stopped by last night after you took Dahlia to the hospital."

"Who?" I ask.

Garrett speaks up. "Ivy Taylor. She wants in."

I stand up and slam my drink down on the bar. My lungs constrict and I have to raise my arms and cradle my head to breathe. Twisting my body, I mindlessly circle the room until I can finally speak. "No fucking way," I yell at them.

"Xander, you and her happened a long time ago. Don't let your history with her cloud your judgment," Nix says.

"I'm not saying no because of our history," I reply with a scowl.

"Then why?" Garrett asks.

"First of all, she doesn't even sing in the same genre as the band."

Nix rolls his eyes. "Come on, Xander, you know her. She'll be able to sing our songs without a problem. For Christ's sake, you played with her for years."

"Even if she can, she's managed by that prick, and I'm not fucking working with him," I tell him very matter-of-factly. I want to be close to her in the worst way, but not when she's with somebody else—that's something I would never be able to stand.

"She says she won't be for long. She's trying to terminate their business relationship," Garrett says.

I stop pacing.

"How much sweeter could this be? We've all known each other since high school, and we're all in it for the music," Nix says, trying to persuade me.

"Xander, come on. We're flirting with disaster, and she pops in as our saving grace. People would follow her into a fire, and she came looking for us," Garrett declares, and I stand there waiting for the punch line, but there isn't one.

"Ellie agrees. She says she'll talk to the label and she thinks they'll be fine with it," Nix tells me.

"Well, Ellie doesn't manage the band," I respond, running my hands through my hair.

"No, but it's not just your band," Garrett says, a little shakily.

My head snaps up and I know my eyes are focused and clear. I take a deep breath. "What did you tell her?"

"Ellie or Ivy?" Garrett asks.

"Ivy," I bark.

"To come over and talk to you with us." His face is determined. It's a look that says it all. They've already made the decision.

"You shouldn't have done that." My voice wavers with uncertainty, but before I can put my issues on the table, the doorbell rings. My eyes flash to his and the pounding in my ears drowns out the sound of the bell. Walking across the dark hardwood floor in my bare feet, I take a deep breath and keep my face blank. Of course I want to see her. Fuck, I want to be with her. But she doesn't want anything to do with me, even though apparently she wants something to do with my band.

When I open the door, there she stands—and she's absolutely gorgeous. I tuck my hands in my pockets to control my nerves. Her beauty is only accentuated by the sunlight. Her hair is silky, her skin seems to gleam, and the sapphire earrings that my grandmother gave her follow the angular lines of her jaw . . . I can't believe she still wears them. But it's her eyes that capture me. They look darker, fiercer, more expressive, and they are focused on me. I can't help but take her all in.

"Hello," I say, ushering in her inside.

"Hi," she says back softly, with a forced smile.

She's biting her bottom lip and if I could have her right here, I would. Thoughts of her being mine race through my head. With her proximity, it's hard not to regret having hurt her.

She stands in the entryway and looks around. "Nice place."

I grin at her. "Thanks." I wonder if she knows this condo was my grandparents'—the place they moved to when they left the house where we spent so many days and nights. This place is much smaller than their house—just two bedrooms. But it works for me. I hired a decorator who made a few minor changes when I moved in, but not much. Just enough to toughen it up.

"Are Garrett and Nix here yet?"

My eyes lock on hers. "As a matter of fact—they are."

I motion toward the living area. "In there."

"Hey, before we go in, I just want to say thanks for yesterday, and I'm sorry for being so rude."

"Ivy . . ." Then I stop myself from blurting out the truth about the past. This isn't the time or the place. "I was just concerned about you. That's all."

"I'm fine. Really, I can take care of myself." She walks ahead of me before I can say anything else.

"Hi, Ivy," Garrett says, almost like he has a schoolboy crush on her.

"Ivy." Nix nods.

She fidgets. "Hey. Thanks for inviting me. So, have you guys talked to Xander about my suggestion?"

"We were just discussing it." I'm trying to ignore how good her legs look in denim shorts.

"Great," she says. "And my attorney confirmed that although my contract with Damon prohibits me from making any deals on my own, it does allow me to collaborate with other artists—he says it's a loophole."

"Yes!" Garrett says, pumping his fist in the air.

"Ivy, not that I don't appreciate the offer. But what does your fiancé say about all this?" I ask her.

Nix clears his throat. "Hey, Xander, we didn't get to that part of the news yet, but she broke it off with him."

Ivy's eyes collide with mine. For a moment I wonder if she's doing this for us, but only for a moment, because I have to quickly look away from the hate I see in her face. "Damon aside, why would you want to 'collaborate' with us?"

"I want back in the music industry and I can't do it on my own right now. Garrett and Nix told me River wasn't exactly keen on hitting the road, so I wondered how you'd feel about having the two of us? I could stay on the road full-time and he could pull off whenever he needed to."

"A few things have changed," Garrett says. "River won't be joining us after all. Dahlia has a complication and can't go on the road."

"Well, then, it looks like the situations we both find ourselves in seem to be a win/win. It's a simple case of I help you, you help me," she responds.

The room goes silent while I study her. It sounds like a business deal between two strangers, but we are far from that. Or are we? I bow my head, not sure what to say other than yes, because I sure as hell want her. "Okay, so if we do this, what's next?"

"We start rehearsing. We have time to nail most of the tour songs before we have to hit the road again," Nix says to all of us, and I'm not sure if he's trying to persuade himself or me.

"I can meet you in the studio with Leif as early as tomorrow."

We all turn our heads her way, but Nix is first to question her. "Leif? Who's Leif?"

"Leif Morgan. He's been with me from the start. He plays keyboard and bass," she says softly, then adds, "And he travels with me. If you don't mind?"

I nod and Nix and Garrett tuck their apprehension aside. There is nothing diva-like in her request. I know she'll mix with us well. She's the same girl she always was.

"We have ten days. It's a piece of cake," Garrett says confidently.

Her eyes find mine. "Look, Xander, we can give it a shot. If it doesn't work out, what are either of us out?"

What can I say? She's right—we have nothing to lose and everything to gain. We spend the next hour mapping out a strategy and discussing playlists. Changing from a male to a female lead means some minor lyrics changes. We decide I'll go through those songs while the band rehearses the others.

"Anyone hungry?" Garrett asks.

"I wouldn't mind something to eat," Nix chimes in.

"I could throw together my famous Enchilada Bake," Garrett says enthusiastically.

"What the hell is that?" I ask.

"You've had it before—a can of black beans, a jar of enchilada sauce, and a tube of biscuits."

"How about we order pizza?" I counter and look over at Ivy. "You in?"

"I can't. I'm sorry. I actually have to get going. Logan's in town for the night and I told him I'd meet him for dinner, but I'll see you all tomorrow. And thanks again." She walks over to Nix and Garrett and hugs each of them in turn.

She turns toward me and pauses.

"I'll walk you out." Standing near the entryway, I wait for her. She walks nervously my way. When she reaches me I automatically press my hand to the small of her back to guide her to the front door. When I realize where my hand is, I pull away, but I swear I see her shiver.

She reaches for the doorknob and my hand covers hers. I leave it there as I ask, "Logan—he joined the service?"

"Yes, he's a marine. He joined up right after high school, actually."

"Hmm . . . I thought he was going to Washington State?"

She looks up at me. "He was, but his parents divorced and money was an issue, so he decided to enlist. He's a sergeant now and stationed at Fort Bragg. He has a wife and three kids. He's really happy."

"That's great. Tell him I said hi."

"I will."

She smiles that forced smile at me that I hate and I step just a little closer. My body burns with a need to see the real one, and I allow the fire to consume me. In a moment of weakness, I pull her snug to me. Her breath heats my skin and with my lips just barely brushing hers, I ask, "Ivy, are you sure about this?"

Silence hangs between us until she boldly steps back. Her voice is low and raspy, but her eyes are clear, focused, and still on mine. Her intentions are not the least bit questionable as she answers, "Yes. I'm sure. The past is the past, Xander. Let's leave it there. We can move forward and do this."

I stare at her, trying to read her for a different sign, but it's not there, so I decide to do as she asks—leave the past behind. When her eyes break away from mine, she again reaches for the doorknob.

"Let me," I say, motioning toward the door with my hand as she moves hers away. I pull the door open and she walks out.

"Good night, Xander," she calls and looks back at me. "Thank you."

"Good night, Ivy," I respond and with a strong sigh I close the door—frustrated, confused, and maybe just a little optimistic.

My face is flecked with two-day-old stubble and my thick brown hair is a mess. I slept like shit. I have a lot on my mind and I had a hard time getting started this morning . . . Maybe I was just procrastinating while trying to figure everything out. There's a battle going on in my head—*Why is she really doing this?* I understand she has limitations due to her contract but is there more to it? Did she feel what I felt the minute I saw her again—that what we had so long ago was still there? She could have joined up with any band, so why this one? Did she do it for me? Because I'm not sure I buy the win/win explanation.

Blinking the sunshine out of my eyes, I'm still trying to sort my thoughts as I walk through the doors of Tyler Records. We've come and gone in and out of the glass-and-steel building for years. Actually, ever since my mother started seeing Jack, he's let us use the studio whenever we needed. My stepfather has been a huge asset to us, with his keen knowledge of the business and his unwavering willingness to help.

The band is so deep into rehearsing a song from our first album, they don't even notice me as I quietly slip into the live room. I stand off to the side and check out the scene—Nix has a Fender strapped around him, Ivy is at the microphone singing "I'll Find You" with unbelievable depth, Garrett's at the drums, but the cymbals sound a little washy next to the electric keyboard. And at the board stands a tall guy with a spray of freckles across his nose and dirty-blond hair that I can only assume to be Leif Morgan. He's wearing a pink button-down, and his wavy hair looks somewhat controlled by a slew of hair products, no doubt. I had pictured someone completely different—older, more fatherly, not a guy that looked like he modeled for Abercrombie and Fitch. Why, I'm not sure, but I think it was because of the fondness I saw in Ivy's eyes when she said his name.

I listen for a moment and I'm immediately impressed—his playing is spot-on. We just need to work on getting everyone in the same scale. All in all, not bad for the first time they've all come together. Shadows from behind the glass pique my curiosity. No one was supposed to be here today. I stride toward the front of the studio, and the sound engineer waves me into the control room. The heavily equipped space is state-of-the-art, including the latest digital audio workstations. I glance at Phil. "What's up?"

He presses the speaker button. "Hang on, guys. Give me a minute," he tells the band.

Ivy rocks back and forth, smiling at him and unleashing her soft laugh before she stops singing and replies, "No problem. We're not going anywhere."

I can't stop myself from turning at the sound of her low, creamy voice through the intercom. Her profile is nothing short of perfection. She sets her guitar down, and when she lifts her head our eyes collide. For the briefest of moments I think I feel the stirring of her heart in mine. She blinks and gives me an obligatory nod before shifting her gaze. I do the same, but my nod is slow, wistful, wanting, and I don't look away. I watch as she studies the music sheets in front of her. Her deep blue eyes practically dart with enthusiasm as she points to the papers on the stand and starts explaining something to the guys. She glances quickly at me again and notices my stare. But she immediately averts her gaze and continues with her conversation, tapping her leg to her own beat. She looks beautiful—every curve of her body is visible. She's wearing fitted jeans that hug her narrow hips and a tank top that clings to her perky tits. She is perfect.

Phil extends his hand as I approach him. "Hey, man, good to see you." Phil is the kind of guy who punctuates every sentence with *man*.

"You too."

He gives me a friendly thump on the back and with a broad grin he leads me over to his desk.

"We're just in here for rehearsal time," I let him know because I see him slithering into recording mode.

"I know, man. But I couldn't help but listen in. I think we should record a track and remix Ivy's voice in with River's."

"Glad for your enthusiasm, Phil, but we're not ready for that."

"No, man, you have to hear this. I've already played around with it. Just listen."

He pulls up a sound bite on his computer and hits PLAY. Her voice surrounds me, followed by River's, and I have to tell him, "It sounds fucking amazing."

"I know, man, I told you. Imagine what it will sound like if we pop that sweet tart in an isolation booth."

I suck in a breath and hold it to keep myself from pounding a guy who's always been a friend. Letting it out, I slide my eyes toward her. "Her name is Ivy, man."

He laughs. "Yeah, man, I know her name. I just like the sound of the words *pop* and *sweet tart* mixed together with *isolation booth*, if you know what I mean."

Anger flashes through me as I shoot fire at him with my eyes. "I wouldn't talk like that. It might get you in trouble."

"I didn't mean anything by it. I was only kidding around," he says, with concern ringing clear in his voice.

I turn to leave the room, throwing over my shoulder, "I'll get back to you on the remix."

Garrett pounces on me when I push on the large steel bar across the heavy door to exit the studio through the rear. "Where are you going?"

I gesture down the hall toward the alley. "I need to get some air. I have a fucking headache and the air in the studio is stifling."

"How about an aspirin?" he asks.

"I'm good."

He crosses his arms over his chest. "Everything okay?"

"Yes, I just needed some fresh air. And what's with the fifty questions?"

He eyes me. "Your past with her isn't going to be an issue, is it?"

"No, Garrett. I'm just beat."

"If you want to talk about it, I'm here."

"Thanks, but I'm fine."

He puts his hands up. "I'll leave you alone, but how about we grab some dinner tonight?"

"Sounds good."

He turns around and walks back toward the studio. I keep going and open the last door leading me outside. The sun shines bright and the sound of the music fades as I take the three steps to the sidewalk, where I can finally breathe. Blurry from exhaustion and hungover from too much booze, I give in and stumble backward. Sitting on the bottom step, I cradle my head in my hands and pray I can do this—that I can handle being around her every day and still do my job.

CHAPTER 5
What If

Ivy

Music has always been my everything. But when I was young, it really was all I had—it was my shoulder to cry on, my confidant, my best friend. I was an outcast in school because I kept to myself. I was always writing lyrics, and the other kids didn't know what to make of me, so they made fun of me instead. I didn't really care. I didn't have time for friends. My mother kept me busy. She wanted me to be an actress and she made me go on audition after audition. I hated the thought of pretending to be someone else in front of a camera. I hated the thought of acting, period. That wasn't what I wanted to do. I just wanted to share my music with others. But my mom saw it differently. We had very little money and she worked two jobs and odd hours to make ends meet. She thought if I acted we'd be secure. So if I wasn't running lines for a part I didn't want, I was going on auditions. I'd gotten a few parts here and there, but nothing permanent. I was also responsible for taking care of my younger sisters. So, like I said—I had no time for friends.

Then I met him—he got me, understood me, accepted me, guided me, showed me who I could be. Before I knew it, music and Xander Wilde—they became my world and stayed that way all the way through high school. I loved him. He was everything I didn't know I wanted and everything I needed. But my world turned upside down the day he betrayed what we were, what we had. I was shocked, surprised, and heartbroken, but somehow I think I always knew I wasn't enough for him. After that I left LA and never looked back. I couldn't be what he needed, so I never sought him out again. And why would I, anyway? All I felt toward him was hatred. I locked him away in my mind and tried so hard to never think about him. Now, without warning, he's come back into my life, and my world feels like it's been turned upside down.

A shiver ran through me and somehow I knew he was there—it was the strangest thing. I felt his stare and when I looked up into those eyes blazing with an intensity I once knew so well, they were boring into me. I felt a sharp jab of pain for what we had shared as the eyes of the boy I once loved quickly morphed into the eyes of the man I hated. The eyes I spent years looking into—the ones that sometimes look green but if you study them long enough you'll see their hypnotic flecks of brown.

He was the same, but different in a few ways. His startling hazel eyes, his tousled brown hair, sharp jawline, and strong, lean frame hadn't changed that much. He was so good-looking—not in a pretty or adorable way, but more in a rugged, handsome way. But he looks harder, even more closed off now. Then again, I'm sure I do too. Staring at him across the pool, I got lost in my thoughts. He was a boy no girl could ever forget. My mind filled with all the things I'd missed about him—our conversations, his protectiveness, his cocky grin, his charm, the way he said "fuck" just because. So many things I didn't want to remember, but they were all right here in front of me.

I never looked back and wondered if I made the right decision.

Even now I know leaving Xander is something I shouldn't be questioning. But the moment our eyes connected at the pool, all the hate I had been carrying around for years dissipated instantly. It scared me. How could just one look erase the bad memory and replace it with all the good ones? He was giving me the same look he used to give me when I'd cross the school grounds and spot him waiting for me—with his smile so genuine that his eyes lit up. It was the look that told me how much he loved me. I only stifled the need to run to him by remembering my fiancé was by my side.

Confusion tangled deep within me, but I couldn't resist setting my sights on him again. A hint of a smile crossed my lips. God, he was magnificent—broad shoulders, lean waist, toned arms. It might sound clichéd, but even when we were both fourteen and I noticed him for the first time I thought he was tall, dark, and handsome. And I couldn't help but fall for him. With his first grin in my direction—I melted. When he first played his guitar for me—he scored my mind. When he first kissed me—he stole my heart. And when he cheated on me—he took a piece of my soul. I was broken. His love broke me, and music was my only refuge.

I reminded myself that I hated him. I had once trusted him, confided in him, given him what I'd given nobody, and he stomped on us like we were nothing. I thought I was over him—I'd moved on long ago. But seeing him just brought it all back. The feelings I had for him were still there in my heart. I realized it the instant his stare reverberated through me and butterflies fluttered in my stomach. But I pushed those feelings aside—hate felt better than love, especially when I saw who the girl was that was standing next to him with her fingers in his hair. A wave of jealousy swept through me—I wanted to be the one running my fingers through his hair.

But seeing him was like a sign I didn't know I was waiting for. I finally knew it was time to break off my engagement to Damon. It had been time for a while—in fact, I never should have gotten engaged to him. The man I was going to marry was not the man I wanted to marry—that man was standing across the pool.

But breaking my engagement wasn't because of Xander—I had decided to do it before I saw him. The simple truth was Damon and I were never right for each other. I loved him in my own way. He had nurtured my talent and helped me with my career. I had trusted him in a world where trust was hard to find. But I had matured, grown up, figured out what I wanted—and we didn't want the same things.

He wanted me to put out another album—just like the first one. He also wanted a family right away. I wanted the independence to make my own decisions. I wanted to give my career time to grow before starting a family. That left us at a crossroads in our relationship when he suddenly asked me to marry him. He wanted me to take a year off and create the album of my dreams. He said he'd help me get it out there, help me sell it, and I loved him for supporting me.

Yet his job demands had intensified, and suddenly he was insisting that I travel everywhere with him—he wanted me by his side. I had written the songs for my album, but they weren't being produced. Damon was adamant that he knew what was right for me. Somehow I had become his arm candy and all we were doing was arguing. I was so unhappy, and I knew what we'd had for each other was gone—I just hadn't figured out how to tell him we were over. And then, without even knowing it, Xander made it all so clear. My relationship with Damon was one of comfortable love, not true undying love. And I wasn't going to settle.

The next day things unexpectedly came crashing down with Damon. We were at the pool and my gaze steadied on Xander again. I couldn't help but be drawn to the sight of him. To his strong, stubbled jaw that I wanted to cup in the palms of my hands, to his pale hazel eyes that were pinned on me, to all of him. Damon saw me staring, and he must have sensed what I was feeling, because he exploded, dragging me from the pool. When I finally told him the name of the person

I was looking at, he slapped me. That was it. I wasn't sticking around any longer. I was done the moment his palm struck my face. I wasn't going to be anyone's punching bag. My father used to hit my mother and me until one day he just up and took off. I wasn't going to repeat my mother's mistakes in any way, shape, or form. Xander's seeing me afterward made me so angry, and his concern made me furious—the hate I had for him was back in full force. I didn't need his help—I didn't need him.

As soon as I got back to the room, Damon was full of remorse. We discussed our situation, and he surprisingly took our breakup better than I could have imagined. He wanted me to keep the diamond ring— but I couldn't. I should have never accepted it from him to begin with. So I left it and left him.

Our personal relationship was over—but dissolving our business relationship wasn't as easy. For some reason he didn't want to let that go. I contacted my attorney, and he told me he would start the litigation needed to terminate our contract, but it wouldn't be quick, easy, or cheap. I hadn't earned any money in the past year and didn't have much money left. I was supporting my mother and my sisters, and my accounts were draining fast. One of my sisters was in med school and the other two were in college. I couldn't let them down. So when Zane Perry was diagnosed with a mild form of vocal cord paralysis and the Wilde Ones needed a new lead singer, I thought it would be the perfect arrangement.

When I left Xander's house the night we'd all agreed I'd replace Zane, I went to meet my cousin for dinner. Logan was really tired and I was glad because Xander's touch was still burning through my body and I couldn't stop thinking about him. Arriving home early, I struggled to sleep. Images of Xander, on top of me, under me, beside me, in me—I couldn't erase them. Even after all these years I remembered how we were together. I could see the sensuality of his raw, naked body. I could smell him. I could hear the groans he made when he came. And in the darkness of my own room, I used those memories to help relieve the need that had surged within me from the moment I first saw him again. I held my breasts and slid my thumbs over my nipples. I ran my hand down to my sex and touched myself. I imagined it was him touching me, pressing his thumb against my clit—taking me to the edge and back simply because he could. My heels pressed into the bed and my fingers gripped the sheets so tightly I nearly tore them as my body finally found its release.

But I refused to give in to that kind of need again. I had to stop thinking about him that way. For the past two weeks I've tried to avoid getting too close to him. For reasons I don't want to think about, though, I want to be near him. Then every time I am near him, I teeter between love and hate. It's a fine line and I'm taking baby steps to avoid stumbling. I have to say, he threw me when he hadn't said yes right away about my joining the band. That bothered me. I wanted him to welcome me, at least make me feel like he cared. But what bothers me the most is he hasn't really tried to discuss what happened between us. I know I said the past was in the past, but I never thought he'd listen. He never used to let barriers keep him from discussing the things that were important to him. The fact that he seems so detached from the whole situation is eating at me in a way that's causing me to lose focus. We're going to be sharing the confined space of a tour bus and before I get on that bus, we need to clear the air. We are both grown-ups. We can do this—talk it out and then put it aside for the sake of business. At least that's what I keep telling myself.

I'm staying with a friend in Beverly Hills, so the drive to his house is short—too short. As I pull up to the beautiful architecture of his Canon Drive condominium building, my pulse races in a way I'm not familiar with. I walk slowly to his door, telling myself I can do this, not to be nervous. Just as I'm about to ring the bell, the door opens. I drop my gaze to the ground and I swear my heart jumps out of my chest. I think about running, but I'm not sure my jelly legs will take me any-where. I draw a deep breath and when I can finally focus, I look up and almost laugh because it's not him—it's his brother. When I saw River at the announcement party I knew who he was right away—the light brown hair that looks almost coppery and the insanely green eyes hadn't changed. To me he'll always be Xander's cute kid brother, but he's grown up to be equally as handsome as Xander. The difference— River borders on adorable, while Xander exudes ruggedness. Their hair and eye color may be different, but there's no mistaking they're brothers.

"Ivy." He greets me, pulling me for a quick hug.

"Hi, River. Is Xander home?" I ask nervously.

"Sorry. He's not. I just stopped by to pick up a few things he bought for Dahlia."

I must look at him skeptically because he explains, "He was out and picked up some old albums, CDs, and movies he thought she'd enjoy."

"That was nice of him. I heard she's been put on bed rest. I'd say I'm sorry, but really that must be kind of nice. The two of you get to spend time together doing things you like to do."

An almost wicked grin crosses his face. He's so much like his brother. My cheeks turn pink and I feel the need to clarify my com-ment. I point to the stack of albums under his arm. "Like listening to some awesome music."

"Yes, we've actually been making the best of it," he says with a laugh.

Backing away from the door, I say, "Well, it was great to see you again and it was really nice meeting Dahlia at the press announcement party. Please tell her I said hello. I'll catch up with Xander later at rehearsal."

"Ivy," he calls in a tone that sounds a little too real for me to want to hear any more.

I stop just before the steps. Turning around, I clutch the railing. "Never mind," he says, and I just smile, then leave.

The sun brightens the east side of the stadium, with blazing-hot rays beating down and making it hard to see anything but what's right in front of you. It's our last rehearsal before hitting the road tonight, and Xander insisted on making it as realistic as possible. We're at the Greek Theatre, the stadium is empty, and I'm clutching the microphone . . . my face carefully blank as I mindlessly search for him. It's upsetting me that he's occupying so much of my mind space. Before I went to his house, I thought having it out with him would take care of it, but now I think status quo might be best. My nerves overtook me when I was there, and I'm not sure I can actually discuss the past with him.

I just have to clear away all thoughts of him and focus on my career. But that's easier said than done because every time I see him, he's back in the forefront of my mind. Even right now he's searing me as he strides down the aisle. He looks amazingly sexy in all black—black T-shirt, black jeans, and black work boots. I'm standing in this huge stadium with so many other people around and he's still all I see. Moving toward me with his dark good looks and arrogance, he's just the same eighteen-year-old boy I couldn't wait to see, talk to, kiss, and wrap my arms around. But today, even though his hazel eyes appear tired and his dark hair looks a little more disheveled than usual, he's still undeniably gorgeous. What's wrong with me? One minute I don't want to lay eyes on him ever again, and the next I can't wait to see him.

The sound system is on the fritz and he immediately takes control of the situation. He points to the stage and yells to someone. He struts even closer and his walk is as full of confidence as his tone. Hearing his voice, now the voice of a man, makes my heart beat a little faster, my breath quicken, and gives me that feeling of comfort in my soul that it once did. Screeching crackles from the speakers pierce my ears. The scratching sound would normally make me cringe, but right now it's the sweetest hymn of music because it helps distract me.

After he gives a few more directives, the sound system seems to be working again and he moves on to his next task. Ellie, the tour manager, calls him over and he approaches her with the easy grin and flirty manner that used to make me see green when he talked to other girls. It has the same impact on me now. I feel like that same lovesick teenager, and my reaction just makes me furious with myself.

When we finally finish what has to be the longest rehearsal ever, I swing my purse over my shoulder and make my way to the restroom. My phone rings the minute I cross the threshold backstage, and I fumble through my bag to pull it out. The screen flashes DAMON and I automatically hit IGNORE. He's been calling and texting me for the last two weeks—begging forgiveness one minute and threatening legal action the next. He wants me back, but whether it's for personal or business reasons, I'm not sure. I haven't asked because I have no intention of going back. I'm not sure what's going to happen when he finds out I joined this tour. Xander is making the announcement today that I've joined the Wilde Ones. I guess I'll have to talk to Damon tonight, but I'll wait until we've hit the road.

The bathroom backstage is old and definitely needs to be remodeled. The mirror is cracked, but I steal a glance at myself anyway. Hot, sweaty, and a mess. Oh, well. I try to stick the pieces of my hair that have fallen out of my low-slung bun back into the elastic as best I can and then head out. I'm a little nervous about starting this journey and a little excited at the same time. Singing is what I love, so getting back to sharing my music is exciting, but having Xander so close has put me on edge. My feelings for him are unclear and crystal clear at the same time—that's why I'm nervous.

The smell of hamburgers fills the air, and I smile when I see that the food has been put on the tables previously set up in the orchestra section of the amphitheater. Since I'm starving, I make a plate and join the guys. Xander is not here. See, I'm still thinking about him—crap. I take a seat in the metal folding chair next to Garrett. His slightly long blond hair covers his gray eyes, shielding them from the sun. I just grin at him because his hairstyle and boyish face make him look like he's still fifteen, and he really is cute. His lip ring only adds to his youthful appearance, and his tall, skinny stature certainly doesn't help him look any more grown-up. When my phone rings again, I ignore it and switch it to VIBRATE.

Garrett asks, "Not going to answer that?"

The sunglasses on my face not only keep the sun from blinding me but also keep Garrett from seeing the stir of nerves within me. Damon's continual calls are wearing on me. Smiling, I tell him, "It would be rude to answer at the table."

He smiles back and takes a bite of his burger.

I push the unidentifiable salad around on my plate. "Do you think these are potatoes?"

He shrugs his shoulders and takes another bite of the mound identical to mine on his own plate. "It tastes like macaroni to me."

Suddenly, the heap of food on my plate becomes very unappealing and I'm not hungry anymore. I push it aside. Nix is sitting across from me, sipping his beer. "He eats anything," he mumbles, rolling his eyes.

Nix is an attractive dark-haired guy. In high school he always had a girlfriend but never seemed interested in any of them. He's tall, but not as tall as Xander, and he has an athletic build. His hair is short, his eyes are chocolate brown, and his skin always looks tan. He looks the same as in high school, just more mature and more built. But he now wears a very detailed tribal tattoo that circles his biceps with an intricate feather design draped down his arm. It's always peeking out from under the short sleeve of his T-shirt. Garrett told me he got it right after graduation—he went to visit his great-uncle, who lives on an Indian reservation, and came home with it. Garrett said he never really explained to them why he got it, but he figures it has something to do with his family heritage.

I stand up and toss my plate in the trash. My phone rings again, but this time it's my mother and I decide to bite the bullet and get it over with.

"Hello."

"Ivy, it's your mother, honey," she says, as if I didn't have caller ID or recognize the sound of her voice.

"Mom. Hi." I drop down to sit on the steps.

"I've been calling you. Why didn't you call me when you broke off your engagement with Damon? I had to hear it from him."

"I'm sorry. I just have a lot going on right now."

"Well, sweetie, I'd like to have lunch this week if possible."

I take a couple of deep breaths. "Mom, I'm going on the road with another band for a few months and I'm busy getting ready, but I promise I'll call you as soon as I get settled."

"Ivy, honey, it's important. Your sister's tuition is due and I don't have the money and somehow I missed the mortgage payment last month."

"Mom, I'll see what I can do. Money is tight right now."

"Oh," she responds. "Do you think you could ask Damon?"

"No! I should be able to get you some money in a few weeks."

"I can't wait that long. The bank will take the house."

I squeeze my eyes shut. "Listen, come get my car. I'll text you where it is. I'll leave the keys and the signed pink slip under the mat. That should hold you over for a bit."

"Ivy, that would help tremendously."

"I have to go, Mom. I'll call you soon."

"Thanks, honey. I knew I could count on you." She hangs up.

Her response was as automatic as mine. She knew all she had to do was ask. But what bothers me is that she didn't even ask where I was going or with whom. That just wasn't as important as getting a check.

My body fills with so much tension I feel paralyzed. I put my head in my hands and sit alone for the longest time, wondering how I'm ever going to free myself from her. Finally, I stand and head backstage to the bathroom to splash some cold water on my face. The floor is slatelike and my heels click against it with each step, but that's not the only sound I hear—I hear Xander's voice. With just one simple word he's back in the front of my mind again and I stand frozen in place in the almost nonexistent space between the stage and backstage.

"Fuck," he says, and the way the word rolls off his tongue catapults me back in time.

I had missed a week of school and band rehearsals. I was in the tenth grade and Xander had just gotten his license. I was sick, but I still had to babysit—my mother was working. The doorbell rang and when I opened it all I could see was a finger hooked around a hanging plant of ivy. I slammed the door shut, thinking it was the neighbor kids playing a practical joke and almost caught his finger.

"Fuck!" he yelled, and I immediately opened the door again.

He came into view and handed me the pot. I raised an eyebrow and just looked at him.

He grinned. "What?"

I eyed the ivy plant.

Shrugging, he said, "Roses are so cliché." Then he kissed me and snickered. "I prefer Ivy." He made the statement sound simple, but it was so full of meaning. His gift was a symbol of our love and it was something that could last forever . . . like I thought we would. He stayed that night to help me babysit. Once the girls fell asleep, we watched the Grammys and we talked about our dreams for each other—his was that I would be up on that stage one day. That made me laugh and made me cry. After that night he'd bring me ivy plants of all kinds—sometimes as a gesture to make up, sometimes for my birthday, sometimes just because . . . and I loved them all. I planted them in the garden I started with my sisters or hung them in my room, and they never died, but I did dig them all up and throw them away the night I saw him with Tessa.

Shaking off the memory, I divert my attention away from him and try to push him out of my mind. But when he yells, "Come on, motherfucker!" I can't help but steal a glance. He's talking to some guy I don't know and the motherfucker in question is a coin. Watching him as he throws his muscled arm up to release the coin and yells, "Heads," subconsciously I yell, "Heads" in unison. I know his call—it hasn't changed. The way his lip curves around the word as he says it gives me a sudden urge to suck on it. Turning, he looks at me and his eyes lock on mine. His mouth forms that same slow, easy grin that always made me weak at the knees. But I can't smile back . . . I want to, but I'm afraid that if I do I won't be able to compartmentalize him anymore. What's between us has to stay professional; if not, things will get too messy. A flash of something mars his finely chiseled face, but he catches the coin without faltering. Covering it with his other hand, he cocks his head and bobs his chin, calling me over. I stay where I am. *I hate him. I hate him.* I have to keep saying it or I'll forget.

Shrugging, he lifts his hand. "Heads it is."

The tall, skinny man standing next him sighs. "Okay, we'll drive straight through to Denver, but if I crash the bus I'm blaming you."

Xander lets out an exaggerated laugh and slaps a hand on the man's shoulder. "First of all, you have Brad, and second, you won't crash the bus. You've made runs like this a million times."

"Whatever you say, boss man," replies the man I can now identify as John the bus driver.

Xander walks away. "See you on the bus," he calls over his shoulder, maybe to me, maybe to John, maybe to both of us, I don't know. What I do know without a doubt is that I want him. The sound of his voice alone makes every nerve in my body tingle, makes my nipples tighten, and causes an ache between my legs. I stand there and watch him move with that ease he has about him, and I know this is going to be so much harder than I've convinced myself it would be.

Later that night, we board the bus and I run for refuge. I have to escape my attraction to him. Being near him only heightens it. I hop in the shower and then get ready for bed. I lie on the mattress in the back bedroom of the bus with my door locked and close my eyes. The movement of the bus should lull me to sleep, but it doesn't. I can't stop thinking about him. I picture his long, lean body, his face, the sounds he used to make, and even the way he says the word *fuck*. I remember the sound of his husky voice in my ear, the way his tone oozed sex. My hands slide down my own body and into my pajama bottoms. I tug the elastic down and kick them off, then spread my legs. And as I lie there alone in the darkness, my hands become his—doing what I want him to be doing so badly at this moment. I come in a shattering climax and sleep finally consumes me.

CHAPTER 6
Talk to Me

Xander

The outside passes in a blur as I walk into the front lounge from the galley. As usual, I'm awake before any of the guys. I did my typical tour bus workout in the back lounge—sit-ups, push-ups, and weights that we keep back there. I'll run tonight before the show. It's hard to keep a routine on the road, but I try. It helps relieve stress and keeps me focused.

Entering the room, I get a feeling like I've been slapped in the face. Jack White's "Love Interruption" is playing. It's an awesome slow-burn blues ballad, and the lyrics seem to reflect the way my relationship with Ivy ended. I flip the light on and see her sitting there on one of the benches. Holding a cup with both hands, she's drinking coffee and staring out the window. I hear soft, quiet notes as she sings along to the song, but she stops when the lights flicker. Her gaze darts to mine for one brief second, and then her eyes swing immediately back to the window.

I clear my throat. "Hey. Good morning." It seems odd to see her on the bus.

She glances back toward me. Something flashes across her face, but it's gone before I can pinpoint it. "Hey. Morning." Her expression is neutral and her voice is low.

"How'd you sleep?"

She sets her cup down. "Great. The quiet of the engine seems to lull me to sleep every time I ride on one of these." Her tone is sarcastic and I fucking love it.

I offer a smile, holding back my smirk. "Yeah, try sleeping on the bottom bunk with the floor vibrating underneath you."

"I'll pass," she says and turns back to look at the cornfields and lush greenery of the Midwest surroundings.

I pour a cup of coffee and look over my shoulder. Lifting the pot, I ask, "Refill?"

"I'm good," she answers, covering the top of her cup with her hand.

I move to sit across from her. "Mind?" I ask.

She shakes her head. I want to ask her a million questions. I want to know everything she's done for the last twelve years, but when one of the songs from her first album comes on the radio, I settle for asking one simple question that has been eating at me. Her song "Hit It" surrounds us. The lyrics are about dancing but can very easily be misconstrued as being about sex. Since it doesn't seem like a song she'd have sung, let along written, I nod toward the speaker and ask, "What made you take that road?"

Her eyes narrow on mine. "What do you mean by *that* road?"

"Ivy, you know what I mean."

She turns to look at me full on. The look she gives me tells me right away that she's offended, and her answer only confirms this. "No, I don't. Why don't you explain?"

Okay, if she wants me to spell it out, I will. I pause for a moment before answering, trying to figure out the best way to phrase this, but decide to just say it. "Why did you choose pop music? You were never one for the verse-chorus structure or catchy hooks like this." When the hook plays, I lift my eyes to the speaker and add, "You have so much artistic depth. I just never thought you'd sell out for mass appeal."

With a sigh, she stands up. Hurt quickly passes over her face before hate presents itself. Bracing her hands on the table, she leans forward. "You don't know what I have anymore," she says with a shaky voice. Then adds, "I'm going to get ready." With that she brushes past me.

Rising from my chair, I call, "Ivy, wait. I wasn't trying to be an asshole."

But she doesn't stop. Instead she hastily pulls the curtain back to huff forward. It's then that she finally comes to a dead standstill. I'm on her heels and almost barrel right into her. She's stopped, just staring, and I glance inside the galley to see what has captured her attention. It's Garrett and he's awake, doing his morning exercise.

"Is that a sex swing?" she asks him wide-eyed, her cheeks turning pink as soon as the words leave her mouth.

I burst out in laughter. I can't help it. For some reason being near Ivy makes everything that's mildly funny seem funnier. It always did.

A devilish grin appears on his face. "No. It's a yoga swing. But thanks for the idea," Garrett tells her.

"Fuck, no, not in here," Nix calls out from behind one of the curtains. "No one wants to see your naked ass in the act."

Leif comes out of the bathroom wearing some kind of sleep pants that make me laugh equally as hard—they're baby blue with an elastic waist, and I wonder if they're Ivy's. Holding my stomach, I try to calm myself. Garrett gives me a perplexed look. I know he must be thinking he's probably never seen me laugh this much, and I don't remember the last time I did. Leif, with his toothbrush in his mouth, shrugs past as if nothing out of the ordinary is occurring and disappears into his cubby. Nix pops his head out and starts talking to Garrett about setting some new rules.

I take the opportunity to get Ivy's attention. Moving directly behind her, I clutch her arm and pull her back to me. "Can I talk to you back in the lounge?" Her laughter stops when I whisper in her ear, "Please."

She turns to look at me, her eyes unreadable. "Okay."

I turn and she follows. I fight the urge to hold her hand. We enter the front lounge again and she moves to one side. I lean against the small counter opposite her. "I'm sorry. That was a shit thing to say. I didn't mean it like it sounded. What I meant to say was what made you decide to debut with a pop song?"

She sighs and sits back down, sipping from the mug she'd left behind. Silence is all around us before she answers, and the room seems much bigger than it actually is. "First, yes, it was a shitty thing to say. But to answer your question, it was my only choice. I'd been back in LA for six months and hadn't found a job. I was singing at the coffee shop my mother worked at. Damon had been going in there for years and she had told him about me. He came to one of the open-mic shows and afterward asked to meet with me. When I first met him, I was determined to put out the album I had always dreamed of. He disagreed with my vision. He said the marketability of what I proposed wouldn't work in the climate we were in at the time. So I left. Then about a week later he talked to my mother. He called me back and agreed to cut a demo of one of my songs. It took another three months before it went out, and I still hadn't found a job. He finally sent it out, but we never heard back from a single label. In the meantime I'd managed to get a job working for an advertising agency writing jingles—I hated it. A year later I decided to do it his way. And even though the album didn't hit the top of the charts—I was still happier."

"That doesn't make sense. No one was interested in your first song, but he found a label to pick up the album after that?"

She looks up at me with her blue eyes, the softness in them draining by the second. She rises and walks to the small sink next to where I'm standing. She rinses her mug, sets it down, and turns her head toward me. "Xander, I'm not sure what you're implying, but Damon has always had my best interests at heart. In fact, we're working on a new sound now—or we were."

It's unlike me to hold back on how I feel, but I'm aware she doesn't trust me yet, so I put my hands up in surrender. "I didn't mean it that way."

She reaches for a banana and peels it, not responding to my comment. I'm really curious why Damon would switch gears, so I ask, "What kind of new sound?"

"Well, not new. Old might be a better explanation."

I nod, understanding what she means.

"We both agreed I'd take a break and refocus, redirect my music to what I envisioned when I first started singing. I've written songs and hit the studio attempting to produce them. We've tried a few different producers, but I'm still not happy with the results."

"Can I listen to them sometime? You can tell me what it is you don't like and maybe I can help you."

She chews a bite of banana, swallows, takes another bite, as if strongly considering my request. "I'd actually really like that."

She makes the simple statement and I want to press her for more. I want to listen to her new songs now. I want to talk to her more about her music. I don't want this conversation to end. But silence rises up between us again. She throws the banana peel away, and then her head drops and she stares into the sink. When I brace my arms back on the counter, our hands are so close all I'd have to do is move my thumb a fraction of an inch and we'd accidentally be touching. But instead I do something I know I shouldn't. I lift my hand and gently grasp her chin, pulling it toward me. "Ivy?" I ask. "You okay?"

"Yes," she answers, closing her eyes.

I breathe out. She breathes in. I can feel my skin touching hers and I want to hold her, rest my forehead on hers, I want to brush my lips across hers, I want to whisper in her ear that she can trust me. Having her this close twists me, turns me, makes me think about my actions. I don't want to upset her. It's been almost two weeks since she joined the band and our conversations have mostly been work-related until now. This is the first personal conversation we've had, and talking to her again has everything inside me screaming for her. Everything she does sets my blood on fire. I drop my hand and back away. I'm going to give her some time because that's something we have—three months' worth of it.

"I'm really going to get changed now," she says, her voice smooth and low.

I nod and she turns and leaves the lounge. I watch her until she disappears. Then I open the fridge and grab an apple. Taking a bite, I chew it and grin—all in all, that didn't go that badly.

Time seems to tick by so slowly the rest of the day. Staring out the window at a stream that meanders through fields on its own sweet time, I kick myself for not pushing it with her. Why wade through the stream instead of jumping over it? Yet I know I have to take it slow with her or she'll keep retreating—and I want her around. I've lived on this bus for six months with eight other dudes, and it's been nothing but comfortably boring. Having Ivy on board has already made everything different—I feel a buzz of energy in the air and everything seems more alive.

By the time we finally arrive in Denver, I'm ready to blast into action. We get right to work, which I'm glad about because it takes my mind off her. I'm in a hurry to get in as much rehearsal time as I can. And at least the tension between Ivy and me melts away when she's onstage. We both act professional and don't let our past interfere with the music. I use today's sound check as more of a rehearsal, so it lasts three hours. The guys are ready to be done, but I think we need more practice. I want their performances to be perfect. A lineup of forty songs means learning a shitload of material, so we keep going over and over them. Leif switches between keyboard and bass, depending on the song. His versatility has proved to be a great addition to the band.

"Okay, let's call it for now," I yell.

"It's about fucking time," Nix snarls at me.

Leif thumps his shoulder and heads to the keyboard with the corner of his mouth turned up. Leaning over it, he closes his eyes and hits some notes. He seems to be playing a song, but the words that leave his mouth sound more like a rap. The melancholy of it draws me in. I take a seat and just listen until he's done.

"That's a showstopper," I comment, meeting him at the bottom of the stairs as he walks off the stage.

"Yeah, well, it's not meant for the audience Ivy sings to."

I shoot him a small grin. "You're full of all kinds of surprises. But really, I liked it."

He shrugs. "Thanks, man. Had a buddy years ago and rapping was his thing. What can I say—he taught me well."

"Not to change the subject, but what's your take on learning all the band's songs in such a short period of time?"

He sighs with what looks like an authentic worry line creasing his brow before he confesses, "Honestly, I'm not sure it's going to happen."

That's not what I wanted to hear.

He turns and heads backstage to get ready for the show, throwing over his shoulder, "Gotcha, dude! We got this nailed."

I grin with relief.

Showtime comes quickly and ends just as quickly. There are good shows and bad shows and this one is definitely not great. The arena is filled at about seventy-five percent—not bad, considering we've switched leads in mid tour. But Ellie has arranged for some special effects to welcome Ivy, and the streamers just seem to take away from the set, and the guys are off the rest of the night after that.

Fresh from the stage, the band and the crew are digging in to the food backstage. Leif has a penchant for wine and opens a few bottles of red. He sniffs the contents of a bottle and then pours a glass. After he takes a sip he pours some for everyone. By eleven thirty we all smell like red wine and are pretty drunk. Knowing it's time to leave, we take the backstage door and head to the bus, which pulls out at midnight. We won't be staying in a hotel until we get to Lincoln.

Garrett walks beside me, complaining about the streamer gimmick. Just as we start to cross the parking lot, at least two dozen fans come rushing over to Ivy, begging for pictures and autographs. I stop and glance at Leif. The others keep moving—all except for Garrett, who's still talking.

Leif stops as well, crossing his arms over his chest. "I'll wait for her."

I nod, already having decided I'd wait for her.

He pulls out a pack of cigarettes and taps it against his hand, then pulls one out and hands the pack to me.

"No, thanks, man," I say. "That's one vice I never took up."

"Good thing, because it's a fucking hard habit to break."

"I'm sure it is."

"I only smoke when I'm drinking and never inside," Leif clarifies, as if I cared.

"I'll take one of those," Garrett says.

I just look at him and shake my head. He lights the cigarette and inhales, then exhales smoke in a huge cough.

"You're such a fucking retard," I tell him.

"What? I used to smoke."

"Yeah, when you could sneak one behind the school grounds in the sixth grade." I laugh.

Garrett stubs his cigarette out. "I'm going to make like Tom and Cruise. You coming?" he asks me.

Shaking my head, I tell him, "I'll stick around with Leif and wait for Ivy."

I have an uneasy feeling about leaving her with just Leif. She's pretty tight with him and he seems to watch over her, but if something happens, he'd never be able to handle it himself—from what I can tell he's definitely more of a lover than a fighter. I make a note to myself to talk to Ena about additional security. I'll have her call River's security guy, Caleb, and get some recommendations.

When the crowd finally clears, the three of us head back to the bus. Leif's phone rings, and glancing at its screen, he stops. "I've gotta take this. I'll catch up with you later," he says, stepping away for some privacy.

Ivy and I walk the remaining few feet in silence. She's wearing a pair of tight black jeans, a gray shirt with the shoulders cut out, and a pair of spike heels that look more like boots. Her flawless body is a perfect match to her songbird voice. We're both a little drunk, and it shows when she climbs the steps to the bus and one of her heels sticks in the rubber matting, causing her to stumble. Next thing I know, I've fallen on top of her. My mouth is next to her ear and I can smell the fresh scent of her hair. I don't move because I can hear her breathing and I can almost feel her pulse racing beneath me. At that moment I know for sure—she still feels about me the way I feel about her. And in this one moment everything changes.

"You want me, don't you?" I whisper under my breath and I can feel my mouth tip to one side.

She flips around and my body instantly falls, molding to hers in a heartbeat. The heat between us is undeniable, at least to me.

"No, I don't," she says a few moments too late. "Please get off me," she adds in a voice that refuses any rebuttal. Our locked gazes keep me glued where I am, but when she averts her eyes, I can't help but grin. It's so apparent what that means. She forgets how well I know her.

"You're lying."

"I'm not the liar," she hisses.

I want to say I'm not either, but I don't, because that would be a lie. So instead I stand up and wipe my palms on my jeans before extending my hand to help her up. She refuses my help and pushes herself up.

"I can manage myself," she snaps as she turns and walks up the steps.

And I stand here smug as shit because now I know—I have to tell her what really happened. I just need the right time and place.

The Lincoln, St. Paul, and Des Moines shows come and go without any noteworthy events. We're headed to Springfield for Summerfest. Summer festivals are a blast to play and we have about four more lined up on this tour. I've been extremely busy with press releases and promo changes. Rehearsal schedules have been ramped up and we have very little time to do anything but sleep and work, so everyone is looking forward to the festival.

We reach Springfield on the third day of Summerfest. I'm backstage at sunset and the band is just coming off the stage.

"You rocked it," I tell Leif, giving him a high five. He had a solo on the keyboard and really tore it out.

"I'm going to check out Eminem a few stages over. Anyone coming?" Nix asks.

"I will," Ivy answers and I'm surprised. Since when does she like rap?

"Yes, I'll join you as well," I add.

The other guys head over to see the Sheepdogs and the three of us cross the field as bands on five stages churn out majestic jams. Walking through the crowds, I stay close to her side, occasionally guiding her with a slight touch. Nix stops to talk to someone he knows and we keep moving. It's hotter than hell and the crowd is a sweaty mess. We reach the stage area as the song ends and everyone is screaming for more. Another song begins to play and we stand together and listen. It hasn't been just the two of us since the first morning on the bus. A comfortable ease slips between us as we watch the performance. Feeling the time is right, I step closer to her. Close enough that we're shoulder to shoulder. Then I dip my head and ask, "Want to have a drink someplace quiet? Someplace we can talk?"

She bites her bottom lip and looks away. She opens and closes her mouth a few times until she actually answers me. "I don't think that's a good idea."

Her breath is sweet and warm on my neck, and I want her to change her mind. I want to hear her say yes. I want to push her, but I don't. As I study her—her body language, her perfect face—my lips twitch from trying not to laugh at myself. I'm a guy who has always gone after what he wants. I want what I want now . . . but with Ivy it's different. I need to earn her trust before I can tell her the truth.

"What?" She looks up at me with an innocence that makes my heart beat dangerously fast.

I can't hold back my laughter anymore and I let it out. "Nothing, nothing. How about we grab some funnel cakes over at the midway?"

She nods with a small hint of excitement, and I have to cross my arms to keep my hands from clutching her face and just kissing her for the sweetness that I see in it.

Ivy and I spent the night listening to bands and just hanging out, but we never talked about the past—about us. I danced around the topic, but every time I did she tensed up and seemed to withdraw. So I decided to put it aside and focus on things between us now. The guys eventually caught up with us and we headed back to the bus and pulled out for our next show. We're on the way to Cleveland with a stop in Cincinnati for a night out. Leif's buddy Casper is a boxer and he invited the band to come watch his next fight. Leif's convinced that Casper will be the reigning heavyweight champion in no time. His career record so far is 23 and 0. Although I haven't been keeping up with the sport, I'd have to agree with Leif—his record speaks for itself.

The traffic is crazy on the way to the Horseshoe Casino and we're running a little late. Ivy's sitting next to Leif in the SUV and I'm sitting behind them with Garrett. Nix is up front. Ivy's almost too much to take in at once. Her strapless yellow top shows off her perfect figure, but I want to cover her bare shoulders and pull her top up a little to eliminate all that exposed skin. Her hair is wavy today, a style I've never seen her wear, but it looks really sexy on her. She shakes her voluminous curls when she laughs at something Leif says, and I take a deep breath—fuck, she looks amazing.

We enter the venue just as the fight is being announced. She's by my side and jumps a little when the speaker blares with the announcer's voice: "Ladies and gentlemen, here he is! I know you all know who I'm talking about—so without further ado I give you Casper 'the Ghost' Holland." I place my hand on the small of her back and guide her down the aisle. A slight shiver makes her body shake and I grin.

"This way," I whisper in her ear.

Just as we reach our seats the crowd roars, "Ghost!" and a guy in all white comes trotting down the aisle. The back of his robe is labeled just what the crowd is chanting—GHOST. He climbs into the ring with one fluid jump and moves to a corner, where someone helps him remove his robe. Shit, this guy is ripped. Ivy's standing between me and Leif, and when I look her way, I see her eyes are glued to his body. Leaning over, I whisper, "You might want to close your mouth. Leaving your tongue hanging out is a little obvious."

"What? I'm just looking at his tattoos." But she's blushing. My eyes travel down her body and my hands want so badly to follow suit. Leif leans over and she tilts her head to hear what he's saying. I can't help but notice how close the two of them are, and I'm glad he has a girlfriend. When Leif pulls his phone out, she steps closer to me. Her fresh scent wafts through the air and I breathe it in. My urge to kiss the skin on her bare neck has never been greater.

When the lights suddenly dim in the stands, she turns to me. "I'm not sure watching two guys beat each other up is my thing."

"Just look away if you don't like it, and if it's too much we can leave anytime," I tell her, thankful for this sign of the innocence I sense she still possesses. I feel an urge to pull her to me and let her bury her head in my chest, but I resist.

Two burly guys try to get by so they can stand on the other side of me and she pushes her body into mine as she moves out of the way. I stifle a harsh breath. The sound of the gruff voice overhead is the only thing that breaks the spell she's cast over me. When the crowd goes crazy, I instinctively grip her side and move her to stand in front of me. So much for resisting. She leans back slightly, almost leaning against me. The feeling of her body so close to mine just about sends me over the edge.

The announcer continues: "And now, ladies and gentlemen, may we have a round of applause to welcome, Eddy 'Bikini' Bottoms." He too almost trots down the aisle. I look into the ring and see that Casper seems to be circling it—waiting for his prey. His opponent takes his place with ease, and both fighters flex their fingers at their sides, their hands taped so their bare knuckles are exposed. I have a feeling this is going to be a good fight. Each of them slides his gloves on and the crowd explodes in cheers around us when the two opponents meet in the middle and the bell rings. Casper's opponent swings first. Casper ducks and jabs Bottoms's side with a right, then a left. A few more rounds pass, and then out of nowhere Casper lands one straight punch to the jaw that knocks his opponent down just like that.

Ivy gasps in disbelief when Bottoms tries to lift himself up on his arms as the counting begins. With each number, she pushes herself farther back into me. Does she know what she's doing to me? I couldn't even tell you what's going on in the ring. I feel like that eighteen-year-old boy that got hard with every move she made. The counting stops and Bottoms's trainer is by his side, as he lies flat on the mat. I think the ref has already called the fight. But I'm not sure until Bottoms fails to rise and the ref approaches Casper and yanks his arm up in victory while the announcer boasts, "The victor, ladies and gentlemen! I give you, your one, your only, Casper the Friendly Ghost!"

Ivy twists her head back and looks up at me with those feline eyes. "Is it over?" she asks.

With her warm breath on my neck and her lips so close to mine, I'm having a hard time concentrating on anything but her. When I lean forward so she can hear me, I accidentally press myself into her and I swear I hear a small whimper escape her throat. I murmur in her ear, "I'll take you back to the bus if you're ready to go."

She looks over at the other guys, who have their eyes glued to the ring, and then turns backs around, now dangerously close. "Are you sure you don't mind?"

I chuckle and nod. "I'm sure."

Just as we move to leave, Leif notices and cups his hands around his mouth. "Pssst . . . Ivy, where are you going?"

Ivy turns. "Back to the bus."

"You sure? I promised Casper I'd introduce him to you and we planned to go out later," Leif responds.

"Next time?"

"Yeah, no problem. I'll set something up."

She smiles and waves goodbye.

We make our way back to the bus quickly and when we hit the front lounge she turns toward me. "Thank you for bringing me back. I'm really tired and just want to sit around and do nothing for a few hours."

"Hey, it's no problem. I'm feeling the same way."

"Want to watch a movie or you going to go to bed?"

"Watching a movie sounds great."

"Terrific. There's a new movie with that actress Jules Atwood on demand I've been dying to catch."

"Jules Atwood?"

"Yes, she's the actress cast in *No Led Zeppelin*."

"Right," I reply with a smirk. "My cousin's movie."

She nods. "Just give me a minute to change and I'll meet you in the back lounge."

I make a skeptical noise over her choice of movie and she flashes me a grin before leaving the room.

"Okay, Mr. Push-ups, let's hear your story," she mock demands as she enters the dimly lit lounge I'm already sitting in watching the all-time classic movie *Stripes*.

I swivel around in my chair and glance up. "Chicks dig me, because I rarely wear underwear and when I do it's usually something unusual." I grin, quoting John Winger's most awesome line from the movie.

She giggles and flops into the chair next to mine. "God, I haven't watched this movie in years."

"Me either." I almost say *Not since the last time I watched it with you*, but I don't.

"Can we watch this instead?"

I give her a charming smile. "Sure, if you insist." Like she has to ask me twice about skipping what I can only imagine to be a chick flick.

She has no makeup on, but she doesn't need it. And when her face is a blank canvas, her eyes seem to always sparkle. Her hair is piled loosely on top of her head, and as she swivels to hoist her feet up on the table, the oversized neckline of her sweatshirt exposes a hint of lace. Fuck, we haven't been alone like this until now, and I want nothing more than to pull her off that chair and onto my lap.

We sit next to each other for the rest of the movie and even talk over it at times. But the closest our bodies come to touching is when I kick my boots up on the coffee table next to her bare feet.

"Don't put your shoes on the furniture," she comments and taps her toes against my boots, shoving my feet down.

I make an amused face. "Yes, ma'am. We don't want to mark up the fine furnishings."

She giggles and I toe my boots off, then kick my sock-clad feet back up, where her toes remain very close to mine. *Friends,* I keep reminding myself. *I can do this—establish what we had through friendship first.* But no matter how many times I say it in my head, that doesn't stop me from feeling the way I feel toward her.

The credits roll. Her feet graze mine for a few long moments—on purpose or by accident, I don't know, but my body reacts instantly to her touch. She looks at me, biting her lip, and the sight sets me on fire. I rise from my chair, ready to pounce, but she stands at the same time and yawns. "It's late. I'm going to call it a night. Thank you for watching that with me."

"Good night, Ivy. I really enjoyed the movie and the company."

She scurries out of the room without turning back, and for a minute I consider chasing after her, but I head to bed instead.

I awake from a deep sleep. Some nights I sleep like a baby, others I find myself tossing and turning most of the night. Tonight is one of those in-between nights. I open my eyes and find myself spinning the gun on his desk as someone taunts me: "Pull the trigger. I dare you. You're such a sorry excuse of a son. Just do it." The shadow hovers over me, a face I can't make out. My heart is pounding and adrenaline pumps through my veins as he urges me to just do it.

"Xander, man, wake up," Garrett says, touching my shoulders, shaking me.

I look up to see him, not my father, standing over me. Fuck, I haven't had a dream like that in a long time.

"Are you all right?" he asks.

"I'm fine. Thanks. Sorry if I woke you. Just a bad dream." He lets the curtain fall back and I shift restlessly for the next few hours.

After a breakdown on the road, we're headed to Cleveland, and can finally get off this bus. I'll be glad to stay in my own room and get some decent rest. I'm too tired to get any work done today. My head is drowning with the same regrets I always have after dreams of my father—mainly one regret—why didn't I keep my mouth shut? Of course, in my dreams it's always my father tempting me with death in some way—but three therapists later, the dreams mean the same thing. I have to let my guilt go or the dreams will continue to haunt me. I have no fucking idea how to do that, and seeing a shrink was not my thing—talking about feelings and evaluating everything in my life since I was born is something I ultimately passed on.

Unable to sleep, I hop out of bed and check my e-mails, but find nothing of concern and no fires to put out, so I decide to go back to bed. Around noon I finally haul my sorry ass up. I skip any kind of workout today—I'm just too drained. The galley is quiet as I walk through it and into the small bathroom. Turning the hot water on in the shower as high as I can, I try to erase the nightmare from my mind and for once just let thoughts of Ivy consume me. The mirror starts to fog up and I think about last night. Shit, all I want to do is make her mine.

Stripping off my clothes, I'm already half hard just thinking about her, her perfect body, and how much I want to be with her again. I step into the pint-sized shower with my cock in my hand. I want her hand to curl around me so she'll feel how hard she makes me. I close my eyes and gently rub, first around my cock, then my balls. Fuck, that feels good. I picture her doing this—in the shower, with us exploring our bodies in any way we want. I want to feel her hands gripping me. I think of her, her face, her body . . . the ways I want to touch her, where I want to touch her. I imagine driving my cock into her sweet pussy, and it makes me want to come hard and fast.

My fist pumps at a quicker pace and I lick the water from my lips. The pressure wells deep and a tingling radiates from my cock. As my orgasm starts to build, so do the contractions—it feels like electricity is shooting through me. My dick twitches and I can't hold on any longer. As I start to come, practically spasming, the incredible feeling builds and I finally let myself go, crossing that threshold over and over until I'm spent. My chest rises and falls and I slouch back against the shower wall.

Once my breathing returns to normal, I lather up with soap, rinse it off, and get out of the shower. I don't bother to shave. Wrapping a towel around my waist, I wipe the steam from the mirror. The ink on my side was always the hope for my future, but I fucked it up because I never went after it. Hazel eyes and brown hair reflect back and I try to see my life differently from what it really is—I'm thirty fucking years old and I have nothing—nothing that matters, anyway.

Throwing on a pair of jeans and a T-shirt, I attempt to shake off the morning. I print out the daily schedule and post it, then head over to get a cup of coffee. Nix and Garrett sit in comfortable silence in the lounge. Nix is reading the paper and Garrett is eating something that resembles nachos.

"Want some? There's plenty," Garrett says, crunching a chip.

"No, thanks. That looks disgusting. What is it?"

"It's classic is what it is—a can of chili con carne, a jar of nacho sauce, and a bag of chips."

I pour a cup of the coffee that looks like sludge. "Flynn, your eating habits need some serious help."

"Hey, watch out—the next time you're craving my pizza, I might just tell you to make it yourself."

I shake my head and laugh. "Remind me again when I ever asked you to take a stale-looking hunk of bread and slap a jar of sauce on it?"

He just grins at me and crunches another chip. I take my coffee and stumble blurry-eyed into the back lounge to catch ESPN. Leif's in there, and he looks me over.

"Rough night?" he asks.

I rub my hand over my stubble. "Just ready to get off this bus."

He's in the club chair, twirling while watching TV. "I know the feeling. Want to play some ball?"

Since my mind is shot and I can't do any work right now . . . "Why not?"

An hour later, I'm killing him. I've always been a competitive guy. I don't fuck around . . . video game or real game, it's all the same. When my team is beating his, 95 to 72, I yell, "Yeah!" and pump my fist in the air.

He sets the controller down. "Bastard! I'm done."

"Yes, you are—you sad son of a bitch. You lost! Rematch?"

Shaking his hand, he says, "No fucking way. Are we almost there?"

I glance at my watch and see it's a little before three. "John said we'd be there before five. What's your rush?"

"Just wish there were chicks on this bus so I could get a handy while we wait."

Unable to believe his candor, I have to laugh. "What about that girl of yours you're always talking on the phone with?"

"She dumped my ass."

"That's why you've been so punchy. Makes sense now."

"Yeah, but tonight I'm not only getting stone drunk, you can bet I'll be taking as many BJs as are offered my way."

"Why did she break it off?"

"My girl?"

I grin at him. "I'm not talking about your dick."

"Fuck you," he says.

Leif and I have really hit it off and I enjoy having him around.

"No, really, what happened?" I ask.

"She's pissed that I'm on the same bus as Ivy."

This piques my interest. "Why? Do the two of you have something going on?"

"Fuck, no. She's like my sister."

"Did you explain that to your girl?"

"Man, I've talked about it so much that last night after another fight, I was over it and just said fine, believe what you want. You want to believe I'd cheat, believe it."

"No, he's definitely not the cheater," Ivy chimes in. She's standing behind my chair and I whirl around. Her words assault me and her eyes flash to me in an accusatory manner, but the moment passes quickly. She moves next to Leif and picks up his controller, then adds, "Just give her some time and then call her back—she knows you're not the kind of guy who'd cheat." She tips her head to the side and Leif moves out of the chair. She flops down in it and when she does her knee grazes mine, and every muscle in my body clenches. I want that two seconds of contact to happen over and over. She looks at me. "Go for the championship?"

I quickly focus my eyes on the TV. "Bring it, baby." The word *baby* slips out. Ivy remains still for a moment, but Leif doesn't seem to notice.

With the Lakers just catching their stride, Garrett, in all his annoyance, stands in front of me. "Hey, why don't you make like Michael Jackson and beat it? My turn."

"Beat it yourself, asswipe. We're not in elementary school."

"Right! So take your loss like a man and move on out so a real player can beat a chick," he says, snatching the remote from me.

I stand up. "This ought to be good. You haven't beaten me in anything since . . . oh yeah, never. Unless you cheat, that is."

"Yeah, whatever," he says and starts to play.

I lean against the window to watch. But under her breath I hear Ivy mutter, "That's the pot calling the kettle black."

I've had just about enough of leaving the past in the past. It's time to have that conversation I've been holding back on. So when Nix walks in the room, I ask him, "Nix, why don't you take over for Ivy? I need to talk to her about something."

She glares at me with a fierceness in her eyes I'm not used to seeing, but I'm ready—it's time to come clean. I nod toward her bedroom and she stands with a huff, throwing the controller down. "Xander, I told you let's leave the past in the past," she tells me in a whisper.

Leif's phone rings and when he looks at the screen, he heads our way. "Mind if I go in your room, Ivy? It's Amber and I think I should grovel in private."

"Take your time. I'm fine out here," she tells him, directing all her coldness my way.

Garrett looks up at me. "Everything okay?"

"Peachy," I answer and head for the front lounge for another cup of sludge, but as I walk I wonder if telling her the truth even matters.

Less than an hour later we pull into the Hyatt Regency at the Cleveland Arcade. I'm in the galley on the phone with Ena making sure the merchandise for this week's shows will arrive on time, not late like last week.

"It doesn't fucking help to have T-shirts at a concert once the concert is over," I tell her.

"I know, Xander, but I can't control the pace at which UPS decides to move."

"Ena, just overnight the shit for next week. We're missing out on a huge financial opportunity."

"Okay, I will. But just remember when you pay the bills, it was your idea."

"Right. I gotta run. I'll check in tomorrow." I hit END and hoist my bag onto my shoulder—so ready to get off this bus.

Entering the hotel, I glance around. This place is completely cool. It's two large buildings linked together by a wall of glass-framed windows. By far one of the most beautiful pieces of architecture I've ever seen, with its old railings and wooden trim. In its day it must have been a place to see.

I get us all checked in and luckily we each have our own room. Garrett takes the room keys while I sign for everything. When I turn around, everyone has disappeared. The lobby is oddly quiet, but the bar is not. A happy hour sign reads TWO FOR ONE. The elevators are to the right of the bar and Leif stands near them, just staring off into space.

Approaching him, I ask, "How'd it go?"

"Not well. She's in love with someone else. That's the real reason she wanted to break up."

"I'm sorry. That sucks. But better to find out now. How about I take you out tonight? Get your mind off everything," I ask as I press the UP button.

"Just tell me where and when."

"There's a club in the warehouse district with a band playing I've heard a lot about. I'm going to check them out later. Meet me in the lobby around ten." The elevator doors open and we get in.

"I plan to get really shitfaced. I'm just warning you now."

"Nothing I can't handle." I remember the shit River and Dahlia went through last year when I had to take care of his sorry ass after he tried to drown himself in booze rather than tell her what he knew. Not that I haven't done the same many times. So, shit, a guy whose girl broke up with him—I can handle that.

CHAPTER 7
Blurred Lines

Ordinarily, I love staying in a hotel—a room to myself, privacy, a decent shower, and a comfortable bed. But by the time I exit the elevator a few hours later, I already miss having Ivy close. So I'm not only surprised but somewhat elated when I hit the lobby and see her sitting in a plush chair near the lounge. I didn't realize she was coming with us—not that I mind. She's on the phone, so I just nod a quick hello to her. She gives me a slight smile in return. She's a knockout in a black minidress and flat sandals. Her hair is down and straight, with a few strands draping over her eyes. I wish I could push them aside so I could see the deep blue of her eyes. I find Nix and Garrett standing near the bar, deep in conversation. Leif doesn't seem to be down here yet. The bar is open to the lobby, so as I walk up to them I catch the conversation.

"Who's Phoebe?" Garrett asks Nix.

"That teacher I met at the party at the Pelican. She's from San Francisco."

"Sorry. No recollection of you hanging with any girl, especially a smart one."

"Fuck off," Nix snaps.

"What's all the talk about a girl?" I ask them.

Garrett knocks shoulders with Nix. "This guy over here invited a chick to fly out and meet him, and she arrives tonight."

"No shit. Are you serious?" I'm somewhat impressed that Nix cares about anyone enough to make an extra effort. It's the first I've ever seen him do something like this.

"Fuck, I remember her now. She was the one wearing that slinky purple number with the really low-cut neck, wasn't she?" Garrett makes a gesture with his fists on his chest and shakes them.

Nix scowls. "You're so immature, Flynn. Get a life and get out of mine."

Leif walks across the lobby wearing neatly pressed jeans and a starched button-down—slightly more dressed up than the rest of us—Ivy excluded, of course. Who the hell irons their jeans anyway? Ivy notices him and quickly gets off the phone, and they both approach us at the same time.

"Are you doing okay?" she asks Leif.

He nods. "Never better. I'm ready to let off some steam on the dance floor."

"Are we going to a dance club?" she asks, looking my way.

"I'm not sure if it's a dance club per se, but they must have a dance floor since there's a band."

She giggles. "Still don't dance?"

I give a slight shake of my head and our eyes find each other and lock together for a moment. A flush passes over her face. Was her question a slip? This is the first acknowledgment she's made out loud in front of others that she knows me from years ago. The softness in her voice and the look in her eyes tell me she remembers how she used to try to get me on the dance floor. Her only victory was her senior prom, where I danced every slow dance with her.

"Let's hit it. I'm ready to party." Leif steps in, oblivious to the connection Ivy and I are sharing.

When Garrett adds, "Yeah, let's party like it's 1999," our stare falters and laughter overtakes all of us.

Outside, the night is warm and the sky is clear—a perfect summer evening that holds the prospect of a good time. This is just what we all need after the vigorous schedule we've been keeping. The waiting SUV approaches and Nix hops in the front seat while Garrett and Leif climb in the back, leaving the middle bench seat open. "Your carriage awaits," I joke, bowing and motioning with my hand that she is next.

She laughs. "I wish!"

When she disappears into the vehicle, I can't help but notice how perfect her ass looks. I step in and before I even settle in my seat, I feel it—the energy that zaps through my body whenever she's close. The guys are talking about the city and what they plan on doing tomorrow, but I'm lost in my own thoughts. I glance down, unable to stop myself from looking at her. When I do, I find that her minidress is riding up so high I can see the lacy bottom of her boy shorts. I run my hands over my face—the sight of her skin mixed with the lace does things to my body that I have to make myself suppress. I'm also pretty sure I could see the crotch of her panties if it were light enough in here.

Leaning over, I whisper, "Don't you think your dress is a bit short?"

She laughs and tucks into my side. Her warm breath on my neck makes me grip the seat to stop from running my hands between her thighs. "I like it that way. You never know when it will come in handy," she purrs.

My jaw clenches and I shut up—I'm not used to hearing her talk like that, and I don't trust what might come out of my mouth if I say anything else. I know she doesn't mean it. I know she's not that kind of girl. I also know I'd never let anything like that happen.

We arrive at the Black Dog later than I planned. It's a bit off the beaten path, so I'm already expecting the hole-in-the-wall that we walk into. It's dark, dingy, and smells like smoke, but jam-packed. We push our way through the pulsating throng of people and toward the bar. "Five shooters," I mouth to the bartender. He nods and melts away into the cries of the other thirsty customers. My eyes adjust to the darkness as I look around. Bright lights from the neon signs on the wall illuminate the faces in the crowd, but I can't locate the band. There is a floor above us that seems to be a loft of sorts with tables and chairs, and a floor directly below us where I can see the tops of people's bopping heads, which tells me there's a dance floor down there.

When the band starts playing, my ears go on instant alert so I can zero in on their sound. I hear a trumpet in the mix of a guitar and drums, and it reminds me of something my dad would appreciate. Anything out of the ordinary, anything that would bring attention and help speed a single up the charts. Something he would latch onto and study—that was just his thing.

"Is this the band you were telling me about earlier?" Nix asks.

I blink myself out of my thoughts. "Yeah. I think they call themselves Echo, and the trumpet player also plays keys. A buddy of mine told me I had to look them up. I figured I'd listen for myself when he said he was surprised they hadn't made it bigger over the years."

"Great concept. I really like the horns mixed in," Nix comments.

"I need to hear a few more songs, but yeah, I agree." It's a memorable sound, and I'm glad I found the time to come listen. Soon the bartender returns with our drinks. I hand the shots around and let my fingers graze Ivy's hand as I pass one to her. Her face remains stoic, but her body responds instantly. Her nipples harden and I can see them through her tight dress. Leaning over, I ask her, "Are you cold?" She smirks at me and in the most casual way she gives me the middle finger. I nearly drop my glass trying not to laugh. I've never seen her do that.

Leif raises his shot glass. "Here's to everyone getting lucky tonight."

I shake my head, knowing he's out to get laid and hoping he stays sober enough to get it up. I order another round of shots adding beers as well and we all stand around shooting the shit. After a couple more drinks Leif turns toward a redheaded chick in a tight pink dress sitting at the bar and starts talking to her.

Garrett starts telling Ivy about the girl Nix has joining him. He seems oblivious to the tension between the two of us, but Nix has been homing in on it. "Everything okay with you and Ivy?" he mutters so she can't hear.

"I don't really want to talk about it."

"That's cool, but if you want to, I'm here to listen."

I nod and take a swig of my beer. The four us stand huddled together at the bar, talking, listening to the band, and having a few more drinks. Before I know it Nix is jetting off to the airport to pick up the girl he's flying in. I glance over at Leif and see that he seems pretty happy. The redhead is sitting on his lap with her hands all over him— doesn't look like he'll be dancing tonight. The band takes a break and dance music is piped in. Ivy raises her eyes and laughs. "See, we are at a dance club," she says.

I can't help but laugh back. She excuses herself to use the restroom and after ten minutes when she hasn't returned, I grow concerned and move around to look for her.

Garrett and I check out the place and end up near the railing overlooking the dance floor, where I spot her immediately. The sheen of her tan legs, the sparkle of her earrings, and the glimmer of her sandals—she seems to shine under the beaming crosses of light reflected from above. She's dancing with some dick in a white tank top whose hands are all over her ass. Tattoos cover his arms and multiple piercings ornament his ears. He just looks like trouble. My breathing reaches an alarming rate, my heart pounds, and my brain tries to maintain its cool as songs change from one to the next. We stay glued to the same spot, just watching her.

When the guy she's dancing with pushes her up against a wall and grinds into her, I lose all control.

Garrett puts a hand on my shoulder just as my foot perches on the rung of the railing. "Let her handle it, Xander. She's pushing him away."

I ignore him and hop the rail in front of me, jumping the four feet between levels and crossing the floor to reach her. The asshole still hasn't let go of her, even though she clearly wants him to. He's about my build, but I know I could take him in a heartbeat. I grip both of his shoulders and pull him back, yanking his hands off her body.

"What the fuck?" he yells.

"Don't touch her like that," I growl, seething.

He looks at me, a little surprised, and flashes a mouth full of brilliant white teeth my way. "You don't know who I am, do you?" is all he says. Then he turns and shuffles through the crowd without a word. That was easy enough.

I look into her eyes. "Are you okay?"

She nods but looks a little shaken.

"Come with me." I take hold of her arm and step toward the stairs.

"Let go of me!" She tries to yank her arm away.

I flip around and lean close to whisper in her ear, "I will after I talk to you." I slide back and my eyes narrow in on her.

"Fine," she says, relenting. "But I could have handled him myself."

"It didn't look that way," I mutter, again turning and leading her to the second floor, where I saw tables and chairs earlier. I indicate a chair with a dip of my chin and she sits. I do the same.

"I was just dancing with him. He owns the club, and besides, we were only talking."

"I don't care who he is. And it didn't look like he was just talking. It looked more like he was trying to take you in the back room."

"Even if he was, it's my choice if I go. Not yours."

I nod, because that's all I can do. Fuck, I knew I couldn't do this. I knew Ivy joining the band was something I wouldn't be able to handle. I lean back in my chair and my gaze spears her, but words escape me. Fuck, I want her to choose me.

"What do you want from me?" she asks, with more pain in her voice than I've ever heard. I want to say *you,* but first it's time to come clean.

I squeeze my eyes shut. "Ivy, I want to explain everything to you. I want you to listen and really think about what I'm going to tell you." I'm nervous as hell about telling her the truth, because if she doesn't believe me it could undo the relationship we've built in the short time we've been together on tour. And if she does believe me but doesn't care—well, that's what scares the shit out of me the most.

She's fidgeting. First clasping her hands together, then moving the candle around in the middle of the table. She blows it out, then looks at me. "Xander, I don't need the dramatics and I really don't need to talk about you and Tessa, or for that matter, you and Amy or any other 'friends' from that circle." She air quotes the word *friends* and I know seeing Amy with me must have stung, but it wasn't like that. It's not like it carried on from high school to now. We met back up years after high school, and it was more of a convenience than anything else for the both of us.

I take her chin in my hand, and even after all the alcohol her eyes are crystal clear and piercing. I take a deep breath and go for it. "That's just it. It wasn't what you thought. That night we were supposed to meet at my grandparents' . . ." The music suddenly stops and the lights turn on, cutting off my words. There's a commotion from below and I stand up and look downstairs to see what's going on.

"Stay here!" I tell Ivy.

Her eyes flip to mine. "What's the matter?"

"Just stay here. Leif must have pissed off the wrong person."

The stairs are a few feet away and I take them two at a time. When I reach the bottom, three brutish dudes, each weighing at least two hundred seventy pounds, approach me and clutch my arms, dragging me into the back storage room.

"What the fuck?" I yell.

They stop just inside the door, and I look around to see where I am. The room is lined with boxes, some tossed, some stacked, some filled with empty liquor bottles—it's a fucking mess.

The brute with a studded black leather belt cinching his jeans stands in front of me and smiles. He's missing a tooth and another one is capped in gold.

"What the fuck?" I yell again, trying to break away, but I can't.

"You need to learn some manners," he hisses.

I swallow hard and take small breaths as the two of them hold me and Missing Tooth swings at me. His fists are like sledgehammers as they hit me. My face. My chest. My stomach—fuck, that hurt.

"Leave your hands off a guy when he's making his move on a chick. Got it?"

"Who are you?" I ask, just fucking curious as to why an owner feels the need to sic his bulldogs on patrons of his bar.

"The question is who do you think you are?" he grunts.

I don't answer but instead spit on the ground. Probably not the best idea. The bald guy punches me one more time in the gut. With a murky laugh, he says, "Get him out of here" to the guys holding me.

It happens in unison. They both tug my arms and drag me back into the bar. Before they drop their hold, the asshole with the lip piercing says, "You heard him. Get the fuck out of here and don't ever come back."

My eyes swivel around, looking for Ivy, and I make a move to head back up the stairs. I've decided to keep my mouth shut not because I'm worried about what they might do to me but because I need to find Ivy.

"I said get out," one of them growls as the other moves to stand next to him.

"One on one, dude—just you and me," I hiss back.

"I don't think so. The owner wants you out and I hope you got his message. Oh and he already removed that hot piece of ass himself before he ran into your posse."

I try not to let him see me flinch. He motions to the bar, where Leif is getting the shit kicked out of him by some other dirtbag who probably weighs twice as much as him. People near the bar are scurrying out of his way.

I hear the dirtbag scream, "Tell your friend she might want to think twice before being a cock tease again."

Breathe, I tell myself. I need to find Ivy, and the only way to do that is to stay calm and get the fuck out of here.

I put my hands up in surrender, though it kills me not to kick the shit out of these guys. "I'm leaving. Call your friend off mine and we'll get out of here."

The one with the dark hair that flops in his eyes smiles, and I want to rip his teeth out of his mouth. He whistles and the dirtbag looks up. He slices his finger across his neck and eyes me, pushing me to the door. I turn and just as I approach Leif, the dirtbag shoves him at me. "Don't forget this piece of shit."

"Fuck. We can't just leave," Leif coughs out.

"Shut up. Now," I hiss under my breath and exit the door with Leif by my side.

"Xander, what's going on?" Garrett yells to me from just outside the door.

My eyes search for Ivy as the fury builds within me. If she's not out here I'm going to kill those bastards. When Garrett jolts toward me to grab Leif, I spot her sitting on the curb. Rushing over, I jump in front of her as cars honk for me to get out of their way. I take her hands, pull her up, and move us to the sidewalk as my eyes scan her from head to toe. "Did they hurt you?"

"N-o-o," she stammers.

"Are you sure?" I ask, caressing her cheek.

She looks at me and her fingers touch my lip. "I should be asking you that question," she says with tears in her eyes. "I'm so sorry."

I pull her to me and tuck her head into my shoulder. "What are you sorry for, baby?" I ask.

"I shouldn't have said yes to dancing with that asshole," she cries.

"Ivy, are you all right?" Leif calls out.

Hearing Leif's voice, she pulls away from me and turns around.

Running to him, she takes his face in her hands. "Why did you go back in after they asked us to leave?"

Even though he's bleeding and Garrett's holding him up, he manages to babble, "Because I had a chick waiting for me."

She shoves his shoulder. "You're a dumbass."

He laughs. "Yeah, you're right, but one minute some hot piece of ass has her hands in my pants and the next I'm getting the shit kicked out of me. Talk about a cock block," he says, looking down at his open zipper.

"You okay?" I ask, surveying him for anything more than superficial wounds.

"I was better with that chick's hand wrapped around my dick."

"Leif, you're so drunk. Are you sure you're okay?" Ivy asks, placing his other arm over her shoulder.

His tone sobers instantly at the sound of concern in her voice. "Yes, I'm fine. What happened, anyway?"

She's suddenly more composed, wiped clean of emotion. She's the same resilient, undaunted girl she always was. She takes his arm over her shoulder and tells him about the guy she was dancing with. I don't need to relive it, so I turn away and call the driver. "Yeah, Scott, we're ready to get out of here."

Every inch of me is tense and the pressure in my chest keeps increasing. It's eight thirty in the morning and I'm standing outside her door. I didn't sleep all night. I got up way too early and went for a run in a useless attempt to push thoughts of her aside, but I couldn't—I have to talk to her. When I knock she doesn't answer, so I keep pounding, louder and louder. She finally cracks the door open, leaving the chain on it.

"Xander, what's going on?" she asks in a low croak.

"I need to talk to you."

"It's a little early."

"Just get dressed and meet me downstairs in the coffee bar."

"Fine, give me thirty minutes." She huffs loudly and slams the door.

Her favorite drink was always a vanilla latte, so I take a chance and order her one. I grab myself a coffee and down a red-eye. Leaning over the railing, I think about us and wonder how different things might have been if I'd told her the truth way back when. The line for coffee grows as the room starts to fill with people, but I spot her as soon as she enters the atrium. She looks incredible—white shorts, a tight red tank top that hugs her body in just the right way, and some kind of black wedge sandals. The sight of her makes my pulse race so fast that my fingers are trembling.

She enters the coffee bar just as I turn around. Spotting me, she walks slowly. Her gaze is fixed on mine and for a moment her face is soft, calm even, but the closer she gets the more unflappable she becomes. When I reach out to offer her the latte, she smiles and takes it.

"Vanilla," I tell her as I run a nervous hand through my hair.

"You remembered," she says with the first genuine smile I've seen cross her face.

"How could I forget? We drank our way through late nights and early mornings with them."

"Do you still drink them?"

"No. I changed to regular coffee. Couldn't take the sweetness after a while."

Her fingers touch my lip, and my body comes alive. "Does it hurt?"

I cock my head and press back my smile. "No. Not at all."

"Well, for what it's worth, again I'm really sorry. I shouldn't have danced with that asshole."

"It's worth a lot." After a few seconds of silence, I add, "I checked on Leif and he's actually fine."

"I know. I checked on him too." She clears her throat and the easy back-and-forth of our conversation is over. She takes a sip of her latte and asks, "What did you want to talk to me about?"

My brain is warring with my lips to keep me from leaning down and kissing her as she licks the excess froth from her mouth.

"Xander?"

I lose myself for a moment, but the softness in her voice brings me back. "I actually want to take you someplace."

"You mean the band?" she asks.

"No. Just you and me."

"I don't think that's a good idea. I've told you this a few times."

"I won't talk about anything you don't want to. Just come with me. I promise it's a place you'll love."

She wavers and takes a deep breath. "Fine. But only because I'm dressed and have nothing else to do. And you're buying me a muffin first."

I laugh. "Ah. I can definitely do that."

Last night another wall came down between us, and although Ivy is still guarded, she actually seems to be warming up to me. My plan was to talk to her after I took her out for the day, but now that I've promised not to talk about the past, I'll just have to take the conversations as they come. I already believe she's who I need, but I just need to convince her I'm who she needs. I wanted to take her someplace I know we'll both enjoy.

The sign reads: OHIO HISTORICAL MARKER—BIRTHPLACE OF ROCK 'N' ROLL. From afar, the Rock and Roll Hall of Fame building is truly stunning. Ivy's face lights up when she sees it.

Pointing to it, she says, "Look, Xander, it looks like the pictures of the Louvre you sent me."

And it does. The building is made up of geometric shapes resembling triangles that seem to shadow the lake. And although Ivy's enthusiasm puts the biggest smile on my face, it's the sound of her voice that melts my heart—the way she just said, "Look, Xander."

As we exit the cab I know without a doubt . . . I'm still in love with this girl. And nothing can sour my mood. We enter the building. "Where to first?" I ask her.

She's studying the map and points to a small red dot. "Right here."

I laugh. "Could you be more specific?"

"The Beatles exhibit. I really want to see John Lennon's acoustic guitar."

"The Beatles it is." I take her hand without thinking and lead her to the exhibit she selected.

Morning stretches into afternoon as we pass from Metallica to the Rolling Stones memorabilia. We talk about each artifact, spending the most time in the Jimi Hendrix forum.

When we get to the Janis Joplin area, Ivy studies the jewelry pieces on display. I lean against the glass and just watch her eyes twinkle. "Hey, guess what River gave Dahlia as a wedding present."

She looks up at me and bites her lip. "What?"

The heat I've felt between us all day—the ease of two people having a great time—seems to flare. "The gold bangles that Grandpa gave Grandma. Remember, the ones Janis wore all the time and gave to my grandfather when she found out Grandma was mad at him."

"I remember them. That was a really sweet gift."

For a moment sadness crosses her features, but it quickly passes.

"Let's move on. The Who or Michael Jackson?" I ask.

"You know, I'm pretty tired. Late night, early morning. What do you say we call it a day?"

"Sure," I say, a little disappointed that our day is already ending. "Let's just slip in the movie theater and watch a few minutes of Dick Clark's *American Bandstand*."

She raises an eyebrow.

"Come on, you have to admit it. Best damn television idea second to none. It was reality TV before reality TV."

She wrinkles her nose. "Five minutes."

Boarding the escalator, we head to the second floor and enter the dark theater. We take seats near the back and watch as eager teenagers try to get the attention of a very young Dick Clark. We watch the show and I lean closer toward her. She stays put and never glances over toward me. I rest my hand on the arm of the chair and force my eyes to the screen. My breathing takes effort and I hear my own heart pounding. Heat rushes through me and my boldness comes alive in the darkness.

"Ivy," I whisper.

She swallows and meets my gaze. "Shh . . ."

The way she turns is slow and sensual and it completely steals my breath away. I lean back a little in my chair and give her another glance. I feel like a kid again in the movie theater, wanting to make out with my girl, and the tent in the middle of my jeans is a dead giveaway. What the hell is wrong with me? I reach over and drop my hand to the bare skin of her leg. She stiffens.

"Ivy," I whisper again.

She turns her head and I focus on her face, her eyes. I stare at her lips. I imagine sliding my tongue down the smooth curve of her arm and shoulder. I sit here as long as I can until I can't take another minute of wanting her. I lean over and pull her face toward mine. I don't think she's breathing. I stop short of her lips and just hold her close to me. I feel the rush of adrenaline as my need for her spikes with every passing second.

Then, just as I brush my lips over hers, she stands up. "I can't. Please don't do that again. I want to be your friend, but that's all," she says and rushes out of the theater. I run after her, but before I can catch her, she hops in a cab and is gone. And just like that, so is our perfect day.

CHAPTER 8
Radioactive

After the Cleveland show the dynamics of the bus changed—I had a lot of work to get done. Ivy hadn't committed to staying with the band after the tour, and I doubted she would, so I was putting some feelers out trying to see who might be available. And the guys' social lives were running rampant. Not only did Nix invite Phoebe to join him for the rest of the tour, but Leif seemed to be on a mission to get laid in every city as much as possible. This often meant a stowaway on board from one stop to the next. It also meant I ended up staying out of the galley as much as possible. Nix and Phoebe aren't exactly quiet and Leif doesn't care who hears.

Spending more time in the lounges hasn't been all that bad, because surprisingly, Ivy seems to be doing the same. She wasn't kidding about wanting to be friends. At some times it's exhilarating and at others it's exasperating, but at least we're spending time together . . . We talk about nothing that matters, we eat together, we play video games, and even watch TV, but now we never do any of these things alone. Garrett is always with us, and the minute he leaves so does she—my guess is the friends thing is just as hard for her as for me, because while most of the hostility between us seems to have eased, the tension hasn't.

Unfortunately something else has changed as well—Ivy can no longer go out without being recognized. The first few weeks with her trademark locks cut shorter, plus having been out of the limelight for almost a year, we were able to move around each city easily. But after the Detroit show, her performance was so dynamic that it went viral. Ivy has gotten in the habit of singing a cover at each performance, and that night's cover was "I Knew You Were Trouble." Her rave-y, edgy performance unhinged the audience and they went crazy. The way she sang that particular song made it come alive. She turned it into her own and I fucking loved it. It was catchy in her key and she gave it a rhythm and flow that rocked the audience. It exploded all over the Internet, and overnight the Wilde Ones became Ivy's band and Ivy was being sought out. The next three stops after that we all stayed on the bus, and tonight is no different.

I'd fallen asleep early with my headphones on, and another fucking dream woke me up. My dreams come more and more frequently lately. For some reason my dad is weighing heavy on my mind during this tour. I'm not sure if it's the fact that he wanted this life and I wonder why he did when he had a family or if it's because I've started to think about what kind of life I could have while doing this. Getting out of bed, I throw a shirt on and head to the front lounge to grab a bottle of water, and as I do, I hear voices and laughter from the back lounge. Heading that way, I take a whiff of the air and the smell of cigar smoke has me more than curious as to what's going on.

Pausing in the doorway of the back lounge, I take in the scene. Everyone is sitting together and playing cards. Garrett is leaning back in a metal folding chair holding a drink in his hand with a cigar resting over the edge of a bowl. Nix is reclining comfortably in one of the club chairs tapping one hand on the table while holding his cards in the other. Ivy, sitting in the other club chair, is wearing black sleep pants with some print all over them and a white tank top. Again she's wearing no makeup and has her hair pulled back—she looks so much like she did when she was eighteen. Fuck, she's gorgeous. Even when she throws her cards on the table with a disgusted look on her face she's still sexy as fuck. Leif glances around the circle with a huge-ass grin on his face and fans his cards out almost methodically before laying them down. "Full house, aces high," he says and pulls the pile of guitar picks his way.

Garrett slams his drink down. "I'm out fifty bucks, thanks to your sorry ass. I think you're cheating."

Leif just laughs at him and continues to rake in the pot. Phoebe throws her cards in and gets up from her chair to sit on Nix's lap. She's an attractive girl—average height, maybe a little shorter than Ivy, with chin-length dark hair. Her skin tone is very close to Nix's. I'd guess that she's either Italian or Hispanic.

I stand silent in the doorway, continuing to watch them, but mostly watching Ivy. She pulls her legs up in the chair and wraps her arms around her knees. When I cover my mouth to stifle a yawn, she glances my way. A small smile forms on her lips, and her eyes sweep over me before they lock on mine. I grin at her and button up my shirt before joining the group. She drops her eyes and stretches her legs out over the empty chair next to her. I wonder what she's thinking when she looks at me like that and why when I catch her doing it she always looks away.

Garrett looks up. "Hey, man, glad you decided to wake up. Welcome to the party."

He looks like such a clown gripping that cigar between his teeth and talking around it. He motions to the chair Ivy has her legs on. "Perfect timing. We need another. Phoebe quit playing and I'm about to unless my luck turns." He takes a puff on his cigar and coughs a little. I bite back the laughter. Phoebe's not happy as the cigar smoke wafts her way. She waves it out of her face and makes an exaggerated choking noise before resting her head against Nix's shoulder.

"John's going to beat your ass for smoking in here," I scold him, more mocking than serious, although John just might do that.

He sets his cigar back down in the bowl. "Then I'll have to explain to him that a fine cigar is just like a woman. If you don't light it up at the right time and suck on it with a certain ferverence, it'll go out on you." He waves his arms to the right, where the window blinds are pulled up. "And besides, I opened all the windows."

Everyone laughs, even Ivy. I look around at the glasses on the table and I know they've all been hitting the wine pretty hard. Glancing sideways, I notice there are at least four empty bottles in the sink of the bar area and another open one on the small counter.

Nix looks at Garrett dumbfounded. *"Ferverence? Is that even a word and where the hell did you pick it up? Wheel of Fortune? Jeopardy!?* Either way, you're watching too much fucking TV."

I don't say anything to that. I just throw two twenties on the table. "Deal me in."

Nix reaches around Phoebe to take my money and shoves a bunch of picks my way and I notice the glass in front of him has an amber-colored liquid in it—definitely not wine.

"And I'll have what you're drinking," I tell him.

I glance down at Ivy's legs stretched across the chair. Her feet are bare and her nails are painted red. "May I?" I ask. My gaze fastens on hers. I wait for her response.

She pulls her legs off the chair and sinks as far as she can back into her own seat. "Welcome to the game."

I sit down and lean forward, inching my way closer to her to take the drink Nix hands me. I take a sip before setting it down on the table and notice she's still watching me. I divert my eyes only when Leif asks, "No wine, man? It's the good stuff. I picked it up at a local vineyard yesterday."

Raising my glass, I say, "I'm good."

He feigns offense.

I try not to stare as Ivy raises her glass for a sip, but when my eyes catch her mouth, I can't keep from watching. She licks her lips and says, "I really like it." I know she's answering Leif, but I feel like she's talking to me, and I can't help but smile—my mind wandering to thoughts of what I know she likes.

Slamming his hand in front of me, Garrett slips in, "I'll take your money any day of the week."

I look over toward him as he gulps the rest of the liquid in his glass. "I doubt you'll be taking my money because if memory serves me correctly, I'm the one who taught your scrawny thirteen-year-old ass how to play this game."

"Yeah, but we didn't use money back then, just beer bottle caps, and I was usually the one who drank most of the beer."

"You were so funny when you drank. You just couldn't handle your alcohol," Ivy blurts out. It's the first time any of us has talked about being together when we were younger, and I notice that her gaze flitters from Garrett's face to mine before she looks down at the table. When she reaches out to push some chips forward, her hand grazes mine. The skin on my arm prickles and the electricity between us sparks immediately. She quickly moves her hand away and crosses her arms over her chest, but I already noticed her nipples harden from our encounter. I want more than anything to sit in that chair with her on my lap. To slip my arm around her waist and pull her close to me like I always did when we played poker with River and his friends.

"Cold?" I ask, wishing I could drape my body over hers and warm her up.

Flushing, she rubs her arms. "Yes, I am. I'll be right back. I'm going to get a sweater." At least I didn't get the finger.

She stands up and I watch her step across the room and then disappear through the doorway. A few minutes later she's back with a sweater wrapped around her and when she sits down, I can smell her sweet scent in the air.

Nix shuffles the cards around Phoebe like he's a dealer in Vegas.

"You smell good," I mumble in her direction.

Her cheeks turn pink again and I just smirk at her. I know she sprayed some kind of perfume on when she grabbed her sweater.

Nix continues to shuffle the cards and his eyes dart to Garrett. "You in or out?"

"In," he says with a scowl, and adds, "But if I lose this one, I'm done, busted, broke, annihilated. Do I need to go on?"

"Whatever, dude, just stop whining and ante up. You're holding up the game."

Garrett throws his picks in the middle of the table, and Nix sets the deck down next to Ivy. She cuts it and finally he deals. She gets the first card, since she is to Nix's immediate left. I get mine next. I stare at the two cards beside each other on the table and try to block memories of playing this game alone with her years ago in my grandparents' pool house. We didn't play for money, though—we played for clothes. I'm sure she remembers. Once the cards are dealt, she leans a little my way and I can smell that fresh, soapy scent even more. I get lost in it and those memories come flooding back.

"Xander, snap out of it. What are you doing?" Nix calls me out.

I blink, realizing I haven't even looked at the cards in my hand. "I'll raise," I say, tossing four picks in the middle.

Everyone starts laughing except Ivy. She leans toward me and whispers in my ear. "I checked."

"Fuck," I mutter under my breath.

Her body stiffens and she sits back in her chair.

I turn my attention to the guys. "So I'm tired. Give me a fucking break. I meant to say I'd open. Either way, see it or fold, assholes."

Needless to say, the first hand ends with me losing. As the game continues, Garrett's luck seems to have changed. He's raking it in.

About two hours later, the room's a little fuzzy and if Ivy moves any closer to me I think I'm going to lose it in my pants right here. Shit, I have to get my dick under control.

"Last hand of the night," Nix calls and deals the cards.

Nix makes his way around the table, but Leif tosses his hand down. "I fold."

Garrett lights the tip of his cigar again and inhales before showing us his cards. "Call it a straight, baby, all the way," he boasts.

Ivy smiles and lays her cards flat but upside down. "I fold too."

"I'm out of this fucking game," Nix calls out, running his fingers down Phoebe's bare arms.

I look at the cards in my hand. Rubbing my nails on my chest, then blowing on my cards, I grin. "Four of a kind. Pay up, buddy." I slowly fan my cards out. Garrett's face falls like the cigar he's stubbing out.

"What the fuck, Ivy?" he blurts out.

Everyone looks her way and back at Garrett, who has his hands up in surrender, grinning ear to ear. Nix gestures Phoebe off his lap and Garrett's up and running. Leif and Nix fly after him.

Ivy quickly pushes the scattered cards on the table into a pile. Her cheeks are bright red. She's so busted. Here I'm thinking she wants to be close to me. That she doesn't even know she's driving me nuts when in actuality she's signaling my cards to Garrett. I glare down toward the floor and spot a number of cards under the table. Looking back up at her, I say, "Ivy?"

She glances up at the sound of her name but quickly averts her gaze. Bending under the table, I pick up the cards and slide them to her with a smirk on my face. Her fierce eyes catch mine and they are cautious, focused, nervous even, as her stare tries to break mine. I notice that the color in her eyes is more liquid blue than gray today. Beautiful. It's inviting me, calling my name, so I don't look away. Instead I keep her pegged and stand up to hover over her. Her breathing picks up speed the closer I lean in, and I'm well aware of the attraction between us.

With no one around to pay any attention to us, I corner her and cage her with my arms. She's waiting for me to look into her face, but I cut my eyes away. Our faces are close and our bodies are like magnets, drawn to each other. I finally fix my attention on her. A piece of hair has fallen in her eyes and I push it aside. Tucking it behind her ear, I whisper, "Ivy."

She murmurs something I can't understand, then closes her eyes. I swallow, my mouth dry. I want to ask her what she said. I want to tell her to open her eyes and look at me. I consider kissing her—I'm pretty sure she'd let me, but I don't. Instead I get close enough that her breath passes over my skin like a caress. I let my pants rub against her stomach and a small sigh escapes her throat. When I'm as close as I can be without actually lying on top of her, I whisper in her ear, "Who would have thought?"

I'm not sure why I chose to call her out, but when she pushes me away and runs out of the room, I really wished I had kissed her.

The next afternoon, the bus is hauling ass to Jersey and I'm spending a rare moment alone in the galley. I'm in my cubby playing around with a song on my guitar when I feel her stare on me. When I glance up, she looks younger again. She has no makeup on, she's wearing a pair of sweatpants and a T-shirt, and her hair is pulled back. She's gorgeous.

"I thought I heard you. What are you playing?" she asks.

"Actually I'm working on something for you."

She laughs. "Oh yeah. Since when do you write songs?"

I chuckle. "I don't, but I have this idea that I've been wanting to run by you."

"Okay, I'm intrigued. What is it?"

I pat the spot next to me on my bed, and her eyes grow cautious. "I'm not going to attack you, Ivy. I just want to show you something."

She crosses the space and sits next to me, then looks around. "I've never seen where you live," she jokes.

Grinning at her, I say, "Well, it's not home. That's for sure."

"Movies, music videos, a picture of your family—it's enough to see you're still the same guy."

"Same guy I was in high school? I think I'd have to disagree with that."

"Well, I think you are."

I bow my head and look at the strings on the guitar. One thing I know for certain is that I'm not, but it's nice that she thinks I am.

"Garrett told me you just started playing the guitar again on this tour. Why did you stop? You loved it, and you were so good at it."

"Ivy, there is so much you don't know."

She turns to face me, propping a knee up as she twists sideways. "You mean about your father's death."

My throat tightens with emotion. "No, I mean about his suicide." The words come out harsher than I mean them to.

She nods. "I know, but I wish I did."

We stare at each other, communicating without talking. We've been walking this line between friends and not, between friends and lovers, between I don't know what since this tour started. She knows she's digging deep and I'm not sure I'm ready to uncover the things I've buried.

She rests her hand on my leg. "Xander, you can tell me anything. You can talk to me."

I wait a beat before answering. My pulse is racing, but I'm not sure if it's from our contact or the conversation. "Let's talk about you and what I've been working on."

She pulls her hand to her lap and smiles automatically. It's a cross between forced and genuine—one I've never seen before. "Okay. Spill it," she says, her tone neutral.

I'm not sure if she's relieved or offended. I take a breath to steady my voice. "I want to make a video. Take a song like 'Last Time' and maybe add percussion, strings, and then I want you to chant over them."

Her eyes go wide and a huge, genuine smile crosses her face. "You want me to be the girl being sung about in the song, don't you?"

I nod.

"That's brilliant," she responds. Full of enthusiasm, she takes my guitar. "Here, let me show you. Something like this, right?"

She plays a few chords and I get caught up in her movements—the way her fingers dance over the strings, the ease with which she moves her body to the rhythm. This is the real Ivy—the one not putting on a show. The girl who loves music like I do. The reason I fell in love with her to begin with.

She points her finger at me. "You missed your cue."

I laugh. "You want me to sing the song?"

"Yes. Just take the lead and I'll interject," she directs me and starts playing again, tapping her foot.

I have to stop myself from watching her, from thinking this is what we could have been doing together for years. I sing the first verse, but I'm not a singer, so I'd say I talked the first line.

We can't keep doing this going back and forth thing that
we do.
You get mad at me and then slam the door.
I apologize and you open it back up.
But, baby, we keep doing it, and this time it's the last
time.

Ivy bobs her head and closes her eyes, letting the words just flow out.

I know we're so dysfunctional that it can't be any good.
Sometimes love just isn't enough.
But for us it should be, because two wrongs can only make
a right.
So, baby, let's keep this and make every time the first
time.

She stops and opens her eyes. My thoughts are racing. The words she can create off the cuff blow me away. And her talent—the way she blends sadness, tenderness, and passion, making them feel like one emotion with just a change in her tone, is why she is the singer that she is. I'm so lost in my awe of her I don't even notice that she's set the guitar down until her hands are on my face and her lips are on mine. With a sharp intake of breath I feel their softness, their familiarity. She tastes like peppermint and smells like heaven. My head spins with raw need—a need to devour her, consume her, own her, and make her mine, this time forever. I pull her onto my lap, my hands cupping her ass, placing her right where I need her. I want to touch all of her at once. My fingers slide under her shirt and dig into her flesh, then around to feel her perfect nipples. She wraps her legs around me and my cock throbs so much it hurts. All I can think about is stripping off her clothes, being inside her, and fucking her for days.

"Um, Ivy, sorry to interrupt, but Damon's on the phone and he says it's urgent," Leif says in a rather uncomfortable tone.

She jumps off my lap immediately. "Okay. Tell him I'll be right there."

Leif leaves the galley and I grasp her wrist and tug her back to me, but she resists.

"Ignore the call," I tell her, standing up and stepping closer to her. She backs toward the door.

I put a hand on the wall next to her head. "Ivy, don't leave."

"I'm sorry, Xander. I shouldn't have done that. I just can't be that close to you."

I look down at her. "Why not? I've gone along with the friends thing, but clearly we both want more."

Her voice cracks as she whispers, "Because, Xander, my body might want you but my heart doesn't."

The pain in her voice collapses everything I am, everything I have to give. She turns and walks out without a single backward glance . . . leaving my good mood shattered and a knife twisting in my gut.

. . .

It's a rainy, miserable day when we arrive in Jersey, and the weather does nothing to improve my mood. The heat and humidity are unbearable and the rain just fucking sucks. We're late and rush into the stadium. We do a quick sound check and head backstage.

"Are you as sweaty as I am?" Ivy asks Leif.

"My balls are sitting in a puddle of water. Does that answer your question?" He grins at her.

Leif directs his gaze my way and asks, "What's with the air in the building?"

"How the fuck would I know? Do I look like the maintenance man?" I snap. His response to Ivy got under my skin, but really I'm pissed that he interrupted us this afternoon for her to take a call from that prick.

"Sorry. I was really just making a comment, not asking you directly."

I nod and steer the band toward a padded blue table in the NFL training room at New Jersey's MetLife Stadium. I throw the playlist on the table. "I'll be back in a couple hours," I tell them all as a general statement. Ivy and I haven't spoken to each other since this afternoon. I'm feeling really fed up with the whole situation, so when Amy texted me and told me Breathless was spending the night in Jersey and could I meet her for a drink before the show—I said yes.

The streetlights flicker on as we exit the bar and cross the road. The sun has set, but the sky is still overcast and the clouds are situated in a way that prevents us from seeing the moon.

"Do you want to have dinner or do you have to get back?" Amy asks.

I glance at my watch and calculate the minutes until the show starts. I'm trying to decide if I should leave now or just skip it. Even if I leave now I'll be late, so I opt for skipping it and calling to check in instead.

"Dinner sounds great."

"My hotel has a great restaurant. What do you say?"

"Anywhere is fine with me. I just need a few minutes to check on things."

We walk to Amy's hotel and she goes ahead to get a table and I stop in the lobby and make a few calls. When I hang up I feel comfortable that the show is going to run smoothly without me and go to seek out Amy.

We're seated across from each other in a booth in the dimly lit restaurant. I order my third scotch on the rocks of the night and decide to drink this one a little slower than the first two.

She chats about her job and we compare the cities we've both been in. Then the topic of conversation suddenly changes.

"Damon Wolf is buying up as many small production companies and record labels as he can," Amy tells me.

The mere mention of that asshole's name makes me want to grind my teeth together. She seems to have some kind of preoccupation with him and I'm trying to keep my cool. "I really don't give a shit about Damon Wolf," I snap.

She gives me an easy smile, ignoring my hostility, and changes the topic. "So how's the new lead singer doing?"

I shrug. "She's doing pretty good. Her and the guys got most of the songs down." I leave it at that and gulp the rest of my drink.

She eyes me. "Everything with you going okay?"

I nod toward the waiter. "Yes, it's great. I'm just hungry. I don't think I ate anything all day."

The waiter approaches and we order our food and I order another drink. For the first time, I don't want to be out with Amy. Our relationship has always been casual and we've always gotten along really well, but tonight she seems to be pushing all my buttons.

She passes the rolls, and conversation with dinner seems to go better. We talk about music and bands, and the topics stay neutral.

Once I pay the bill, I lean my head back in the booth and close my eyes. "I should get going." My words come out slurred.

"Are you drunk?" Amy asks, the word rolling off her tongue in a nonaccusatory way.

"Yes," I answer proudly and open my eyes. "I think I am."

She reaches across the table to place her hand over mine. "Why don't you come upstairs with me and sleep it off?"

I have to grin, because a night out with Amy always ends up the same way. "Sure, why not? But the bus is pulling out first thing in the morning for New York City and I have to be back."

"Xander, I'm sure you'll be up, and if not, the bus is moving less than twenty miles away. You could always take a cab."

I laugh. "Yeah, when you put it like that it does sound kind of ridiculous. I just wonder if the bus would wait for me."

She giggles and stands up from the table. "Come on, let's go."

The elevator ride seems to last forever and the walk to her room seems even longer. When we finally arrive, she unlocks the door and ushers me in.

"Want a drink?" she asks.

"I think I'm good," I reply.

I sit in one of the chairs, hoping that will stop the room from spinning.

"I'm going to brush my teeth. I'll be right back," she says, disappearing into the bathroom.

I close my eyes and start to fade away, but her voice jolts me up.

"You seem off tonight. Are you okay?" she asks for the second time this evening.

I straighten up and look over at her. "Yes, I'm fine. Just tired. I haven't been sleeping great lately." I try to focus on her. She's got a toothbrush in her mouth and she's leaning against the bathroom door wearing nothing but some sexy underwear. She looks hot, and my body responds before my mind can think. She turns back into the bathroom and after a few minutes she turns the light off and crosses the room. She kneels in front of me and presses her palms on my thighs. She slides her hands upward to my zipper and tugs it down.

"Let me help you get undressed," she says.

There's nothing I want more at this moment than to forget Ivy, but I can't do that to Amy. If I do this with her it would just make me more of an asshole than I've already been tonight.

"Amy, no," I whisper, trying to sober up and stop her before she frees my half-hard cock.

She looks at me wide-eyed. "Why?"

"I just can't right now. I've had too much to drink."

"You look fine to me," she says, staring at my erection.

"Not because of that."

She stands up with a sad smile. "Oh. Right. I get it."

"I think I should get back to the bus and see how the show went."

"Xander, you can talk to me, you know. Tell me what's going on."

"Amy, really I'm just tired," I lie.

"Okay. But at least let me drive you back. Jane rented a car and had me run errands earlier, so I still have the keys."

I nod. "Sure. Thanks."

She pulls out a shirt and a pair of shorts from her suitcase and slips them on, then pockets the car keys and we leave.

With a crash and a bang, I manage to pull the door to the bus open and climb the steps. I stand there in the entrance to the front lounge and brace myself against the doorframe. Amy slides under my arm. I think she thinks I need help walking, but really I'm just more tired than drunk.

"I'm home," I announce. As the words come out, I can hear my speech. It's slightly slurred. My eyes are glassy, I'm sure.

Garrett raises an eyebrow. "You're drunk, man. What happened to you?"

I shrug and stand there silently as I look into Ivy's eyes. She's sitting at the table watching me. Her eyes fill with hurt as she studies the situation.

"Hi, Garrett," Amy says.

"How are you? How'd you get stuck with him?"

Amy laughs. "I asked him to meet me for a drink."

Narrowing her eyes on Amy, Ivy stands up.

"Hi, Ivy," Amy says to her. "How's the tour going?"

Ivy glares at her with a look I've never seen before. "It's great," she says benignly. "I was just going to bed," she adds and hurries out of the room.

Garrett comes over and hoists me up, relieving Amy of my weight, which I seem to have bestowed upon her.

"What's with her?" I ask Garrett.

"You. You're an asshole."

My lip curls. "Clue me the fuck in. Why am I an asshole?"

"We were worried about you. You've never missed a show. We've been calling you. Why didn't you answer your phone?"

I pull my phone out of my pocket and squint at the screen. "Never heard it. It's still on VIBRATE from rehearsal." And laughing, I add, "I never felt it, either."

He rolls his eyes at me.

"I didn't know I needed to check in."

"You don't, man. Forget it. Come on, let me help you to your bed," he says, moving toward the door. The air still smells like Ivy and I breathe it in.

I turn around. "Sorry about tonight," I tell Amy.

"Don't worry about it. You were actually a lot of fun and pretty entertaining."

"Well, thank you for everything." Meanwhile I'm wondering how the hell she thinks I was the least bit fun.

She places her hand over her smiling mouth like she's putting on a show. "My pleasure," she says, then adds, "I think I saw on your schedule that we're both in Bristow, Virginia, next month. Call me and you can make it up to me then."

"I will." I'm starting to feel like the asshole Garrett just called me.

" 'Bye, Garrett," she says.

"Thanks for the delivery," Garrett responds.

She climbs down the steps and disappears, waving to me as she goes.

"You're a real knight in shining armor," Garrett says mockingly, shaking his head.

I break loose from his grip. "I got this, man. I need a shower before I have to lie down and listen to the porn show going on."

He laughs. "I'm guessing you were too drunk to get laid, then."

"You could say that," is all I say before hitting a cold shower for the second time today.

CHAPTER 9
I'm Alive

The black Escalade idles in downtown Manhattan. Rain pounds on the roof. Our show was rained out, so the band is heading to a Panic performance in New York's Bowery Ballroom instead. We're all ensconced in the chauffeured SUV outside the W, all except for Ivy. We've been waiting for her for at least twenty minutes. She got a phone call from Damon as we were walking out of the hotel and decided to take it in private. I try not to think about what that douchebag is talking to her about.

I'm in the front seat, turned around talking to Leif. We're discussing the shredding abilities he demonstrated at last night's show. Ivy sang a cover of "I Kissed a Girl" and out of nowhere Leif riffs during the chorus, making the song even more appealing to the audience.

"Hey, Xander, what's with Panic's underplay? I didn't think they needed any promo assistance," Nix calls to me.

Phoebe looks at him. "Underplay?"

He answers, "It's when a big-name band performs in a small venue and instantly sells out. It helps get a new album noticed."

"I think they're a little nervous after coming off the momentum of their first two albums and because of the split. I think they just want to make sure they keep their groove going."

The door finally opens and Ivy, covered by an umbrella, climbs in and sits next to Leif. She seems a little nervous and she's definitely been crying. Leif leans over and whispers something in her ear. She answers him and he makes a face.

The driver slides the SUV into the traffic and spins a tight circle before accelerating. I stay twisted in my seat, my eyes glued on Ivy. "Is everything okay?"

She frowns and looks out the window, muttering, "Nothing that you need to worry about."

My eyes flash to Leif's and he shakes his head, making sure his eyes are locked on mine. He's signaling me that everything is not okay. I turn around in my seat and watch the people on the street and the lights turning red and green, just waiting to get out of this car and talk to her.

We arrive at 6 Delancey Street, and it's a mob scene. People are everywhere, waiting in line to get in, scalpers hovering to sell their tickets at a markup, and fans are camped out hoping to catch a glimpse of the lucky ones who got tickets and maybe even the band members themselves. Ellie somehow managed to get tickets for us. She's been really on the ball and I'm thankful for her help.

The door opens and immediately we're ushered through the crowds and into the club. Garrett and Nix stop at the bar to get drinks.

"Do you care what we get?" Garrett asks me.

I shrug my shoulders. "Anything is fine with me."

I've had enough to drink the past couple of nights, so I'll lie low on the alcohol tonight. I turn to ask Ivy what she wants, but she and Leif already went ahead. The place is split in two—one side is the bar and the other side is the club. On the club side, the room is decorated with big white wreaths and candelabras set on the balcony tables, and a violinist is standing to one side of the stage. A band I don't know much about is already playing, but my mind isn't on the show. It's on Ivy and what's going on.

As soon as I get the opportunity, I make my way over to her and stand behind her. Her hair's pulled up on top of her head, and she's wearing a tight sleeveless white dress with high-heeled silver sandals and her sapphire earrings, which sparkle in the light from the stage—she looks fucking amazing. But she's also a little twitchy and constantly tucking pieces of her hair in place. I can tell the conversation with Damon really got to her.

"What's going on?" I whisper in her ear loud enough so she can hear me but not loud enough so anyone else can.

She turns her head. "That was a really shitty thing to do!"

I whip her around to look at me. "What are you talking about?"

"Not showing up for the show so you could go out on a date with Amy."

I sigh. "That's not what happened."

"Did you sleep with her last night?"

My jaw tenses. "No," I snap and peg her with my eyes. "If I did, would you be jealous?"

"No." She exhales. She presses her bright red lips together. "It's none of my business anyway. Guess I was just curious. I shouldn't have asked," she says, shrugging and then looking back toward the stage.

"You can ask me anything, Ivy. You should know that."

She doesn't answer in any way—no words and no body language as she focuses on the stage.

I take the silence to mean that conversation is over, and so I shift back to my original question. "I asked you what's going on with Damon. Why are you upset?"

She twists her head back toward me and her body leans into mine as her lips brush my ear. My hands move to her waist and I squeeze my fingers a little.

"Drinks for everyone," Garrett says, shoving glasses toward both of us.

She steps forward and turns toward Garrett to take the glass. Wanting to close the last few inches she just put between us, I take a step in her direction and snatch the drink that Garrett practically shoves in my face.

"What the hell is this?" I ask, pointing to the pink straw extending out of the glass filled with ice and a blue liquid.

"It's a mind eraser."

Within moments Ivy sucks all of the liquid out of the glass in one swallow.

I follow suit and the cold liquid slides down my throat. "Fuck!" I yell. "That gave me a head rush."

Ivy actually laughs, loudly. "It's supposed to. That's why it's called a mind eraser."

"Well, I'm done with those."

She laughs again and I smile at her. For a moment there is no hostility, no tension . . . just us having a good time. I think I miss that most of all—the ease of being with her. Doing anything or nothing, we always had fun. She always made me laugh.

Garrett goes into detail about what the bartender put in the shot we just drank and then lists a multitude of other shots that have quirky effects. I'm not really listening to him—I'm thinking about Ivy and why she'd ask me about Amy, and about what's going on with Damon. I just can't stop thinking about her.

Finally, Panic takes the stage. It's just them—no elaborate stage settings, no theatrics, just pure music. The kind of music I love. Ivy dances her way over toward Leif before I can bring us back to the conversation we left unfinished. He clutches her hips and starts dancing with her. He's been pretty hands on since breaking up with his girl, and I'm starting to wonder if they do have something going on. As I watch them, the tension in my body starts to strain my muscles.

I try to direct my attention elsewhere for as long as I can. I watch the band, the people in the club, talk to Nix and Phoebe, compare notes with Garrett on the sound in the room, but my eyes keep landing on Ivy. Running my hand over the stubble on my jaw, I look at her with unrestrained longing, and she catches me. My heart skips in my chest when she sings along with the band and smiles at me. Watching her makes me weak in the knees. We stare at each other and I rock on my heels. She averts her eyes to pull her phone out of her purse. She glances at it and her smile fades quickly. When she shows the message to Leif, I can't take it anymore. I'm going to drive myself crazy unless I talk to her.

Walking up to both of them, I address her. "Tell me what happened. I can tell you're upset." My voice comes out harsher than I intend.

"Everything's fine," Leif says, squeezing my shoulder.

I turn to him and with a scowl on my face, I hiss, "I was talking to Ivy."

He puts his hands up in surrender and my gaze goes back to her. Her steely eyes stare into mine for the longest time, like she's searching for something. Then finally she leans into me and on her tiptoes she whispers against my cheek, "It's nothing, really. Damon just wants me back or he's going to start legal action against me."

Every muscle in my body freezes. How dare he threaten her! "Did you tell him to go fuck himself?"

"Xander, no, I didn't. He's serious. He doesn't screw around. He says regardless of what my attorney says I'm in breach of contract—that I can't just go out on my own without having the financial agreements prearranged. He's going to sue me for everything I've earned on this tour."

"I'm serious too, Ivy. You can do whatever you want. He doesn't give a shit about the money—he just wants to control you. I hope you told him to take it all."

Any softness in her gaze instantly drains from her eyes. "No, I didn't. It's none of your business anyway. I shouldn't have told you." She turns back toward Leif, who grasps her hips again as she runs her hand up his chest, leaning forward to whisper in his ear.

The front man's voice booms through the room. "I am so relieved to finally be back," he says. He's dressed like the other three members of the band, in a vest and skinny tie. Personally I'm not one for band costumes, but from the cheers and screams the crowd seems to disagree with me. Applause drowns out his voice. He hits the floor with a bevy of dancers costumed in black and gold lamé, brocade with leather and feathers. The place turns into mayhem.

He starts his first song in the set and everyone sings and dances along, including Ivy. My eyes sharpen as I continue to watch her. She's moving to the beat. When she raises her arms over her head and I see Leif's eyes flow down her body—I'm done. I can't take her flirting with other men, I can't take the back-and-forth between us, I can't take skirting the issues. I'm pissed as hell and I need to get out of here. I turn to Garrett. "I've had enough. Just make sure Ivy gets back safely and don't forget to stop by my room. I have changes to the playlist for tomorrow's gig."

"Sure, no problem. But you're not coming to the festival?"

"I'm not sure what I'm doing," I tell him and turn without a second glance her way. I know it's time again—time to let her go. But I can't stop thinking about the choice I made so long ago—the one to set her free. As I push through the crowd of people, I don't see any of their faces. Rather, I'm swept back to the first time I let her go.

It was nine forty-five p.m. I couldn't find my fucking car keys. I was supposed to be at my grandparents' at ten. We hadn't talked much and definitely hadn't had phone sex. I just couldn't bring myself to talk to her, so I told her my mother said the phone calls were too expensive and that my aunt wouldn't appreciate the bill. That may have been a small lie—my aunt would never have cared about the money.

Anyway, I soon figured out that River had taken my car without asking. Again. My mother was sleeping and it took me forever to find her keys. The whole trip to my grandparents' I was still trying to figure out how I was going to tell her I wasn't going to Chicago, that she had to go without me. She couldn't stay in LA and let her mother continue to guide her career—she needed to get away from her. At one point I even considered begging her to stay in LA with me, telling her how much I needed her, but I knew that was selfish. No, I had to tell her she had to go without me. I knew I had to do right by her.

Just as I was signaling to pull into the driveway, she went speeding by me in her mother's car. At first I thought she had to get home because her mother never let her take the car, but when I pulled on into the driveway, I saw my car parked there. I walked around back and through the window I'm sure I saw what Ivy had seen—River with Tessa. I sat there forever, contemplating going after her, figuring out what I'd say. Wondering why she'd left in such a huff. In the end, I decided not to. If her mother was home, she'd be pissed as hell at me for showing up that late, and she'd take it out on Ivy. No, I would go home and call her. But when I got home and tried to call her, no one answered. Just as I was hanging up the phone, Bell came rushing into the kitchen.

"Xander, there you are," she squealed. "Ivy called. She said you and Tessa can have a nice life. What's she talking about?"

Her words told me everything. I walked out of the kitchen without answering Bell. Why would Ivy assume that was me with Tessa? I would never do that.

But in a moment of both anger and clarity, I decided to seize this chance. To use this to my advantage, that maybe what happened would be for the best—it would get her to Chicago. That stupid poem came to mind. I didn't know the whole thing, but the part I knew was enough—*If you love someone, set them free.*

And I did. She ended up going without me—it wasn't the way I planned or wanted. But once it happened, I let it. I let her go. How was I to know I'd be left feeling like half of me was missing after I did it?

As I exit the club, the smothering night not only suffocates me, but also threatens to steal what I have left of my composure. I'm tired, worn, and seething with anger. I've had enough. I'm pushing my guilt aside and letting all of this go. As of right now, I don't give a flying fuck what any of them do—Ivy included. I move from the shelter of the awning above me. It's still pouring, but I decide to walk back—letting the rain cool me off.

CHAPTER 10
All I Want

Ivy

Everything is closing in on me—my mother's constant calls for more money, Damon's harassing texts about my career, Xander's unyielding scrutiny. It's all too much. Tossing back drink after drink, I let myself go. I surge into the crowd and sway my hips. And as the music starts to breathe life back into me, all I want to do is forget the world. I think about the outdoors—the sound of the never-ending rain, the strength of the wind, the ominous color of the sky—I focus on those calming things. But Xander's features that draw together in a dark triangle whenever he looks at me tonight, that's all I see and I want so much to be the one to smooth them out.

Leif moves close and together we find the beat. We dance to forget—two friends who need each other. We've been companions for so long, he's really the only person besides Xander who I've ever really confided in. I'd have been lost without him to talk to these last few years among the stresses of album production, demands on my career, and the need my family has for more and more money.

I try to push all my stresses and worries away, but I can't push Xander from my mind. I don't want to. Spending this time with him has me questioning everything. I feel like we've grown close, reestablished that friendship we once shared, but I've kept it on the surface. I'm afraid to let it go any deeper. He's tried to talk to me, but I can't handle talking about him with another girl. I know he wants me and I want him so badly, but I can't let go of the past. Whenever he gets close, I see him with her. And I also can't handle a casual relationship with him. He seems to have that with Amy, and who knows who else— That's not what I want from him.

Everything is hazy, the room is hot, and I'm sweaty, so I excuse myself to use the bathroom. I splash cold water on my face and try to wipe him from my brain. I found the strength to forget him before and I have to find it again. I have to fight these feelings I have for him that just won't go away. But when I follow the crowd back into the room, I can't help but look for him. I scan the area. I see people drinking, dancing, groping. I spot the band. But I don't see him anywhere. My gaze flickers around and finally settles on Leif, who's talking to Nix and Phoebe. Popping over to him, I stand in the circle, but don't really listen to the conversation. Instead, I continue to search for Xander.

When a sweat-clad Garrett taps me on the shoulder, he interrupts the conversation. "Hey, there you are. I think it's a good idea for us to get out of the club before everyone else starts to leave. To avoid the crowds as everyone exits."

I nod at Garrett, and he motions toward the door with his chin and takes my elbow. "Come on, this way," he shouts over the music.

I'm not really ready to leave, but since he seems to have decided it's time, I follow him to the car. When we start to drive away, I become alarmed. Turning around toward Nix, I ask, "Where's Xander?"

He shrugs his shoulders. "I don't know. I haven't seen him since the band started playing." His lack of concern just pisses me off.

But Garrett seems to know. He mutters something about him being in a shitass mood and leaving, telling him to stop by and pick up the materials for tomorrow's show when we got back.

"Why? Is he not coming?"

Garrett seems annoyed and just throws his head back. "Who the fuck knows?"

Since I'm pretty sure Xander's foul mood has something to do with me, I tell him, "I'll stop by his room. I need to talk to him about something anyway."

"You're the one opting to walk into the ring of fire. Just remember, I'm not the one who sent you."

I give him a halfhearted grin as I think about how Xander hasn't changed. His temper, his mood swings—they've only intensified. I need to apologize to him for snapping when he asked me about Damon. I think I should explain my financial situation and how important it is that I work things out with Damon in an amicable way. And now is probably the best time. I can tell he doesn't care for Damon or trust him, but that rush I felt over his protectiveness that first morning on the bus has kept me from discussing Damon with him. I don't want him to make any trouble for the band because just like Xander, Damon can be hotheaded. And since Damon's demands keep coming and his calls get more frequent, I'm just not sure what he wants from me, but I know he wants something.

As soon as the car parks in front of the hotel, we make a run for it through the rain, none of us waiting for the doorman or an umbrella. Leif and Garrett decide to hit the hotel bar for one last drink, and Nix and Phoebe head to their room. I ride the elevator with them and exit at Xander's floor.

Walking down the hall, I notice the slide bar of his dead bolt holding the door ajar. I knock lightly and swing it open. "Xander, it's me. I don't want to fight with you. And there are some things I think you should know . . ." I'm stunned into silence. I stop for a heartbeat as my gaze tumbles over him. He's standing in the hotel room, his long, lean body turned to the side, as he shrugs out of his unbuttoned shirt. My eyes graze his body—he is still the most beautiful man I have ever laid eyes on. My breath catches at the sight of him. Seeing the lines in his muscles makes my heart beat so fast, and watching the flexing of his biceps has me biting down on my lower lip. The way his abs ripple down into the waistband of his jeans causes my body to clench with need. My memory of him isn't nearly as powerful as the real thing.

I savor the sight, trying not to pant. I make sure not to deflect my stare, but rather I make it clear that I'm studying every single inch of him. I even notice the fraying of his shirt, which on most men would make me think they should mend it or buy a new one, but on him the imperfection only makes him all the more appealing. When that shirt drops to the floor, I watch it intently, and as the hem skims the ground, a small noise escapes my throat.

His eyes sweep to mine and our gazes lock. He turns, leans slightly forward as if considering picking up the shirt, then decides differently. "Ivy." He says my name not as a question, not as a statement, not in surprise. It's sensual, full of longing; it's a sound I remember from him, from before, and one I could never forget.

I feel pummeled by his rugged good looks—God, he has a face that would melt any woman's heart. His pale but intense hazel eyes, the sprinkling of stubble across his chin, the lushness of his lips, and the wave of his thick brown hair that always had me itching to run my fingers through it—all features any woman would pine for. I take a step in, letting the door slam against the slide bar behind me. Neither of us says a word. The burn of his stare has me longing to escape the intensity of the moment. I let my gaze slip but feel my lips part—and his do the same. I lower my lids and immediately notice the way his jeans sit so low on his hips, and a shiver runs down my spine. Then something more beautiful than anything I've ever seen catches my attention. At first it looks like a tribal design running vertically down his right side, but as I narrow my eyes on it I can see it's a straight line of black inked letters.

Gasping, I slowly cross the room. I stand in front of him, trembling. I touch my shaky fingers to his bare skin, to the *R* right at the apex of his rib cage. It's warm beneath the pads of my fingers, and my body is electrified at the feel of his skin against mine. Xander looks down at my hand, and I peek up at him. His face is completely unreadable. It's filled with an emotion I've never seen. But when he nearly loses his balance from the contact, I think he's feeling what I'm feeling—euphoric. Shuffling his feet, he recovers quickly. His head remains bowed and his chest rises and falls rapidly as I carefully trace each one of the letters. Every letter is a work of art, forming the phrase—

Tears fall and sobs I can't control escape me as I place my trembling finger on the tiny ivy leaf, the mark used instead of an accent to stress the *E*. It's only then that his gaze falters. His eyes flutter closed when I touch him there. Then I drop my hand and his eyes open.

"When did you get this?" My voice dips low, but I manage to get the words out.

He's gazing down at me. His voice is deep and sexy in the dim room. "Right after you left for Chicago. If I couldn't have you, I wanted to always have a part of you."

"Why? Why would you do that?" My voice quavers as I ask.

He inhales a deep breath and sighs. "Because I loved you and knew I always would."

All the tension I've been feeling. All the pain and anger I've held on to. I blurt it all out in what I believe to be the truth. "No, no you didn't. You didn't want me. You wanted her. This"—I say, drawing a line down his tattoo—"doesn't make any sense."

His hand grasps my waist. "Ivy, I have something to tell you."

I pull away and he lets me. "Tell me what?"

"It wasn't me that night."

"Xander, this is why I didn't want to discuss our past. Please don't lie."

Everything about him goes rigid. The intensity in his eyes grows even stronger. He pauses for a moment, then almost hisses, "I've never lied to you, Ivy. Ever. And I NEVER will." He puts emphasis on the word *never*.

I take a step backward toward the door. Afraid—afraid he's lying . . . afraid he isn't. Everything about that night suddenly comes crashing back—everything I've fought so hard to forget.

His fingers tuck a piece of hair behind my ear as he says, "I was an asshole then. I let you believe things I shouldn't have."

"Things like what?" I squeak out.

He pauses, then asks, "What did you see that night?" The question comes out quiet, sounding almost sad.

I move back. Certain about what I saw, but suddenly unsure about the facts, trying to remember everything. "I saw your car parked in the driveway, and when I went around back I heard voices. I looked in the window and saw Tessa's face almost staring back at me, so I turned and ran."

Xander let out a low, shuddering breath. "It wasn't me with Tessa that night. That wasn't me in the pool house. River took my car. He was the one with Tessa."

I look at his face now, into his eyes—and truth is all I see. "Why would you let me believe it was you?"

He shrugs. "Fuck, I don't know. I was confused. I didn't know what to do and I was mad."

I'm shaking from head to toe. "You were mad? Why would you be mad?"

He steps forward and runs his fingers down my arm. His mouth thins. "Why would you automatically think I cheated?"

"Because we were apart for so long. I just thought you couldn't wait."

He entwines his fingers with mine. "Couldn't wait to fuck someone I didn't care about? Ivy, you knew me better than that."

Tears slide faster down my face. "Why wouldn't you just explain? I still don't understand why you let me go to Chicago thinking you cheated on me." Anger, sadness, regret—they all resonate within me. None of them taking control. I'm mad that he let me believe a lie for so long, I'm sad that I didn't confront him before I left, and I regret letting my own insecurities cloud my judgment—overshadow what I knew we had.

He squeezes my hand and I squeeze back. He catches my chin between his thumb and finger with his other hand and caresses it. "Because it was the easy way. I had to let you go . . . you had to get away from your mother, and that was the only way. I had so much other shit going on in my head. I couldn't go with you, baby, even though I wanted to so badly. My mother, my brother, my sister—they needed me."

My tears are out of control and I push him back. Anger finally takes over. I turn and head for the door, my voice rising as I cross the room. "I needed you."

He follows on my heels, clutching my hand and twisting me to look at him. "I know," he says in barely a whisper. "I know. But I knew you were stronger than you thought. I wanted you to make it. To become the powerhouse singer that you deserved to be. And you did it. I had so much going on in my head then, I couldn't think straight, and at the time it was the only way."

I stare at him and he doesn't falter. More anger clogs my throat. "You shouldn't have decided that on your own."

"I didn't know any other way. I was struggling with so many emotions, emotions I still struggle with. Things about my father I can't seem to forget."

"I was there for you. I would have been with you."

"That's why I let it happen. You couldn't stay and I couldn't go."

"But I missed you every day. When I started singing, every performance I thought of you, I looked for you, not for congratulations but for support."

He steps into me and any buzz I was feeling from earlier is gone. He brings his hand to my face and wipes away my tears and I let him. Silence falls between us as we communicate with only our eyes for a few seconds. He draws even nearer and the attraction can't be denied and neither can the love. He kisses my forehead and again I let him. I want him to. I want to feel his touch. I love him. Yes, I love him. I always have.

Pressing his forehead to mine, he whispers, "Baby, I was always there for you. I watched you. I never forgot you. I sent a piece of my heart to your first show and even though you never responded, I didn't give up for the longest time."

I'm breathing so fast my heart can't keep up. "What do you mean? What are you talking about?"

"The plants. I sent ivy plants with a card that said this." He points to his side, to the beautiful letters.

"I never got any of them. I promise. God, if I had gotten them, gotten one—I would have responded." *Did Damon circumvent them? Did he keep them from me?*

Cupping the back of my neck, his strong fingers press against my skin. He pulls me even closer and grazes the very corner of my mouth with his lips. With just that one simple touch, a need that's been buried for years surfaces, in the most out-of-control way. I lift my mouth toward his, sealing us together, and his response is immediate. His lips are warm, full, inviting. It's a forceful kiss, and when we both pull away, breathless, his eyes are simmering. My fingers tremble as they dance across his abs over to the letters. He takes a deep breath.

I bend down and drop my mouth to his tattoo, tracing the letters with my tongue. I peek up at him and see his eyes close and his head fall back. I lick his skin, taste the ink, inhale his sweet scent. His muscles tense under my lips with every touch. Once I reach the ivy leaf, I slowly stand up on my toes and bring my mouth to his ear. "Remember after our first performance when I fell on the bus stairs and you whispered, 'I want you'?"

"Uh-huh."

I slide my hand to rest on the button of his jeans. "All you had to do was take me and I would have been yours."

"Fuck," he breathes through his teeth and his hands slide down my back to my ass. "Well, I want you now, and I'm not asking."

"You don't have to."

His lips part and form an incredible smile. He clenches my hips in his strong hands and turns us around. Pushing me against the wall, he grinds into me with his hard cock, and everything in the world as I know it is gone—I have all I want, all I need, right here. His lips are at my ear and he says my name over and over. I skim my hands along the bare skin above his jeans, this time unbuttoning them.

He pulls me close to him—as close as he can—and holds me. Just holds me, for the longest time. Then his lips brush my ear and in his sexiest, huskiest voice, he says, "Fuck, you feel incredible. I want you, now."

His whisper floats into the air and shivers run down my spine. Oh God, I want him so much. "Xander, yes!"

I'm frozen in anticipation of what's to come as he grins down at me before sealing his lips over mine. This time the kiss isn't as forceful, but it is equally as breathtaking. His mouth is wet and soft . . . just like I remember, and his tongue probes deep inside my mouth . . . just like I remember. We seem to dance a familiar dance with our tongues. I'm so hot for him, I moan with every touch. Pulling my dress up, he reaches between my legs and I writhe against him with a primal need. He cups my sex with one of his strong hands and cups my breast with the other. And then I finally get to bury my fingers in his hair. I am done pretending. I want him and he wants me. I pull on his hair to make sure this is real, and he grits his teeth with a strangled gasp. My dress keeps sliding down and he keeps pulling it back up. His fingers are back in my panties and the moment they circle my clit, I call out his name. "XANDER!"

His lips and tongue are everywhere. I'm lost in the feeling of him. My dress drops again and I don't even notice.

"Take it off," he growls.

I lift the dress over my head and before I have it completely off, his hands smooth down the bare skin of my abdomen. I'm wearing a simple white bra and matching thong. He stares at me with such intensity— I don't even remember kicking off my shoes and pulling my hair down.

"You're gorgeous," he tells me.

I see the appreciation in his eyes and touch his hair again. "You're all wet."

"I walked back from the club," he tells me, running his mouth down my neck.

"Why did you walk back?" I manage to say with shaky breaths.

He pushes my hair over my shoulder and his tongue slides up and down my neck. "I needed air," he mumbles.

I start to ask why, but he silences me with that mouth I've wanted all over me for so long. And it works, because all I can think about is him.

"Take your panties off," he says in a hoarse, low voice.

I nod and shimmy them down with trembling hands. I've never let anyone tell me what to do during sex except him. Never since him have I allowed anything but mutual dominance, but with him I love it when he takes control.

When I move to unhook my bra, he whispers, "Let me."

His soft but callused hands first cup my breasts, then slide around my back and with the precision he always had, he quickly unfastens my bra. I gasp when his cold, wet mouth finds its way to my breast at the same time his hands slide the straps down my arms. With his mouth still sucking one of my nipples, his hand caresses the other one. He takes a step back and I swear I blush from the look he's giving me. I extend my hands to unbutton his jeans, but before I can tug his zipper down, he pulls out the desk chair next him.

"Sit down," he says, chewing his bottom lip.

He's watching me, his jaw relaxed, relieved of all the tension he's possessed since I first saw him at the pool. I slouch back and spread my legs like I know he wants. I want it too. When he drops to his knees, the anticipation of what's to come has me squirming with an uncontrollable need to touch him. He draws a line with his tongue up my inner thigh and when he reaches my sex he circles it just one time before moving right to my clit.

"Oh, Xander," I call out, and his eyes flare to mine.

Watching me, he kisses, licks, and sucks me in a way no one but him ever has. The feel of his stubbled face against my sensitive skin is like heaven. I completely lose control when he inserts first one, then two fingers inside me. My head falls back and I arch my body as I come hard and fast, shattering into what I can only think are pieces of the last twelve years of missed time.

Lifting my head to look at him, I can see he's got a huge grin on his face. He wipes his mouth on his arm and toes his boots off before pulling his pants down. I watch with a ravenous hunger as his thick cock springs free. The tip glistens, and all I can think about is tasting it. I don't wait for him to kick out of his jeans before I lean over and lick the precum off of him.

"Fuck," he says, pulling me up out of the chair. He claims my mouth with his and a groan escapes his throat when I take his throbbing cock in my hand. Pulling away, he removes a condom from his wallet and rolls it on.

Once it's in place, he growls, "I want to be inside you, right now."

He pushes me back onto the desk and in an instant he thrusts into me, filling me in one swift motion. His hips jerk and mine follow. He brushes his lips along my collarbone, up my neck, and to my ear, where he whispers, "You feel so good."

My fingers dig into his skin as a feeling of complete satisfaction takes over. The passion between us is so fierce that my muscles are convulsing around his cock way too quickly. I don't want this to end. I try to slow my impending orgasm, but when he rolls my nipples with his fingers, I can't hold back any longer. Instead, I just close my eyes and get ready to experience the joy I haven't felt in so many years.

"Ivy," he yells out, pounding into me at an unrelenting pace. "Look at me."

Opening my eyes, I delight in watching him, but I can't hold it off another minute. Lifting my hips, I grasp hold of his arms and move with him. Leaving no space between us—we come together, shouting each other's names in unison. When he stops moving, he buries his face in my chest, practically panting. He licks his way up and I can feel his warm breath near my neck and hear his heart pounding against mine. Stepping back slightly, he slips out of me and I feel a sudden, overwhelming loss.

I pull him to me. "Don't leave."

He drags his teeth along my jawbone, sending a shiver down my spine. "I'll be right back," he says as he pulls me off the desk, and then he goes into the bathroom.

I stand there watching him—the boy who made love to me over and over is now a man that I don't think I can ever get enough of. The feeling of having him inside me is something I've never forgotten, and I never thought I'd feel it again. It's a feeling I now know I can't live without. When he comes out of the bathroom, he rakes his eyes down my body in a way that makes my heart skip a beat. I stare at his tattoo as he walks back into the room and grabs the door handle, pulling the slide bar back and letting the door close on its own.

I start laughing uncontrollably, and he looks at me, then does the same.

"It might not have been so hysterical if Garrett had walked in on us," he says, crossing the room with a confidence that makes my stomach flutter.

I bite my lip and stare into the depths of his eyes as he stands in front of me. Wrapping his arms around me, he inhales a deep breath. He runs his hands down my body and I relish his touch. When he presses his cheek to mine, his soft stubble makes me shiver. His body moves flush with mine, and I brush my fingers down the length of his side, blindly tracing the letters.

"I must be dreaming," I tell him, leaning back and looking into his intense greenish-brown eyes. My voice is hoarse, but not the least bit weak.

He places his fingers under my chin and lifts it, tilting my face just enough to press his lips to mine. "No, baby, it's not a dream. This is real." He plants sweet kisses around my mouth, and his words undo me.

He walks me backward until the backs of my knees are touching the bed. "This time I want to take it slow. I want to make love to you, and I think the bed is a better choice than the desk."

I open my mouth to agree, but he pushes me back and I fall with a laugh onto the soft mattress, looking up at him. The pulse beating in his throat makes me smile. We stare at each other for the longest time—me lying on the bed, with my feet on the floor, and him standing over me, with the corners of his mouth turned up in the sexiest grin. Then suddenly the mood seems so serious and my laughter stops.

"I missed that smile," he tells me.

I don't say anything because I know if I do I'll just cry again. He could always make me smile—not the fake one I have to put on for the sake of my career—and the mention of everything we once had together swells my heart. He licks his lips and I back up slightly on the bed, inviting him to join me. The mattress dips as he crawls onto it and settles beside me. I trace my finger around his moist, full lips, he smiles, and I whisper, "I've missed yours too."

Tucking his head into my neck, he kisses his way down my body, then rolls us around. We touch, stroke, and lick every inch of each other for what doesn't seem nearly long enough. Both breathing heavily, we're tangled in the sheets and he's hovering over me—his eyes roaming every uncovered inch of my body. The lights are still on and I'm glad, because I want to watch him, see him, make up for all the days that have passed that I never got to see his beautiful face.

He hovers over me and hesitates for a moment. He presses his forehead to mine, and I ask, "What's wrong?"

"I want to feel you. Really feel you—like I used to."

I stare at him, knowing what he wants but not sure he wants to hear what I have to say. "Xander, I'm on the pill, but I haven't been tested since—"

Lifting himself up, he cuts me off. "I'm clean, Ivy."

"Make love to me," I answer, giving him the go-ahead not to wear a condom.

With a soft groan, he centers himself and heat floods me. His face smolders when he looks down at me, and I can feel my need for him all the way down to my toes. His teeth clench and he bites his lower lip as he slowly pushes into me. His cock—long, thick, and hard—fills me. Skin to skin—the feeling is magical, and both of our bodies tremble with the intimate contact. My arms circle his back and my fingers press hard into his muscles as we move together in the same rhythm.

I pull his mouth to mine and softly kiss him. Returning my kiss with the same tenderness, he pulls out of me and I search him for an answer as to why. My question is answered when he rolls onto his back, bringing me with him. Straddling him, I guide his cock back inside me and he lets out a guttural groan. My legs squeeze his body as I sit up and press my hands to his chest for support. His hands find my breasts, and he rolls and fondles the nipples into hard peaks. With his hands on me and his cock inside me, I just close my eyes as bliss washes through my veins.

When his fingers stop massaging my chest, I open my eyes and look into his face to see that it's full of desire. I gasp when his hand slides between my legs and his thumb rubs circles around my clit. "Do you like this?" he asks.

Moaning, I arch my body and throw my head back. "Yes," I scream, moving my hands behind me and clutching his knees. I want to wait for him, but the higher I lift myself off his cock and the harder I slam down on him, the more intense the feeling. When he rubs my clit harder and harder, moving his thumb in smaller and faster circles, my body starts to tremble and I can't hold back any longer. "Oh God. Yes!" I scream, and everything in the world seems to stop except for this feeling of pure heaven.

"Fuck, Ivy, yes!" he yells.

I open my eyes as my orgasm rolls through me. Watching him, I know he's coming too. His eyes close and with one final thrust I can feel him filling me. When he opens his eyes and looks at me with that look I could never resist—I melt.

"I love you." The words just tumble out without any advance thought. I regret saying them immediately. "I'm sorry. I shouldn't have said that." I shift my eyes away from him, knowing the words were automatic and true, but it's too soon to actually say them. I roll away and throw my legs off the bed, but before my feet hit the floor his hands clutch my waist and his hard chest nestles against my back.

"Where are you going?"

Without turning toward him, I answer, "To the bathroom."

"Not yet. Turn around, Ivy. Look at me."

He sits down on the bed and pulls my legs off the floor and lifts me back on his lap. "Okay, now we're going to do this again. You start by saying 'I love you.' But this time when you say it, keep looking at me and don't turn away as soon as the words come out."

"Xander, I shouldn't have said that. I don't know why I did."

"Look at me, Ivy," he commands, and I do. "You know why you said it—it's because you feel the same way I do. Look, we could play the game—pretend we both didn't feel what we felt the minute we saw each other at the pool, but I'd rather not. I loved you when I was fourteen. I loved you when I was eighteen and had to let you go. I've loved you for the last twelve years. And I love you now. Ivy—I love you."

Hearing those words from his lips seems surreal. My stomach flutters and I throw my arms around his neck. "I love you, Xander. I love you," I tell him, holding him and wanting to never let him go.

He holds me close and I don't even question his words, not for a second. I don't need to. I can feel it. I can hear it. I can see it. It's written all over him—it's even etched on his body. It's real and right. It's everything I've been missing and everything I want. He's mine, and this time I'll never let him go. We were always so much alike. We covered up our feelings, pushed them aside, wore a strong armor to face the world, but with each other we were bared—no shields, no masks—just what was real and what was true. And the emotions I'm feeling between us right now tell me that hasn't changed—they tell me I'm home.

He swats my ass a few minutes later. "Now let me get up and get something to clean us up."

I lean back and smile at him. He bends down and bites my lip. "Or come with me and we'll take a shower."

Tightening my grip, I let my body answer for me.

"Shower it is," he says as he moves off the bed with my legs wrapped around his waist.

Thirty minutes later we're lying in bed in the pitch-dark room. I'm spent, sated, and happier than I've been in such a long time. Pulling me to him, he hugs me like he used to—arms and legs wrapped around me, squeezing so tight.

"I love you, Ivy Taylor," he whispers.

"I love you, Xander Wilde," I whisper back. And then I close my eyes, feeling so full of raw emotion I could burst with happiness.

CHAPTER 11
Feel Again

Xander

Daylight threatens to break at any moment. We're lying here together, and it seems unreal. I can hear our heartbeats in the silence between us. In all the years we've been apart I've never found anyone that makes me feel like she does. It's as if my heart closed off after our breakup and it took her letting me back in to reopen it. Hearing her say those three words to me last night and telling her I felt the same—it was the truest and most honest feeling I've ever shared with anyone.

I'm rubbing circles along her back and she's tracing the lines that are inked down my side. We slept only a few hours, but I feel more rested than I have in weeks. I woke up this morning ready for her, so I put my hands between her legs and did everything to her I've wanted to do over the past month.

Now she's lying on my chest and the sapphire earrings are still in her ears. "My grandmother would be happy that you still wear the earrings she gave you."

She clutches one and twists it in her ear. "I never take them out. They're the most special gift I've ever received."

My hand catches the back of her neck and I tilt her head toward mine. Her statement makes me equally as happy and sad.

"I loved her too, you know. I'm sorry I didn't make it to her funeral."

"Yes, I miss her, and my grandfather. At least they didn't have to be apart long. The six months my grandfather was alive without her, he was lost. I moved in with him when his depression took over. Really he just didn't want to live without her. And at eighty—who could blame him? He had been with her for so long and he just really loved her."

Silence takes over and we lie here together.

"Tell me something?" she asks, flipping onto her back and staring at the ceiling.

"Anything."

"How do you see this going?" she asks, motioning between the two of us.

My lips twist into a sad smile as I pull her onto my chest. "We'll take one day at a time together. Twelve years is a long time and we have a lot to learn about each other. But I'm not planning on spending any more days apart."

"Do you think relationships can work that way?"

"What way is that?"

"That something once broken, irreparably, like us, can be so easily mended?"

I shift to hover over her, taking her wrists and pinning her arms to her sides. Kissing her neck, I slide my tongue up to her mouth before answering. "I think all relationships are different and each one has its own dynamics. There are no rules to follow. So, yes, I think if we both want this bad enough there's no reason we can't have it."

Her eyes flicker from my eyes to my lips, and I take that as a sign not only that she agrees but also that she wants me to kiss her, which I most happily do.

We've spent the morning naked in bed, ordering room service and just talking. We talked about my brother and his decision to leave the band. I even told her about the difficulty I had accepting his decision. She told me about her years in Chicago and that she hasn't seen her family in some time. She told me why she stopped singing last year, and I was really proud of her for taking a stand and trying to gain control of her own career. Then she finally told me about her money worries and why she doesn't want to piss Damon off. We got lost in so many conversations that when I finally pick up my phone to check the time, I bolt straight up. "Shit, it's almost eleven."

She pushes up onto her elbows and looks up at me. "I have to go. We're supposed to meet on the bus in less than an hour," she says, rushing out of bed and quickly pulling her dress over her head.

I nod and stand to stretch.

She stares at me—her dark eyes gleaming and her mouth twisting into a smile that I can't resist returning. Then I pull her to me so I can kiss her. She tugs on my lip and presses her body to mine and there it goes. Fuck, I have to get this under control.

"I have to get ready," she breathes.

"I know." I'm already pulling her dress back up over her head. "But you can be fifteen minutes late. The bus won't leave without you. I promise."

Ivy's full of confidence and poise onstage without her trademark guitar. Both of her hands are on the microphone stand and her head is down, waiting for the music. She's wearing a short one-piece black outfit with lace sleeves. When she slipped it on this morning, I thought we were going to be really late for the show. And when she started out the door with it on I had to stop her.

She smirked at me. "What?" she asked.

"Why are you wearing your pajamas to perform?"

She laughed so hard it took her a few minutes before she could say, "It's called a romper, and it's clothes, not sleepwear."

As her sound fills the open space, the crowd cheers her on. It's a midday show and the sun beats down on the stage, causing everyone to squint. But even though she's only five seven, her voice is a powerhouse. She begins to sing a simple ballad. She pats her chest with her palm while singing, "With the beating of your tiny heart."

Today I notice the band has really come together as a group—from Ivy's adorable, awkward banter with the audience to Garrett making shadow puppets on the wall while Nix tunes his guitar. Leif seems introverted at times, turning his face and his guitar away from the audience at the deep emotional parts of certain songs, as if getting lost in the music, but it works. They've mastered the union of a band in such a short period of time—it's incredible to watch.

My gaze automatically slides back to Ivy and my body starts to tremble when I think about how everything has changed between us in the last twenty-four hours. The only thing assuring me that it's all real is her sideways glance at me and that smile she gifts me with before saying to the audience, "I want to come back next year. I love it here. Upstate New York, you rock!" The crowd yells louder and louder, and once again she's a hit.

We got to New York's Mountain Jam early enough that we could enjoy the other shows, but we can't stick around. She exits the stage with Nix, Leif, and Garrett following her. The minute her foot crosses the threshold behind the curtain, she smiles at me and I can't help myself. I pick her up and swing her around in a circle. Once I've set her down, she grasps my cheeks and pulls my face toward hers. My hands drift down her back while I press my lips to hers.

Garrett clears his throat. "Ummm . . . Xander, would you like to tell us what the hell is going on?"

Ivy laughs and we break free of each other. The guys are standing around us with their eyes wide open and their jaws hanging.

"Yeah, Xander, would you like to tell them?" Ivy mocks.

We played it cool on the bus ride over, since we hadn't discussed telling the guys. And once we got here we went in different directions—I had to take care of a few things and she and Leif had some bands they wanted to watch. Ivy and I discussed Leif last night, and she assured me they're only friends, so her hanging out with him doesn't concern me anymore. Garrett and Nix know we used to date in high school, but that's about all. I was going to tell them we were back together before the show, but there was no time. And when I saw her exiting the stage in all her glory, it made me feel like that eighteen-year-old boy . . . and all I wanted was to have my arms around her.

Now all I can do is smirk. I clutch her waist and pull her away from the guys. Leaning over, I whisper in her ear, "I think they can figure it out for themselves."

She doesn't know it, but I rented a car and have a short sightseeing trip planned for us. Ever since my father killed himself, I've kept such a tight grip on things. I control my emotions—containing things when I'm angry, pissed, or frustrated. I control my life—I decide where I go, who I go with, and what I do. Everything is planned. I never waver. There's been such a driving force within me for so long, I hardly acknowledge it. But with her I can let my guard down; I don't have to control every little thing. I feel free—free to have fun and explore the emotions I've locked away for so long.

Once we're alone in the car, I pull out a blindfold.

She stares at it. "What is that? Part of Garrett's sex swing?"

I smirk. "I'll never tell. Now come on, I want where we're going to be a surprise. So turn around."

She laughs and does as I ask. I tie it around her.

"I hope it's a short ride," she says.

"It is." I put the car in DRIVE and we carry on with our conversation like she's not wearing a blindfold. I can't help but steal glances at her the whole way.

When we come to a stop she asks, "Where are we?"

I put the rental car in PARK and open my door. "Stay there."

"Where am I supposed to go? I can't see anything."

One thing I know is that I have a lot to make up for, and I'm not letting any more time pass. Striding around the car, I can't help but admire how gorgeous she looks with that blindfold on. Her blond hair is sticking out everywhere with the small piece of fabric strapped around her eyes. It's a perfect match to her ruby red lips. The material actually is a small piece of Garrett's yoga swing that I snipped off the top. I considered bringing the whole thing and trying it as a sex swing, but I didn't have time to figure that contraption out.

Slowly I open the door and take her hand. She pushes herself against me, snaking her arms around my neck. All the air leaves my lungs. "You have a habit of doing that. Not that I want you to stop." I don't tell her I have to work on controlling the hard-ons she keeps giving me the minute her body touches mine.

She giggles and it's so fucking sweet I want to remember this moment forever. I feel more alive than I've felt for years. My body hums with an energy she's instilled in me. She's biting her lip and I take a moment to mimic her gesture.

Staring at her lips, I trace them with my finger. "You ready?" I ask.

She brings her hands up to her covered eyes and I clear my throat. "Not yet." I slip my hand in hers, my heart thumping at the boundary between happy and happier. Caressing her soft skin, I tug her forward in anticipation. The closer we get, the louder the roar becomes. Cold water plops on us from everywhere and drops glisten against her skin. One falls right on the corner of her lips and when I bend to lick it off, she catches my tongue with her mouth. The heat that arises between us is enough to ward off any chill from the icy water. Panting and out of breath, I slide my fingers up her cheeks and under the stretchy fabric, removing the blindfold and turning her around to see the crystal cascades of the roaring falls. We lean over the railing, both of us silent and staring at Niagara Falls. The air is warm and full of moisture, but the sky is darkening and the slight breeze seems to make her shiver.

"What do you think?" I ask.

When she doesn't answer, I place my hands on the curve of her hips and turn her back around to face me. We're chest to chest, and as my gaze meets hers I see tears streaming down her face. "Why are you crying? What is it?"

She shakes her head and manages to say, "They're happy tears, not sad ones."

I'm not the kind of guy who cries. In fact, I don't think I've ever cried, not even at my dad's funeral. I may have shed a tear or two for my grandparents, but I swear I have to rely on all the self-control I can muster not to let one slip past me now. The joy I see in her eyes is enough to bring me to my knees. I take her face in my hands and kiss away each and every tear.

"I don't want you to cry, gorgeous. I brought you here so we could experience something we both enjoyed together once." Leaning back, I lift her chin so I can look in her eyes. "Talk to me, Ivy."

She gets up on her toes and touches her lips to my ear. "This is the single best surprise I've ever received in my life."

"I'm glad," I tell her, and then I kiss her hard and hold her tight. We stand like that for a long time.

The smell of food wafts over to us from the nearby restaurants, and after the intimate silence I clear my throat and ask, "You hungry?"

"Very."

"Me too. Come on, let's find someplace to eat."

Walking down the busy sidewalk, we reach the crossing. The light is red, so we wait with a bunch of other people. Cars screech to a halt behind the white lines that etch the road, and out of nowhere a driver slams on his brakes, obviously thinking twice about running the light. He comes to a standstill in the middle of the crosswalk, and I instinctively step in front of Ivy, who was closer to the car. I pause for a minute to look over at her, and it hits me. After all this time it's not that I couldn't love someone, that I wasn't capable—it's that the one I needed wasn't there for me to love.

As we start walking again, I lean over and whisper in her ear, "I can't wait to get you alone. To get your clothes off and do everything I didn't get to finish last night."

She looks up at me and a rosy blush covers her cheeks. Then out of nowhere someone screams, "You're Ivy Taylor. Oh my God," and snaps a picture before either of us can turn away. I move to go after the woman, but Ivy pulls me back. "Ignore it. It's fine," she says. So we keep walking and I reach for her hand as we look in the windows of all the tourist-trap shops that line the street. When we walk past a cheesy diner with a pink flashing sign that says ROSIE'S, we smile at each other. Diners were always our thing. In high school we searched them out for the best breakfasts, milk shakes, and burgers. Just as we walk into the restaurant, her phone rings and she retrieves it from her purse and holds it in her palm.

"Aren't you going to answer it?" I ask.

"No," she says quietly.

My eyes narrow on her. "Who's calling that you don't want to talk to?"

"Xander, it's nothing." But she's still stopped on the sidewalk, gazing down at her phone.

I take it from her. Ten missed calls from Damon Wolf. "Why is he calling you nonstop?"

"He wants to discuss our contract termination. My attorney says to let him take care of it."

"I'll take care of it when we get back." I can feel that I'm glowering, but I can't help it.

She shakes her head. "No. It's best to let my attorney do it."

I nod. Like hell I will. "Sure, gorgeous. Come on, let's eat." I lace my hand with hers and lead her to the diner I spotted.

We walk in and it's like a scene out of *Happy Days*. The front counter is lined with classic candies—Sugar Daddys, Bit-O-Honeys, Sixlets, Oh Henry! bars, candy necklaces, Sky Bars, and Cherry Mashes. Betty Boop memorabilia is everywhere. The waiter waves us to take our own seat, and we find a booth in the very back. The restaurant looks like it hasn't been remodeled since it opened in the 1950s. The booths are ripped and the table is sticky, but I could care less because we both look up at each other and grin. There's a shiny chrome Seeburg Wall-O-Matic jukebox sitting at the end of our table. Jackpot!

I ask the waitress for some change and when she brings it to the table, I push it all over to Ivy. "Your choice, baby."

We both order pancakes with bacon and then she selects a number of songs. We listen to the singles spinning round and round somewhere we can't see, while we wait for our food. Once we've eaten, she uses the restroom and I snag a candy necklace for her, pay the bill, and stuff the little sugar beads in my pocket before she comes back.

We spend an hour or so walking around Niagara Falls and really talking. Telling each other the things we have done in our lives—what we feel we've accomplished, what we haven't, and what we want out of life. As strange as it is, I think we both want the same things. It's too early to talk about a future, but I see mine with her in it.

Back at the small private cottage I rented on the lake, she pushes me flat on my back on the bed as soon as we walk in. I give her a knowing look as she peels off her top and then removes her bra. The tears are long since gone and an entirely different emotion has taken over. I raise my head to suck on one of her nipples, but she pushes me back down. I try not to laugh and decide just to roll with it. She runs her hands down my arms and I try to grab her fingers, but instead she lifts my shirt up slightly. Again I let her. She traces the letters inked along my side. Another moment passes and she drops her lips to my skin to kiss each and every letter of my tattoo. A raw ache from her touch emanates from every nerve in my body. When she sits up, her hair rests on her shoulders and she takes it and swirls it around as if knotting it.

Even in the dim light I soak up the curves of her body, the angles of her face, the way they light up the room. I move to sit up, so she straddles my lap and I pull her close to me. She tugs hard on my hair and I kiss her even harder. Her breasts rub against my bare chest and I clutch her ass and press her more firmly into my lap. By the time I break away, after she rocks forward on my erection, I'm nearly panting. With boldness she never exhibited in our moments of intimacy before, she unbuttons my shirt and takes it off, then pulls my undershirt over my head but leaves it tangled around my wrists.

"Are you okay with this?" she asks, her voice shy but smooth.

I grin at her and then close my eyes. I'm so turned on by this side of her, but I don't want to ask whether she's done anything like this before, because I might not like the answer.

My cock is so hard against the fabric of my jeans that I decide the "have you ever" question will definitely have to wait. I tug the shirt the rest of the way off and capture her hips. "Yes, I am," I tell her as I roll us over so she lies beneath me. I'm just not okay with giving up control. I reach into my pocket and pull out the elastic candy necklace. "I got you something," I murmur to her. But instead of putting it over her head where it would sit snugly around her beautiful neck, I pull her wrists to me. She stares at me with a glimmer in her eye and I know she's fine with this. After all, she started it and it's a tame, harmless first attempt at something I've never thought about doing until now.

She draws a line with her tongue from my mouth to my ear. "Go ahead," she whispers in a sexy, ragged voice. "But I can't use my hands if you do," she adds.

I smile at her as I wrap the elastic in a figure eight around her wrists and then stand up, kicking off my boots, and taking my pants off in record time. Hovering over her, I remove her remaining clothes—everything except her lacey black thong. Then I slowly pull her arms over her head and pin them there. With my other hand I slide my fingertips down her bare stomach to the edge of her panties. Creeping along their edge, I feel her wetness and quickly slide my hand inside them to cup her pussy.

She gasps. "I want you inside me."

I answer against her skin as I lap my tongue over the peaks of her hard nipples. "I want that too." My lips move farther down the swells of her breast. "Keep your hands pressed together," I groan as my lips move toward her taut stomach and I let go of them.

"Xander, I want you inside me," she moans.

"I know, Ivy. Soon. But first I want to devour you until you can't stand another minute."

My tongue dances around the lace of her panties and I peek up at her. She's staring at me with her hands where they're supposed to be. Her sexy, hooded eyes make me throb even more. "I'm so hard right now," I whisper as my tongue continues down over the lace. Her hands start to move. "Keep your hands together over your head."

"Xander!" she screams out when my hands tug so hard on her underwear that the crotch rips apart.

I laugh against the wetness of her pussy as she pushes herself toward me. With my mouth, my lips, my tongue, I can't get enough—she tastes so good. "I've wanted your sweet pussy in my mouth, around me, on me . . . all day. I'm going to feast on you."

She giggles and I'm sure she must turn red. Talking dirty to her is something I know she likes. But as I slide my finger inside her and circle her walls, she stops laughing and I can feel her muscles tighten—she feels so good. I circle her clit over and over, licking her and stroking her at the same time. I want to devour her, every inch of her . . . lick her all up and then do it again and again. The way her body reacts to my touch, the need between us—it's raw and real and I never want it to end. But I settle on savoring her—slowly bringing her to the brink and pulling back to do it all over again.

When she starts to tremble, she digs her heels into the bed and I know she's climaxing—that puts a huge grin on my face. I run my tongue up her body all the way to her lips, and she attacks my mouth greedily. She twists the necklace off her wrists and tangles her fingers in my hair. "I want to suck on you," she says, letting her fingers slide down my back, pressing into my skin.

Rolling over onto my back, I bring her with me. I catch both her wrists and try to make my voice sound serious. "You let your hands free."

She bites down on her lip. "I want to suck you. Please," she says in that same sexy, raspy voice.

Her look melts my insides. "Fuck," I growl, lifting my ass off the bed, offering my hard cock to her. Her warm lips are on my neck, my chest, my stomach. Her hand wraps around my base and her lips lick around my tip. Fuck. I might lose it before she even starts—I have got to get the horny teenage boy under control. Her tongue licks down my shaft before her mouth wraps around me. That feels so unbelievable. I throw my head back and brace my hand on her head. A low groan steals past my mouth and I can feel her lips move in an upward curl.

The next minute she's taking all of me and I close my eyes and just let this feeling that I wish could last forever take over. I try as hard as I can to hang on, but I have to let go and feel what comes next—that feeling that puts me on top of the world, the one that is unlike anything else I've ever felt. I start to shudder and release at the very same time my phone on the nightstand starts to ring. I ignore it and continue to ride out the feeling as she swallows everything I have to give. I never let my phone go to voice mail, but today I do. The message light flashes, but my attention is for her right now. "Fuck," I mutter, pulling her up to me. I kiss her hard, feeling out of breath and completely satisfied.

The smell of sausage and bacon wafts through the small one-room bungalow. I sit up, immediately blinded by the assault of light from the large picture window with a view of the lake. Rubbing my eyes, I sniff again and the sound of percolating coffee catches my attention. I glance around and see her, not very far away, but still not close enough.

"Good morning," she says.

"Come here," I say with a grin.

She walks toward me with a coffee mug in her hand and I accept the cup, but immediately set it on the table beside the bed and pull her down to me.

"Why are you dressed?"

"Did you want me to go the store naked?"

"No, but I'd like you next to me when I wake up."

"I am now." She starts to kiss me.

"But you're not naked."

She stands up and takes her layers off before sliding in bed next to me. "I am now," she repeats.

My hands slide down her body. "Morning," I whisper in her ear, pushing my erection against her stomach.

"Good morning again." She giggles as her hands follow a similar path to mine.

An hour later I sip the cold coffee and tie the laces of my boots. "What do you want to do today?"

"Are we staying here?" she asks with a hopeful tone to her voice.

I cross the room as she's stirring batter in a bowl. "Yes, it's the Fourth of July, so I thought we would. We don't have to be back to the bus until tomorrow. Is that okay with you?"

"I'd love to stay here. It's beautiful."

I pull her hips to mine. "No, you're beautiful."

She blushes, but the crackling of oil has her easing out of my grip way too soon.

On the counter sit a box of pancake mix and a bowl of blueberries. I know I must be wearing the biggest shit-eating grin when I see them. She's busy taking the bacon from the pan when I open the drawer and grab a black rubber spatula. I hide it in my back pocket and once she's finished, I scoop her up and set her on the table.

"You know what you haven't had in a while?" I ask her.

"No," she says, with more giggles.

I pull the spatula from my pocket and move it back and forth under her ass. "*The Aunt Jemima Treatment.*"

She laughs some more, and her blue eyes match the color of the water in the lake. "No, no, stop it!"

Channeling my best Bill Murray from *Stripes*, I ask, "Who's your friend?"

"You."

"Who do you love?" I question.

She places her hands on my cheeks and in a moment that takes my breath away she says, "You, you, always."

We eat breakfast on a blanket out on the grass and then take a walk around the lake. The water looks like a mirror—clear and calm—and we decide to take out the small rowboat that's tied up to the dock. We stop in the middle of the lake and lie back, absorbing the sun and each other. With my arms stretched behind my head, I can hear fish breaking the surface of the water, and it takes me back to when my grandfather and my father would occasionally take River and me fishing. Those days were good ones—dropping a pole in the water, sitting back, waiting for the fish to bite.

"What are you thinking about?" she asks, raising her head off my chest.

I wrap my arms around her and look straight at her. "River. He was so impatient when we would all go fishing. He'd put his pole in the water for about five seconds and then get upset that he hadn't caught anything."

"I've envied what you have with him and Bell."

My hand finds hers and I give it a squeeze. "Did you stay close with any of your sisters?"

"No, not really. Not the way you are with your brother and sister."

I kiss her head. I have no words to respond. I am lucky in that way—in the way that I have a family that will do anything for one another. It's always been that way. Even when my dad was a drunken mess, even when I caught him in bed with his guitar student and he claimed their relationship had not escalated to sex, we stood together— my brother and I and my sister.

"Ivy, I have some things to explain to you about my family. Things I probably should have told you years ago."

She sits up and I pull her back to me. I want her close as I tell her about my father's suicide. I tell her everything, everything except the fact that I'm to blame and what his last words to me were—that he muttered the name of her ex-fiancé before he died. And it's strange, but in a moment of clarity I suddenly get why River didn't want to tell Dahlia what he knew about her ex-fiancé—that Ben Covington had cheated on her with our sister, Bell. I get it. *Damn it, River. I get it.*

She lifts her chin, offering her mouth to take and do with as I want. I kiss her for a long time and then we lie quietly as the boat rocks us back and forth and I'm lulled to sleep.

The next thing I know I can feel her soft touch creeping up my chest. I snatch her hand and roll her over, but the rocking of the boat has me second-guessing my agility. I'm not sure I can actually fuck her in here and not tip it over.

"We should get back and figure out what to eat for dinner," she says.

I look down at her, now pinned beneath me. She is so incredibly gorgeous, especially right now—her blond hair shines in the sunlight, her eyes reflect the color of the water, and the warmth from her body makes me wish we could stay like this forever.

"I know what I want for dinner," I growl in her ear.

"Blueberry pancakes?" she asks.

"No," I say, pushing my hard-on against her pussy.

"Bacon?"

"No, try again."

"Me." She giggles as I dip my tongue in her belly button—having decided I may not be able to fuck her in this boat, but I can certainly put my face between her legs.

When her cries of passion subside, I manage to row us back to shore. We take a shower and she very nicely relieves me of the tent I've had in my pants for the past hour. Then we finally get dressed and head to a small local pizzeria for dinner. Being together like this and having fun—it's the way it used to be, and the way I hope it will stay.

Later, fireworks blaze above the lake as we watch bursts of color paint the sky through the open windows. The air is warm and we lie together in bed, entangled in each other's arms, discussing our remaining stops and the things we want to explore in each city. When my phone rings, I pick it up and glance at the caller ID. It's my sister.

"It's Bell. Let me just see what she wants," I tell Ivy.

She nods, her fingers skimming the letters down my side.

"Hey, Bell. This isn't the best time to chat. Can I call you back?"

"Xander." I tense at my sister's tone. It sounds like she's crying, but then she falls oddly silent.

"Bell, what's wrong?"

"It's bad, Xander. It's really bad."

"Bell, just fucking tell me."

"It's Dahlia. She's on her way to the hospital. I was over there watching movies with her one minute and then the next minute there was blood everywhere. So much blood."

I sit up, as alarm and concern course through my body.

"What are you talking about? What happened?" A sick knot forms in my gut.

"I don't know. I was talking to her and the next thing I know I see blood seeping through the bedsheets. I called nine-one-one, and the ambulance just left. Xander, it's too soon for the baby."

I feel myself tremble. "Where's River?"

"I called him. He's on his way to the hospital. Xander, you have to come home. We need you."

Ivy lifts her eyes and I take her hand, holding on tight, wanting to never let go.

"I'll be there as soon as I can. Call me when you get to the hospital." I stare silently at Ivy after I end the call. "I have to go home," I tell her, wrapping my arms around her and pulling her to me.

We leave Niagara Falls in a blur. The one-hour car ride is an emotional one. I don't want to have to leave her, but I can't pull her off the tour. For some reason I bring up my father's suicide again. We discuss it in more detail than I've ever told anyone—breaking down, I tell her I think I pushed him too far and that I'm the one who broke him. She's quiet for the longest time and then she leans over and says, "Xander, people make their own choices—don't blame yourself for your father's."

I squeeze her hand, remembering all those sessions in therapists' offices when they would say the same thing. The difference when she says it is that I actually want to believe it. She runs her fingers through my hair and around my ear. "I wish you would have told me then, but thank you for telling me now. I understand so much more now."

We fall quiet as we both immerse ourselves deep in our own thoughts. I blink when I feel her smoothing her fingers through my hair. "I need you. You know that, right?"

My throat tightens as I shift my eyes to hers. "I'll be back as soon as I can. I'd bring you with me if I could."

"I know," she whispers quietly, fidgeting in her seat in the dark.

I stop at a light and turn toward her. I tip her chin to look at me and run my thumb over her lip. "Hey, we are going to be together. We might not know how or where, we might not know what comes after the tour, but we're going to figure it out and we'll figure it out together."

Tears spill from her eyes and I gather her close to me. By the time I pull up next to the bus, I'm a fucking wreck. Thoughts of her and of my father are mixed with worry for my sister-in-law and my brother.

When we finally arrive it's really late and everyone is asleep. As soon as I set foot on the bus my phone rings. "Bell, what's going on?" I answer.

"Oh, Xander, Dahlia had a miscarriage. She lost the baby. She was hemorrhaging and the doctors had to perform an emergency C-section."

I can't breathe. I have a hard time saying anything as I sit down and bow my head.

"How is she?"

"I don't know," Bell says between sobs.

"I'll be there soon," I manage to say and then I hang up.

Ivy's hand finds my shoulder and I place mine over hers and a few moments later she leads me to the galley. She helps me throw a few things in a bag and within fifteen minutes I'm ready to set off for the airport to catch the red-eye. Tossing my bag in the trunk, I slam it shut and turn to her and pull her to me, holding her tightly. Anxiety and nervousness pulse through me at the thought of leaving her. It's an incredibly familiar, yet somehow still foreign, feeling.

I place my fingertip over her lips and outline them, then cup the sides of her face and lean in to kiss her. "Bye, gorgeous. I'll see you in a couple of days."

She nods reluctantly. Her expression softens as she runs her hand down my cheek. "Call me when you land, even if it's early. Okay?" Exhaling deeply, she adds, "And, Xander, I'm here for you if you just need to talk. Remember that. I love you."

Her words catch me off guard—I'm not used to people baring their feelings to me and I'm not used to baring them back.

With a heavy sigh, I tighten my grip on her. Kissing her hair, I whisper, "I love you too" into her ear. Then I notice she's wearing the candy necklace. I bend down and gently bite a piece off. Chewing it, I say softly, "I'll call you," and without looking back, for fear of not being able to leave, I quickly get into the car.

CHAPTER 12
Disappear

Dark clouds surround me, and the first flash of bright lightning zigzags across the sky. Thunder follows with a loud crash. The rain pelts down, smashing against the plane's windows, and another burst of lightning flashes, immediately followed by a low rumble. After hours of circling, we finally land and I just want to get the hell off this plane.

Once I hail a cab, I go straight to the hospital. I text Bell and she tells me where they all are. The ping of the elevator alerts me that I've arrived. I exit and see Mom standing in the open doorway to a small room. I rush to her and she holds me tightly. The waiting room is bathed in darkness, with only a single lamp in the corner to light the space. Bell enters the room from the other side and runs to join us.

"What happened?" I ask my mother.

She explains the medical terminology of Dahlia's condition and the reason for the emergency C-section. She tells me the baby was just too little to survive the premature birth. When she finishes, I ask, "Where's River?"

She shows me to Dahlia's room. My hand stills on the doorknob. I suck in a breath and open the door, looking in before entering. It's dark and the hissing of the blood pressure machine is the only sound when I walk into the room. River is nestled in the chair next to Dahlia's bed, and she's sleeping. He shifts his gaze to the door and as soon as he sees me, he stands up.

I study his face—it's worn, tired, but most of all heartbroken.

"I'm—I'm sorry about the baby," I stammer.

He chokes down a sob. "The baby was a boy," he tells me in a trembling voice.

I can see the nakedness of his grief. I put a hand on his shoulder and then pull him to me. We stand together in silence for the longest time. "Has Dahlia woken up?"

He stares at me intently before scrubbing his eyes with the palms of his hands. "Just once. She was hysterical, so the doctor gave her a sedative. She should sleep for a while, he said. They had to cut her open to deliver the baby."

"I'm so sorry." I can't find any other words to soothe his pain because right now his pain is my pain.

I clear my throat. "Why don't you go take a shower and get something to eat? I'll sit with her."

He shakes his head no and pushes back in the chair. I grab a chair from the other side of the room and just sit next to him for hours. By the time I leave the hospital the rain has stopped and the day has faded into night. I take Bell's car—she got a ride from my mother and Jack. As I drive to Beverly Hills, I look up into the sky at the stars and wonder why things happen in life the way they do.

At my house, it's dark and I'm alone. I make my way to the bedroom and throw myself on the bed. Pulling out my phone, I hit Ivy's name. I texted her when I landed, but she hasn't responded. I figured they were preparing for the show, but it should be over by now. There's no answer, though. I lie in bed listening to her voice mail message and start to get nervous. "Where the hell is she?" I leave her a message and fall prey to exhaustion while waiting for her to return my call.

When I wake up, I check my phone—four a.m. here, seven there, and still no call. My nervousness quickly turns to annoyance as I dial the number again. *When did I turn into a chick?* I ask myself and lie back down.

I wake up again to my cell phone ringing. Blurry-eyed and groggy, I can just make out that the screen is flashing RIVER. I answer it.

"Yeah."

"Hey, sorry to wake you up so early, but Dahlia woke up and wants to go home this morning. The doctors cleared her. Do you think you could run by the house and pick up her car? Mine will be too uncomfortable for her. Her keys should be on the hook near the garage door. And Mom ran over to the house this morning and packed a bag for her. She left it in my bedroom, if you could pick that up too."

Wiping the sleep from my eyes, I throw myself back on the bed. "Sure, bro, I can do that. I'll be there as soon as I can."

I hang up and jump out of bed, shower, snatch my phone, and hop in my car. Bell's car is parked next to mine and I have to get it back to her. With the sun blinding me, I search for my sunglasses and then squint at my fucking phone. Still no call from Ivy. I swing the car around the corner and turn onto Sunset Boulevard. Glancing down at my phone to call her, I look up and come to a screeching stop. Fucking LA traffic.

At River's house, I park in front of the garage and wonder whose car is blocking the steps to the front door. I check my phone one last time and then squeeze between the concrete wall and the car. The door is ajar—cleaning lady maybe?

"Hello?" I bellow, pushing the door open with my foot.

A roar from the TV catches me off guard and my gaze shoots to the figure moving in the kitchen. A head full of long dark hair rises above the counter. Her slender figure is wrapped in an apron over a navy tank top. "Xander." She smiles at me.

"Amy? What are you doing here?" She tries to kiss me, but I turn my cheek as she gives me a hug.

"I ran into your mother at the supermarket this morning and I told her to let me take care of the food so she could concentrate on your brother and Dahlia. She let me in and said she'd be back in a bit. I'm so sorry to hear about the baby."

She glances at the door. "I left the door open because I burned the brownies."

I stifle a laugh. "Well, it's nice of you to do this. I'm sure they'll appreciate it."

"We've all been friends for years. It's the least I can do. It's no big deal."

I nod my head and take a step back, throwing my keys and phone on the counter. My gaze drifts to the TV, where the news is flashing a picture of two men being escorted in handcuffs to waiting police cars. The screen alert reads: OPERATION SHADOWDANCERS COMES TO AN END. It draws my attention because I think Caleb mentioned something about Ben Covington being involved with that case.

I focus on the woman reporting the news: "Two more members of the Mexican drug cartel have been arrested. Along with the bust— more than one hundred pounds of methamphetamine, ten pounds of cocaine, and half a pound of heroin were seized in the raid—vice squad detective Jason Holt said he estimates to have removed nearly five million dollars of trash from the streets. The almost five-year-long investigation culminated late last night when a long undercover operation targeting the remaining members of the Cortez family was executed. The Department of Justice said that they believe the trafficking organization run under this family is now completely shut down. In related news, Josh Hart, believed to be linked to the cartel, who was found guilty of aggravated assault and battery back in March, was sentenced to three years in prison today."

She scans the stations and stops on *Entertainment Today*. "Oh, look, there's your picture with Ivy."

My head snaps back to the TV. It's a picture of Ivy and me in Niagara Falls together.

"I didn't know the band played there," Amy comments.

I shrug, not clarifying that we didn't play there. Then I focus on the banners scrolling across the screen. One reads: "Today marks the thirtieth anniversary of Dylan Wolf's death. He was the prodigal son of Sheep Industries' founder, Josh Wolf. His fraternal twin, Damon Wolf, now sits at the helm. Dylan's life ended tragically when . . ."

"I didn't know Damon had a twin brother." I toss the comment off to Amy, ignoring the rest of the newscast.

"Yes, I think I heard he had a drug problem and overdosed." She claps her hands together. "Okay, I'm all done in the kitchen."

"What are you doing in town anyway?" I ask.

"The band has a few days off before heading to Bristow. Are you staying in town? Maybe we could go to dinner? You do owe me."

I shake my head. "Actually, as soon as I make sure River and Dahlia are settled I have to get back. I'm leaving tonight, or first thing in the morning."

I step around the counter and Amy crosses to the sink to rinse the bowls before loading them into the dishwasher. "We'll catch up in Bristow, then," she says with a smile.

I know I should tell her about Ivy, but I need to get out of here. "Listen, River's waiting for me. I'm just going to grab some things." I direct the statement her way, already walking down the hallway toward the bedroom. When I come back out she's sitting at the breakfast bar drinking a cup of coffee.

"Pour a cup to go if you want. I just made it," she says, motioning to the pot.

I do, then snatch my stuff off the counter, say goodbye, and jet.

My nerves are buzzing by the time I walk in my house well after ten. I'd picked River and Dahlia up at the hospital, helped him get her settled, sat and just talked to him while Dahlia slept, talked with my mother, with Bell, and with Jack when he came over after work with dinner in hand. At least Amy was gone by the time we got back from the hospital, so I didn't have to deal with that guilt. The pain I feel for River and Dahlia, plus my mother's crying, and Bell's strange behavior, on top of not having talked to Ivy yet, are putting my temper into overdrive.

I flop down in a chair in my living room and run my hands through my hair. Then I decide to call Garrett. Fucking voice mail again. I'm the band manager—they should be answering when I call. I hang up and slam my phone down, then throw my head back, just closing my eyes.

I hear a faint ringing noise. Glancing at my watch, I notice I've been asleep for thirty minutes. It's my phone. I quickly answer it.

"Yeah."

"Hey, man, sorry I missed your call."

I sit up and focus. "Anything going on I should know about? I've been trying to get hold of Ivy since I got home and she hasn't picked up."

He clears his throat. "I'm not really sure what's going on. I would have called you, but I can't find her."

Standing up, I start to pace the room. "What the fuck do you mean you can't find her? Did she do the show?"

"Yeah. I don't know how to say this, man, but Damon showed up just before the show and they disappeared into her room. She came out, did the show, and vanished. None of us have seen her since."

"Did you talk to Leif?" I can hear the irritation in my voice.

"Yes. He doesn't know either."

The blood pounds through my veins. "Why the fuck wouldn't you have called me the minute that asshole showed up?"

"Xander, you weren't here and there was nothing you could do."

"Just fucking keep looking for her and call me the minute you know anything. I'll be there as soon as I can," I tell him and hang up.

I leave all my shit and just grab my keys. I peel my Porsche onto the street. The engine roars and the tires squeal. Slamming on my brakes only when I need to, I run every red light. I circle through the airport garage but find no empty spots, so I park in a handicap space. Fuck it—let them tow it. Right now I'm pissed as hell, and the last thing I care about is my fucking car. I hustle to get into the terminal and somehow manage to get on the red-eye to New York City.

"Sir, can I get you something to drink?" the flight attendant asks when I take my seat.

"Yeah, a Jack and Coke. No, make that two Jack and Cokes."

CHAPTER 13
Through the Glass

Bars surround me. I'm wearing an orange jumpsuit. "I did it, Dad. I'm sorry. It's my fault."

His face fades in and out, but I can see he's frowning. "You'll have to pay the price for your sins, son. Your apology can't help you."

Fuck. I wake up in a cold sweat just as the wheels touch down at JFK. The effects of the alcohol have long since worn off; I push that dream far from my mind as I exit the plane and scramble to rent a car. It's seven a.m. and once I'm flying down the highway, I call Garrett. The band is playing in Hartford and I'm humping ass to get there.

"Hello," he answers groggily, obviously asleep.

"I'm just leaving New York City. I'll be there in two hours. Did you find her yet?"

"No, man. I'm sorry. No sign at all. She didn't come back to the bus. We waited as long as we could. Leif said she told him after the show she'd meet us in Hartford. We still waited as long as we could before pulling out of New York."

"Did she say anything else to Leif?"

"No. He asked her what was going on, but she said she didn't want to talk about it."

"Okay. Call me if you hear anything else."

"You know I will."

"Thanks."

Fuck, fuck, fuck. I hit the accelerator and pound my palms against the steering wheel. *What the hell is going on?*

Just shy of two hours later, I pull into the XL Center in Hartford, Connecticut. There are two tour buses there—one of them ours. I slam the car into PARK right next to it and pound on the door. John opens it. "Hey, buddy, where you been?"

I give him a cursory nod, but say nothing and head toward her room, crossing through the front lounge first. No one is around. I quickly stride to the galley, and find that it too is empty. When I hit the back lounge, all the guys are huddled around the table. Rubbing my hand over my stubbled jaw, I assess the room before walking through the door. She's not in here, but three mouths drop open when the guys turn to look at me. My eyes catch Garrett's first and I stare him down. He looks nervous as he stands up and heads my way. Stopping in front of me, he places his hand on my shoulder. "Hey, can we talk outside?"

I jerk away, feeling agitated and unnerved. "No, we can talk now. Where the fuck is she?"

"She's here," he mumbles.

I dart to her bedroom and fling the door open, but it's empty. I spin around toward Leif, who's behind me. "Where the hell is she?"

"I think you should sit down and let us explain."

"Where is she?" I ask again, getting closer, my eyes flashing with fury.

He swallows a few times. "In the other bus, but we need to explain."

I don't need to hear any explanation. I take off like a bat out of hell to the other bus I saw when I pulled in. My heart pounds and my stomach is in knots as I approach. Pulling the doors open, I take the two steps in one and find myself face-to-face with a burly dude at least twice my girth. He levels a serious stare at me and I return the same to him.

He comes right up to my face and grabs my shirt with his fist, almost picking me up off the floor. "Any reason you felt you couldn't knock?" he mutters, his lips flapping over his set of double chins.

I laugh. As if anything he thinks he can do is going to intimidate me or stop me.

"It's okay, Johnny." A voice colder than ice comes from behind the ninja assassin.

Johnny steps aside and then directly in front of me I see the asshole himself—Damon Wolf. I lurch forward to drop him on the spot, but his bodyguard stops me. He's got my arms twisted behind my back, so I use my feet and kick his shins—hard.

He doesn't make a sound or move a muscle, except to pull tighter on my arms. It feels like he might pull them out of the sockets if he pulls any harder.

Turning my head, I try to spit in his face, but he picks me up and quickly slams my head into an overhead compartment. I can feel a faint trickle of liquid oozing down my face as he sets me down.

With my head throbbing, I stare at the man in front of me. "Where is she!"

"She's safe with me. You don't need to worry about her." Hearing this, I want to punch the smug look right the fuck off his face.

"Ivy," I yell and again flatten my work boot against the guy's shin. This time he clocks my face on the small counter and I think my nose just might be broken. "Fuckkkk," I yell and when I look up I see her.

"Stop it!" she screams.

I wipe the blood from my face and stare at her. She's wearing a tight white dress that hugs her curves perfectly. The neck is high and so is the hemline. Her hair is pulled back and her sapphire earrings sparkle in the morning light shining through the windows. I let out a huge sigh of relief that she's all right. Searching her body for signs of abuse, I see none—none that appear physical anyway. But she looks at me with a deep sadness I've never seen in her eyes before and my heart slams out of my rib cage. Adrenaline spikes through me and I manage to somehow free myself. I shove Damon out of my way and move toward her.

"Come with me," I tell her, wiping my palms on my jeans before trying to take her hand.

"I can't," she whispers and pulls her hands behind her back.

My knees buckle at her words, and the ninja is on me again.

"Leave him alone," she orders in a much sterner voice. She then looks at Damon. "You said you'd leave him alone."

"And I will, my angel, when he leaves us alone."

Us. I feel like I might puke right here. I look at Ivy and then I can see it—her eyes are red and swollen, her face looks lifeless, but she regards me with what I think is pity.

"That's not going to happen." I direct the statement to Damon and shift slightly before finding her eyes again. "Ivy, what's going on?"

She doesn't answer me, but repeats herself, this time screaming at Damon. "You said you'd leave him alone."

My eyes are narrowed on her and I'm moving closer now that there is room. "I don't need you or anyone else to fight my battles." The closer I get to her, the faster my heart beats. Without any hesitation, I run my hand down her cheek. But before I can talk to her, the wind is knocked out of me by a swift punch in my side, and then my arms are restrained again. Sucking in a painful breath, I narrow my eyes at Damon. I would kill him in a minute if I knew I could get away with it.

"How about you and me outside—now," I hiss.

"Xander, Xander, Xander. So much like your father."

My eyes slam to Ivy, who noticeably flinches, and back to him.

Everything about him is revolting. His words infuriate me, set my blood on fire, and I turn, trying to move toward him, consumed by a rage I haven't felt since the day I saw my sister's fingers bleeding. But again I'm blocked by his bodyguard. "Now, listen, Xander. You don't want to end up like your father, do you?"

My father's last words haunt me—*Damon Wolf.* I spit in his face and this time I hit my mark. "What do you know about my father?" I spit out.

Removing a handkerchief from his pocket and wiping his cheek, he says, "I'll give you that one, but now you need to walk away and know she'll be happy with me."

Ivy's cries turn into sobs.

"Ivy, angel, stop crying and come here."

She doesn't move.

"Ivy! Come over here so we don't have to shout," he commands, his eyes speaking to her in a language I don't understand. She walks with trepidation toward him. She's shaking and I know she's scared. He takes her hand and I cringe, again trying to free myself.

"We have an announcement and you're going to be the first to hear it. In fact, you can be the first to congratulate us. We got married today."

Her face pleads with me for something—understanding, maybe— and the sudden pain that strikes my body is unbearable. I try to struggle free, but the adrenaline surge I had is gone.

She looks at me a moment longer before his barking voice commands, "Angel, tell him how much you missed me. Tell him how you begged me to forgive you, to take you back because you loved me. How much you regretted leaving me. Tell him how it took him to make you see I was right for you."

"Damon, please stop," she says to him, with tears streaming down her face.

My gut twists with disgust. "Ivy?"

Her body trembles.

Still unable to believe it, I finally ask, "Is it true? Did you marry him?"

She nods her head.

"Why?" I don't even recognize my own voice at this point.

"Let it be, Xander," she pleads.

I look around at the posh surroundings. "Does this have to do with money?" I ask her.

Her face turns to anger.

"You need money. Is that why you joined the band so eagerly? Is that what this was all about?"

"Yes," she cries out, but for some reason I feel like she's saying no.

Damon laughs. "Keep trying to figure it out and you'll keep coming back to square one. Love speaks for itself. She just couldn't stand to be without me. She loves me. Has for years. Her mother told me about you two when the picture surfaced and I've forgiven her for her slight misjudgment."

I flinch. I'm the misjudgment? That makes me want to laugh.

"I'm sorry," she mouths silently, and when our eyes connect for that one moment, I know she's trying to tell me something. I know she is, but I can't get any sound to come from my throat to ask what.

He grabs her hand and shoves the ring in my face. "I think your visit has lasted long enough. Ivy will be performing tonight and she should rest. We'll discuss the rest of the tour tomorrow. Oh, and Xander, Johnny will be with her at all times." He nods to Johnny, who drags me down the aisle of the bus.

"Ivy, talk to me," I yell. "How could you do this to us?"

"Xander, this is how it has to be," she says in a soft voice, covering her face with her hands.

Damon steps closer and she steps back. It's clear that what he says is love is not. Why did she marry him? I don't have a chance to find out anything more, because the muscle throws me out of the bus and I land on my ass. In a haze I stand up. *Ivy married Damon Wolf?* I puke right there as thoughts of his hands on her send me to the pits of hell and devastation careens through my body. Looking around, I see Leif, Garrett, and Nix staring in disbelief and I stare back with the same feeling.

"Fuck, man, let's get you cleaned up," Nix says, throwing my arm over his shoulder. I walk with him, pissed and confused about what just happened, but knowing it is far from over . . . knowing something isn't right . . . knowing sure as shit that Damon must have something over her. Because there is no other explanation I want to think about.

CHAPTER 14
Underneath It All

Morning had stretched into afternoon and before I know it, it's evening. I spent the morning trying to convince myself not to turn my back on her like I did before. She loves me—or I thought she did. Fuck, for twelve years I've been flirting around, never finding anyone else who could light up my soul like her. I never paid much attention to it, either. Then once she was back in my arms, it was all there—she was the one I'd always needed. She brings out parts of me I never thought I had. I had spent the afternoon talking myself down off the ledge—I wanted to kill him, with my bare hands, strangle every last breath out of him. But then who would win? I have to keep my cool.

We're huddled together for our drink and a prayer. But no one is praying tonight. I regard them all steadily as I sit in a chair and lean over. My head throbs, my nose hurts—the painkillers Leif gave me are wearing off. I'm starting to feel more than a little bit agitated and annoyed. The show begins in minutes and she's not here yet. What the hell is going on? Did I imagine what we had? Why would she marry him? The questions are on constant repeat in my mind and I feel like I'm going to puke again.

The feeling gets even worse when I hear Damon's voice taunt me. "Don't tell me you're feeling sorry for yourself."

"Fuck you," I say, not bothering to raise my head.

They walk in together, with the ninja right beside her, but I already felt her nearness. My body has come alive and her presence gives me the strength I need. I flick my eyes toward her. She looks just as sad as earlier. I need to talk to her—alone. But it's too late—the music sounds and the band is announced, so she makes her way onstage with the guys. Thank fuck Damon disappears, but he forgot the ninja and the guy stays front and center at the curtain.

Since backstage is as empty as I feel, I watch for a bit and then suddenly feel like I can't breathe. I'll be back before the show ends. The outside air is hot, muggy, almost suffocating, and I try to block out everything as I make my way back to my small cubby on the bus. The walk feels like miles and when I look up toward the sky I see thousands of stars there to light my way, but the darkness is everywhere. The bus doors are open and John is asleep in his seat. I finally make it to my bed and throw myself down, then call my brother. I want to check on Dahlia, but when he asks me what's wrong, I tell him. He tries to persuade me to keep my cool and not do anything stupid, but at the same time I'm sure he knows he's talking to the wind. I want to kill that son of a bitch, I want to scream at Ivy and ask, "What the fuck are you thinking?" I want answers. And I'm going to get them.

An hour or so later I'm back in the empty area backstage and she's announcing her last song. "How about 'Sorry' by Buckcherry?" she asks the crowd. They go crazy, like they always do whenever she sings a cover.

Vamping chords, then a wailing bass introduce the song. "I'm sorry I'm bad," she croons into the mic with her eyes closed. Her voice goes even lower and she sounds raspy, beautiful, inspiring, as she continues with "I'm sorry about all the things he said to you."

And there it is—*he*. She said *he*, not *I*, like the song is written. What the fuck is going on? She turns slowly, fixing her gaze on me. She swings the mic gently and she sings the song to me.

With each verse, her voice grows stronger and louder and the ache in it more pronounced. Her passion and the love heard within the lyrics of the song infect everyone in the audience, but no one more than me. I want to wrap my arms around her and feel her body against mine, tell her we can fix whatever it is he did. Because I know it's something he did. This time I will take care of her—I will not set her free. She needs to know this. I have to tell her. And now I know I'll do whatever I have to to get her back—I'm not going to let her go this time.

When the song ends, the crowd explodes. Whistles, cheers, and yells fill the air as she walks offstage toward me. Before she reaches me, Ninja steps between us. Her demeanor changes as she approaches. "Johnny, Damon said not to let him within five feet of me. But he didn't say we couldn't talk. I need to discuss our upcoming shows. I'm sure Damon would never jeopardize the performance."

I'm actually impressed at the way she turns the charm on and works him. Shit, did she do that to me? No. Now I'm only second-guessing myself. My mind is so fucked right now.

Ninja nods at her. Is he hot for her? I'm going to kill him right after I kill Damon Wolf. He steps back and I stay where I am. I consider grabbing her and making a run for it, but what good would that do. She's married to the bastard.

In a low whisper she says, "Leave this alone, Xander. Leave us alone. I wanted to marry him. He makes me happy."

Fury courses through me. My pulse races and my blood pounds.

"Why are you doing this?" I practically spit out the words, angry, repulsed.

"I'm not doing anything. Just move on. You've done it before. You can do it again."

"Bravo. Bravo," the bastard's voice calls from behind me.

I turn around. I want to rip him into a thousand pieces and let him spend his days putting himself back together.

"Since we're all here now, you'll save me the time of having to call you tomorrow. Look, Ivy doesn't need you to manage her—that's my job," he says, and his words rock my body with a jealousy I've never felt before.

Once I can focus again, I look straight at him and say, "I manage the band and she's in the band, dickface."

Ivy moves to stand next to him and he tries to grab her hand. If that happens, I know I'll lose all control. Thank fuck she pulls her hand away. But she's still standing beside him.

"Listen. Let's make this simple. I see it like this. Your whole band is Ivy. Keep your name for now, since there's less than six weeks left on the tour. But you need to disappear. I'll give you until after Bristow to arrange it. We don't need you around causing trouble and chaos. This is our honeymoon after all," he says, this time wrapping his arm around her waist.

I rip my gaze from him in time to see the tears escaping her eyes, but I can't feel anything right now but hatred. I fight the urge to tell them both to fuck off. I glare at her as she frees her body of any contact with him. I don't want to leave, but I have to. I can't take it. I can't take his grimy hands on her. I can't even think about his hands on her. I inch a step toward him, ready to tear his wagging tongue right out of his mouth, but the ninja is up my ass within a nanosecond. Like I didn't see that coming. I shrug my shoulders and push past them both. I've had enough of this. Turning around, I walk toward the door. When I reach it, I punch it hard, wishing it were his face. The pain pulses through me and it feels like such a relief.

CHAPTER 15
Mirrors

Ivy

My ravaged eyes stare back at me in the bathroom mirror of the ridiculously glamorous tour bus. With a built-in coffeemaker, plush sofas, an enormously large shower, and even a vanity in the bathroom—it really is over the top. Damon insists we remain here and not in a hotel even though we're not traveling for a couple of days. I'm sure he's afraid I won't keep my end of the bargain if I spend too much time with the band, too much time with Xander. But what I don't think he really gets is that it's my overwhelming love for Xander that pushed me to make this decision—my primal instinct to protect him from getting hurt, not my need for money.

Holding the can of spray near my hair, I suddenly feel faint. The memory of his piercing dark eyes fades in and out and I know I should sit down and put my head between my knees. But I don't want to appear weak. I take a deep breath, spray my hair, and let the breath go. I wish I were stronger than I am—to stand up to Damon, but I can't.

Instead I close my eyes, hating myself. Hating myself for knowing him, for marrying him, for hurting the only man who understands me . . . who loves me for me.

Grinning, maybe gloating, Damon watches me put my red lipstick on. "Let's go," he says, snapping his fingers. "You're going to be late and I flew her all the way here just to interview you so we could put some hype behind these performances. Next week you'll meet with Mara and I'll make sure it's a double blast—Sound Music and Sound Entertainment together will really garner some attention."

I open my eyes and finish putting my makeup on, ignoring how his gaze rolls down my body. First down the front through my reflection in the mirror and then down my backside. He insisted I wear what he picked out—a push-up bra, a low-cut white cowl neck blouse that just skims the top of my breasts, tight skinny jeans, red high-heeled sandals, and a huge matching flower in my hair. He wants to take publicity photos later, but I can't help but feel like he's getting off on playing dress-up and it revolts me. It reminds me of how my mother insisted on dressing me whenever I went on auditions. I like to wear sexy outfits, but only because I want to, not because someone else wants me to.

"Please don't stare." My voice pulses with hatred.

"Angel, I've always enjoyed the way you look. That will never change. You're a beauty. But I'd like it if you'd watch the way you speak to me. I've treated you with respect and I'd like the same. In fact, I think I've been very understanding. I've let you have your own room and although I am your husband, I haven't insisted that I share your bed, not even on our wedding night. I'm hoping our business transaction helps us find our way back to each other, but if it doesn't in six months, you'll be free of me."

I'm saved from having to reply when his phone rings. "I'll take this in the lounge. You have five minutes. And, Angel, you look exquisite." He smiles before leaving, closing the bathroom door behind him.

I close my eyes again. He was never like this when we were together, was he? God, if he was, how did I never see it? And what must Xander think? He threw me yesterday. I thought I knew what to expect from him when he found out I'd married Damon. He's an all-or-nothing, black-or-white kind of guy. I thought he'd walk away hating me, but he didn't. Instead he searched me, for answers, for love, maybe even for hope. I didn't expect that and he just broke my heart all over again—this time in a different way. He asked questions I hadn't anticipated and the words stumbled out of my mouth, but not the right ones, not the ones that mattered—not the truth. That I couldn't tell him. He has to leave me alone and I have to be the one to push him away. I can be strong for him—this I know without a doubt. He did it for me twelve years ago—I can do it for him now.

The pitch of Damon's voice rising tears me out of my thoughts. "Angel. We have to go. Now!" he snaps. I put on my facade and walk out of the bathroom.

White linen tablecloths embroidered with gold threads dress the dining room of the downtown Marriott Hotel. Soft lighting sets the tone for intimate conversations and the distance between the tables lends itself to privacy. We're escorted to a secluded table in the corner and served coffee right away. Sipping his coffee, Damon is explaining to me how to answer the interview questions in order to fast-track my career. That's the bottom line; he needs money and for some reason he sees me as his golden ticket—although he didn't quite put it that blatantly. He finessed the words—but I think it's more. I wish Xander and I would have kept our reunion between ourselves, but we didn't, so I'm doing what I have to to protect him.

Damon keeps talking and I easily distract myself from the monotony of our conversation by staring at the magnificence of the high ceiling. Its beautiful tinwork catches my eye and the molding is truly a work of art.

"Ivy, are you listening?" he asks.

"Yes," I answer. "You want to get a single out right away to help launch me back on top of the charts."

He pushes his cup away. "I'm hoping to have one of the songs selected by the end of the week. That should make you happy."

I nod. I just let him go on thinking that I'm fine with our bargain—that trading Xander's career for money is my motivation. My mother called him even after I sent her what she asked for. I guess it wasn't enough, because she told him I was suffering from financial difficulty. From that conversation he got the perverse idea that I'm getting something out of our arrangement. As if the money ever mattered to me. I guess he really never knew me—all I wanted was to earn enough to help my sisters finish college.

A beautiful petite woman approaches us. She pulls her wavy blond hair back and fastens it with a clip she fishes out of her purse. Greeting us, she extends her hand and I scan her outfit. She's wearing a pale gray suit, all buttoned up with a hint of black lace peeking from above the lapel of her jacket. Her high-heeled pumps scream "I'm a corporate bitch." Right away I know she must be one of Damon's "Yes, sir, whatever you say, sir" lackeys and I try not to roll my eyes.

"Ivy, this is Aerie Daniels. She manages *Sound Music Magazine* for me."

"Aerie Daniels?" I question. "You're the niece of Ian Daniels, aren't you?"

"Yes." She smiles. "I'm also a music journalist."

"Oh, yes, of course. It's just I've been following the movie reports on the progress of the planning of the *No Led Zeppelin* film. And I can't wait for it to start filming and then for its release."

"Ivy, Ms. Daniels is here to interview you, not the other way around."

"Of course. I'm so sorry, Ms. Daniels."

"Ivy, it's fine," she replies.

Damon's phone rings. "Excuse me one moment, ladies." He scoots his chair back quickly, nearly knocking it into the waiter. "Yes," he answers, then pauses for a few seconds. "I'll call you right back." He hangs up. "Ladies, I have to return this call, but please carry on without me. Hopefully it won't take very long. Johnny is right over at the next table if you need him."

Damon bends to kiss my cheek and I feel the tip of his tongue on my skin. His mouth actually repulses me, but he doesn't notice as he quickly leaves the restaurant. I absentmindedly wipe my face with my napkin and catch Aerie staring. The look on her face tells me she knows what I'm doing. Women pick up on stuff like that. I should have been more careful. But I watch her face as she stares at the doorway where Damon breezed out moments ago. The crease in her brows and the pucker of her lips tell me I might be wrong about her. The look on her face seems to perfectly match mine. It's a look of distaste and disdain. Maybe she isn't the savagely ambitious "Yes, sir" journalist I thought she was.

In the next moment it's like a switch is flicked and she yanks her laptop from her oversized bag and turns it on. A grin dances across her face.

"What?" I ask.

"I'm just proud of myself. I wasn't wrong," she answers.

"What do you mean?"

She moves the bud vase and two votive candles from the center of the table and then turns her computer around so I can see what she's looking at. It's the picture of Xander and me in Niagara Falls and it's flashing across a gossip magazine Web site. The caption reads, "Ivy Taylor moves on to a new love." A huge smile that I can't contain crosses my face as I remember my body snug against his muscles, his face so close to my ear that I could feel his warm breath, and the way his arm curved around my shoulder protectively when the woman jumped out in front of us and snapped the picture.

Aerie turns the screen back around and says, "I told Jagger I knew there was more to this picture. But he laughed it off."

"Who's Jagger?"

"Oh, sorry. Jagger is Xander's cousin and my boyfriend. He's also the lead in the movie about my uncle." She has a sparkle in her eye that softens her demeanor when she says his name.

"You know Xander, then?" I ask, surprised.

She laughs. "Yes. Not well, but I know him. Not only am I dating his cousin, but his brother is married to my best friend."

The waiter approaches. "Can I start you both with a drink?"

Aerie glances at me and I nod. "Absolutely."

We both order a glass of wine and my comfort level continues to increase as she fills me in on her friendship with Dahlia Wilde. I ask how she's doing during what must have been a hard time for all of them. I wish I could have been there for Xander. I also ask her questions about her boyfriend and the movie.

The waiter brings a basket of Brie with crackers and two goblets of Chablis.

"So am I wrong about the picture?" she asks.

"What do you mean?" I start to feel nervous, so I drum my fingers on the table. She notices right away.

"You can trust me, you know."

My eyes search hers and I stifle a laugh. "You work for Damon, my husband. Of course I can trust you."

"That's not what I mean. Look, Ivy, you don't have to tell me anything, but I get the feeling that something isn't right. That today's headlines stating you've reconciled with your true love don't reflect the real story."

I stay quiet. Damon warned me not to say a word. The deal was simple—Xander's career would remain untarnished as long as I cooperated. Otherwise Damon threatened to dismantle the band and ruin Xander's future. I have to put out an album and keep quiet about our real reason for the reconciliation. Six months I have to give him—I can do that.

"Do you love him?" she asks.

"I married him," I answer, not wanting to lie.

"I know. It's just that the look you're giving Xander in the photo looks like love. The look you gave Damon when he walked away looked more like disgust."

I look at her, stunned, and before I can stop them the words tumble out. "Damon threatened to ruin Xander and the band's career like his father did to Nick Wilde . . . unless I married him. I couldn't let that happen to Xander or the band. So I did what he asked."

"Really? Nick didn't stop touring because Xander's mother, Charlotte, got pregnant?" she asks, and I quickly answer.

"No. Damon said his father fired Nick for poor sales performance and that the Wilde Ones' sales have been anything but stellar, so he could do the same."

"From what I know, Josh Wolf is a decent man. I can't imagine him killing anyone's career unless the sales were nonrecoupable. And I've actually seen those sales reports not too long ago, and I don't think that was the case."

"You have? How? Why?"

"I have them in my possession. My uncle never married and I was his sole heir. When he died, all his possessions were willed to me. I was going through his stuff a few months ago to help Jagger prepare for his audition and I came across the sales reports. I thought it was strange that they were in with his things, but then, my uncle was a silent partner with River and Xander's grandfather's store, Avery's. So I figured the documents just got placed haphazardly in the wrong stack. I did look at the numbers out of curiosity and remember thinking they were actually phenomenal."

I look at her, trying to figure this all out. My head is spinning. Why would Damon lie about that?

She reaches across the table and takes my hand. "I can help you. Do you trust me?"

I nod. "How?"

"I know a freelance writer who specializes in financial investigation. Can I contact him? Ask him to look into this? Maybe he can find something you can present to Damon as a counter, a way out, who knows?"

Again I nod. A *counter*—the word sounds so strange, but then again, my situation is anything but normal.

She sets her phone on the table and hits CONTACTS. I watch her as she selects BEN and texts, *I have a job for you. I'll e-mail you the details later.*

"There, done." She hands me her phone. "Give me your number and I'll let you know if we find anything. And, Ivy, if you need to talk, just call me."

I type in my contact information and slide the phone back across the table. "Thank you."

"Listen, it's none of my business and I don't know Xander that well. But from what I do know, he seems like a tough guy. I think he can handle Damon."

"Who can handle Damon?" his voice inquires from behind me. His lips are on my cheek as he pulls up a chair. The spot where his mouth touched my face feels damp and clammy, and I want to wipe it away.

Aerie doesn't stumble in her response. "Ivy's security." She smiles and looks over at Johnny. "I was joking about having a glass of wine"— she raises her glass—"while conducting the interview and asked if he"— she points to Johnny—"would get in trouble. Then I corrected myself when I looked over at him again and said I think he can handle you."

Damon isn't amused. "Well, are you ladies finished? I have a lot of pressing business to attend to today and I want to get my wife back to the bus."

"I think we are," Aerie says, closing her laptop. "I'd like to send Ivy the questions and responses before I publish, though. If that's okay with you?"

Damon seems extremely distracted. "Of course. Just run them through my assistant and she'll see to it that Ivy gets them." He scoots his chair back, reaches for his wallet, and throws a fifty-dollar bill on the table like it's confetti. Then he takes my hand and tugs me to my feet with a smile, as if I'm a child not following directions. More disgust flows through me.

I extend my other hand to Aerie. "Nice to meet you, Ms. Daniels," I say as nonchalantly and as formally as I can.

"Mrs. Wolf, it was my pleasure. Damon, thank you for the opportunity." I'm so sickened by the sound of his name as mine that I can feel the bile rising in my throat.

"Good afternoon," Damon says for the both of us before placing his hand on the small of my back and guiding me forward. She glances down when her phone beeps with a text and I hope it's the information she was talking about.

My disgusted reaction toward him only grows with every touch, and again I question what I ever saw in him. We reach the waiting car as Johnny trails behind us. On the way back to the bus, Damon says nothing while he reads e-mails on his phone and I relish the silence. Looking out the window as we approach the two tour buses in the parking lot, I see Amy boarding the Wilde Ones bus. The pit in my stomach grows, and I start to wonder if I am strong enough to do this—even for Xander.

CHAPTER 16
Something to Believe In

Xander

Damon Wolf has been here for two days. I can't get near her and it's killing me. I have to find a way to get past his security—I need to know if she did this because she wanted to or because she had to. Either way, I don't understand her actions but I'm not ready to give up. Hatred has been consuming me and I exhale his name as a curse before mustering the strength to get out of bed.

Slowly sitting up, I turn my phone on—too many messages to check right now. My head is pounding and I feel like shit. The bus is unusually quiet. No one seems to be around. I tack up the daily before hitting the bathroom. Then I jump in the shower, slip a pair of jeans on, and head back to the galley, where I lie back down and close my eyes, trying to figure out what the hell I'm going to do next.

"Xander, there you are. I've been calling you. Why aren't you answering your phone?" Amy calls from across the room, holding the daily sheet in her hand.

I lift my head. "What are you doing here?"

"Jiffy Lube Live is a double bill, remember? You were supposed to call me?" She points to the sheet I prepared days ago but never bothered to look at today before I posted it.

I throw my head back. "Shit, I completely forgot Breathless is opening for us tonight."

She laughs. "Yeah, I know. I called Ena and she didn't know anything about it."

"My head's been in my ass lately. I'm really sorry. What do you need me to do?"

"I took care of it all. The guys are finishing up in the amphitheater now."

I nod. "Thank you."

Technically, coordinating with Breathless would have been Ellie's job, but as soon as Damon showed up he told the label to let her go, quoting cost cuts. She was actually really happy about it—she said she had wanted to move to New York City for some time and the severance pay would give her the time she needed to find a new job.

"Want some company?" Amy asks me with a smile.

I throw my hand over my eyes. "I'm really beat and I have a lot on my mind. What do you say we catch up later?"

There's no response, so I move my arm and rise on my elbows. She smiles at me and reaches her arms around her head to unwind her braid. Then in an extremely bold move she steps forward and straddles me on the bed. The smell of her hair hits me and the feel of her body on mine makes me want to forget everything and just let go.

She runs her fingers up my bare chest.

"Amy, what are you doing?"

Again nothing—just silence. She slowly starts to unbutton her blouse, but I gently take her hand to stop her.

Again I ask, "Amy, what are you doing?" but this time my voice is cool in a way I've never spoken to her before.

"I want you."

I sit up and carefully slide her off me. I take her chin in my hand and tip her face up to mine. "Amy, I have to tell you something I should have told you a while ago."

"What is it?"

"I'm in love with Ivy."

"But she's married to Damon," Amy snaps.

"I know, but that doesn't change how I feel about her."

Tears fill her eyes.

"We've had a casual thing going for a long time. It had to end eventually."

"I've wanted more than casual for a while and I thought you did too."

"Amy, believe me, you're gorgeous and I enjoy your company . . . but I'm not in love with you."

She takes a deep breath and stands. With a frown she says, "Fuck you, Xander Wilde. Don't call me ever again."

I throw myself back down on the bed as soon as she leaves. I can't even go after her right now. I feel like an asshole, but I never promised her anything.

The guys come back around thirty minutes later and drag my ass out of bed. They ran into Amy, who was spitting nails. Garrett puts his arm around my shoulder. "Look, buddy, I think I told you once—chicks don't do casual."

I shake my head because I don't really have a response and he pours me a drink and tells me all about how chicks don't do casual. After drinking more than we should on the bus, we head over to the arena, all in foul moods. We watch Breathless perform and drink a few more beers. I know I'm being irresponsible, but I just don't give a shit right now.

Breathless is ending their set and it was flawless. Jane's love for the audience and of performing made for a great high-energy show.

Scarcely taking a breath between songs, she powered through soaring ballads, bounced excitedly through new songs, and scorched the place with a cover of Katy Perry's "Roar." Her charm and undeniable strong pipes had the half-packed house crazy in love with her.

The band has fifteen minutes before taking the stage. Again Ivy doesn't show to huddle with us, but this time we know she's in her dressing room because her fucking bodyguard is standing outside it.

Leif, undaunted, walks up to him. "I need to talk to Ivy. Get out of my way."

The brute crosses his arms and completely ignores him.

Leif gets right in his face. "I said, I need to talk to Ivy."

"Not happening before the show," he grunts.

"Why the fuck can't I talk to her?" Leif curses fluently at the ninja.

With my face still battered from my last encounter with Johnny, I make my way over there. I want Leif to make it onstage; I don't give a fuck what happens to me.

"Come on, man, no use trying to budge this asshole," I tell Leif.

Just as the door opens and I think I finally have my chance to talk to her, I see that it's Damon, not Ivy.

"What are you still doing here?" he asks me, staying close to his bodyguard.

I just stare at him while ways to kill him run through my mind.

The cue for the band to take the stage sounds, and I look at Leif. "Go." He hesitates and I growl at him. "Go."

"This is fucking bullshit," he shoots at Damon and finally walks away, leaving me with Damon and his bodyguard.

"Are you letting her onstage or what?" By this point I'm scowling at them both.

"Look, boy, you need to learn how this is going to work. I hold the cards. I say where and when Ivy makes an appearance. I say who she talks to and who she doesn't. Do you get it?" He enunciates every syllable in case I don't understand him.

I glare at him. "Fuck off." My voice is cold and my intentions are made clear.

There's fury blazing on his face but not as hot as mine.

"You will be gone before morning—or you and your band will be on your bus headed back to LA. A few calls to the remaining venues about a conflict among the band members, some drugs found on the bus, whatever the hell I want to make up, will have them accepting Ivy graciously in your band's place. Do you hear me?"

I lunge for his throat, but Johnny grabs me by mine with one hand and gives me a swift punch in the gut with the other. Damon nods at him toward the set of doors leading backstage. "Let him watch his last show," he orders, and I'm assisted backstage, in case I couldn't find it myself, in some kind of hold that I can only assume is a martial arts move.

The Wilde Ones' show sucked. By the time Ivy took the stage, the audience was yelling about why it was taking so long. They started up with hits, but their performance lacked energy, there was no excitement, and they all seemed completely drained of any artistic ability. Even Ivy's last song, a cover mix of a combination of both Kelly Clarkson's and the Script's "Walk Away," just wasn't enough to excite the audience. The show was a bomb. Immediately afterward Ivy was quickly taken from the arena. As I'm staring at her back as Damon's personal security leads her away, Leif grabs my arm. "Come with me. We're getting the hell out of here."

"Where are the other guys?"

"They all went back to the bus. It's just you and me."

I haven't told the guys I have to leave before the bus takes off at six a.m. I was going to tell them right after the show, but maybe it's best this way. I decided to go, not because I give a shit about Damon's threats but because I want the guys to finish the tour and if they know my reason for leaving they probably won't agree to finish. So putting all that happened tonight out of my mind, I follow Leif into what looks like an abandoned warehouse. It's incredibly loud and hot in there and I regret agreeing to come the minute I set foot inside. I can feel the pulsing bass lines travel up my leg and uniform glassy expressions are on everyone's face. This place screams illegalities. From having to call ahead to get in to the fact that there are no lines, no signs, and no ropes outside.

As soon as we walk through the main part of the club, there are beautiful girls surrounding us. Leif has his choice and he takes what's offered along the way—running his hands down women's chests and occasionally even up their skirts. I pass on the walking and grazing. We take the stairs and end up in an even darker part of the club.

"Fuck, is this some kind of strip club on steroids?" I yell over the beat of the wild music.

He looks around with experienced eyes and I know he's been to places like this before. Laughing, he says, "No, it's an underground nightclub. No rules. Sex. Drugs. Threesomes. Whatever you want, it's here."

"You're not joking, are you?"

"Nope," he says with a grin.

"That explains the practically naked women dancing on the tables."

He raises his eyebrows. "Let's have a seat and take a better look. Order a drink and I'll show you how it's done here."

Once we sit down, I raise a finger and quirk it my way. He leans forward and I say, "You don't have to show me anything. But I'll definitely take a drink."

"Calm down, man, I didn't mean anything by it," he says as he whips out a pack of cigarettes and lights one up. Exhaling the smoke in a ring, he motions a waitress in our direction. She's at our table before he even takes another drag. The voluptuous brunette is wearing fishnet hose and a see-through bra with her tits pushed up. She bends down enough to give me a perfect view of her nipples. She asks me what I'm drinking and once I tell her she shimmies over to Leif and does the same thing. I shake my head when he tucks a twenty between her breasts. A few minutes later her tits are back in my face and she's sliding a gin and tonic my way. "Thanks." I slip her a twenty across the table.

"Anything else?" It's easily understood she's talking about things not on the menu.

I shake my head. "I'm good," I say and lean back in the booth. I start to relax a little when the cold and icy mixture hits my lips. I hold the liquid in my mouth and let the ice slide across my tongue as I watch Leif place a hand on the waitress's hip, then slide it down to her ass. She whispers in his ear and then dances off into the crowd, letting at least a dozen other shitfaced men touch her in the same way.

Leif slams his drink back. "I'll be back in ten," he says with a sly grin.

"Don't catch anything," I mutter.

"Man, it's just a hand job. What could I possibly catch? And if you change your mind, just ask any of the girls down here. A hundred bucks and it's yours."

"Sorry. I've never paid to have someone touch my dick and I don't think I will tonight."

He shrugs his shoulders. "Sometimes it's just easier. I don't feel like charming some chick right now, and my guess is neither do you. But serve yourself." He laughs and walks away mimicking jerking off.

Two thoughts hit me almost simultaneously . . . I need to enroll in Jedi training classes before approaching the ninja again and I have to get the hell out of here—out of both this club and this town.

I awake in the darkness, glancing quickly at my watch to see it's eight a.m. East Coast time. After leaving the bar last night, I went to the bus, packed my shit, and left a note for the guys that said I wanted to check on River and Dahlia and I'd be in touch. That was all they needed to know. I took a cab to Dulles International and waited for the next flight to LA.

Sitting here, I remember I probably won't have a car when I get back—I make a mental note to call Ena and tell her to do whatever she has to do to get my car out of impound and have it delivered to my house. I think today is Sunday, but I've lost track of the days. Once the wheels touch the ground I turn my phone on to check the date and there are more than twenty missed calls and messages. Fuck. I turn it back off. It is Sunday—a day of rest—and I think I'll take advantage of it.

I manage to exit the secure area of the terminal in record time. There's some kind of commotion in the airport. There are at least twenty reporters and photographers in the vicinity. Cameras are to eyes and microphones are in hands as soon as I exit security, and they all head toward me. A woman shoves her microphone in my face and asks, "Is it true that Dylan Wolf was your biological father?"

That stops me in my tracks. There are more strangers surrounding me, yelling out ridiculous questions that seem more like statements. It hurts to breathe. I swallow hard as cameras flash repeatedly in my face. "Come again. What?"

"Haven't you heard? Josh Wolf passed away this morning, and his son Damon announced that you are his nephew."

A sick feeling unlike anything I've ever experienced before overtakes me. Still, I just stand there and stare at her. What the hell is she talking about?

"Do you have a comment? Dylan Wolf died before you were born but were you close with Josh Wolf? How do you feel about sharing control of Sheep Industries with Damon Wolf? Are you in love with Ivy Taylor? Did your mother love your father . . ." Questions from all directions and of all kinds surround me and I can't answer a single one. How is this happening? I only just learned Damon had a twin brother who overdosed and now I'm hearing his name again. Where the hell did this come from? What are these people talking about?

"Xander!" I hear Jack's voice calling my name.

I look ahead and see his face through the crowd. My heart pounds in my chest and threatens to break in two—why is he here to pick me up? His expression looks pained, and right away I know that what these people are yelling out can be nothing but the truth. He approaches me with a team of airport security behind him. Clutching my arm, he tries to thread us through the vultures.

"Come on, follow me," he directs, and I do, only because I need to get the hell away from the chaos that's trailing behind me.

His car is parked out front and he opens his door. I get in, feeling numb. He stops and talks to one of the men on the security team, then climbs in the car.

"Xander . . ." Jack reaches across the car to touch my shoulder.

He pulls me out of my trance and I jerk away. "What the hell is going on?"

"I want your mother to explain this to you."

Through gritted teeth I say, "Jack, I need you to tell me what the hell's going on."

He pulls out of the airport and speeds onto the highway. "Josh Wolf died today and his son Damon decided to make a public announcement."

"I fucking gathered that. Is it true?"

He grips the steering wheel and hits the gas. A minute passes and he still doesn't answer me.

"Is it true?" I yell.

"Yes, son, it is."

"Pull over now. I need a drink."

"Your mother is waiting for us at home."

A scowl tightens my mouth. "I'm not your fucking son and I said I need a drink. Either pull off at the next exit or stop the car so I can get out."

Veering off the highway, he takes a right. He pulls into a dive bar just outside the city and I bolt out of the car. He follows and catches up with me inside the joint. "Look, I want your mother to explain everything, but you should know a few things."

I glare at him from where I'm sitting at the bar. "What exactly are 'a few things'? I think there is one thing—that Nick Wilde wasn't my father and she never told me."

"You're wrong, son. Nick may not have been your biological father, but he was your father in the ways that count."

"Scotch, neat. Make it a double," I order. The bartender pours the amber liquid in a tumbler and I pound it back, then slam the glass down. I nod and he pours another.

"What do you know about it?" I ask Jack, after I've finished off the second glass and motioned the bartender back over.

"Two shots of tequila," I tell the bartender, deciding a couple of shots might help faster than another drink.

"I only know what your mother told me today."

I shrug my shoulders. "So she kept you in the dark, too. Why is that?"

"Xander, I understand you're upset—and you have every right to be—but I think you need to let your mother explain everything to you."

I lick the back of my hand and salt it. I tilt the shot back and suck on the lime, then toss back the second one straight up.

"What happened? Did she cheat on Nick when he was on the road? Was that the catalyst behind his career tanking?"

His hand grips my shoulder and this time he's not trying to comfort me—he's warning me. "I get this is a shock and I'll let you take the brunt of it out on me. But I'm telling you right now, you will listen to your mother and treat her with the respect she deserves."

"She cheated on Nick. What does that deserve?" I spit out.

"Xander, I can tell you this. She never cheated. She and Nick broke up right after he went on the road. She was seeing Dylan Wolf on and off for a while when you were conceived, but he died before he ever knew she was pregnant."

Anger washes over me and I know I should just shut my mouth. My hand flies up in the air without conscious thought. "Bartender, another," I yell. I don't want to hear another word because already the use of the word *conceived* makes me want to puke right here. I am so fucking relieved when the conversation finally disappears from my mind and into the next tequila shot.

CHAPTER 17
You're Not Alone

A ray of moonlight through my window brings me to consciousness. I sit straight up, staring into his face, wild and fierce, full of hate. It takes me a moment to realize he is me. I struggle to find the floor and then stumble to the mirror over the dresser. I peer at the reflection; it's murky, but I can see it now—I look like him. If I look like Damon, he must look like his brother. How did I not see it?

Devastation, anger, and remorse run through me in a cacophony. I head to the bathroom and splash cold water on my face. I squeeze my eyes shut as a rapid succession of faces flies across a blank canvas in my mind. My family, the ones I belong to . . . but not really. I shake off that thought and try to persuade myself that my conception doesn't change anything. But I know it does. If it didn't, why did no one ever tell me?

Was Dylan Wolf a monster like his brother? I scream at that son of a bitch buried in a coffin somewhere—*you bastard*. Gripping the sink, I break down when I realize that no, I'm the bastard. What kind of fucking irony is that? Along with rage, should I be feeling shame? What do you call that combination of emotions?

I bend over and purge myself of my thoughts and the alcohol. Vomiting profusely, I fall to my knees and wrap my arms around the toilet. A rush of memories that I haven't thought about in years surfaces, only causing me to want to expel the toxicity even more. I spit in the bowl one last time, making sure every ounce of wretchedness is gone.

"Feel any better?" my brother's voice asks from behind me.

I slowly turn my head, not sure if any of my senses are functioning. It's River, leaning against the bathroom doorframe. His eyes are red, bloodshot, even more so than when I left him two days ago.

"What are you doing here?"

He narrows his eyes at me. "I'm here for you."

"You should be home with your wife."

"Bell's with her and I should be here with you. I want to talk to you. I've been calling you and when I called Mom for the hundredth time Jack finally got on the phone and filled me in."

"I don't want to talk to anyone right now. I just want to be left alone."

He stares at me. "Not happening. We can talk . . . or not. Your choice, but I'm not leaving."

My heart rate picks up speed as I try to stand up, and he extends his arm to help me. I take it. He feels like my brother. He's the same guy he always was— except we no longer share the same father.

I get a close look at him. "You look like shit."

"You don't look so hot yourself." Then with his voice full of sarcasm, he adds, "You want another drink?"

"Fuck off," I tell him. "And I'm not talking about it. I'm going back to fucking bed."

"Suits me. I'm pretty exhausted myself." He follows me into my bedroom.

I kick my boots off and peel out of my jeans before sliding into the sheets. He stares at me and throws himself on the bed.

"Are you fucking kidding me? You're not sleeping in the same bed as me."

"The fuck I'm not," he says and toes his shoes off.

I roll over with my back to him and close my eyes. "Whatever."

When I next open my eyes the sun is filtering through my bedroom window and I'm alone. For a moment I'm the person I always was, but then the recent revelations come back to me. I feel the pain as soon as I lift my head, but I don't give a shit how my head feels. Kicking out of bed, I glance over at my phone. I turn it on to see missed calls and messages from late last night and most recently an hour ago. My mother, Jack, Bell, the guys, and Ivy have all called. I turn it back off—I can't deal with any of them right now, not even Ivy. Instead I walk out of my room and through the living room into the kitchen. River's sitting at the kitchen table that used to belong to my grandparents . . . the people I thought were my grandparents anyway. He's sipping a cup of coffee and thumping his fingers on the wooden tabletop.

He watches me cross the room to the coffeepot. I pour a cup and move to head out the back door onto the balcony.

"Where are you going?" his voice asks calmly.

"Outside. Where does it look like I'm going?"

"Xander, let's talk about this."

I pause at the door but don't turn around. "Everything in my life that I thought was real was a lie. Fuck, even this house that belongs to me is a lie. It was willed to me by the two people I admired more than anyone in this world and they weren't really mine. So what's there to talk about?"

"Stop being such a fucking douchebag and sit down and talk to me."

I open the door. "Fuck you."

"You're my brother and I'm concerned about you. Please talk to me." His voice sounds just as shaky as mine.

Closing the door, I lean my head against the cool glass.

"You and me—we're the same as we were two days ago. Nothing has changed. We're always there for each other. We always have been. Come on, Xander, we're the same two kids that grew up together, fought with each other, went to school together, took care of our drunk father, watched over our sister, looked out for our mother. We started our careers together. We know who we are. Whose DNA runs through your veins doesn't change any of it." His voice rising slightly, he adds, "None of it!"

I turn around and close the distance between us, taking a seat across from him.

I look at him for a long while before speaking. "You know, it's weird, but I don't feel any different. Both men are dead, so what's it matter?"

"It doesn't matter. That's what I'm saying."

I nod and try to put everything in perspective.

He looks me in the eye. "You know I love you, right?"

I roll my eyes. "I was just starting to think you had stopped being such a pussy and now you're going to talk about feelings?"

River takes a serious tone. "No, Xander, I'm serious. I want to talk to you about Mom."

One solid fucking hour we spend talking about how I need to go talk to my mother. I tell him I'm not ready. I mean, I'm still digesting that I'm not who I thought I was. All he keeps saying is that I'm the same person I've always been—and fuck, I know he's right. I just need time. We slam our fists on the table, throw both our coffee cups across the room, and I almost walk out about a dozen times, but the storm passes and now we're both lying on the huge L-shaped sofa in the living room reminiscing about our youth.

"You should take that 'Vette out of storage," he says.

"I hate that fucking car," I tell him.

"Really? Then why have you held on to it for all these years?"

"Because Grandpa bought it and he helped me get it running again after it sat in his garage for so long."

"Xander, come on, I know as well as you do that you loved it that Dad gave that car to you. Do you know how pissed I was when I was finally able to drive and I begged Dad to make you share it with me and he said no. He actually said it was yours and yours only. Then when you wouldn't even let me drive it—that pissed me off more than anything."

"I forgot about that."

We're both quiet for the longest time, and I try to remember the last time I even set eyes on that car.

River sits up and breaks the silence. "Xander, I've got something to tell you."

"Please, no more feelings. I can't take any more of it."

"Fuck off! I'm being serious."

"Okay, what?"

"Damon shut the tour down. Everyone arrived home this morning."

"What an asshole." That's all I can come up with because I can't even think about work or the band.

After a few more minutes of silence, I'm tossing a basketball above my head. "Can I ask you something?"

"Sure."

"Do you know anything about Dylan Wolf? What kind of person he was?"

"No," he answers softly. "Can I ask you something?" he counters.

"Maybe," I answer.

"Why do you think Damon made the announcement?"

My heart starts pounding and I bolt upright, tossing the ball aside. River's eyes flare to mine. "I don't know. But I'd wager it has something to do with money," I say with a lump in my throat that I can't swallow.

River frowns and crosses a leg over his knee. "Go on."

"With everything that's been going on with Ivy and the tour, he still kept it going. It had to be for the money. He could have given a shit about the band. Then his old man dies and he cancels the remaining shows even after I left. When I confronted him, he kept throwing things out there about me being like my father. I assumed he meant Nick, but he must have meant his brother."

The doorbell rings. Blood rushes to my face and my shoulders stiffen. "Don't answer it," I bark.

River shrugs. "Don't be a dick. You can't stay locked up all day. People are looking to talk to you."

"By *people*, you mean Mom?"

"Yeah, Mom, Jack, Bell, the band. Everyone that cares about you."

"I'm not ready to talk to Mom."

"It's not her anyway. I told her I'd call when you were ready. I made her promise to give me the time I needed to talk to you. But, Xander, she's a wreck. Don't make her wait too much longer."

I stand up and stare at him. "When did you become so mature?"

He shakes his head at me.

Walking over to the door, I look through the peephole to see who it is. It's Aerie.

As soon as I open the door she rushes in. She's dressed more casually than I've seen her before. She's wearing some kind of track suit. Her blond hair is pulled back and the sneakers on her feet make her seem really short. She's almost a whole head shorter than me.

"Xander," she greets me in total business mode.

"Aerie, what are you doing here?" Then I remember she asked for an interview. "Now is not the best time for that interview."

"That's not why I'm here."

"What's going on?" I ask her as I close the door.

"Can we sit down and talk?"

"Sure. Come in." I move past her, escorting her toward the living room.

River's still sitting on the couch and stands up the minute he sees her.

"River," she says softly and crosses the room to hug him. She holds on to him tightly. "I'm so sorry I had to run out on Dahlia. As soon as I explain everything to the both of you I'm heading back over to see her. Jagger's meeting me there with lunch from her favorite place."

"She understands. I'm sure she'd love to see you," River responds.

She pulls away. "Mind?" she asks, looking at me and pointing to the large graphite-colored chair that used to be my grandfather's favorite.

"No. Have a seat." I wonder what could be so urgent that she would come over here to talk when I know she's obviously seen the headlines. "You want a cup of coffee?"

"No, thank you, I don't drink coffee. I'm fine really."

Aerie takes a deep breath, pulls some papers out of her bag, and sets them on the large glass coffee table. "Well," she says, "I have something I want to show you."

"Okay. Shoot." I'm a little agitated that she's not just getting to the point, but I think I get it. "Fuck, did Damon send you over? What does he want now? For me to sign some kind of huge-ass contract?" I say, pointing to the stack of papers on the table.

"Xander, relax, man. Let her finish."

"Didn't you hear?" she asks.

I shake my head. "Hear what?"

"Damon no longer owns *Sound Music Magazine*. If it hasn't been announced yet, it will be later today."

River raises an eyebrow. "Really? Why'd he sell it?"

Aerie snickers. "Well, he didn't really have much of a choice. We were in poor financial condition. I actually think it was a takeover. I'm not sure about the details, but I've been reassured that the company that bought it intends to keep the magazine intact. I've never been more thankful in my life on both counts."

"Who bought it?" I ask her.

Aerie shrugs her shoulders. "A company by the name of Plan B. It's a small private company. *Sound Music* is its first acquisition, but I know another magazine is being shopped."

"Interesting," River responds.

"Are you concerned?" I ask him.

"No, just curious."

"Sounds like perfect timing if you ask me," I interject.

"It is," she says, looking a little nervous. Then, "I can't divulge the details just yet. I'm sorry."

I shrug. It's no skin off my back.

She fumbles through the papers on the table and my agitation level only grows.

"Well, I don't want to keep you. I just wanted you to have these," she says after she's located what she's looking for. She rises and walks over to where I'm still standing at the bottom of the steps in the living room.

"What are they?" I have to ask because I have no fucking clue why she's handing me a stack of papers with numbers all over them.

"Sales reports and various supporting documents from when your father was signed under Sheep Industries' Little Red label."

I hand the papers back to her. "What do you want me to do with these?"

She pushes them toward me. "Look at them."

"Aerie, I have a lot going on right now. Can this wait?"

"Xander, I wouldn't be here if it could wait. I talked to Ivy yesterday and she told me everything. I know your mind is probably in a million places, but these reports are what she needs to get out from Damon's hold."

"Damon's hold?" I question.

"Yes. Damon is blackmailing her—or he was. I wanted her to have the information either way."

"Fuck, I knew he was up to something. I just wasn't sure what. Do you know what he's holding over her?"

"All she told me was that he'd said he ruined Nick and he would do the same to you. But I overheard him on the phone with his attorney just before the takeover became official, and he said at least the marriage clause was executed before his old man passed. I know it has something to do with the will, but that was all I heard."

"Josh Wolf's will going public has to be news to everyone. I can only guess the bastard wanted to be the first to report it. Put his own spin on it," River muses.

Aerie flips through the stack and hands me two sheets of paper. "Well, here is what I found. This report is from Little Red's records," she says, pointing to the column on the right. "And this one I just got," she says, pointing to the one on the left, like I have any idea what that means.

I look at both pieces of paper. My eyes scour the numbers. They're different. I read the handwriting on the bottom and have no problem deciphering what this means now. "Where did you get these?"

"What are they?" River asks, standing and crossing his arms over his chest.

Aerie explains. "One set was in the basement of Sheep Industries, the other is from a box of old papers that I found in my uncle's things when Jagger and I were going through everything a couple of months ago."

I want to question her further, about how she got documents from the basement of Sheep Industries and why would sales reports of a record label be among her uncle's things, but right now I don't give a shit where the information came from. I stand there dumbfounded as River comes over to us and looks over my shoulder. "They're for the same period of time, but there's a huge discrepancy in reported earnings," he manages to say, shock evident in his voice.

"Exactly!" Aerie says.

What kind of person does that to someone? I have to sit down, and once I do, I read the handwritten note again, but it begins to blur. River sits next to me, both of us staring at the series of numbers in front of us. Spots cloud my vision and my heart pounds for the man I always knew as my father—the one who wanted his whole life to be successful and thought he'd failed . . . when in actuality he was a superstar in his own right.

Utter silence falls in the room. River and I both sit there in shock, absorbing the information that might have changed both our lives . . . Maybe we both take the quiet to fast-forward that life in our minds, or maybe we're barricading ourselves from the truth, maybe we're just trying to stop the black fury that comes with the truth—or maybe those are just my feelings. I push aside the papers in my hands and lean over the others on the table, noticing that my hands are trembling. I look to my brother—his face is white, his expression blank.

I take a deep breath, adjust my focus, and pull myself together. I drop my hands to my sides and flex my fingers. When Aerie's wide eyes meet mine I can finally say, "Thanks so much for this. I have to run, but call me for anything."

River nods, still seemingly in a trance. Then he stands as well. "I'll walk you out."

She gives me a sad smile. "Call me for anything, Xander. I'll leave you all this," she says, pointing to the stack of papers. "It's mostly collaborating documentation in case you file a complaint with the FCC."

For a moment I stare at her. "I think I'll handle this in my own way," I tell her with no edge to my voice at all. Do I want to turn him in or do I want to use this to get him to leave Ivy alone? That's a question I don't even have to ask myself.

River leads Aerie to the door. I hear them whispering in the foyer. I cradle my head in my hands and know I have to see my mother before I do anything else. The biggest question being . . . selflessness or selfishness? The two conflicting feelings struggle within me and I'm not sure which will win out.

Thirty minutes later I've sent my brother packing and I'm climbing into my sister's car, which is still parked in my driveway. She never came to pick it up. She must be driving my mother's car. Fuck, I never called Ena and told her to get mine, but right now I don't give a shit about my car. There's no sign of the press and I'm fucking thankful. At first I lurch full speed down the road in my sister's Cabriolet, but with no pickup in her chick car I change my mind and lay off the gas. Gripping the steering wheel tightly, I quickly decide to turn around, trading Sunset Boulevard for the scenic route, the longer way. While I drive, I think about everything that has happened over the past days. I think about my life. I'm a guy who likes control. I follow a plan. I have a schedule. I'm all about structure—not chaos. And lately my life has been full of instability.

As I drive through the wooded streets, I stare at the beautiful manicured lawns and large homes that belong to families who I bet know who they are. I think about Nick—did he know any of this? If he knew the truth, why did he never treat me any different from River and Bell?

Pulling in the driveway, I park the car, whip off my sunglasses and toss them in the passenger seat. I look at the large two-story house tucked away behind a bounty of trees that my mother shares with Jack. I'm suddenly thankful that this isn't my childhood home. I always thought it would have been cool to visit my mother with my kids at the place I grew up in—but now it's a relief not to have to see that house again, since my childhood was a lie.

Turning off the ignition, I wipe those thoughts from my mind and get out of the car. I jam my hands into my pockets and pace the shadows of the sidewalk in front of the house. My stomach is in knots. I'm not sure I can do this. What can she say to take any of the pain away? Nothing can make me feel any better. I notice a strange car in the driveway and wonder if Brigitte got a new one or if someone is visiting. *Fuck.*

I stall as long as I can, pondering leaving in case someone is here, but I take a deep breath and go for it, hoping it's just Bridgette's new car. I walk slowly along the cobblestone path that leads to the back entrance, before slipping in through the door. The gleaming black-and-white marble floor of the rear entrance blinds me and I pause a moment to reconsider having this conversation with my mother. I'm still furious despite my heart pounding with fear, but I know I have to do this.

The kitchen smells of freshly brewed coffee and I look around for our housekeeper, Brigitte. Since she's been with our family for years, I wonder if she knows. The room is empty, though; she doesn't seem to be around, so I make my way through the house. The stab of irritation I'm already feeling quickly turns to trepidation when I hear Ivy's voice—she's here talking to my mother. The sadness in her tone makes me stop in my tracks. As if in slow motion, I come to a stop just outside the family room and listen.

My mother's voice is raspy as she speaks. "You did what you had to—Xander will forgive you. I know he'll understand."

"I hope so. But he looked so hurt and betrayed. It killed me to see him like that."

"Ivy, Xander is strong and perceptive. It's easy to see through Damon's manipulative ways and I'm sure he did."

"God, I feel so dumb. How did I never see that side of him until recently? If I had I would have never been with him. Never." Ivy starts to cry and her words only serve to strengthen not only my fury but also my fear.

It sounds like my mother's comforting her. Then Ivy continues. "Damon told me after he received the call that his father passed that Josh's will had a clause in it that Damon had to be married to collect his inheritance. That's why he insisted we get married so quickly. I thought it was money from my performance he wanted. He said he only needed us to stay married for six months, enough time to produce an album. But really he knew his father didn't have much time and he wanted to be sure he got what he thought he'd earned."

"Oh, Ivy, no one could have known, darling," my mother says amid sobs.

Ivy's voice is low and I can't make out what she says.

"You don't know how it hurts me that you had to go through that," my mother tells her.

"Charlotte, I'm so sorry to come over like this. I just didn't know what to do. Xander won't answer my calls. I can't believe Damon made his father's will public. I heard him on the phone with his attorney, completely shocked that Xander was in the will and the marriage clause wasn't. I guess Josh changed his will, or Damon was told incorrect information. I don't know. But as soon as he was behind the microphone making that announcement about the will, I knew I had to be with Xander. But now that I'm here I'm afraid he won't forgive me."

With my mother's sobs weighing me down and Ivy sounding so emotional, I can't stand to stay hidden listening any longer. I swing around the corner, almost manic. My mother turns toward me and I meet her gaze. Her face is full of concern and love, whereas I know mine must be a picture of confusion. She rushes over to me as I stand in a daze.

"Xander!" She pulls me in for a tight embrace. Then she pulls away and clutches my face in her trembling hands. "Xander." She begins weeping again.

I shift on my feet, not sure what to ask. Not sure I want to know anything. I take a step back and nearly collide with the doorframe. The moment is awkward, and for the first time in my life I don't know what to say to my mother.

Ivy clears her throat. "I'm going to leave you two alone. Thanks for talking to me, Charlotte." I meet her gaze and her sad eyes, but I can't talk to her now. I wish I could think of a way to let her know I know what she did and why she did it—I hope she understands I'm telling her I get it.

"Ivy, don't go yet," my mother manages, but I see Ivy turn and leave the room, then hear the click of the door. My mother is in such a state that her tears won't stop. She's sobbing so hard that her breathing is out of control.

"Take it easy, Mom," I whisper.

"I was afraid you wouldn't come. That you'd never talk to me again. I was so scared I wouldn't be able to explain everything to you."

I take her hand and lead her to the sofa. "Sit down, Mom. I'm going to get you a glass of water. I'll be right back." She tries to stop me, but she's so hysterical I can't even understand what she's saying. I hate seeing her like this—because of me. I pour some water in a glass and gulp it down, then fill another and take it to her. She drinks it, and once she sets the glass down, she takes my hands.

She looks at me helplessly. "I want you to hear the truth from me. I should have been the one to tell you, and I'm sorry I wasn't."

I squeeze my eyes shut and then open them to look at her. "I'm ready."

With a deep sigh, my mother starts to explain. "I never told any of you that your father and I spent some time apart before we were married. That was a dark time for me. I was lost and alone. I had dated your father all through high school, and then we broke up shortly after he left to go on tour. I missed him terribly. Dylan and Damon went to UCLA with me. We were friends, but I had allowed Damon to fill my head with stories of what it must be like on the road. I loved Nick so much, but jealousy tore us apart. After we broke up I spent a lot of time with Dylan and Damon. I started to date Dylan, but it didn't last long. Once we broke up—well, Damon—he was there for me. He made me think he was taking care of me—that my well-being was what mattered to him. He made himself trustworthy, he was a friend, a confidant even. And then one day he turned on me. Even now his name is a painful reminder. I never say it. Never talk about him or his brother. I let it go—I had to. But I'll never forget . . ."

"Mom, you don't have to go on. It's okay." My voice fades, but I know she hears it. She seems to forget I'm there, even though her story continues.

"I woke up the morning of Dylan's death with a feeling of terrible anticipation—something had startled me out of what I thought was a horrifying dream. I sat up and realized I wasn't in my own bed. My stomach was in knots from one too many drinks the night before. I groggily scanned the area for clues, trying to remember why I was in Damon's room." Her voice goes hoarse and I hand her the glass of water again.

"Damon rushed into the room—opening the door and closing it behind him just as quickly. He spoke haltingly as he opened the blinds and let the light flood the room. His tone was unusually grim and his haste caught me off guard. He told me he took care of everything. I didn't know what he meant. I was scared. Shivering, I pulled the covers up closer to me and asked him what he was talking about. But even as the words left my mouth, hazy memories of what had happened came rushing back to me. I looked out the huge window at the daylight and tried to piece together where the previous night had led." She stops again and I'm feeling poisoned by my own thoughts. Sitting up straighter, I try to calm my breathing so I can speak, but she starts again before I can say anything.

"After a few moments I cleared my dry throat and told him I had been out with my girlfriends and I'd had a little too much to drink. I'd called Dylan from the bar to see how he was doing. We had run into each other earlier that day and he looked terrible, so I wanted to check on him. He had asked me to come over and I couldn't say no. When I got there he cried for me to take him back and when I refused he was so upset. I tried to talk to him, but he wouldn't listen so I thought it best that I leave. I told Damon that when I tried, Dylan begged me to stay, so I did."

I feel sick—my head is pounding and I'm not sure I want to hear any more, but my mother seems intent on telling me the whole story.

Swallowing, she goes on, but the words stick in her throat. "He was a mess and he needed someone. Please don't judge me, Xander."

"I'm not, Mom, I'm not. I promise," I assure her. Because I am certainly in no place to judge.

"I started to feel sick when I was telling Damon what had happened—I felt so incredibly hungover, so I slowly edged toward the bathroom, but I stopped at the dresser to look in the mirror. My hair was a mess, my eyes deeply shadowed, and my face pale, but what concerned me most was Damon's reflection staring back at me—the crease in his brow and the anger in his eyes scared me."

And once again my mind entertains thoughts of wanting to kill him.

She goes on. "The rest happened so fast. Damon told me Dylan was in the hospital, I'll never forget the icy-cold edge to his voice. I looked at my hands and saw red stains and I screamed. Just then the phone rang and he answered it. The expression on his face darkened as he hung up the receiver. In that instant I felt like I had to get out of there. For the first time I was afraid of him. As I moved, the room started spinning, but I managed to make my way to the door. I swung the door open to the family room, the room I had been in the previous night. He caught me before I crossed the threshold and told me Dylan had died and I cried as I ran out of his bedroom and the nightmare of the previous night set in. The last thing I remember is the floor rushed up to meet me and unconsciousness consumed me."

My mother pauses and seems to snap out of whatever trance she was in. "When I woke up I was home alone. He had brought me home. I remembered everything then. Dylan had gotten up and a few minutes later I heard a thud. I ran into the living room and there he was lying on the floor in a pool of blood. He must have fallen and hit his head on the coffee table. A syringe was on the floor next to him. Damon came in as I hovered over him and found us. He called for an ambulance and they came and took Dylan to the hospital. Damon stayed with me. Dylan died of an overdose before Damon made it to the hospital. Nick flew back for the funeral and we went for coffee and started talking. We kept talking even after he left again and we ended up reconciling while he was still on the road. He even asked me to marry him over the phone. He was always so impatient. God, I loved that man." She pauses again, taking another breath and squeezing my hand. "After Nick left again to get back on the road, Damon kept coming around, but his mood was darker, grimmer. I thought it was because his brother had died and I didn't want to turn my back on him. One day he asked me about Nick and I told him we were back together. It was like a switch went off. He started blaming me for Dylan's death. He'd call me and ask if I wanted to go to dinner one minute and when I'd say no he'd ask if I wanted to go to jail. I knew what he was doing—he was trying to scare me into marrying him. I knew I hadn't done anything wrong—but I still worried."

"What made him finally leave you alone?" I ask.

"He didn't right away. First, he tried to convince me to marry him, and when that didn't work he threatened me. But my father overheard our conversation and when he asked me about it, I broke down and told him everything. My father intervened and after that I never heard from Damon again—I honestly don't know what happened."

My ribs ache from breathing so erratically as I listened to my mother. I take a good look at her for the first time since sitting down next to her. She's wearing tan linen pants that look like they've been slept in. Her white blouse looks rumpled and is covered in coffee stains. Her naturally long brown hair is messy and her eyes are swollen. Seeing her like this . . . I can't fight what's in me. I want to be mad, upset, yell at her, curse the day she gave birth to me, but she's my mother and I love her. I've always looked after her, protected her, and I can't change that now.

The words just slip out. "It's okay. I understand why you didn't tell me," I tell her.

She takes a deep breath and her tears start to wane, but her chest seems to be heaving at a greater rate. I draw her into my arms and kiss her hair.

"We're going to be okay, Mom. Don't cry."

She wraps her arms around me in return and rocks me back and forth. In her comforting arms everything I've been feeling melts away. This woman loves me for who I am. After a beat, I pull away and wipe the tears from her cheeks.

"Xander, Nick will always be your father. Please tell me you know that."

I don't say anything.

"I wanted to tell you about Dylan, but once you knew, you couldn't unknow it. And I just knew it would have mattered to you so much more than it should have. You were always my and Nick's firstborn. You were his son and he loved you."

My words come out as the question of a young boy. "Did you love my father, my real one?"

"Nick's your real father, Xander. Dylan and I had a short and turbulent relationship and he died before he ever knew about you. So Nick—he *is* your real father."

"Did he know? Nick, I mean?"

"Yes, of course he knew."

"How could it not have mattered to him?" I ask, looking into her eyes—the eyes that none of us had inherited. Mine are more brown, like his, I'm sure, and River's and Bell's are greener, like Nick's.

"Your father and I loved each other, and the time we were apart took its toll on both of us. Once we were finally back together, we vowed we'd never let anything tear us apart, and I tried to keep that promise." She cries a little more and her words trail off. She doesn't have to finish. Walking over to the mantel, she lifts a crystal-framed photo of River, Bell, and me. "When I told your father I was pregnant, he stared at me for the longest time. We both knew whose baby it had to be. I expected anger, or worse. But instead he put a protective hand on my belly and with a calm and certain voice he said, 'We're going to have a baby, Charlotte, so now you have to marry me.' That's what he said."

"How do you not hate me?" I ask her.

"Why would I ever hate you? You're my son. I love you. You healed me."

At her words my gut wrenches. I swallow hard. "Healed?"

"Healed, mended, made me the person I wanted to be. You made me grow up and, Xander, I loved my life with your father. I loved him. I know he had his flaws and I know you saw him in a way that high-lighted those flaws, but he was a good man. He loved us. He loved you, Xander. You were his son. It made no difference whose blood ran through your veins. And I think he was more afraid of you finding out and not loving him than anything else. He was so proud of you. He loved you so much."

I wince at the raw emotion in her statement and stare at her, at a loss for words. I hated my father for so long I never looked at the good in him. I buried those memories the day he killed himself. But he was my father, not the man with the brown eyes, but the one with the green ones. And he loved me. He did.

Everything is a jumbled mess in my head. I can't look at my mother anymore because she's right. I feel a need to flee from any more emo-tional conversation. I stand up and cross the room to the sliding doors, go out onto the deck, then across the wet lawn. The sprinklers are on, but I sprint across the yard and fall to my knees. Holding my head in my hands, I think of Nick taking us to every concert, instilling in us everything he knew about music, teaching me to drive in the Corvette he never drove anymore because it wasn't a practical family car. He was my father, but over the years I'd forgotten all the good things.

"Xander!" The slight wind carries her shaky voice, but I can hear it. I can hear the worry and concern.

At first I don't move. She calls to me again. I raise my head and see her wiping her tears, the tears I'm causing to fall, and I lift myself up. And in this moment of clarity, I realize I don't give a shit who my bio-logical father is. And I know with everything I am that I loved Nick Wilde and that I have to tell him. But before I go I have to tell my mother about the falsified sales reports—the reports that not only changed Nick's life, but all of ours.

The memories that hit me as I enter Forest Lawn Cemetery are oddly not memories of the many times I've been here, but ones of the people it holds. All of my grandparents, both my mother's and my father's, are buried here, and of course so is my father, Nick. It's an older place with large tombstones . . . some toppled, some crumbling with age, others new. It's eerily quiet and I can hear the birds singing as they land on top of the marble and stone that line the rows.

It seems wrong to come here and not visit my grandparents. A young boy is selling cut flowers and I stop to purchase a wrap from him. I ask him what kind of flowers they are, and he says, "Today I have lilies, but tomorrow I'll have wreaths with a mixture of flowers." I just grin at his enthusiasm—an entrepreneur in the making.

The grass between the carved headstones leads to people I don't know, but I read their names etched on the stones as I pass and scan their markers. Some of those buried here lived long, full lives. Some of their gravestones read, BELOVED HUSBAND AND FATHER or BELOVED WIFE AND MOTHER. Others aren't so descriptive, with just their date of birth followed by their date of death. Wilted bouquets of flowers lie below some of the gravestones and others have rosary beads draped around them. A far greater amount show no sign of visitation.

I stop at Nick's parents' graves first. Pulling two lilies from the stemmed flowers I'm holding, I place one on my grandmother's grave and then another on my grandfather's. Finding words has never been easy for me, but today my thoughts pour out and I thank them for loving me.

Once I've told them all I can handle right now, I stand and make my way down the path toward Nick's grave. I think about him, about our life as a family, and about the turn his life took because of a man that hated him. Stopping in front of his headstone, I stare at it and silently recite the last words scripted on it: "A beloved son, husband, and father rests here where no shadows fall." It's a simple inscription but full of so much meaning. More now that I know the truth. I've never actually come here to visit him. I came with my grandparents to help take care of the area, I came with my mother when she needed to visit, but I've never come for me—just to talk to him.

I shuffle on my feet, feeling uncomfortable, and stand in front of the industrial gray marker. I run my fingers through my hair, then skim them over the smoothness of the stone. Glancing around, I'm surprised at how well tended the site is. My mother or Bell, or possibly even River, must still come here. I don't know—I have never asked. I've carried this anger toward him deep inside myself for so long that once in a while I can douse it, but it has never gone away. I didn't think I would ever get rid of it, but right now I don't feel it anymore. The trees lining the cemetery sway back and forth as a slight wind ripples through the air. I inhale and let it out. I clear my throat and try to find my voice. This is so much more difficult than I ever thought it would be. I take another deep breath and sit down.

Dad,

My old man killed himself and left me to take care of the family. That was my "tagline" whenever anyone asked me about you. That basically summed up everything anyone needed to know about you as far as I was concerned. I hated you—not only for taking your life and leaving us, but also for leaving me feeling guilty in the wake of your death. I was never the same—our family, your family, we were never the same without you.

River and I said once if our life before you died was a puzzle, you took a piece of that puzzle with you—a piece that can never be returned. It took me until now to see that you were a product of the tolls life took on you . . . that you were a good man who had more than his share of obstacles thrown his way. But you and me—we shared a bond and I felt like you destroyed it when you took your life. I was mad at you a lot, but I was a teenager, you were the adult. You should have had faith that I loved you, no matter what. I mean, come on, you knew me better than anyone else—and I always wondered why. Was it because you wanted to make sure I was more like you than him? If so, I hope you are proud of me because I am proud to be so much more like you.

My view of the world has changed since your death, but I remember when I was young and naive and you taught me everything you could about music and helped me believe in the magic of the world. We looked for four-leaf clovers for hours and when we found one, you laminated it for me to preserve that small wonder. When I had questions, you answered them. You were always there for me.

Then after the funeral, that all changed. I lost my parent, my hero, and my teacher. I thought a lot about death and dying and who was to blame. In the end I blamed you rather than myself, but now standing here talking to you—I blame no one. I just wanted you to know that—I blame no one. And, Dad, know this—I love you.

That's how I feel about him—finally I can accept him for him. I get to my feet and brush off the grass. Then I pick up the flower pack and pull the lilies out one by one and lay them on the ground. As I turn and walk away, birds sing and a bell tolls in the distance, but all I can think about is this man who I called Dad, even with all of his flaws—he was my dad and I loved him.

CHAPTER 18
I'm Alive

My eyes blink against the silvery glow of moonlight as I open the door. Her earrings glimmer and her shy smile makes it hard to breathe. I'd fallen asleep on the couch and the sound of the doorbell jolted me awake. I'm surprised to see her—why, I'm not sure. Maybe because I acted like an asshole, maybe because I feel like I should have taken her away from him. I haven't had time to figure out where exactly my guilt is coming from, but as I stand before her I know it doesn't matter.

We look at each other for the longest time until I notice her eyes tilt to my chest and I realize my shirt is unbuttoned. She's staring at my skin, at my side, where the ROSES ARE SO CLICHÉ tattoo is inked—the tattoo I got for her because I knew I'd always love her. I know that not even what has happened the last few days can change that. She stands in the doorway before me, quiet and utterly gorgeous. She's in a pair of jeans and a simple white T-shirt. She's not wearing any makeup, not even her trademark red lipstick, and her hair is pulled back by some kind of band. My heart races at the sight of her and I let out a long breath.

"Ivy," I manage as the love I feel for her whirls around and cocoons us.

Her cheeks flush at the sound of her own name.

"Xander, I'm so sorry. Are you okay?" she asks in an impassioned voice.

I nod. But I don't want to discuss Nick or Dylan any more today. After a beat, I ask, "Is everything all right? What are you doing here so late?"

She crosses her arms tightly over her stomach and grips her elbows. "I needed to see you. Make sure you were all right. Can we talk?"

My breath catches on the smallness of her voice—the uncertainty in it tears a hole through me. She holds my gaze, and my gut twists in a funny way. She inhales deeply and blurts out, "It's my turn to say I'm sorry. I left Damon. I never loved him. I only married him to protect you."

"I know," I whisper and close my eyes, standing silent for the longest time. It's like my body turns to stone at the mere mention of his name. When I open my eyes and look at her, I let everything go and just pull her to me and hold her.

"I love you, Xander," she cries.

"I know," I whisper again, but that doesn't change the fact that she's married to him. I swallow, trying to catch my breath and then pull away. I move aside and motion for her to come in. She reaches for me again, but I retreat and instead place my hand on the small of her back and guide her into the living room. This slight, seemingly intimate touch makes me come alive. I want to feel her skin all over mine, touch her, taste her, sink into her. I want to forget about the day and just get lost in her. But she's married. We take the step down into the living room. My stuff is thrown on the coffee table and the pillows from the sofa are tossed on the floor. Normally I'd have an urge to pick up, but I really don't give a shit right now. When my eyes shift from the floor to her, I see it—the innocence she possesses—and my guilt is back.

"I want to explain everything, Xander," she says softly.

"I understand why you did what you did. You don't have to explain." I pause, then add, "Fuck, I just wish you hadn't . . . After everything, I can't believe you didn't . . ." I stop as the words keep catching in my throat.

"Didn't what?" she asks.

"You should have called me the minute he showed up. To be honest with you, I can't even think about you with him without wanting to kill him."

"I did call you, Xander. I did," she cries. "But Amy answered and I hung up. Did you run to her the minute you got home?"

I whirl around to face her. "Fuck, no! Of course not. I didn't even know you called." I try to figure out how Amy would have answered and then I remember being over at River and Dahlia's and leaving my phone on the counter. "I headed over to my brother's to pick up some things and left my phone on the counter. She was there helping my mother get some food ready. That's all."

Alarm flashes across her face. "I believe you. I do. But I needed to talk to you then. Damon was threatening you and the band. I tried to reach you and she answered your phone and I had no idea what that meant. Before I knew it, he was whisking me off to get married. He told me if I didn't do it he was going to tear you apart with lies—your life, your band, your family. He was on the phone with TMZ. He gave me five seconds to make my decision. I knew I'd regret not stopping him for the rest of my life—so I agreed to his terms—I had to appear happily married to him for six months. Once I said yes, we were married before I could even think twice about it. In hindsight that may not have been the best decision to make, but it seemed right at the time. Xander, I'm so sorry, but I hope you understand and forgive me."

I sit a safe distance from her. "There's nothing to forgive. You did what you felt was right. I may not agree with it, but I understand. I get it, but that doesn't change anything right now. You're still tied to him—not me—and I can't stand it. I have to figure this out. You need to give me some time. I need to get a handle on how to proceed." Looking at her, I want nothing more than to thread my fingers through her hair and pull her mouth to mine. But I can't. I swallow the lump in my throat. I don't want to ask the question because there can be only one answer that will make us all right. Bending down, I cradle my head in my hands.

"Xander, talk to me," she begs.

"I just need to know one thing right now."

Her eyes search mine and she never lifts her gaze. "What do you want to know?"

I shift uncomfortably before I even ask the question. But I'm tired, beat, shot for the day, so I just ask, "Did you let him touch you while you were together on the bus?"

"No. No. No. No, Xander. I would never. Not after you and me. Not after what we finally had again. I don't want anyone else. Just you."

Suddenly she seems so far away. I stand up and close the distance between us. She smiles at me and I wrap her in my arms. We hold each other for a long time. I kiss her head over and over. "Come here," I whisper in her ear, and I sit down, pulling her onto my lap. I slump back against the couch. Relief floods me, and now that that burden has been lifted off my shoulders exhaustion overtakes me. "Ivy, I know we have a lot of talking to do, but I just can't right now. I'm just wiped out."

"It's okay. I understand. We can talk tomorrow."

I nod with a small smile and claim her mouth as mine. "Ivy," I breathe against her lips.

"Xander, take me to bed. Please."

"No, Ivy. Not while you're someone else's. I want you, but we need to figure all of this out." I stare into her perfect face and know I'll do anything to make her mine.

She pleads, "Please let me stay here."

I don't have to contemplate what to do—I lift her off my lap and stand up. "Come with me," I tell her and lead her to my room. She changes into one of my T-shirts and I get her settled in bed and kiss her on the forehead. "Good night, baby."

"Where are you going?" she asks.

"I'm going to sleep on the couch."

She clasps my hand. "No, stay with me. I just want to be near you. I need you."

"Ivy, don't make this more difficult. You're still married to him."

"We were married for three days."

"It doesn't matter. You're still married and until we can take care of that I think we should keep our distance."

"Please, just stay with me. Just lie down with me until I fall asleep."

Tired, worn, and so in love with her, I give in, against my better judgment. Seeing her lying on the bed, I feel like my willpower has already crumpled and being this close to her is crushing it. I bite down on my lip to keep from stripping her clothes off and fucking her right now. She pats the bed next to her and I give in and crawl in beside her. She rests her head on my chest and I wrap my arm around her. I squeeze her against me and she's right where she should be. I close my eyes and finally find peace.

The bathroom light illuminates the room a bit when I wake up to her fingers trailing down my stomach. I take a deep breath. "No, Ivy, I told you. Not while you're married to him. Don't make this any harder." Her touch is breaking me down. I have to find whatever strength I have left to deny the need to bury myself in her. I want to slide inside her and just let time slip away. But I'll hate myself if I do.

"Even if we can't be together, we can be close in a different way," she whispers.

Her fingers brush the side of my cheek. "Xander . . ." She shifts her body so she's lying on her back.

My pulse races as her hands drift down her own body.

"I'm going to touch myself and I want you to do the same," she says in a soft, quiet voice, and even in the barely lit room I can see her cheeks flush violently. I'm shocked by her words, but it's her actions that floor me. I sit up, but don't say a word. I'm mesmerized by the look on her face. She stands up and I watch her every move. My breathing is so accelerated I'm not sure if I can ever catch my breath. She lifts my T-shirt over her head and runs her fingers over her pink bra. She reaches behind her to undo it and she slowly lets the straps fall down her shoulders. I lick my lips at the sight. The bra falls from her body and her perfect breasts are all I see. I want so much to touch them, squeeze them, suck her nipples into small peaks, but I can't—I won't.

Instead I continue to watch her, captivated not only by her actions, by her beauty, but by her body language as well—by the way I can tell she wants me to know she loves me. She moves her hands to her panties and I hold my breath. Exhaling, barely able to speak, I ask in a hoarse, low voice, "Fuck, what are you doing?"

She reaches inside the lace and her back arches as her hand disappears. A low, slow groan slips from my lips. "I told you. I'm going to touch myself. I'm going to make my hands yours the way we talked about so many years ago," she says. "You can stay or you can go take a cold shower and come back after, but I need you, even if I have to imagine you're the one getting me off."

"Fuck, Ivy," is all I can say.

"Join me or don't," she whispers so sweetly and so full of seduction. I can feel the sound echoing in my cock.

When she hooks her thumbs into her matching pink lacey underwear, I chew my bottom lip. Fuck, do I look like a pervert if I do this? When I was eighteen it sounded hot—now I'm not so sure. But I want to do it in the worst way. No, what I want in the worst way is for her hands to be my hands, but I'm not giving in. I'm not fucking her when she's married to him—I won't be the other guy.

Her eyes close and she strokes and tweaks her nipples. I can see them harden and my cock grows harder with each passing second. The room is so quiet, I can hear my heart pounding in my ears. "Use your thumbs," I tell her, and her eyes open but remain hooded. She smiles and does as I tell her. I'm almost panting at the sight. "Lie down," I direct her. But she doesn't do it right away. Instead she slides her panties off and her whole body flushes everywhere. Once she's naked, then she lies on the bed. Her head rests on a stack of pillows and my body molds into the mattress. When she spreads her legs and lifts her hips, I want so badly to be the one to fill her that I have to close my eyes.

"Xander." She calls my name, and my eyes fly open just in time to see her hand cup her pussy. She runs her fingers through her folds and all my muscles clench with need. It's an urgency unlike I've ever felt before—it's a need for her.

Her hands continue to move. Fuck, she's really going to do this. I have two choices: enjoy it or leave and endure the torture of wishing I'd stayed. It's an easy choice. I unhook the button on my jeans and shove them down just enough to free my cock. I kick them the rest of the way off, then whisper, "Are you wet?" and she lets out a small whimper while nodding her head.

She presses the heel of her palm against her clit and then I watch as her fingers circle it over and over. I start stroking myself; concentrating on the fact that it's her hands, not mine, bringing me closer to exploding. I bite down on my lip and let my head tip back as I feel the intensity of her stare on me and the sounds of her rapid breathing. Once I start and I know she's watching I don't stop. I'm doing this for her, for me, for us. Stroking myself, I push my hips forward and thrust my cock into my closed fist.

"Are you okay?" I ask.

"More than okay."

"Talk to me. Tell me what you like me to do to you and then do it."

"I want your fingers inside me," she says shakily.

"Inside you where?" I ask, stroking myself faster. Pumping in and out, wishing it was her I was thrusting into.

"I can't say it," she says.

I grunt at the sound of her voice. The innocence in it and the thought that she's doing this with me almost sends me over the edge.

"Add another finger," I tell her. "Then with your other hand rub circles around your clit, massage it. Find the spot and when you do, pretend my tongue is on it."

"Oh, Xander," she moans and lifts her hips, pressing her heels into the mattress. Watching her fall apart makes me come hard with a shuddering release. After a few seconds, she collapses to the bed, and I do the same.

"I need to jump in the shower, alone," I tell her and she nods at me.

Just as I hit the threshold, she purrs, "Thank you."

I turn around. "You never have to thank me for that." I grin.

When I get out of the shower I throw a pair of sweatpants on and head back into the bedroom. She's back in my T-shirt, under the covers and half asleep. I climb in beside her and find her hand, lacing my fingers in hers and pulling her against me, my front to her back.

I hear her give a sigh of contentment.

I squeeze her tight.

"Good night, Xander. I love you," she says.

Leaning over, I whisper into her ear. "Good night, baby. I love you."

I allow myself a soft, sweet kiss to her cheek and slide my mouth to her lips before throwing my body back on the mattress. I close my eyes knowing she knows I'm right—us being together before her ties with him are severed will just muddy up the relationship that we've worked really hard at. But knowing this doesn't make any of it any easier.

Fingers creep across the pillow and push my hair away. I open my eyes to peer into her beautiful ones. "Good morning." I grin.

"Good morning." She smiles, inching closer to me.

I glance at the digits on the old clock radio on my nightstand and hop out of bed.

"Where are you going?" she calls softly, her sleepy eyes gleaming.

"I'm going to take a shower."

"No, don't go yet. Come back to bed," she says, rolling over onto her stomach and rising on her elbows.

"I can't. When I lie next to you like that, all I can think about is being inside you. I need to take care of the Damon situation."

She rolls back over and tosses the pillows off the bed. "I'm going to have to touch myself again. Aren't I?"

"Fuck, Ivy. Don't talk like that. The shower can't get cold enough for me already."

"You could let your crazy thoughts go and spend the day in bed with me."

"Ivy, stop. Please."

"Xander, his father is being buried today. My attorney said he'd take care of it as soon as he could."

I look at her. "Ivy, I'll take care of it much sooner. I can promise you that."

Looking out the car window, squinting against the brightness of the sun, I think I have to get my fucking car back. And what is Bell doing without a car anyway?

Turning the corner to my mother's house again, I resolve not to be so emotional. I need to know what she knows about Damon and his family.

I step in the back door again. This time Brigitte is in the kitchen. Her shoes clatter against the floor as she runs to greet me. "My Xander. My Xander," she says, hugging me.

"Brigitte. How are you?" I respond.

"Very well," she answers. "Your mother will be so pleased to see you."

I kiss her cheek and make my way through the house. I find my mother sitting in her leopard-print chair at the oversized desk in her office. This room is her domain. The carpet is the lightest of beiges. The walls are a deep red with three large shadow boxes strategically placed behind her desk. They are lit from within. One houses my first basketball jersey, another River's pint-sized first guitar, and the third one holds Bell's pink ballet slippers. Our most prized possessions that she just couldn't part with. Photos plaster the walls. On one wall, photos of the three of us kids are hung, and on another, photos of her parents and sister. There is one large photo of my mother and Jack on her desk.

She looks up at me from over her reading glasses. She opens her mouth to say something, but I've already crossed the room and planted a kiss on her cheek. "I love you, Mom," I tell her, because I know I don't let her know this often enough.

She stares at me, squeezing the hand I leave on her shoulder.

"I'm okay, Mom. I am. But I need some help."

"I know all about Ivy and Damon," she says.

"Mom, I need to understand him. What makes him tick?"

"Power and money." She looks at me and then picks up a letter on her desk. Running her finger over the edges, she hands it to me and says, "I think this is what you're looking for."

I take a shaky breath. My hand grips the envelope tightly for a few seconds. "What is it?"

"It's your inheritance."

My mind is running in circles. "What do you mean, my inheritance?"

"Josh Wolf was a good man. He never knew Dylan was your biological father until Damon blurted it out one night in the heat of anger. He came to see me afterward. You were around seven. I made him promise to leave you alone, and he did as I asked. His only request was that I send a photo of you once a year on your birthday with a few words about you written on the back. He wanted to know you even if he couldn't really know you."

She looks at me, studying my reaction before continuing. "This came this morning. It's a letter from Josh's attorney telling me it was Josh's wish for me to use my best judgment in determining if you are ready for this. Ironic that his son couldn't even let him die in peace. He had to tell the world about you before his father could. I'm really sorry for that."

"Mom, I told you I'm okay. And I am." I take the letter and have a seat. I open it and a number of pictures fall out onto the thick carpet. I bend to pick them up—they're of me, with words written on the back. A picture of me in a Poison T-shirt at eight years old with the words "Loves Ninja Turtles" on the back. Another of me with my new guitar, the words "Loves to jam" scripted on the reverse side. I pile them all together and sit back in my chair.

"I stopped sending them when you turned eighteen. At that point I figured you were a man and I couldn't stop him from telling you if he wanted. I thought about telling you so many times after Daddy's death because I was afraid Josh or Damon would, but I couldn't get the words out. Like I said, Josh was a good man and he respected my wishes."

I understand why she couldn't tell me. I don't have to ask. She knew how much I hated Nick then. And she didn't want me to hate him. She wanted me to love him like she loved me. She was right not to tell me because I'm not sure how I would have reacted back then. I shuffle the stuffed envelope between my hands until I decide to pull the letter out. The note itself is a short handwritten one . . .

I've watched you grow into a young man. I've watched you
take control of your life. I wish I could have been a part of your
life, but you have a family that loves you more than anything,
so it's only in my death that I'm able to tell you how proud of you

I am. By all rights what I'm giving you is yours. Take care and never forget who you are.

Love, Your Grandfather

I unfold the thickly folded pieces of paper and read the bottom line—he's left me half of Sheep Industries. I stare in disbelief. I stand up with a huge grin on my face.

"Xander, where are you going?" my mother asks.

I look at her. "To take back what's mine. Do you know where the funeral is taking place?"

The afternoon sun is warm on my face. I take a left turn and slam right into the congested part of the city. I quickly change lanes, wishing I had my own car because every time I accelerate, this little putt-putt car goes nowhere. Exiting the highway, I see a steady line of cars pulling into Evergreen Cemetery. The media are following right behind, but a police barricade turns them away. I turn on my headlights and slip into the funeral procession without a problem. Once I'm in, I ease off toward the east side of the cemetery with the processional cars heading south. I park and watch as men in suits and women in dresses spill from their automobiles. They're all engaged in their own conversations as they walk through the cemetery to Josh Wolf's final resting place. I watch the pallbearers pull the casket from the black hearse and an uneasiness creeps through me. I didn't know the man lying in the long rectangular box, but he was my grandfather and he left me half of his company.

I sit in the car and watch until everyone assembles for the burial ceremony. Once everyone has gathered, I see him. He stands front and center—smug, black suit, sunglasses, and a rose in his hand. Fuck, a rose. I laugh to myself, thinking *Roses are so cliché.* Getting out of the car, I lean against the door and just watch. The sound of his muffled voice courses through my body and lures me closer. From a distance I watch as people with tearstained faces throw roses on top of the casket. The ceremony is soon over and everyone seems to disperse quickly. I take the opportunity to blend into the crowd and make my way toward Damon. His bodyguard is a few feet away and I wonder why he has one—I thought he had hired the ninja for Ivy.

Weaving through the tombstones that will last far longer than the lives they mark, I near the gravesite. The casket is resting in the hollowed-out earth and Damon stands next to it talking to a silver-haired woman dabbing her eyes with a white handkerchief. As soon as I approach, the ninja is on me. Damon excuses himself and with a staggered gait that can only be for show, he confronts me. Through gritted teeth he says, "What are you doing here?"

"I want to talk to you." There's a calm control to my voice that I'm surprised by, considering I want to pound the shit out of him and bury him in the hole.

He's glaring at me through his sunglasses. His hate for me is so apparent. "This is my father's funeral. How dare you show up here!" His blood pressure must be out of control because his face turns beet red.

My eyes hold his. "Meet me in your office in one hour. Alone."

"Why would I do that?" He flinches, trying to find his composure.

"Because you and I," I tell him, anger coursing through my veins at an uncontrollable speed, "have business to discuss."

He works his jaw. "Go to hell."

Before walking away, I sneer and say, "That's where you'll be if you don't meet me."

Rush hour is barely beginning as I approach the city. With one hand I grip the wheel; with the other, I verify the address. I know where I'm going, but I want to be sure. Taking the next left, I pull into an underground garage but decide not to take the elevator leading straight into the building. I want to see it from the outside. I take my time entering the large black marble building with gilded doors. The number reads "1619" and the words above the door spell out SHEEP INDUSTRIES in big block letters. Entering the lobby of the building that is home to most of Sheep Industries' holdings—Little Red, Front Line Management, and House Records, I'm not surprised at what I see. The lobby is nothing less than posh. Several seating areas span the vast area in color variations on the building itself—golds, whites, and blacks. Plaques, certificates, and various recognitions cover an entire lobby wall. The reception desk in the middle of the jet-black marble floor is the home to three women, all with headphones hooked over their ears. I approach them with a strange trepidation—this building, these furnishings, the businesses under this roof are half mine. I'm connected to them by a bloodline I never knew flowed through my veins.

Approaching the oldest of the women, who's wearing a black blouse and has short gray hair, I smile and say, "Hi, I'm Xander Wilde, and I'm here to see Damon Wolf."

She almost cracks a smile but keeps her businesslike demeanor. "Yes, Mr. Wilde, he's expecting you. Take the elevator to the twelfth floor and his receptionist will show you the way from there."

"Thank you," I reply and then make my way to the elevator. My nerves start to pop and my legs seem to be shaking—what the hell am I nervous about? Stepping into the elevator, I can only think, *Keep your poker face on, mean what you say, and own it.* The doors close and I close my eyes. The doors open and I'm not even paying attention until the bell dings. I snap my eyes open and hustle out of there. Game on.

My fingertips tap the dark wood of the reception desk and a cute redheaded girl smiles at me. "You must be Mr. Wilde. Flo told me you were on your way to see Mr. Wolf. Let me show you in. I've already told him you had arrived."

She opens his door and holds it open for me to enter. I walk into his over-the-top office—a huge mahogany desk, floor-to-ceiling windows with a view, four large-screen TVs on a red wall, a sheepskin rug with a large leather sofa on top of it. All very designer chic, all very impersonal. He's standing at the bar, pouring himself what looks to be a scotch. He raises his glass. "I'd offer you one, but you won't be here long enough to drink it and I hate to waste hundred-year-old Balvenie."

Striding across the room in two seconds flat, I decide I've had enough of him. I snatch his shirt, but stay in complete control of my actions. I push him roughly, slamming his back up against the wall. "You disgust me." I stare hard into his cold brown eyes and repeat myself. "You disgust me . . ."

He struggles to free himself from my hold. "You're just like your father," he hisses.

I flinch and let go of him. "You're right. I am. Nick was a decent man. Nothing like you."

He gives a sad laugh. "You're wrong. He was weak. Easily manipulated. But what I meant is that you're like Dylan, my brother. He wasn't so easily fooled, but he was easily feathered. It's been fun watching you get so riled up. I could do it to my brother with a simple word, and I looked forward to perfecting my technique on you. It's a shame everything came to an end sooner than I had hoped, but now I can show you what a great uncle I can be. And I'll start by telling you how well I can take care of my wife."

He gives me a cocky grin and although I want to knock it off his face, I'm choking, shuddering at his audacity. I catch a glimpse of myself in the mirror behind his bar and rein my temper in. *For Ivy*, I keep reminding myself. *Keep your cool for your girl.*

"But before we discuss my wife, let me start by telling you a little bit about the man that owned this company—the great Josh Wolf, my father, your grandfather. He was a man who ruled with an iron fist, always logic and numbers, never any emotion. So getting Nick Wilde fired was easy. I knew all I had to do was show poor performance—no matter how much my father liked Nick, he was a businessman through and through and nothing but performance mattered in both his personal and professional life. Oh, wait—there was one tiny exception to that rule—Dylan, my brother, your father. The great Josh Wolf loved that boy in a way he loved no one else—Dylan could do no wrong. Ironic, since he was a user, a drug addict who couldn't keep clean. I always tried to help my brother. I lived with him, I took care of him, I picked him up off the floor numerous times. And how did he repay me—by dating the woman I worked so hard to get. I deserved your mother . . . he didn't. Do you know that when he overdosed, my father blamed me? Me!" he screams. "And then your mother—she went back to Nick."

I don't move. I'm caught in the web of the story he's spinning.

"My father never forgave me for Dylan's death and for years I had to prove to him I was worthy to be a part of his business. I had to make my way up the ladder and even after I landed Zeak Perry as a client, that wasn't enough. Only when he took ill did I earn my rightful place. And then in his death I learn the bastard didn't leave me the company—he left me half. I'd been under the impression my inheritance had a marriage clause. I never thought it had you in it. Never saw it coming. He didn't seem to care about you. The night I told him you existed he didn't even blink an eye. I remember it like it was yesterday. It was the anniversary of Dylan's death and he was putting my brother on a pedestal again. I couldn't take it, so I just blurted out that at least I didn't have an illegitimate son out there. You see, he knew about you for years and never did anything, never cared—not until he died anyway. How does that make you feel?"

I don't bother to tell him Josh Wolf sought out my mother—that he knew about me and that he did care. He cared enough to do as my mother wished. His knowing the facts wouldn't change anything. The man in front of me is vile, evil to the core, and I want to rid my life of him as soon as I can. I reach in my pocket and pull out the documents showing my fifty percent ownership.

"Ahhh . . . so you're not here to meet your dear old uncle. I was wondering when you'd get to the point. How long it would take. But finally!" Damon says, walking to his desk. "The reason you're here." He claps his hands together as if congratulating himself. "You're here for your half of the company. What do you think? Should we share desk space? Make decisions together? How do you think my dear old dad saw this going? Did he think we'd make an excellent team?"

I stare at him. He is so cold that I freeze. Falter. Words can't explain how this man makes me feel. Finally I find my voice. "Why did you go see my father the day he killed himself?" I ask the question I've wanted to know the answer to for so long, unconcerned as to what position that puts me in in his eyes—because I know without a doubt that when this meeting is over I will be the winner.

A smile slowly spreads across his face. He touches his fingertips to the desk and leans on it. "For you and your brother. Boy bands were popping up everywhere and I had one in my backyard. I wanted to represent you both, but Nick was adamant that he wasn't going to let me. I may have mentioned telling you about Dylan and then I gave him twenty-four hours to decide. But we both know how he responded to that."

"You're not why he killed himself. He wouldn't have wasted a single breath on you." I'm seething. I shoot across the office and slam his head down on the desk. I'm shaking so much it's making me dizzy. I inhale, then exhale and let go.

He stands up straight and removes his handkerchief to wipe the sweat from his brow. He levels his gaze at me. "How about we discuss whatever it is you so urgently had to call me away from my father's funeral for before I call Johnny in to escort you downstairs." He cocks his head and holds back a smile.

Shaking in my anger, I fist my hands at my sides. "I'm here for a trade."

"A trade. Really?"

I hold the paper in the air. "Ivy for this."

His eyes darken as realization dawns on him. "I didn't play you for the type to put love before business. I have to say I'm surprised. But it's not going to be that easy. There is so much I want from her before I can let her go."

Stepping forward, I stand directly in front of him. Eye to eye. I'm buried in hatred, anger, frustration—wanting so much to wrap my hands around his neck and strangle him. But I have what he wants and I'm pretty sure he wants it more than anything else. I casually walk around his desk and take a seat in one of the two chairs in front of it.

"Maybe you're more like me than my brother. Willing to make a deal," he says with a grin.

"We are nothing alike. Nothing!"

His eyes gleam and he sits in his desk chair, tenting his fingers. "You start. Tell me what you think you can offer me for that beautiful wife of mine."

Vibrating with disgust as the words roll off his tongue, I take a deep breath, knowing I have to keep myself under control. I put my poker face on.

He squeezes the arms of his expensive leather chair and with a clenched jaw asks, "Why are you here?"

I cock my head and suppress a bitter smile. "To tell you it's in your best interest to file annulment papers as soon as your shaky fingers can call your attorney."

His bottom lip trembles. "Why would I want to do that?"

No longer able to hold my smile back, I tell him, "Because for every minute that passes once I leave your office today that you don't, you might not like the results."

"Don't play games with me, boy."

"Oh, see, here's where you're wrong. I'm not a boy and I'm not playing any kind of game. I'm dead serious. I will sell one share of stock to the public for a dollar for every passing minute you don't pick up that phone. You figure it out—you're smart. In about a week, half of Sheep Industries will be worthless. Oh, and when you call your attorney, tell him to terminate your contract with Ivy, effective immediately." I'm quiet for the next few seconds as he sits there with an incredulous expression on his face. Then I look him straight in the eye and add, "And when our business is settled you can do what you want with the company. I'll stay silent. But hear this: if you ever threaten my family again I'll make it my life's mission to ensure you don't have a company left to run." Once I've said all I came to say, I get up and walk out the door—never looking back, never wanting to see his face again.

CHAPTER 19
Dig

One Month Later

There are no degrees or certificates hanging on the walls in the hallway of the Amazing Grace recording studio. Rather, only one wall gleams with gold and platinum records from Tyler Records and Amazing Grace, and that makes me smile. I want Ivy's up there one day. Jack and River have combined the recording aspect of their companies and now Amazing Grace handles production and Tyler Records takes care of distribution. It's clean and easy and gives Jack a little more free time.

I owed Jack a huge apology for the way I acted the night I found out about Dylan. Jack, in his typical fashion, blew it off as a small blip on the radar and graciously accepted my apology. I took that opportunity to talk to him about the guys, and he said that with the merger of the two companies there were a number of positions that needed to be filled. I wasn't sure how they'd react or if they'd want to work there—but they did. Garrett and Nix both decided to join River. It's been great to see the childhood friends who almost launched a band to stardom now helping other bands achieve their dream—pretty awesome if you think about it.

Finishing a call, I tuck my phone in my pocket. I know I have a huge grin on my face as I enter the control room. Ivy's eyes are closed at the microphone and everyone is silent. Leif is on the keyboard accompanying her. He is staying on with her. I'm not sure he will forever, but he seems happy—for now. Pressing the intercom, I say, "Move your music forward, Ivy. Don't overthink it." She peeks over at me and smiles that genuine smile that I love, and I add, "So we can get out of here." The ease with which we have fallen into sync with each other isn't hard to believe. We get each other and we get along—we did before and we do now. It's just that easy.

"I don't want to jinx it."

"Baby, no chance of that." I wink at her.

She's wearing a tight red blouse that buttons up the middle. It makes her tits look all the more perfect. She's also wearing a pair of jeans that when she turns around to cue the band, make her ass look amazing. Shifting on my feet, I think, *Fuck, when am I going to get this under control?*

She and Leif start playing, and concentrates on laying the tracks. He hasn't made a single sketchy comment to me since that first day in the studio and our ability to work together has been spot-on. This is the first album completely under Ivy's control and it's coming together faster than I ever expected. For the past month we've lived and breathed the studio day in and day out. Ivy already had the songs written. Dahlia's designing the cover art and Aerie is working on promoting the album. With any luck it will be ready to launch in six weeks.

Ivy has moved into my grandparents' place with me, but I want us to have a place that we can call our own. We've started looking at houses in my mother's and River's neighborhoods and she found one she loves. It's a restored Mediterranean with a spectacular view of the city. It was built in 1926 for a silent film legend. Ivy thinks it's a work of art. I was about to buy it when fate stepped in and the people who swooped in and bought it out from under us told me about the house they were selling. I bought it immediately without telling Ivy because I know she's going to love it. It will be weird moving out of the last place my grandparents lived, but I know they're smiling over my decision about where to move—a house not only for kids but for grandkids too.

Having Ivy near me, waking up next to her, I've never been happier in my life. I didn't know someone could be this happy. I'm even thinking about my own family now, something I haven't done in a long time. And my dreams, or my nightmares—I haven't had a single one since going to the cemetery and visiting my father's grave. I've accepted him for who he was—both his strengths and his weaknesses. I may never understand why he chose to take his own life, but I no longer hate him for it—in the end he did choose us, his family, over music.

I'm in a hurry to wrap up the day, so I call it much earlier than usual. Everyone else leaves and Ivy and I are the last ones at the studio. She packs her guitar in its case and props it against the wall, then meets me outside. Her eyes glitter. "Why are you in such a rush?" she asks.

I pull her out into the alleyway by one hand. The air is cool and there's a light breeze that blows her hair across her face. I push it aside. "I have something to tell you. . . ."

"What?" she asks, full of excitement.

Lifting her high in the air, I turn her around in slow circles.

"What?" She squirms, pressing herself against my waist and finally I look forward to exploring the incredible attraction that's been building between us.

"It's final," I whisper, my voice hoarse as I trail my tongue down her neck. She quickly wraps her legs around me and I know she can feel how excited I am.

With wide eyes she asks, "The annulment?"

I nod with a huge-ass smile on my face.

In a low, soft voice she cries, "I'm so happy right now!"

"Me too, baby. Me too."

Damon had moved quickly to get the annulment. I was in constant contact with the attorneys. I didn't want Ivy stressing over any of it. Damon used his connections to get it fast-tracked, and I kept my word—I didn't sell a single share and I gave all exercising rights to him. I'll stay part of the company, but as a silent partner. It was a quick and easy transaction and I never want to see his face again.

My red Corvette is only a few feet away, but I can't resist stopping and pushing her up against the wall. "I've missed this so fucking much." My lips find hers and after nearly a month, I can actually kiss her the way I want to. She's finally free and she's all mine. I gently bite down on her lower lip before sucking on it. She lets out a soft moan and I seal my mouth to hers. She presses her lips against mine with equal force. Her hands tangle in my hair and I hold her like I've never held her—in a way that tells her I'm never going to let her go. She bites on my tongue and then flutters hers against the tip of mine . . . driving me insane.

I pull back. "Let's go home," I growl.

"No," she purrs. "It's too far away."

"Fuck, Ivy, don't do that," I tell her as she takes my hands and presses them against her breasts. She kisses my chin, my neck, and slides her tongue over to my ear. I slip my hands up the front of her shirt, which has come untucked, and feel her soft skin. It electrifies me. It's been a month with no actual physical contact. We've imagined each other's hands on our bodies, told each other what we want to do to each other, talked each other through our deepest desires, but now we no longer have to use our own hands and bodies to make love to each other. Running my mouth down her neck, I undo each button with my teeth. When I get to the last one I pull her shirt open and quickly lift her bra. The cool air makes her nipples harden and when I close my mouth around one, fondling the other between my fingers, she moans loudly.

I look around and pull her shirt together. "Come with me."

"Why did you stop?" she questions softly.

"Because I want to fuck you now—and not in the alley."

"Oh." She giggles and follows me as I stride quickly back to the recording studio, fumbling for my keys.

We stumble up the three steps and our lips break apart only so I can unlock the heavy metal door. Once we are on the other side of it, I slam her against the door and run my hands all over her body. I'm hungry for her, starving. I walk us backward toward the studio. "Take your bra off," I growl, knowing that unhooking it and trying to navigate backward to the studio at the same time would be nearly impossible with how turned on I am. My hands find her back, her ass, and finally her freed breasts. My mouth doesn't leave hers even though I want to suck on each nipple and hear her moan. I can't tear my lips from hers. I feel every touch we made to ourselves over the last month penetrating our kisses. My body's singing—and it's alive. I can't wait for the feel of her smooth skin as her fingers wrap around my cock.

The backs of my knees hit the sofa in the recording studio and I fall to it. She lands on top of me. I finally break the connection our lips were fervent to hold. Pulling back, I stare at her gorgeous naked tits. I run my hands up and down her chest, holding each breast, squeezing it, pinching the nipple between my fingers. Bending toward her, I nuzzle one before licking and pulling it in, sucking on it. She arches her back and my hands move to the front of her jeans. My pulse is racing. She tries to pull my shirt over my head, but I want her so badly, I can't tear my hands from her. Finally I manage, "Stand up and take your pants off," and then I pull my own shirt over my head.

She rises and easily slides her jeans down her legs. My hands find the lace of her panties, ripping them off before she even lifts her feet to kick off her shoes. I pull her closer to me. She stands before me completely stunning and again I can't help but think, *She's all mine.* My mouth goes slack as I see her hooded eyes staring down at me. I slip one finger inside her, then another, and then just one more. Stretching her, fucking her with my fingers. Her body starts to shake and as she cries out in pleasure, I remove my fingers and replace them with my mouth. Her hands grip my shoulders tightly.

"Xander!" she screams when I find her clit with first my lips, then my tongue. I pull her closer to me. I don't just want to eat her . . . I want to devour her. Her body trembles and she calls out my name louder and louder with each passing second. She tries to pull away, but I hold her tight. "Just feel it baby. Just feel it," I manage, stopping to blow on the small nub that I plan to devour again in an instant.

Her grip tightens and she cries out, "I love you!" Those words have my cock throbbing to be inside her. I pull away and stand up. She's wobbly and holds on to me. I tear out of my boots and jeans and stand fully ready in front of her. Her fingers wrap around my hard cock and the feeling is so unlike my own hand that I feel myself start to tremble.

I take a few minutes to admire her. Her smooth, tan skin, her seductive, stormy eyes, the cute sprinkling of freckles across her nose, her lush lips, and those breasts—all Ivy, all things I will never get enough of.

"Did you like that, baby?" I ask her.

"I like it," she moans as I take my cock and rub it against her entrance.

"Do you like this?" I ask, running my tongue around the shell of her ear.

"Yes," she cries out as I place my knee between her legs and gently fold her onto the sofa.

I hover over her and she pulls my face to hers. She gently traces my mouth with her soft lips and I nip at her finger. She giggles only for a moment before taking my cock in her hand and guiding it to her. She rubs my tip over her clit and I feel like I'm going to explode if I don't get inside her this very minute, but the look on her face is so full of lust, I grip the back of the sofa and just fall into her. She takes her other hand and grabs me, cupping and tugging alternately while she continues to rub the tip of my cock over her wet pussy.

"That is so fucking hot," I tell her, but when her fingers trail up my shaft, I can't take it anymore and I thrust into her. Both of us yell out in ecstasy and I don't wait another minute before pounding into her over and over. Thrust for thrust, she meets each and every one. My cock pulses and I pump my hips into her. I grip her shoulders, holding on, trying to go deeper, wanting to be as far into her as I can. Everything about her is so sweet. The feeling of being buried deep inside her is one I never want to lose. A groan stutters out of me as I try to hold on for her, but I can't. Letting go, I stop kissing her and look at her angelic face.

She moans, "Oh God," and I can tell an orgasm is rocketing through her, just as powerful as the one owning me right now. All I want to do is hold on to her for dear life because I'm pretty sure I'm going to die from the unbelievable pleasure I'm basking in. We both come in unison. Fuck, it feels so good—I can't hear, my vision's a little hazy, and there's a gentle ache radiating from all parts of my cock—all reminders of the intensity we just shared.

After a few minutes, when I'm able to move, I pull her to my chest. She smiles against my neck and rests her head on my shoulder. I murmur in her hair, "That felt so good."

She lifts her head and her beautiful eyes dance in the light. "I'm so happy."

I smile at her. "Me too. Ready to go home to our bed?"

Her smile fades and I lift her chin and see a tear dripping down her cheek. "Hey, what's wrong, baby?"

"Nothing's wrong. Just the way you said *home*—it couldn't be more right." Her smile reappears and she says, "Xander, please take me home now."

God, again I have to swallow a surge of emotion from the sight of the tear on her cheek and hearing those words. I kiss her tear away and say, "There's nothing I want more."

We head for my car again and this time, for some reason, that stupid poem from so long ago pops in my head, but this time I know the words—"If you love someone, set them free. If they come back, they're yours."

CHAPTER 20
You

Ivy, Three Months Later

The day has arrived. All the hard work and energy and it's finally ready to share. And it's all because of him. He shifts to his feet before me and the mere sight of him makes my eyelashes flutter, my throat burn, and my heart pound. He hasn't shaved and his hair falls forward as he moves, making him look impossibly sexy. The hint of stubble I'm staring at has just rubbed against the sensitive skin of my face, my stomach, and everywhere else, but the yearning I feel for him is raging—I still want more.

He pulls up his pants and zips them, standing before me bare-chested—he looks hotter than sin. He catches my stare and before he buttons them he says, "I've just got a few things to pick up while you get ready. I'll shower when I get back. Do you need anything?"

I lick my lips at the sight of the way his pants hang low on his hips, and I take in the perfection of his chest, the muscles in his arms, the line of his collarbone up to his neck. The jaw I'm desperate to kiss, to taste. I can almost feel my hands sliding inside those jeans and I suck in a deep breath as I imagine the feel of his warm, thick cock—the one I just felt. My heart skips a beat at the thought and when I look at him to answer, I'm not smiling. I don't want him to leave and I can do something about it. A low purr escapes my throat and his mouth quirks up at the corners in response.

I rip the T-shirt off that I just slipped on and sashay across the room. I feel like a lion after her prey. His eyes search mine, and the tone of that hissing noise he makes that just sounds like sex as he watches me makes my pussy clench. I approach him without an ounce of hesitation. "Stay. Take a shower with me. And I promise I'll make it worth your while." I feel a slow blush creep up my throat but ignore it and concentrate instead on tracing each letter of his tattoo. The one he had inked on his skin to keep me close to him. His body reacts to my tender touch and I grin. When I finish, I skim my fingers up his body and then bury my hands in his hair. His fingers grip my hips, but he stands still. I kiss his jaw, then his mouth. My tongue seeks what my body just had and we lose each other in our kiss.

Minutes later he cups my face and says, "Ivy, I have things to do before we leave. What are you doing?" He drops his head back as I do what I imagined doing just a few seconds ago. I push my hands into the front of his pants and feel the pulsing and throbbing of his already thick penis.

"I want you to fuck me again. I want to suck on your cock. Please." My animalistic approach, the fierceness I felt before his body was touching mine, is ruined by the shakiness of my voice and my use of the word *please*. But he doesn't seem to care.

"Fuck, Ivy," he growls. Then he unzips his jeans and in one quick motion shoves them down, freeing his erection. Knowing he has just come inside me not more than fifteen minutes ago and he is already this turned on makes my clit throb. He shakes his head and just grins at me, then leads me to the bathroom. Without a word he turns the shower on and pulls me in.

The warm water hits us both and I push up against him, licking a few drops off his chest as they make their way down to the same place my hands are headed.

"You want me to wash you?" he asks, burying his face into my neck so I can feel his stubble.

I nod. He pours the body wash into his palm and I let my arms fall to my sides as his fingers work lather all over me. His hands move lower and I melt against the cold tile of the shower wall when his fingertips graze my clit. His hands circle and I push my hips forward, moaning in delight.

"You want my fingers in your pussy?" he asks, tracing his tongue around his lips, the lips I want on my body. He uses it to draw a line down my throat to my breasts, where he licks away the drops of water that fall on them.

I nod my head again and the water pelts down against my skin.

"Tell me, Ivy. Use words. I can't see your response," he says as his mouth sucks on my nipple.

I drop my head back and my hair, having grown longer, touches the space between my shoulder blades. "Yes. I always want your mouth on my pussy, your tongue over my clit," I tell him and gasp when his lips descend farther down my body.

He stops and I peek down at him with a look of urgency. "What?" he asks.

I shake my head. "Nothing." I'm panting now.

He climbs up my body and his hard muscles touch my skin, sending shivers down my spine.

"What?" He says the word with such tenderness I feel silly mentioning it.

"Tell me," he says more forcefully and pushes the wet hair from my face.

I close my eyes and just say it. "I want you in my mouth."

He laughs, and it's not a laugh that upsets me at all . . . it's a laugh that makes me laugh too, but our laughter is laced with desire. Our breathing picks up before we stop and I can see the rapid rise and fall of his chest. His fingers twist in my hair and he leans down to kiss me. As he kisses my neck, the water splashes between us like rain. His lips find mine as his fingers release my hair and clutch my head. He turns us around so his back is against the sleek tile, and I smile. Making my way down his lean body, I take my time. I trace the lines of each muscle with my tongue. My mouth eases onto his length and my hand grips his base. He moans at first contact and it's the sexiest sound I've ever heard. He pushes his hips up and I take him all in. I love this side of him—the way he lets go and just feels the pleasure. As I glide my tongue up his length and over his head, my hold loosens as my lips slide farther down. I repeat this movement over and over at a steady pace, but when he makes that same noise again, I move faster and suck harder. Xander takes a long, slow breath and then pulls me up to him.

He turns us back around . . . he's taking control again and I love it. The shower door has turned steamy and the water mists all around us. His hands slide up my shoulders and then down my arms until he reaches my hands. "You're so gorgeous," he says breathlessly into my ear. Water slices down his chest and when he presses his hard cock against me, excitement runs through my body. He lets go of my hands and positions himself at my center. Looking at him, the water on his skin, the way just a few wisps of his dark hair curl onto his forehead, I can't wait another minute to have him. I lean in and my nipples brush against his chest as I thrust my tongue into his mouth, kissing him hard for a long time. Sliding my lips to his ear, I whisper, "I want you," and then I kiss his mouth, his jaw, his shoulder. "So much." I see him quiver. I love how affected he is by my touch. He finally strokes his finger inside me.

"I'm going to take you now," he growls.

I close my eyes and the water sprays against my face. Resting my forehead on his shoulder as he strokes inside me, I lose all thoughts.

"Don't come yet," he whispers and I open my eyes. He quickly presses me back against the tile and pushes my feet apart. He kisses my neck, sucks on my nipple, and I have to clutch his muscular back to hold on. "Don't come," he growls again. "I want to be inside you when you come."

Goose bumps cover my body as I try to hold on—the water, him, it's all too much. I'm still wrapped up in the pleasure of him when he slides into me without warning. I suck in a breath and enjoy his hard cock as he thrusts into me. He moves at a slow pace, much slower than earlier today.

Standing on my tiptoes, I run my fingers through his hair. Then I clutch the muscles of his arms with my hands, pushing myself farther back against the cool marble wall of the shower so he can press farther into me. When I lift my chin I notice the look on his face. That combined with the water dripping in small, even streams from his head to his cheek to his shoulder to where my hands are grasping, squeezing, as he moves in and out, is the most erotic thing I've ever seen. When I drop from my toes, his cock goes even deeper inside me. I moan in pleasure at the feeling and he seems to lose complete control—his hooded eyes and the look on his face is one of pure pleasure.

I scream, "Oh God, Xander," as my back bows and my inside muscles tighten around him.

"Do that again," he pants, his hot breath caressing my ear.

I do it again and another peak rolls through me before the first one's even ended. Then I do it again, and this time the overwhelming sensation takes us both, making me feel like the two of us have become one.

"Fuck, Ivy," he mutters. Resting his head against mine, he manages, "Put your arms around my neck."

When I do he buries himself in me and the pleasure is pure, raw, full of energy. His mouth slams to mine as we experience something that is beyond anything I've ever felt and I hope beyond anything he has ever felt as well. My heart stills, my breathing stops, and I let this feeling consume me. Let him own me with everything I have and everything he has. His body goes limp against my already boneless one and together we stand under the shower trying to recover from something I want to feel over and over.

I cling to him for support and he buries his head in my neck. After a while he lifts my chin. "I've never felt anything like that," he tells me, his mouth lifting slightly as his hooded gaze tells me how much he loves me.

"Neither have I," I manage, relishing the feeling of his stubbled jaw against my skin.

He grins and then runs his fingers through my hair as his lips dance over mine.

I trace the rim of his collarbone, then wrap my arms around him as the water cascades over us. "I love you so much."

He sighs contentedly and then whispers against my lips, "I've always loved you," and his words echo with happiness through me because I know he has.

An hour later it's almost time to leave. Soft music plays from the bedroom and when I glance up from the vanity, my heart beats that familiar thumping. Xander's standing there with one shoulder propped against the wall, just watching me. He can say so much with just a look—the quirk of his mouth and the rise of his brow make my body flush all over.

"Will you zip my dress?" I ask him, trying not to drool at how incredibly hot he looks in his suit, with no tie, of course. Just like roses, he thinks wearing a tie with a suit is too expected. I turn around as he enters. Damp towels are on the floor from our shower, my makeup is scattered across the vanity, and my dress hangs on the hook behind the door.

Xander loves the dark blue sapphire satin because he says it matches my eyes. It's short, sleeveless, and just about backless. First, letting his fingertips skim across my skin, he ties the cord that spans my back and holds the dress in place, and I shiver. He moves to the zipper at my side and with his finger he trails a line from my hip to under my arm. He takes his time zipping it and when he's done he smooths the zipper with his palm and I can barely keep myself upright.

He's quiet. Not saying a word. I turn around to face him and he's pressing his fist into his mouth.

"You said you loved it?"

"Fuck, Ivy, it's sexy as hell," he growls.

I smile and blush at the same time.

"But don't you think there's a little too much skin showing in the back?" he asks.

This actually makes me laugh. I used to think he didn't want me to show off my body because he didn't like other guys to see it. But now I think I was wrong—it's because him seeing so much skin drives him wild, and I love that! I step close to him. "I think it's the perfect amount of skin," I whisper hotly against his lips.

He catches my mouth and kisses me. "Yeah, for roving hands who want to feel you in places where they shouldn't be," he breathes, sliding a hand into the side of my dress and squeezing my breast.

Smiling, I say, "Trust me, you're the only one thinking that way."

I turn around and throw him a wink, but before I can move away his hands are on my hips and when I rock back against him, I can feel the heat and hardness of his cock beneath the layers of fabric. He mumbles something against my skin that sounds like, "Fuck, you'd think I was fourteen again," but I don't ask why because the softness of his mouth in my ear and the feel of his breath against my cheek is all I care about. He turns me around and anchors his hips to mine. He slips his arms around my waist and I place mine around his neck. His feet start to move in a slow circle—he's dancing with me in the bathroom. I strain to hear the lyrics to the song playing as his fingers trace the exposed bumps of my spine. He draws me closer and I can smell his cologne—a mix of the sea, the sun, the earth, and a Mediterranean breeze. I breathe him in and become intoxicated by his scent.

"You smell so good," I murmur in his ear.

"You like it? I wore it for you."

"Mmm-hmmm . . ."

My head fits perfectly on his shoulder and I find all the comfort I need for the night ahead right here in him. His hands slide up the center of my back—the skin against skin contact makes me forget any apprehension I'm feeling. He suddenly dips me and pulls me back to him. "We have to go," he murmurs. But instead of letting me go, he kisses me again.

"We have to go," I breathe around his lips. I can feel his sexy smile against my mouth, but I somehow manage to break free and make my way back over to the vanity on shaky legs. I pick up my earrings—the sapphires that dangle with stars at the bottom. He grins at me as I put them in both ears. We stare at each other and I'm sure we're both remembering the woman who gave me her earrings because she just knew I was going to be a star.

I'm still tingling when we get in the car. He hits the gas and takes off, but instead of taking a right to head toward the studio he takes a left. "Where are you going?"

"I'm sorry, baby. I have one stop I have to make before the party."

About thirty seconds elapse and he pulls over. "Oh, I forgot one thing." He grins as he pulls out the piece of fabric from Garrett's yoga swing that he used as a blindfold when he took me to Niagara Falls. "You have to wear this."

I look at him in surprise. "Why? I can't see where you have to stop along the way?"

"Just turn around," he tells me with a smirk, and I do. He ties the fabric around my head and kisses my hair.

I'm not sure how much time passes before he parks the car and turns the ignition off. I rest my hand on the door handle and he says, "Wait for me."

He quickly opens my door and guides me out. I have no idea where we're going. Soon I hear the click of a lock and we seem to be inside somewhere, but then I hear another click and we're back outside. When I hear another lock open, I ask, "Xander, where are we?"

"We're home, baby," he says, and his deep, husky voice resonates against my skin. He quickly removes my blindfold and opens the ornate etched-glass door in front of us. I stand in shock as my eyes roam the very familiar room. The built-in window seat, ceiling fan, light blue walls, and bamboo wooden floor are still the same. It looks just like it did the very last time I set foot in it, twelve years ago, except that the countertops seem to have been upgraded to granite and track lighting now glows from the ceiling. But even with the minor changes there's no mistaking this place he just called home.

"Home!" I cry, turning around to throw my arms around him. "You bought your grandparents' old house? But how?" I ask.

His eyes meet mine and he doesn't answer. Instead he drops to one knee, and I swear the butterflies actually flutter out of my stomach. My heart pounds and I'm a little nervous—no, a lot nervous. Xander's eyes take in every inch of me, but my full attention stays locked on his tranquil hazel eyes. His gaze skims over my dress to the sapphires that never leave my ears, and then it settles on my eyes. In that moment I have no doubts about this man, my life, our life. He pulls a velvet box from his pocket and holds it out. My pulse races as he slowly lifts the lid. What I see in the velvet cushion brings tears to my eyes. The ring flashing so brilliantly there is the ring that his father gave his mother. He's offering it to me—he wants me to be his wife. It's simple and perfect and I always thought it was the most absolutely beautiful ring I'd ever seen.

"Will you marry me, Ivy Taylor?" he asks with the slow and easy smile that makes my heart melt every time.

"Yes!" I cry without a second thought, and drop to my knees next to him before he can even take the ring out of the box. I cradle his face in the palms of my hands and tears stream down my cheeks. "Yes, I will marry you," I whisper. Then I kiss him. I kiss my prince charming with a long kiss that is full of meaning. I don't want to ever stop kissing him. When I lean back to catch my breath I ask, "You bought your grandparents' old house for us? How?"

"Luck, fate, destiny." He shrugs. "Are you happy?"

"Yes!" I say. "Yes, yes, yes!"

His smile is as wide as mine, I'm sure. He nibbles my lip one more time and pulls me to my knees. We kneel together and hold each other and before we stand up he says, "Give me your hand."

I extend my left hand and as he slides the large pear-shaped diamond on my finger, my other hand flies to my mouth. It's perfect. The brilliance of the diamond is just so stunning, I'm completely surprised and so overwhelmed. My tears are still flowing and he softly says, "Stop crying. You're not supposed to be crying." His eyes are gleaming and he kisses my fingers so gently I feel like I'm floating on a cloud. I just want to hold him, smell him, feel him—forever.

We walk into the building where the unveiling of my new album, *My Mended Heart*, is taking place. Both of us are literally beaming. We've decided not to mention our engagement until the end of the evening, so I turn my ring backward for now. We're a little late, but not much, and surprisingly Xander hasn't looked at his watch or even mentioned it. His hand is on the small of my back as we enter the gala, and before we greet everyone I turn to him and mouth *I love you*. This is the album I always wanted to put out but never had the courage to—until he came back into my life. I allow myself to just stare at him—he's the most handsome man I've ever seen.

I breathe in the scent of the flowers that fill the room and then shift my gaze to admire the glimmer of light from the crystal chandeliers.

The room looks as magical as the night already has been. Amazing Grace has been transformed from a concrete hangar into a glittering nightclub. With six crystal chandeliers, dozens of round tables, and more than a hundred vases of purple dahlias and, of course, a splash of ivy, compliments of Xander, this get-together feels more like a welcoming party than a release party.

Bell planned the whole event. I would have thought she'd have been here for hours, but she actually walked in right before we did. Jack and Charlotte dropped her off and she got out of their car with a large bag hanging from her shoulder. We tried to catch up with her, but she was off fluttering around and making sounds that seemed incomprehensible. Xander had just shrugged his shoulders. But his cool facade seems to have evaporated now.

As we make our way farther into the room, his brow creases and I can tell he's nervous. I bite the inside of my cheek, wondering if I should feel more nervous than I do. I decide to try to calm him instead of joining him in the nerves. "It's the calm before the chaos," I tell him, as he stands next to me gripping my hand tightly. Squeezing his fingers, I look around at all the people who are here for me and realize I may have misspoken about the calm. The mood in the room is anything but sedate. It's full of such real positive energy that no forced smiles are necessary.

My stomach flutters when he kisses my forehead. "You're going to be great. Don't let my sorry-ass nerves get to you."

Wrapping my arms around his neck, I pull him to me. "Thank you." Then I seal my mouth to his and kiss him in a way that lets him know that with him by my side I know I'll be fine. Pulling away, we smile at each other. We have both been lavishing these smiles on each other. Smiles that make the world seem all the more perfect. And it is. His thumb traces my lips.

Over Xander's shoulder, I catch sight of his brother. A minute later a chin rests on his shoulder and arms wrap around his waist. He too smiles. It's contagious. I motion toward the door. "There's River and Dahlia. Let's go say hi."

Dahlia looks amazing. She's wearing a pewter-colored halter dress with a chain neck and a large brooch at the center of the deep V. River looks pretty good himself in a suit much like Xander's, and he as well has opted for no tie. He and Dahlia are fashionably late as always, but since today is their one-year anniversary I think it's perfectly acceptable. Their tardiness seems to always drive Xander crazy, and River seems to get a kick out of it every time. Over the past few weeks, Xander has ended up laughing along with us. I actually find his reaction pretty funny myself because for someone so much in control all the time, he seems to be letting some of his barriers down.

Xander and Dahlia have a bond that warms my heart. It seems that when Xander first met Dahlia he acted like a real ass. I'm glad to see that they've moved past their issues, especially since the day he met her was the day I announced my engagement to Damon. He told me he was pretty drunk by the time they were introduced.

"Xander. Ivy," River says in such a drawn-out way that it clues me in that he knows something. Dahlia kisses River's cheek before circling to stand next to him. River searches Xander, and if I hadn't been looking, I would never have noticed the slight nod Xander gives him. River grabs Xander around the neck and pulls him forward, and with a not so subtle snicker, he says, "A phone call would have been nice."

Xander's eyes grow bright with laughter. "Right, bro. Sorry. I'll remember next time."

River lets him go. "That's better."

Xander slants him a look. "If that's not a spade calling a spade."

Before River can counter Dahlia swoops in. "Congratulations," she cries, kissing me and then Xander in turn as she wraps an arm around each of us, pulling us together for a group hug.

River ducks under Dahlia's arm and pops up in the middle. He kisses her on the lips. "Don't forget me."

Dahlia releases us just as Garrett comes over. "Awww . . . I missed out on the hugs and kisses. What, because we all work together now, I get shafted?"

Laughing at him, I have to say he is the funniest person I know. He seems to love his new job, and I think he may have even gone on a date or two with Ena. He nods hello to each of us and then in true guy fashion grabs River by the collar and jerks him backward. "You're late, dick. Come on," he quips. Then he starts to shake his hips and sing, "LA, let's get this party started!" He sounds so much like B. Taylor, I actually want to hear him sing the whole song.

Dahlia and I giggle as Xander shakes his head and we all watch as River gets dragged away and pulled onstage for a jam session with the guys. They're all up there—River, Leif, Nix, Garrett, and even Zane. The crowd rushes the dance floor and throws hands in the air, dancing to a cover of "Hands All Over." I have to laugh because I know how much Dahlia loves Maroon 5. I also know how much River dislikes them. But he must have planned this for her, for their anniversary.

"Excuse me," she says, and moves toward the stage. Mesmerized, she watches them, her hands clasped near her heart. She grins ear to ear as River sings to her—the performance seems to make her very happy.

Bell finds me in the midst of all the excitement. She too looks beautiful. She's so petite, but her vibrant emerald eyes and long coppery brown hair make her look like a spitfire. She's wearing a green strapless romper with metallic flowers on it, and wisps of thin gold chains adorn her neck—she's stunning and it looks like she's also a little sunburned. The red contrast against the silky dark fabric makes her rosy all over. Dragging me over to the photo booth she rented, she has me posing in it for at least twenty different pictures. Then she runs off to use them to decorate the tables so everyone knows who I am—I can only laugh at that.

I spot Xander across the room and wave him over to drag him in with me. I try to get him to make playful faces and whenever I whisper something dirty in his ear, he does. These pictures are for me, not for the tables. When we step out of the booth, I'm a little flushed myself.

Sashaying up to us, Aerie greets us in an extremely bubbly manner despite looking very businesslike—her hair is in a bun and she's wearing a purple pantsuit with pumps, but surprisingly it's low-cut and shows a hint of cleavage. We've spent a great deal of time together since I came back to LA. We get along so well. She's even shown me some of her uncle's music collection. She hugs me and cascades kisses on each cheek, then does the same to Xander, who looks utterly shocked at her exuberant display of affection.

"Where's Jagger?" he asks her.

She gestures toward the makeshift bar with her wineglass. "Oh, Jack caught him on our way in and they're huddled somewhere."

Xander's gaze follows mine across the room. They're leaning against the bar with their heads together, each holding a glass of beer. Xander crosses his arms and lifts his brow. "What's going on?"

Aerie giggles. "Jack wants Jagger to help him move *No Led Zeppelin*'s sound track release date up."

"But it hasn't finished filming yet, has it?" I ask.

She shrugs. "No, but Jack's pushing for an early sound track release around Christmas and then a rerelease when *No Led Zeppelin* hits theaters."

Xander nods. "Makes sense."

"Yes, it's a brilliant idea, but Jagger is still working on perfecting most of the songs," Aerie says.

"Get River to help him," Xander suggests.

"They've been coconspiring, but I think they might be spending more time playing around than actually focusing," Aerie replies, rolling her eyes.

Xander chuckles. "Sounds like I'll need to pay them a visit."

Now I roll my eyes.

Aerie snatches the sleeve of photos I have in my hand. "Nice," she says with a smirk. "I like the one of Xander licking your neck."

He snags the photo strips from her and she laughs.

"Hey, do you think I can talk to you a minute?" Aerie asks Xander.

"Sure," he says.

"There's something I think you should know before it's announced," she adds, slipping back into business mode. Then she looks at me and says, "And you and I will catch up later. And don't forget lunch tomorrow!"

I nod my head. She's such a type A personality. "I'm going to get another drink. I'll leave you two to talk."

As I walk away, I feel a pair of hands grip my waist. "You forgot something," Xander's deep voice says into my ear.

I turn my head and feel the tickle of his whiskers against my skin. "What?" I purr.

He gently pulls my mouth to his, and a soft brush of our lips has me tingling all the way to my toes. He runs his cheek down my neck and groans wickedly in my ear before releasing me. And for some reason, this tiny display of affection seems so much more intimate than just a simple goodbye kiss—it has me flushing.

I can feel myself smoldering as he turns back toward Aerie. I stand there and watch him as the two of them engage in conversation. When I snort to myself and break out of my lovesick trance, I continue my journey toward the bar just as Phoebe turns the corner in a knockout champagne-colored gown. She sees me instantly and waves, motioning me over. I look her up and down. She's dressed so elegantly, she even takes my breath away.

"You look beautiful." I say.

She's grinning from ear to ear. "Can I tell you something?" she asks, practically jumping out of her heels.

"Of course. You know that."

"Nix and I got married today."

"What?" I scream. I can't believe they got married on the same day I got engaged. I'm so happy for her and Nix. It's all so exciting and I want to share my news, but Xander and I agreed to let this night be about the album.

"It's crazy, I know. We haven't known each other that long, but it seemed like the right time. Nix loves his new job and I love my new teaching position. We decided what better way to start our new lives."

"Congratulations, Phoebe! I'm so happy for you. And love doesn't have a meter, so don't worry about how long you've known each other."

"Thanks, Ivy." She's beaming.

"Come on. Let's find some champagne to celebrate."

The night has just begun and I already feel like a princess—but not the molded pop princess that catapulted my career. This time I'm my own person, doing what I've always wanted to do—singing about life as I know it and putting my own soulful twist on it.

With Xander at my side, I finally went to see my mother last week. Before that I hadn't actually seen her in years. I've supported her and my sisters but had no contact with them. I'm not sure where my relationship with her will go. She told Damon about Xander and me and God knows what else—I don't trust her, but she is my mother. In the end we worked out an arrangement giving her some time to work out her finances, but I told her I can no longer be her primary source of income. I'll continue to support my sisters, but that's it. Surprisingly, she agreed.

Charlotte is talking to Dahlia and I start to make my way over to them. Dahlia and I have spent a lot of time together. We talked about her miscarriage and she told me she and River are taking it one day at a time. The pregnancy was unplanned, and right now they want to enjoy each other and not stress about getting pregnant again. I was so happy to hear that, because so many couples go down that road.

They are so happy together, and I know they will face what comes their way together with love—it's so obvious how they feel about each other.

We could not have had any more fun putting my album together. Xander, River, and Dahlia all worked together. Xander took charge and managed every detail. River took care of coordinating with producers he thought would best enhance each song. And Dahlia designed my cover, using photographs she took of me—it really is a work of art. When we weren't all working together in the studio, we were hanging out—going out to eat and even running trails together. Dahlia and I have a common bond—she doesn't have any family, and in a way neither do I. We seem to be drawn to each other because of it.

"Ivy—there you are." Bell appears, interrupting my thoughts.

I haven't spent as much time with her as I have with River and Dahlia, but I've known her since she was ten, so I feel a connection to her as well. Tonight she seems nervous, much like Xander, and I have to bite the inside of my cheek to stop from laughing at the similarities between the two of them—similarities of course that neither would ever admit to.

"No more pictures, Bell," I joke.

She laughs. "Oh God, no, I think Xander might lose it if I ask him to smile one more time." With that we both laugh.

"What's so funny?" he asks, putting his arm around my waist and pulling me to him.

"Nothing. Nothing at all."

Bell's phone dings and I watch as she pulls it out of the pocket of her little romper. A slight rosy color blooms on her cheeks. "Who's that? A guy? Maybe a boyfriend?" I tease.

Xander snorts. "You don't know Bell well enough yet—she always has a boyfriend."

She puts her hands on her hips. "I'll have you know, brother of mine, I have not had a boyfriend since Tate."

Xander raises his arms in surrender. "Wow, calm down. I didn't know. But I'm just teasing you."

She quickly slides her phone back into her pocket and gives him a giant smile before slipping a stuffed mushroom in her mouth. "Ummm . . . these are so good."

"Hey, little sis, aren't those your favorite?" he asks, pointing to a silver tray with scallops wrapped in bacon.

"Very funny."

"Why don't you try one of them for old times?" Xander asks, the tone of his voice dropping.

"No, thank you," she says almost menacingly.

"I dare you," he challenges.

Her gaze flits over him in an assessing manner as she reaches for the appetizer. She squishes her nose in disgust and pops it right into her mouth. I think she swallows it without even chewing. Then she covers her mouth as if to stop from gagging.

"Happy?" she says, suddenly waving her hands in the air.

"What? Are you going to throw up?" Xander asks, now with concern in his voice.

She covers her lips again and I think she's gagging. Her next words are muffled. "I just remembered. I forgot the Bellinis. I'll be back."

She scurries off amid the clacking of her gold and silver heels against the floor.

I turn around and catch Xander shaking his head.

"What was that about?" I ask.

"Oh, long story, but Bell has hated scallops wrapped in bacon ever since she ate too many of them years ago and threw them all up. And here's something else you don't know about my sister—she can never, I mean never, back down from a dare."

I lift a brow.

"What? She's a bundle of nerves. She needed to calm down."

I put my hands on his chest. "So are you. I think we all are." The glimpse of his stubbled cheeks makes my fingers itch and I forget all about the fact that I meant to scold him. Instead I run my palms up the side of his face and look into his eyes. After a few minutes I ask, "Everything okay with Aerie?"

"She just wanted me to know who the new owner of *Sound Music Magazine* is before it's announced on Monday."

"Who?"

"No one I really give a shit about or want to talk about now. I'll tell you later."

I step closer and kiss the place where my hand was just resting.

He stares at me. "Fuck, you look incredible. I know I already told you this, but I can't keep my eyes off you," he whispers.

I can feel the heat blazing in my cheeks from the way he says it. I run my fingers up his shirt, thinking of his tattoo lying just underneath it. The tattoo he got for me. The one I love to trace with my eyes, my fingers, my tongue. I take a deep breath, then rub my hand over his stubbled jaw again.

A wicked grin crosses his lips. "Sorry. I didn't have time to shave. Someone hijacked me before getting ready." My pink flush turns to red instantly, I just know it. "Don't be embarrassed. Feel free to hijack me anytime," he says, unabashed.

With my hand still on his jaw, I rub the slight stubble one more time. "I like it when you don't shave."

He grins and kisses me. "I know you do."

The rest of the evening is enchanting, spent with Xander's family and our friends. But now it's time to debut my new songs and I'm really nervous. But as soon as I hear his voice at the microphone introducing me, my nerves fade away and a contentment washes through me.

"Here she is, everyone—Ivy Taylor," he announces and steps off the stage before I reach him. I know he wants this to be my moment, but I at least wanted to kiss him. He stands right in the front as I bound onstage. The music begins and I start with the buoyant opener "Rollercoaster," then move into the slinky number "Jagged," and then go on to the hypnotic, hitching grooves of "Pure," which is the only song I wrote after Xander and I got back together—it's about us.

I surprise Xander by ending my performance with a vampy cover of Prince's "Little Red Corvette." It seems appropriate since he started driving the car that we spent so much time in in high school. It's the perfect song—it tells our story. When I finish, everyone applauds, but no one louder than Xander. He holds out his arm for me to join him, and his familiar gaze is full of heat. He smiles at me and my whole body goes weak. I smile back as he jumps on stage and swings me around whispering, "Congratulations, baby," in my ear.

We spend the rest of the night talking to the guests. After almost everyone but our close friends and Xander's family has left, I notice that the band takes the stage again. The music begins, and as I try to place it, Xander takes my hand and leads me to the dance floor. Suddenly I know the song. I smile because, oh my God, it's "Marry Me." River begins to sing the lyrics, "He can't help that he likes to kiss you. And he wouldn't mind if you changed your name to Mrs."

No Doubt's song, of course—Xander always said I looked like Gwen Stefani, and we even modeled our first band after them. As River sings, Xander braces his arms around me and for the second time today starts dancing with me. I bury my face in his neck and enjoy the dance. This is obviously his way of announcing our engagement. Just as the song ends, the applause starts. He lifts my left hand and turns the ring around. Looking over his shoulder, I see his mother right away. She too has tears streaming down her face. Wiping my own tears away, I take a deep breath. "Let's go hug your mother."

He gazes at me with those eyes so full of intensity and I know I'm home. "She'd love that," he says.

"Ivy . . ." Charlotte throws her arms around me and hugs me tightly. "I couldn't be any happier right now." She holds me for the longest time and then says, "You really make him so happy."

Jack flashes a grin and engulfs me in a huge embrace. "We couldn't be happier for the two of you," he says, and I swear I see a few tears in his eyes too. He slaps Xander on the shoulder and pulls him in as well, whispering something in his ear that I can't hear, but whatever it is, it makes Xander's mouth quirk up.

River smiles at us as he crosses the room with a bottle of champagne in his hand. Dahlia is at his side, snapping pictures. Bell trails behind with a tray of champagne flutes. They must all have known.

River hugs me. "Welcome to the family."

Dahlia squeezes me. "It's so amazing that you both found your way back to each other."

Before I know it, River tugs on the cork and it goes flying. I jump, startled by the noise. Laughter fills the room when he spills a little on the floor and flashes a grin. "I always say I'm not much of a bartender."

Xander whispers something to him that I can't hear. River nods and then the two embrace, pulling their sister in as well.

River turns back to the crowd and hoists a glass high for a toast. "To Ivy and Xander. To true love." We all clink our glasses and tears of joy well up in my eyes. Bell makes a sweet toast, then whispers in my ear that she has to leave but she'll be calling me to plan the wedding. That makes me laugh—I'm sure she will. Aerie, Jagger, Leif, Garrett, Nix, and Phoebe join us. Several more toasts are made, not only to us but also to a successful album. At this moment life just couldn't be more perfect.

Looking around the room, I see us surrounded by a group of people who have become my family, and the man in the center of this universe who is my life, my love, my happily-ever-after. He wraps his arms around my waist and holds me tight. "I love you," he breathes in my ear.

When I turn to look at him, to tell him how much I love him, I catch a glimpse of that boy I loved so long ago, and it makes me think about my life growing up. I wasn't a little girl who played dress-up, had tea parties, or even liked the color pink—but I was a girl who dreamed of her prince charming and a fairy-tale wedding. That's why the girl who always wore black clothes and combat boots melted when she laid eyes on him for the first time. At first glance, I just knew he was my prince charming, my happily-ever-after. Now, his teeth find my shoulder for a nibble and I shudder. Xander Wilde the boy may have broken my heart once upon a time . . . but Xander Wilde the man, is the one who mended it.

ACKNOWLEDGMENTS

> Where words leave off, music begins.
>
> —Heinrich Heine

My thanks to the artists and musicians who inspired me through each chapter of writing this book. Music is a world within itself. It is a language we all understand. And although I hope the words in this book do not fail you, I also hope the music helps to enhance them. Music speaks to me, tells me a story, and when I listen to songs, I listen to that story. . . . I hope I have succeeded in telling you a story that was brought to life through both words and music.

This section is by far the most difficult to write because it is so very important to acknowledge all of those who have never wavered in their support not only of me, but also of the Connections Series.

First and foremost, I have to thank my family.

I would like to thank my beta readers—without your suggestions this book would not be what it is today.

In addition, a very special thank-you to:

Kimberly Brower of Book Reader Chronicles. She not only beta-read *Mended*, she did so much more. She felt the heart and soul of Ivy and Xander as deeply as I did. Thank you so very much. You've become a lifelong friend.

Mary Tarter of Mary Elizabeth's Crazy Book Obsessions for your overwhelming support from day one. Thank you for all your help and for your friendship—both of which I truly value.

Jody O Fraleigh for friending me, for supporting me, and for helping me with whatever I need. Your SWAG is truly beautiful and represents a piece of each book.

To Amy Tannenbaum of the Jane Rotrosen Agency, who not only believed in *Connected* enough to sign me, but dedicates the time to help me each and every day! You are such an amazing person and I couldn't be more grateful to have you as my literary agent. And thank you to the team at Jane Rotrosen Agency for all you do as well.

To Penguin. When I began this journey with *Connected*, I never imagined I would land a publishing deal, and now three books in, I couldn't love my life more. So thank you, Kerry Donovan, for not only taking my words and making them so much better, but for believing in the romance itself. And thank you to the team at New American Library for so eagerly and enthusiastically helping to get Book Three of the Connections series published.

To all of the bloggers who have become my friends—you're all so amazing! I cannot possibly put into words the amount of gratitude I have for each and every one of you!

And finally, my love and gratitude to my family: to my husband of twenty years, who became Mr. Mom while continuing to go to work every day; to my children, who not only took on roles that I for many years had always done—laundry, grocery shopping, cleaning—but always asked how the book was coming and actually beamed to their friends when telling them their mom wrote a book.

Without the help of those mentioned above, plus all of the support from my readers who have contacted me daily since *Connected*'s release, the writing of *Mended* wouldn't have been possible—a giant thank-you to all of you.

Photo by Studio One to One Photography

Kim Karr lives in Florida with her husband and four kids. She's always had a love for books and recently decided to embrace one of her biggest passions—writing.

CONNECT ONLINE
authorkimkarr.com
facebook.com/authorkimkarr
twitter.com/authorkimkarr

Don't miss the next digital release
in Kim Karr's Connections series!
BLURRED will be available from InterMix
everywhere e-books are sold in August 2014.

The people in Australia say they have sand in their souls. I believe it. Thirty thousand miles of paradise and I've made sure to circle all of it. Now I'm back to the city that I first landed in six months ago, any surfer's wet dream—Bondi Beach. I lie in bed, staring out the open window just listening to the sound of the ocean. It's early, but there's enough light to reveal a hint of what the waves promise today. It's my last day in the Bondi Bubble and I don't want to leave, but I have to. The trial for the drug cartel is about to begin and I've been called to testify.

The time passed here in the blink of an eye. What I'll remember most is that I was able to forget . . . forget about my life back home for the first time since I supposedly died as Ben Covington so long ago. I feel stronger, more focused, and more determined to make this transition in my life—to finally move on. I'm ready. Being here has helped me put things in focus and I can finally accept that Dahl is happy with someone else.

Stacks of *Surfers End* magazines lie on my nightstand. I reach around them to grab my laptop and punch a few keys to bring up my bank account. I officially have less than I paid for my first board in it. Fuck me—where did all my money go? My brilliant plan of living off the rent didn't work out so well. I shut the lid and lean back, thinking about what I'll do for money when I get home. An hour passes before I decide to get up. When I do, I glance out to the majestic shoreline I've enjoyed so much and see families already frolicking on the beach and lifeguards in their signature red-and-yellow swim caps monitoring them for safety. It's a slow and easy way of life here—one I could very easily get used to.

My clothes are neatly piled on top of the dresser, ready to be placed in my bag. My journal is packed, the one I haven't been able to write in. I survey the room for what's left—not that there's much. All I'll have to do before I leave for the airport is grab my duffel, my brief-case, and my board. But I have time, so I quickly shower and head to the Bucket List for breakfast. The diner spills out onto the beach with its wide patio. It's one of my favorite views of the Pacific. I could sit here for hours, staring at the coastline, the glistening sand, and the stone cliffs. The place itself looks like a pirate ship with its faux-fisherman-style decor, complete with lobster pot lampshades on every table and a namesake mural that looks like a map lining the walls—the only difference being the purpose of the mural is to record your bucket list items, not to navigate the sea.

"You're finally doing it today?" my waiter Scott asks, pointing to the Sharpie I have in my hand.

I shrug as if it's no big deal. "I am."

"Way to go, man. You did it." He raises his hand and I slap it.

After I drink a cup of coffee, I approach the iconic wall with my marker and write my checked off items on it. It reads:

Ben Covington
☑ Jog the Bondi Bronte Cliff Walk
☑ Brave the surf at Tamarama

Yes, I did do it. I rode the waves of Tamarama yesterday, despite its ferocious currents and strong riptides. It took me six months to get back in shape but I can now say this: mission accomplished.

Time grows short and I move through town in an effort to say my good-byes—not only to the locals but also to the places. I stop at Icebergs. It's a local bar with its own outdoor pool wedged right into a cliff. The pool refills itself with seawater whenever waves crash against the rocks below it. And the joint itself is filled with happy, friendly people. No one cares what demons you carry. They're just here to have a good time. Not to mention, the deeply tanned waitresses saunter around taking drink orders wearing skimpy bikinis. . . . Talk about living life easy.

Living in the Bondi Bubble . . . life couldn't be sweeter. But my visit here today isn't to enjoy the pool or talk to the waitresses, it's to say good-bye to Kale Alexander, the owner's son. He and I hit it off right from the start. He reintroduced me to what I once loved—writing. Not just the thrill of catching the story that I had become addicted to—he reacquainted me with the passion I once felt for words.

Kale writes for *Surfers End* magazine and is worried he'll be losing his job soon. The publication is tanking in circulation. We've had in-depth discussions as to why. His view was very eye-opening but I didn't necessarily agree with it.

When I walk in he's sitting where he always does—a table near the railing overlooking the water, notebook in hand. He's old-school—no laptop, just pen and paper. Ironically, I think that's the issue with the magazine—they need to enter the world of technology.

I clasp his shoulder. "Hey, man, how's it going?"

He looks up, lifting his shades. "Just trying to figure it all out."

I sit across from him. "That's heavy for this early in the day." I bob my chin to one of the waitresses and hold up two fingers. She smiles and I direct my attention back to Kale. "Care to elaborate?"

He sets his pad down and leans with his elbows on the table. "Surfing is at a crossroads."

"What do you mean?"

"Too many of us out there."

I scrunch my brows together.

He points out to the water. "Watch that."

I do. Two, three, four, five surfers systematically fading with one another in what at first seems to be some strange choreography. However, once the wave rolls over, the surfers are shaking their fists at one another—obviously fighting for the waves and not bothering to wait their turn.

"Why is no blood being spilled over this? You can't just fade someone rail to rail and get away with it," he says, slamming his fist on the table.

It's a thin fabric that holds surfing together. Kale is a former champion and he holds his standards high. I shake my head. "But there are so many unwritten rules out there. Some have long passed their use."

Our drinks arrive and I push one his way.

"Too early, man. I have to get something on paper before I can indulge."

I push it farther toward him. "I'm taking off today."

He sits up straight. "Fuck, how about a little warning? I just got used to seeing your scrawny ass around here."

"Yeah, right." I grin and raise my glass before downing its contents. Then I stand up and extend my hand. "Hope to see you in another life, brother."

He quickly rises and pulls me to him, patting me on the back. "Take care, man, and keep in touch. I'm serious about coming out to see your nephew in action. Who the fuck knows? I might even be writing about him someday."

"Yeah, wouldn't that be something? See ya, man."

"Oh and, Ben, make sure you teach your nephew better than what just happened out there. Courtesy is one rule that should never pass its time."

I nod. "I completely agree."

As I walk away, he says, "In my day, that would never have happened. If it had, someone would have gotten a fucking punch in the head."

I twist around as he snakes his arm around one of the waitresses and plunges his tongue in her ear before looking over toward me. "Sure you don't have a little time?" he asks, his eyes darting to the chick in his arms.

I grin at him before I take a last look around. "Next time."

I have one final stop to make before I leave—the beach herself. As I make my way through the sand, I think about the many hours I've spent here . . . surfing, walking, running, looking for myself. On this beach, I found a part of what I was missing. It was finality, a feeling of closure. Something I had missed over and over with everyone I lost. I'll especially always regret how things ended with Dahl. As I meander down this beach for the last time, I want so much to let that guilt roll off my shoulders. But there are some burdens that just won't wash away. While I wipe the sand from my feet and slip back into my shoes, I try to focus on the possibility of new beginnings, instead of the fact that when I head back to California, no one will be awaiting my arrival.

Just as I enter the gleaming glass doors of the Sydney Airport, my cell rings and I grab for it from my front pocket. I see Caleb's name flashing across the screen.

"Hey, fucker, how's the newly minted agent?"

Caleb snorts. "Hey, fucker yourself. And you're being a little premature with your greeting. I haven't graduated yet, but I am doing fucking amazing. I drove my first surveillance-detection route yesterday."

"Sounds like a kinky fantasy life if you ask me."

"Scraping ice off cars and specialized training classes don't add up to anything whatsoever."

"Sucks to be you, then."

"Yeah, yeah, it does. But not you, I'm sure. How's Australia?"

"Not a waste of time. I can tell you that, but I'm headed home now."

"For the trial?" he asks.

"Yeah."

"Want to talk about it?"

"Absolutely fucking not. But I do want to hear more about your shenanigans. When are they letting you out of Quantico?"

"Soon. Really soon." His laugh is low. "But it's not like I'm in prison."

"I'd say that's up for discussion."

"Over a few beers?"

"Is there any other way?"

"Really, how are you doing, man?"

"I'm managing. I need to get a job when I get back and figure everything out, but right now life is good."

"Hey, one day at a time, right?"

"I'm not in AA, fucker."

"I know, Ben, but when you get back—take it easy. And make up with your sister. Jason said she really misses you."

"Yeah, yeah. One day at a time," I groan, and roll my eyes.

"Listen, I gotta run. I have a simulated bank robbery I have to get to, but I'll call you next week. And, Ben, I just found out I won't be home until the end of the year, but I'll have a month off then—and I'm planning on spending it with you."

"Aren't I a lucky bastard, then?"

"Hey, seriously man, call me if you need me, and, Ben, take care."

"Yeah, you take care too."

I've always liked being independent because if you don't depend on anyone, there is no one to let you down. But Caleb and Trent are the exceptions. I looked forward to their calls. Caleb was the one person, besides Dahl, I had always depended on. And Trent was the one person besides Dahl I'd always allowed to depend on me. The fact that he's doing so well right now is the shiny spot in my life. He's out of rehab and back in school. He's even training for a local surf competition.

The first time I called Trent from Australia was the hardest. I had just arrived and he told me Dahl went to Paris for her honeymoon. For the longest time when we were younger, I had wanted to take her there. I wanted to be the one to show her the Eiffel Tower, which she had always dreamed of photographing. The days that followed that call are all a blur. After that, whenever I called Trent, I quickly changed the subject whenever her name came up.

The airplane door swings shut with a thump and I twist my head toward the window. This is it. There's no turning around—I'm really going back. As the plane takes off, I look at the golden coastline and say good-bye to what just might have been my own piece of heaven. White sandy beaches and crystal blue water blend together and I close my eyes as that life fades away.

When I open them, the wheels are touching down and my old life comes rushing back. Shit, while I was gone I did a great job of not thinking about anything and I only hope I can keep it up. Even Dahl seems to have faded in my memories. Her birthday came and went, and I never remembered it until days later. I'm not sure why—maybe the passage of time, maybe the distance. It doesn't really matter though; whatever the reason, it's working.

Standing stiff with tension, I look around Los Angeles International. Home, sweet home. I had Trent pick up my car months ago and told him to keep it. Now I have no wheels. I shuffle over to the rental office and take the cheapest they have. I hand the attendant my credit card and get a sick feeling, knowing I'm living off of borrowed credit.

I shove my stuff in the shitty sedan and exit the airport, hopping on the 405S. The freeway is jam-packed with cars, but that's nothing new. If it's not an accident or a stalled car bringing traffic to a stop, then it's construction. I mean, really, where else in LA do you get to park your car for free except on the fucking highway? I've always hated this town, and today nothing feels any different.

Thirty minutes later I'm still inching along the road, listening to the radio, when I look ahead and see the bumper sticker on the car in front of me. It reads, "Life is only what you make of it," and those eight words remind me of the advice my mother gave me just before we took Trent to the recovery center.

She looked at me with such sadness and placed her hands on my face before saying, "Please, be happy for the life you have. Make the best of it and don't waste it. Instead, try to put your life back together. Benjamin, please try. If not for yourself, then do it for me. I only want to see you happy."

I grip the steering wheel and jerk my car toward the 110, and away from the road that would take me to Laguna Beach. I silently answer her plea, because I didn't then. *I can do that for you, Mom. I can try.*

With her words ringing in my head, I know what my first step toward a new life has to be—securing a job. So I reluctantly decide to call my old editor from the *LA Times*. She liked me and I'm sure she'll be happy to hear from me. I dial the paper and enter her extension. I get her voice mail and leave a message.

The sun is starting to set as I click my blinker, then take the Adams Street exit. I figure the next thing to check off my list is finding a place to stay. It might as well be near the paper since I don't have a car. When I stop at the light, my mind flips to the last time I drove down this street and stopped at this very same place—the day I "died."

The glow of the headlights shone through the rain. I hated listening to top 40 music, but I turned the radio station to 102.7 for her because I knew she'd like it and it would make her smile. We were listening to Gavin DeGraw's "I'm in Love with a Girl," and I was singing along to the lyrics. She was surprised that I knew the words. Of course I did—I always listened to what she was listening to, after all.

She was watching me—I could feel it—so I turned to look at her. I stopped singing and I told her, "If I ever wrote a song, this is the one I'd have written about you." Then I got off the 110 and headed toward the Millennium Biltmore. I noticed she was still looking at me. So I asked her, "What?"

She grinned at me and reached over the console. She placed her hand on my thigh before running it up my leg and saying, "We're going to be late to your first award party, and it's all your fault."

I grinned and said, "So fucking worth it," because it was. I needed that one last time with her—I had to show her how much I loved her.

Then we stopped at a traffic light and she took her hand off my leg to turn the radio station back. I knew the setup was on. It was time, but fuck, I wasn't ready. I wanted her hand back on me. I wanted to feel her touch forever. But it was too late. Tires squealed. The SUV with heavily tinted windows jackknifed in front of us just as planned. The passenger door opened, and the paid-off shooter in a ski mask jumped out, holding a gun with blanks for bullets.

She screamed, "Oh my God, he has a gun!" but I already knew he would.

She was afraid, and it killed me. I wouldn't let anything happen to her. I sat there trying to decide if I should just tell her. I couldn't take it—but once I looked at her, I knew I had to go through with it. She was too perfect, so beautiful, and all too fragile to take with me. So I said, "Just keep calm, Dahl."

When I didn't get out on cue, the gunman tapped his piece against the window a couple of times and then pointed it to her head, reminding me she'd be dead if I didn't go through with it. So I pretended like I would have tried to flee if I could. I pounded the steering wheel with my fists and said, "We're fucking blocked in."

Her cries only grew louder and she started to shake.

I grabbed her hand tightly one last time while I opened my car door and told her, "Call nine-one-one!"

She sat there in shock and I wanted to cry. But I pulled it together and told her, "Whatever happens, don't get out of this car. Do you hear me?"

She screamed, "Ben, don't!" as I stepped onto the pavement. Then her last words killed me. I didn't have to be shot to feel the pain because I felt it when she yelled, "You don't have to be the hero! Come back!"

Fuck, I wasn't a hero. I wasn't anything of the sort. But I did what I was taught to do when I heard the shot and fell to the ground. She screamed, "No! No! Noooo!" and that was all I heard from her.

I hop back on the freeway, wanting to avoid that street. Clearing my head of the memory, I can't wait to get a fucking drink. I take the next exit I see and pull into the first cheap extended-stay motel I can find. It's some kind of Econolodge in West Hollywood. The perks, the check-in clerk tells me, are I'm close to Melrose and Sunset and they have Internet. The only perk I see is that I'm close to Dodger Stadium and it's baseball season.

I climb the flight of stairs and try to read the sign directing me to room 220. The glow of the moonlight is too dim and the grime that covers the plaque makes it unreadable. With my key in hand, I take a guess and turn right. I pass door after door of peeling green paint and rust. The door to room 216 swings open, and a chick wearing only her panties stands there. She covers her tits with her hands and then turns to slam the door. I think the squeaking of my sneakers against the stick of the concrete made her think I was someone else. I finally reach my destination and open the door, only to be greeted by the pungent smell of stale cigarettes, alcohol, and, if I sniffed hard enough, I'd say sex. The room is a shithole. The carpet is ragged and torn. The walls are dingy. And the TV looks like it's from 1980. I decide it's safer to leave what I have in my bag and drop it on top of the dresser. So with the unpacking done, I hit the street in search of a liquor store to buy some liquid relief.

The sidewalk is crowded—people push and shove one another to move from one place to the next as if that might get them there any quicker. I duck into what has to be a supercenter for booze and peruse the aisle of whiskeys. So many to choose from—tall bottles, shorter ones, blue labels, white labels, darker amber liquids, lighter amber liquids, and then I spot it. Jack Daniel's. I grab a bottle off the shelf by its neck and purchase it with my credit card and a smile. My one friend I can always count on. The one who I already know will fuck me up the ass before I even sign my name on the yellow slip.

The night air is cool, and with my brown bag in hand, I take a small detour down La Cienega Boulevard. In the middle of all the high-end establishments sits a bookstore. I pop into it, in search of something to read. I decide on one of my favorite classics—*Huckleberry Finn*. As I pick up the spine of the dark blue cover embossed with silver letters, a stray memory surfaces. Another one I've tried hard to push away, but once it presents itself I can't stop it. I fight the small smile that crosses my face as S'belle Wilde's red hair and emerald green eyes pop into my mind.

Books surrounded me. The library was large and filled with people, along with hushed whispers. I was a senior in college and I was hiding out in the USC library reading Huckleberry Finn, *laughing to myself as I reread my favorite part when I felt someone's stare. Leaning against the bookshelf, I tapped my heel against the mass of books and watched a curious girl set her sunglasses on top of her head and approach me. She thought she was invisible as she snuck my way. But I noticed her. . . . I noticed her right away. In fact, I stole glances she didn't catch as she shuffled books around. First at her heeled, pointy-toed green shoes that no girl wears to the library. Then at the scarf with quotes on it she had wrapped around her neck. She was slightly overdressed for the library, but she looked fucking amazing.*

I fought laughter as she pushed each book back without even bothering to look at them. I ran my fingers through my hair. My pulse sped up when she swung a glance my way but I quickly averted my gaze. However, the first time my eyes caught on her otherworldly green cat eyes, I couldn't help but stare. When I saw her wild, long, curly red hair bounce with her movement, I became the pretender. I made like I was still read-

ing my book. The cute girl had dropped a book out of her hands and it tumbled to the ground. My eyes stayed glued to her as I bent to retrieve it. My hands grasped it from the floor, and as my eyes swept the title, I couldn't help but smirk. But when she got close enough, my smirk turned into a snort, almost a snicker.

"You're reading about the Kama Sutra?" I raised a brow and tried to feign utter seriousness.

She answered, but her voice sounded distant. "What?"

I pointed to the book with a photo of a woman's body and her panties pulled partially down. "Your book. A Lover's Guide to Kama Sutra?" This time I had to laugh.

"No, no. I wasn't reading that." Her eyes widened like saucers and a look of horror crossed her face. She immediately grabbed the book from me and pushed it into an empty space in the shelf. Then she laughed too.

After a few moments she pointed to my book. "Homework?" she mimicked me, and raised a brow.

I raised my hands surrender style. "No. You caught me. Just hiding out reading one of the classics. Fucking Huck Finn. Something he said turned my mind in a way it shouldn't have."

"What?" she asked, her curiosity piqued.

"Have you ever read it?"

She shook her head no.

"Don't judge me then," I said as I opened the book to any page and recited the line I knew so well. "'That is just the way with some people. They get down on a thing when they don't know nothing about it.'"

She stifled a giggle as she covered her mouth. And when our eyes locked again, I felt something strange—I felt like she got me. I also knew I should leave. I had a girlfriend that I loved. I blinked, remembering that thought, and handed her the book. "You should read this if you have time. It really is one of the best books ever written."

She snickered at that. "Right. It's up there next to Tom Sawyer."

"How'd you know?" I winked.

I walked backward and kept my eyes on her. I stopped at the end of the aisle, put both my feet together and leaned forward slightly. I pretended I was tipping an imaginary hat. "It was nice talking to you. . . ." I paused, waiting for her to fill in the blank.

"S'belle," she finished for me.

"S'belle." I grinned. I stood straight again and quickly disappeared around the corner, knowing I had to leave.

She yelled, "Wait, I didn't catch your name."

I called back, "Ben. My name is Ben Covington," and left the library as fast as I could.

$\mathscr{I}$ clutch the book tightly and push the memory away. I'm getting good at that. The word *ghost* catches my eye, and when I glance at the shelf, I find a book about haunted locations around Los Angeles. I grab it as well. I may despise LA, but certain stories and historical events that occurred in this city fascinate me. As I'm checking out, I see a rack of journals right next to the cash register and pick one up. It's black with gold gilded pages, similar to my old ones. The ones I no longer have. I haven't allowed myself to put my feelings on paper since after my mother's death, since the day I gave Dahl the journal I kept for her, but I think it's time now.

Turning the corner back toward my hotel, I spot a small coffee shop like the one in Laguna. The sign on the window reads FOUR & TWENTY BLACKBIRDS and the name catches my eye—pie. I peer in the window. Pressed-tin walls and communal tables with a few booths create a sense of small-town charm. I know I'll be coming back here. The night's young but I'm feeling wrecked. I still have one more thing to accomplish today before it's over. I pull out my phone and search for her number. Making this call might be risky, but since she hasn't phoned me back, I can only assume she isn't checking her messages until Monday. So calling my former editor at home is my only option.

304 | *EXCERPT FROM* BLURRED

"Hello?" Christine answers.

"Christine, it's Ben. Ben Covington. How are you?"

"Ben." Her voice breaks. And although I know she already knew I was alive, her surprise is still genuine. Her professionalism quickly returns. "I've been meaning to call you."

"Good. That makes two of us. Can we get together and talk?"

"Yes, I'd love that. Unfortunately I'm out of town until Friday afternoon, but I can meet that night. What do you say to Novels at seven?"

"Great. I'll be there. See you then," I say before hanging up.

I'm almost back to the motel when a flash appears in front of me. Fuck me—the paparazzi found me already. I'm not in the mood for their shit, but game on. I weave in and out of stores until I find one with a back door. Once I lose the douche bags, I hightail it to the fleabag motel.

Not feeling nearly as tired anymore with adrenaline coursing through my veins, I pour a drink. I flick on the TV, which surprisingly works, and make my way to take a shower. A few stray hairs in the bathroom make me hate my life even more. I glance at myself in the mirror. What the fuck have I done with my life? I'm twenty-seven, staying in a shit-bag motel with no money and nothing to look forward to. I stand in silence and ponder my decision, questioning this supposed new start of mine.

A few hours later, I'm struggling to get some sleep when a disturbance from next door gets louder. Male, female, I can't tell—the voices are muffled, but the act is undeniable. The lack of light through the broken blinds clues me in that it's either really late or really early. I roll over and cover my head with the pillow, but can't fall back asleep. After a few minutes, I turn back around. The moans and groans are gone, replaced by quiet whispers that can still be heard through these paper-thin walls. I stare at the plaster peeling from the ceiling and watch the fan blades moving around as I try to stop my mind from thinking about how I ended up here. It wanders and I mentally scold myself for allowing any form of self-pity.

I jump out of bed to grab another drink and my journal. I run my fingers along the lines of the page and then let the ink bleed upon it. I write about Australia, how sweet life was there. I write about the upcoming trial. I even write about finding a place to live and calling Christine for a chance at a new job. When I'm done, I close the journal and set it on my lap. New journal. New beginnings. New life. I eventually drift off, spending the rest of my first night back in California alone in a fleabag motel.